Margaret Dickinson

Jenny's War

PAN BOOKS

First published 2012 by Pan Books
an imprint of Pan Macmillan, a division of Macmillan Publishers Limited
Pan Macmillan, 20 New Wharf Road, London N1 9RR
Basingstoke and Oxford
Associated companies throughout the world
www.panmacmillan.com

ISBN 978-0-330-54430-6

A CIP catalogue record for this book is available from
the British Library.

Typeset by Set Systems Ltd, Saffron Walden, Essex
Printed and bound by CPI Group (UK) Ltd, Croydon, CR0 4YY

Visit www.panmacmillan.com to read more about all our books
and to buy them. You will also find features, author interviews and
news of any author events, and you can sign up for e-newsletters
so that you're always first to hear about our new releases.

For my granddaughter,
Zara Elizabeth Robena Jean

I love thee with the breath, Smiles, tears, of all my life!

ELIZABETH BARRETT BROWNING

AUTHOR'S NOTE

Whilst *Jenny's War* is not a sequel, the story is linked to my novel, *Sons and Daughters*. Since the publication of that novel in 2010, several readers have told me that they wanted to know what had happened to the little evacuee girl, Jenny Mercer, and so here is her story. There is, deliberately, an overlap with the earlier novel so that this one, too, is a complete, stand-alone story. I hope those who have read *Sons and Daughters* will understand the need for this and will enjoy the scenes told this time from Jenny's viewpoint.

One

Jenny sat on the battered sofa, shifting herself a little to avoid the spring that poked through the worn fabric. Her gaze was on her mother standing in front of the mottled mirror above the fireplace. 'You goin' out again tonight, Mum?'

'No. Yer uncle Arfer's coming here an' I want yer to be nice to him.' Dot Mercer finished painting the bright red lipstick on to her mouth, fluffed her dyed, brassy hair and turned to face her daughter. 'There, how do I look?'

'Very nice,' Jenny murmured dutifully, absentmindedly scratching her own, rather dirty, blond curls. The contrast between mother and daughter was stark. The child was thin and small for her ten years. Her hair, if washed and cut properly, would have been pretty and there was no denying the beauty of the startling blue eyes in her pinched little face. Bathed and dressed in finery, she could easily have been a carnival princess, but Jenny Mercer would never have that chance.

Dot Mercer was small too, but her figure was shapely and voluptuous. Her clothes were brightly coloured, the hems always two inches too high, the necklines two inches too low. Make-up was plastered thickly on her

1

face, her eyes outlined with black, her lipstick always bright red. 'Yer can go next door to Elsie's and play with her lads, but be home at eight and then go straight up to bed. No coming into the sitting room.' Dot nodded her head towards the front room, where she liked to entertain her guests. Jenny was rarely allowed in there except to pass through it to go out. The door from the street opened directly into Dot's 'best room' and then through that into the kitchen, which the family used most of the time. Beyond that was a scullery with a sink and modern cooker.

Jenny glowered and clenched her teeth. Sitting room? She's having a laugh. The girl knew only too well that, by then, her mother and the latest 'uncle' in a succession of 'uncles' would already be in the front bedroom. Jenny would have to creep upstairs to the tiny back bedroom, closing her ears to the sounds coming from her mother's room.

A loud knocking sounded on the front door.

Dot was suddenly flustered, like a young girl on her first date and not the twenty-seven-year-old who'd had more men in Jenny's short lifetime than the young girl could count on her fingers. 'Oh, is that him already? Go on, out the back way.' She pulled Jenny off the sofa roughly and pushed her towards the back scullery. 'You look like a scruffy street urchin. I don't want 'im thinking I can't look after me own kid.'

They heard the front door being opened and a woman's voice calling, 'Hello, anybody home?'

Dot relaxed. 'Oh, it's only Elsie.' She raised her voice. 'Come on in, Elsie.'

Jenny beamed as their next-door neighbour came into the kitchen. Elsie Hutton was her idea of what a mother should be. She was married – properly married, because

2

Jenny had seen the black and white wedding photo on their mantelpiece – to a hardworking man employed in the nearby East India Dock. Their three sons still lived at home. Ronnie, at fourteen, was now working. The second son, Sammy, was twelve and itching to leave school too. The youngest, Bobby, was a year older than Jenny and her best friend – in fact, her only real friend. They played together, walked to school side by side and it was always to Bobby that Jenny went when Dot's men friends came round.

Elsie came into the cluttered kitchen. She was small and thin with a careworn face that could break into a warm and loving smile and then her hazel eyes would twinkle with mischief. Her hair was smoothed back from her face into a loose bun at the nape of her neck and no one ever saw Elsie without her apron. Her life was simple; caring for her husband and her sons was all she wanted out of life, hard though at times that life could be. But however tough it got, there was love and laughter in their home and the Hutton family faced life's difficulties together. And by the look on her face, there was more trouble coming to her door now. 'Have you 'eard?'

''Eard what, Elsie?' Dot's mercurial attention was already flitting away again as she turned for yet another reassuring look in the mirror and smiled smugly at the contrast between herself and her drab neighbour. For the umpteenth time, Dot wondered what kept Sid Hutton faithful. Elsie never wore cosmetics, never dressed smartly; even her Sunday best coat had seen better days. It'd probably been second-hand when Elsie had got it, Dot thought uncharitably as she smoothed her new silk dress over her slim waist and shapely hips. She couldn't wait for Arthur to see her in it. He'd given her the money and told her to get herself something nice. 'And treat the kid, too. Buy her a pretty frock.'

But all the money he'd given Dot had gone on the dress for herself. It'd been worth it, though. Low cut at the neckline and tight waisted, she knew Arthur wouldn't complain.

'About the kids being sent away?'

'Eh?' Dot's head whipped round. Elsie had her full attention now. 'What yer talkin' about?'

'Evacuated. They're bein' evacuated.'

'Elsie, talk English, will yer? I haven't a clue what you're on about.'

'Don't you ever read the papers or listen to the news on the wireless, Dot?' Elsie's patience was wearing thin.

Dot smiled and winked. 'Got better things to do with my time.'

'Didn't you get the list?'

'List? What list?'

'We all had a list come round about what the kids should take with 'em.'

'Don't remember no list. Anyway, she ain't got much worth taking on holiday. 'Sides, they're starting back to school, ain't they? Summer holidays is over.'

''T'ain't no holiday, Dot,' Elsie snapped. 'Kids, old folk' – she ticked them off on her fingers – 'and invalids are all going to relatives or to be billeted with folks in the country if they'll take 'em. And pets too if you've got any.'

'Got a couple of rats in the roof.' Dot gave a tinkling laugh. 'I hear 'em every night. I wouldn't mind gettin' rid of them beggars.'

Jenny shuddered. Whenever she heard the scuffling above the ceiling in her bedroom, she buried her head beneath the bedclothes. She hated the beady-eyed vermin. And to think they were scampering about just above her.

Dot fluffed her hair again. 'The country, you say? Sounds like a holiday to me.'

Elsie cast her glance to the ceiling and shook her head. 'I give up,' she muttered and turned to go, but it was Jenny's little voice that halted her. 'Aunty Elsie, what d'you mean?'

Elsie turned and her expression softened. She liked the little girl, who, she reckoned, had a rough time of it. Oh, Dot was right enough in her way, but Elsie had serious doubts that Dot loved her daughter – really loved her with a proper mother's unconditional love. Dot had been scarcely more than a child herself when she'd got in the family way. And the father, not much older than Dot, had hopped it, leaving the seventeen-year-old to cope on her own. Elsie didn't know much about Dot's background, but she'd picked up snippets from the gossip about her and even from Dot herself when one drink too many had loosened her tongue. Dot had been illegitimate too, brought up by her single mother who'd never married and had drunk herself into an early grave. Talk about history repeating itself, Elsie thought. She hoped the same thing wouldn't happen to Jenny. Despite her home life – and it was in spite of it – Jenny was a nice kid, a good kid. Oh, she got into mischief, usually alongside Elsie's own Bobby, but the woman had a soft spot for Jenny. She'd always make time for her, which was more than the girl's own mother did.

They were both looking at Elsie now, the same question in their eyes. And it was Jenny who voiced it. 'What do you mean "'vacuated"?'

Elsie sighed, sat down beside Jenny on the lumpy sofa and put her arm round the girl's shoulders.

5

'Listen, darlin', they reckon there's going to be a war and that – that our enemy might – well, attack us in some way, so they're sending all the kids out of the city into the country.'

Jenny's eyes widened. She'd never been out of London, not even on a day trip. She couldn't begin to imagine what the countryside would be like. The only fields she'd seen had been in picture books and there were not many of those lying around the Mercer household.

'Are we all going?' She glanced up at her mother. 'You too?'

'I ain't going nowhere,' Dot vowed. 'What? Leave Arfer to the tender mercies of that trollop at the end of our street? I've seen her in her doorway when his car pulls up. Well, she can think again—'

'Dot,' Elsie interrupted. 'This is serious. Just forget your fellers for a minute, will yer?'

Dot glared at her neighbour, but fell silent as Elsie turned her attention back to Jenny. 'No, darlin'. Not the grown-ups, just you kids.'

'Is Bobby going?'

'Well...' Elsie hesitated and bit her lip. 'I'm not sure. Sid doesn't want them to go. If there is a war, yer uncle Sid's going back into the navy an' he wants the lads to look after me. But,' Elsie went on, 'I'm trying to persuade him to let Sammy and Bobby go.'

'What's everyone else doing?' Now Dot was interested. Elsie glanced up sceptically. Was she really thinking of her daughter's safety or did she think that the girl's absence would make life so much easier for her and her goings-on? Elsie smiled inwardly. Dot had some surprises coming. If Jenny was evacuated, her mother might well be drafted into war work. But for the

6

moment, Elsie kept that little piece of information to herself. Better to let the child be sent to safety than have Dot keep her here as an excuse to escape work.

'I don't want folks thinking I don't do right by my kid,' Dot was saying.

Elsie shrugged. 'Most are going. We've to take them to their school in the morning with their clothes, gas mask and a packet of sandwiches for the journey.'

'Where are they going?'

'Mum—' Jenny tried to interrupt.

'Shut up. I want to know what's going on.' Dot turned back to Elsie. 'It's a bit sudden, ain't it? War's not even certain yet, is it?'

'Looks like it's going to happen. That's what Sid says anyway.'

Dot was thoughtful. Arthur had arrived yesterday rubbing his hands with glee. 'If there's a war,' he'd said, 'I'll make a ruddy fortune.'

Dot wasn't too sure what Arthur Osborne actually did for a living, but he always seemed to have plenty of cash. She'd never enquired too closely how he earned it just so long as he continued to spend it on her. But he didn't seem worried that there might be a war; he was revelling in the mere thought of it.

'Right then, you'll be goin' an all,' Dot decided, prodding her forefinger towards her daughter. 'You'd better get yer things together.'

'They've to have a label sewn on to their coat with their name and the name of their school on,' Elsie added, getting up. 'I'd better go and get the boys' stuff ready, 'cos I reckon Sid'll let the two youngest go when it comes to it. He'll not want them here when 'Itler starts dropping his bombs.'

'Mum—' Jenny began to wail.

'Shut up and do as yer told. Go and get packed.'

That'll take the poor little scrap all of five minutes, Elsie thought as she left her neighbour's house. At least my lads'll have clean clothes and decent shoes. We might not be well off and their clothes aren't new, but they'll be clean and neat. And by the look of the way the child was scratching her head, Elsie thought, I reckon Jenny's got nits again.

For a brief moment, she felt sorry for the country folks who were going to have to take Jenny Mercer into their home.

Two

'I'll take you to school in my car, Tich. You'd like that, wouldn't you?'

Arthur was still there the next morning, sitting at the table and tucking into a huge plate of eggs, bacon and sausage. Dot was standing at the stove, still wearing her dressing gown. The previous day's make-up was now caked and blotchy. A cigarette hung from the corner of her mouth and she screwed up her eyes against the smoke. Before Jenny could answer him, Dot said, 'No, she won't. She can walk with the rest of the kids from our street.'

Jenny slid on to the chair beside Arthur, her mouth watering at the smell of his breakfast. He looked down at her and winked. 'Like a bit?'

She looked up at him, her bright blue eyes regarding him steadily. She'd never really liked him. From the first time her mother had brought him home, she'd been a little afraid of him. And Jenny Mercer wasn't usually afraid of anyone. She was a street kid, born and bred in a poorer part of the city but amongst people with a proud tradition; hardworking men with homemaking wives who loved and cared for their families. That Jenny had been landed with a mother like Dot was her misfortune. Dot, slovenly and slatternly in her ways, was the exception in these streets, not the rule.

'Wotcher, Tich,' had been Arthur Osborne's first

9

greeting as he'd handed her a bag of sweets. And that had set the precedent; every time he came to their house – and it was often – he brought a little something for Jenny. Sweets usually, but occasionally a book or a jigsaw puzzle. Sometimes he gave her enough money for her and Bobby to go to the pictures, though she felt that was only to get her out of the house. But instead of pleasing Dot, his well-intentioned actions towards the child seemed to infuriate her. 'You spoil her. She'll be expecting presents every time.'

But Arthur had only winked at Jenny and said, 'No harm in that, is there, darlin'? I bring yer mam presents too, don't I?' Dot could not deny this and the gifts he lavished on her were certainly more expensive than the tokens he gave her daughter. But despite his generosity, there was still something about him that Jenny didn't like, though she couldn't put the feeling into words. It just felt as if he was trying to buy her approval and the harder he tried, the more Jenny was suspicious of his motives. He was handsome enough in a flashy way. He wore loud-check suits and a trilby hat and sported a thin, pencil-line moustache. He chain-smoked; there was a cigarette still smouldering now in the ashtray on the breakfast table. But she had to admit that he was kind to her, much kinder – and certainly more generous – than her own mother.

'Don't be giving her your breakfast, Arfer. She can have bread and dripping.'

'Aw, go on, Dot, give the little lass a special breakfast. She's going on a long journey.'

A shudder of fear ran through Jenny. She didn't want to go. Didn't want to leave her mum and the familiar streets. She was sure she'd hate the country and everyone in it. This was her home. She'd even put up with

Arthur, if it meant she could stay here. 'Mum, I don't want to go. I don't have to, do I?'

'Yeah, you do. Everyone else's kids are going. Even Sid's letting Sammy and Bobby go. I won't have folks say I don't do right by you.'

Jenny cast a pleading glance at Arthur. She had the feeling that, deep down, he wanted her out of the way too, but maybe . . .

'It'll be all right.' He patted her greasy curls and then wished he hadn't. Jenny saw the look of disgust on his face and knew that her fate was sealed. Neither of them wanted her around any longer and now they'd a ready-made excuse to get rid of her.

'Here, have the rest of this, Tich.' Arthur pushed the half-eaten breakfast in front of her and handed her his knife and fork. He winked at her and said loudly for Dot's ears, 'Yer mam's made me too much.'

Jenny grabbed the knife and fork and began to shovel the food into her mouth, whilst Arthur lit another cigarette and watched her with a mixture of irritation and pity.

Half an hour later, there was a loud knocking on the door and Elsie called out, 'Is she ready, Dot? It's time the kids were going.'

Dot, still in her dressing gown, thrust a dilapidated small suitcase into Jenny's hands. 'Here, go and put your clothes in this. Arfer got it for you, so you say "thank you" nicely to him.'

Jenny put her hands behind her back and scowled mutinously. 'I ain't goin'. I'm stayin' here.'

'Oh, no you're not. If the other kids are goin', then so are you. 'Sides, I could do with a bit of peace and quiet for a week or two. It's only for a bit. It'll be like a holiday.'

Tears sprang to Jenny's eyes. So, she'd been right. They did want her out of the way. Maybe Uncle Arthur was sick of feeling obliged to bring her presents to wheedle his way around her, tired of having to think of a way to get her out of the house for a couple of hours. This way, they'd be able to do what they liked. Go out every night, stay in bed till noon without a nuisance child to look after.

Jenny snatched the suitcase from her mother and ran up the stairs. She stuffed her clothes – precious few – into the case and then gently she laid Bert, her battered teddy bear, on the top. Then she closed the lid muttering, 'Sorry, Bert, to squash you. Maybe it won't be for long but I can't leave you behind.'

As she went down the stairs, Elsie was standing in the kitchen. 'There you are, darlin'. Get a move on, we'll miss the train.'

Jenny stared up at her with wide eyes. 'Train?' she squeaked fearfully. 'We're going on a train? Where to?'

Elsie shrugged. 'I've no idea, but it'll be all right. You'll be with Bobby and Sammy'll be there too. He'll look out for both of you.' She held out her hand towards Jenny, who took it reluctantly. Then Elsie turned to Dot. 'Look lively, you're the one holding us up now.'

Dot pulled her dressing gown more tightly around her. 'I'm not ready, Elsie. You take her with your lads. Off you go, Jen, and mind you're a good girl.' She made no move to kiss or hug her daughter. She just reached up to the mantelpiece for her packet of cigarettes.

' 'Bye, Tich,' Arthur said and made as if to ruffle her hair but then thought better of it. Instead, he touched her cheek with a gentle gesture. 'It'll be fine. You'll be all right.'

But Elsie's anxious frown did nothing to reassure the young girl.

Walking beside Bobby towards the school was what she did every morning. But today was different. Today they would not be coming back home when afternoon school finished. There'd be no games of hopscotch in the street or kicking a ball through makeshift goalposts, whilst Bobby tried to prevent her scoring, or playing cricket with Sid Hutton's weathered bat and ball. No simple game of tag with all the other kids from the local streets. Not even a trip to the nearest stretch of grass that passed for the closest thing to a park and a strip of countryside for the city kids.

How Jenny longed to slip her hand into Bobby's as she walked alongside him, but she knew it would provoke teasing from the other children if they were seen. Bobby wouldn't like it but she felt that, actually, he wouldn't have minded holding her hand. Even he was quiet and subdued this morning, quite unlike her cheeky playmate and friend. Red-haired and freckle-faced like his older brothers, there was always a ready grin on his face. The three Hutton brothers were very much alike and neighbours would say that you could only tell them apart because of their different heights. Bobby was constantly in the wars and permanently scruffy, however hard poor Elsie washed and mended his torn trousers and ripped shirts. But he was fun to be with and he never turned his back on Jenny when he was with his mates just because she was a girl and a year younger.

'Come on, Jen, you can play with us.' And even if the other boys pulled faces and grumbled, he'd say, 'Good as any of you lot, she is. You just watch her dribble a football. She'd be good enough to play for the 'Ammers if she weren't a girl.'

And he was right; Jenny was fearless and fearsome and could hold her own in a game of football against any of the boys, even the bigger ones.

But now those games were finished for, as the youngsters trooped to school on the morning of 2 September 1939, not one of them knew when they'd all be back together again and playing football in the familiar streets.

Three

They assembled in the school playground.

'Are the teachers comin' too?' Bobby muttered as he saw one or two of the school staff with suitcases at their feet and clipboards in their hands marshalling the children into different groups around them. The boy was torn between feeling relieved that a familiar grown-up would be with them, and realizing that a continuation of lessons would inevitably follow.

'Let's hope so,' Elsie said with feeling. 'I'd be a lot happier if they are.' She approached Mr Napier, Sammy's form teacher, and repeated Bobby's question.

'Only to see them settled in, Mrs Hutton. Then we'll be coming back. Once we've handed them over to the billeting officers where they're going, then our job will be done.'

'And where are they going?'

The man shrugged. 'Up north somewhere. That's all I can tell you. But they'll all be given a card and a stamp to write home to you when they're settled. Don't fret, Mrs Hutton. They'll be well cared for.'

Elsie glared at him for a moment and opened her mouth to retort, but Bobby pulled her away. 'Don't, Mam. You'll show our Sammy up an' he won't like that.'

Elsie sighed, understanding her son's concerns. Boys didn't like their mothers arguing with their teachers. She

15

turned to Bobby. 'Now listen, son. You write to me when you get there. You hear? An' if yer not happy, you write at once an' I'll be on the next train to fetch you home, never mind what it'd cost. I'm not havin' my kids unhappy – bombs or no bombs.'

Listening, Jenny wished her mother had said something like that to her. Elsie Hutton was letting her children go because she believed it was the right thing to do to keep them safe, but it was obvious that for two pins she'd keep them here. She didn't *want* them to go, whereas Jenny had the feeling her own mother couldn't wait to see the back of her.

They walked in crocodile formation to the nearest underground and eventually arrived at King's Cross railway station. Now Jenny clutched Bobby's hand tightly, afraid of losing him amongst the crowd of bewildered children from all over London thronging the platforms. Cardboard boxes holding their gas masks dangled from around their necks and labels flapped from every coat or jacket lapel. Some carried small suitcases, others – like Bobby and Sammy – carried their belongings in kit bags or even pillowcases. There were smartly dressed boys in school blazers and caps. They wore good, stout shoes, short trousers and knee-length grey socks. Girls, too, wore neat coats, white ankle socks and shoes. Their hair was neatly trimmed and freshly washed. But others were as scruffy as Jenny, with tangled hair, worn-out plimsolls and no socks.

Sammy stayed close to Bobby and Jenny. Several parents, Elsie amongst them, had followed them to the station for last-minute hugs and tearful farewells. Already, the teachers were looking harassed; they would have preferred goodbyes to have been said in the school-yard. This was just prolonging the agony. Several of the younger children were crying now and even some of the older girls too. A few boys looked suspiciously wet eyed, but were manfully holding back from actually shedding tears. Only one or two looked actually happy to be going, Billy Harrington for one. Billy was in her class and Jenny knew that his mother had died and now he was beaten regularly by his drunken father for any imagined misdemeanour. Anywhere would likely be better for Billy than his own home. But despite his harsh home life, miraculously the boy was always cheerful and friendly. Once at school, he seemed to be able to block out memories of last night's beating or thoughts that more cuffs and knocks awaited him again that night at home. And today Billy was positively beaming. He was tall and thin for his age. His clothes were second-hand, too small for the growing boy and often torn; there was no one at home to mend them. His light brown hair was short, roughly trimmed by an impatient father.

A whistle sounded and there was a sudden flurry of activity. Children were bundled aboard the train and doors were slammed by the guard walking along the full length of the platform shouting, 'All aboard.' Jenny giggled. It was just like she'd seen on the films; she hadn't imagined it could be real.

Mothers remained on the platform, standing on tiptoe to see their children one last time. Now a lot of the grown-ups were in tears too, waving handkerchiefs and shouting last-minute messages. And then the train, with much chugging and puffing of steam, began to move.

'Where's Aunty Elsie? Where's yer mum?' Jenny was overcome by a sudden panic. She had to wave to Aunty Elsie; it would mean she was coming back. Aunty Elsie was her good-luck charm. Bobby, leaning out of the window, was just as anxious. 'I can't see her. Oh, I can't . . .'

'There she is.' Sammy put a hand on both their shoulders. 'Look, she's waving. Give her a wave, Bobby. And you too, Jen. Let her see us go off with a smile.' He bent down and whispered, 'We can have a good cry later when no one's looking.'

Sammy was twelve and feeling very responsible for the two youngsters who'd been put in his charge, but it didn't mean he wasn't feeling the parting from his mother just as much as they were.

Mr Napier was in charge of the carriage with Sammy, Bobby and Jenny along with several other children from his class. Billy Harrington was there too, bubbling with excitement and bouncing up and down in his seat.

'Now settle down,' the teacher said, as the train drew out of the station and gathered speed. 'We've a long journey ahead of us. I hope you've all brought sandwiches.'

Bobby whispered, 'You can share mine, Jen.' He didn't even need to ask if she'd got any.

Jenny's smile trembled. 'Ta, Bobby.'

The carriage grew very hot and Jenny, unused to such a big breakfast, began to feel queasy.

'I feel sick,' she said at last to Mr Napier. The man looked down at her and pursed his lips. 'I shouldn't be having to look after little girls,' he muttered. 'You should be with your own class teacher. Have you got a towel in your bag?'

Jenny shook her head.

'I have,' Bobby said. 'Mam packed us some towels.' He stood up, swaying with the motion of the train.

'Sit down, boy,' Mr Napier snapped. 'I don't want you falling and breaking a limb. I'll get it. Which one's yours?'

Bobby pointed to the luggage rack. 'The blue one, sir.'

Mr Napier reached up to the rack, his hand already on the bag when Jenny spewed up her breakfast. Vomit splashed on to the floor of the carriage.

'Ugh!' the other children in the carriage cried in disgust. 'You dirty little devil.'

Mr Napier looked down at his trousers and sighed. His left leg was stained and the smell now permeating the carriage made everyone feel ill.

'Open the window, Harrington,' he said, motioning to Billy, who was sitting near the window.

Jenny hung her head, embarrassed and angry with herself. She'd so enjoyed Arthur's breakfast and now she'd lost it and there was a horrible taste left in her mouth too. 'I'm sorry, sir,' she whispered.

'Your mother should have known better than to let you eat so much just before a long journey.'

Surreptitiously, Bobby squeezed her hand. 'It's not your fault. We'll use my towel to mop it up.'

Sammy stood up and helped Mr Napier lower the heavy bag from the rack. 'I'll see to it, sir,' he said, winking at Jenny. 'No harm done, eh?'

'I don't know about that,' the teacher muttered, glancing down again at his soiled trouser leg.

Sammy bent and wiped away the offending liquid with an old towel he'd pulled from Bobby's bag. Then he mopped the floor as best he could. Lastly, he rolled the towel up into a ball and shoved it under the seat. As he sat back in his seat, the boy sitting beside him muttered. 'You stink, Sammy Hutton.'

But Sammy only grinned. 'No more than you do all the time, Bates. At least I wash every day and have a bath once a week, which is more than—'

'Now, now, boys,' Mr Napier remonstrated, but with little anger. He was grateful to Sammy for taking charge of the unpleasant situation. He'd noticed that the Hutton boys were taking care of the young girl. He didn't know Jenny – she wasn't in his class – but he knew Sammy well as a kind and helpful lad.

The rest of the journey passed off uneventfully, though several of the children held their hands over their mouths and noses and cast accusing glances at Jenny, but Mr Napier noticed Billy wink and smile at the girl to reassure her. The train stopped at two or three stations, but each time Mr Napier shook his head to the children's questions, 'Are we there?' 'Is this it?'

At last, as the train began to slow yet again, Mr Napier peered out of the carriage window and announced, 'This is where we get off. At least—' The flurry of excitement as the children tumbled thankfully on to the platform drowned the rest of his sentence.

'Come on, Jen,' Sammy said, getting up and pulling her case down from the rack.

'What about my towel, Sammy?' Bobby asked.

'Leave it. It was only an old one anyway. Come on, get a move on. We don't want to be left on the train. We don't know where we might end up.'

'We don't know now,' Bobby muttered, but he grabbed hold of Jenny's case and leapt off the train, then held out his hand to help her.

She scrambled after him and stood on the draughty

platform looking about her and shivering even in the warm September sun. Some of the other children were standing about looking as lost and bewildered as Jenny was feeling, but others ran up and down the platform, shouting and laughing as if they were on holiday. Perhaps they felt as if they were. Removed from the control of their parents and put in the charge of a few teachers who could hardly cope with the number of children in such unusual circumstances, a few were running wild, Billy amongst them.

A whistle shrilled and everyone stopped as if turned to stone. The children looked about them, wide-eyed and fearful. A big man in railway uniform stood halfway up a flight of steps. 'Stop running about,' he boomed in a voice that carried the length of the platform. 'There're trains coming and someone'll get hurt. Now, line up properly for your teachers and behave yourselves.'

No amount of shouting and gesticulating from the teachers could have achieved the same result. The children meekly formed themselves into groups around the teacher who had been put in charge of them. Jenny, clinging unashamedly now to Bobby, joined the group around Mr Napier. Catching sight of her, he said, 'You, girl, whatever your name is—'

'It's Jenny Mercer, sir,' Bobby piped up.

'Yes, yes, Jenny – you're to go to your own teacher's group. Miss Chisholm, isn't it? She's over there.'

Jenny began to move towards her own class teacher, dragging Bobby along with her.

'No, Hutton,' Mr Napier ordered. 'You stay here. I know you're in Miss Chisholm's class, but we have instructions that families are to be kept together wherever possible. You stay in my group with your brother.'

Bobby looked at Jenny apologetically and tried to

release his hand from her grasp, but she clung on all the more tightly. 'No,' she cried. 'I want to stay with Bobby – and Sammy. Why can't I come with you?'

'Because—' the flustered man began. This was all too much. He'd entered the profession to teach not to nursemaid a bunch of uncontrollable children, who were treating the serious matter of being evacuated from danger as if it were a day's outing to the seaside.

Jenny's voice rose in protest. 'I want to stay with Bobby.'

'You're coming with me, young lady.' Miss Chisholm's firm grasp fastened on Jenny's arm and hauled her away. The girl began to scream, but the middle-aged woman was well used to dealing with the likes of Jenny Mercer – and even with Jenny herself during the time she'd been her teacher.

Mr Napier stood looking on helplessly, whilst Bobby and Sammy attempted to follow Miss Chisholm to plead Jenny's case.

'Hutton – stay here, if you please.' Sammy, used to obeying the man, stopped at once, but Bobby went on.

'Bobby, mate, it's no use,' his brother called after him. 'There's nothin' we can do. They're in charge of us. Let her go.'

The last sight Bobby had of Jenny was of her being dragged away with tears pouring down her face. The sound of her cries echoing in his ears would haunt his dreams for several nights.

Four

Now they were put on different trains. Jenny, still crying loudly but held fast by Miss Chisholm, was forced to watch her friends get back on to the train they had just left. Jenny's teacher and a colleague were left standing on the platform with the children from their classes.

'We've to catch a connection to take us to where we're going. It won't be long,' Miss Chisholm said, more gently now. She was a strict teacher and held her class in fear of her, yet beneath the stern exterior there was sympathy for those less fortunate children in her charge. And Jenny Mercer was one of them. She knew a little of the girl's home life; had to deal with the child's dirty appearance on a regular basis, and at this moment felt pity for the little girl who was being separated from the two boys who lived next door to her home and were her friends. Jenny didn't make friends easily and her classmates avoided her. There was often a scuffle in the classroom by the children wanting to avoid sitting next to her. Only Bobby never seemed to mind. Although he was a year older than Jenny, he was still in the same class and Miss Chisholm had found herself allowing him to sit near her, even though it was normal for girls to be on one side of the room, the boys on the other.

But now they'd been separated; they weren't even going to the same destination. Goodness only knew when they would see each other again. And meanwhile, poor Jenny was thrust amongst the rest of her classmates, who flatly refused to befriend her.

'I'm not sitting near "Sicky",' the teacher heard one girl mutter as she shepherded them onto the train.

'Don't call her that.' Billy, who was also now once more under Miss Chisholm's authority, pushed the girl roughly. 'It could've 'appened to any of us.'

The girl flushed but still turned her back on Jenny.

'You sit with me,' Miss Chisholm said softly. 'I shall be staying for a day or two until you're all settled. So come along, dry those tears and we'll find you someone nice to stay with.'

'I want to go with Bobby,' Jenny wailed one last time, even though, as she watched the train carrying her friend move out of the station, she knew it was hopeless.

'I know, I know,' Miss Chisholm said, surprisingly kindly. 'But it'll be all right, I promise.'

But even the powerful Miss Chisholm, who ruled her class with a rod of iron – or rather a wooden cane, if necessary – was no match for the billeting officers with their badge of governmental authority.

They hadn't been on the train many minutes, it seemed to Jenny, before it shuddered to a stop and the guard walked down the down the platform shouting, 'Ravensfleet, Ravensfleet. Next stop Lynthorpe.'

Miss Chisholm was suddenly galvanized into action. 'This is it. This is our stop. Hurry, children, collect your belongings. I must tell them in the next carriage.' She lifted her own suitcase down from the rack and opened the door.

'Don't leave us!' Jenny screamed.

'It's all right, I'm just here on the platform. I'm not far away.'

Seeing that the school parties were alighting, the guard came to help and lifted the smaller children down.

'Where's Miss Jones?' Jenny heard Miss Chisholm ask. 'My colleague?'

The guard pointed. 'Two carriages further along, miss. Now, come along, you lot. Get back from the edge of the platform, there's good kids.'

'Doesn't he talk funny,' one boy said.

Jenny stood feeling lost and lonely. She shivered again. The afternoon sun was dropping low in the sky and there was a chill in the air on the draughty platform. And there was something else too. The air smelt funny. Sort of salty.

Miss Chisholm hurried back to the children standing huddled together. 'Miss Jones and her party are going on to Lynthorpe, but this is our stop. Now—' she looked around her – 'I wonder who's here to meet us.'

As if on cue, a small, thin man, with a receding hairline and wearing spectacles, came hurrying along the platform towards them.

'You must be the party from London.' He held out his hand to Miss Chisholm. 'I'm Mr Tomkins, the billeting officer for Ravensfleet. Now, come along, we have refreshments waiting for you in the school. Of course, it's still closed for the summer holidays at the moment so you'll be bedded down there for the night. And then in the morning we'll start getting you all sorted out.' He beamed round at the children. 'Welcome to Ravensfleet. I hope you'll be happy with us. We're all anxious to make you feel at home.'

Twenty-three solemn little faces with mistrustful eyes stared back at him. He cleared his throat nervously. 'Come along, then. Follow me.'

They trooped after him out of the station and along

the street walking two by two, though Jenny still walked beside Miss Chisholm. Along the narrow street, through a market square and round another corner until they came to a school building.

'Here we are,' Mr Tomkins said cheerfully. 'Come along in. The good ladies of the town have got a meal ready for you.'

The children trooped into a large classroom where trestle tables had been set with knives, forks and spoons. Several women at one end of the room ceased their chatter and turned to stare at the newcomers. One rotund woman came towards them with a beaming smile. 'Now then, my little loves, you come and sit yarsens down and we'll get you summat to eat.'

The children shuffled uneasily and stared at her, but said nothing. They weren't exactly sure what the woman had said. Her way of speaking was so very different to their own.

'That would be most welcome,' Miss Chisholm said politely. 'Thank you.'

'Dorn't mention it, duck. We've all got to do our bit till this lot's over. Sit ya down.'

Within minutes, enamel bowls of mashed potato and vegetables with a little meat had been placed in front of each child.'

'What, no chips?' Billy said.

'Now, Billy,' Miss Chisholm remonstrated gently. She knew the boy's diet consisted mainly of chips from the local shop. She doubted he ever had a proper meal. 'Just try it, there's a good boy.'

She smiled at him, knowing that if Billy would lead the way the other children would follow. She glanced at Jenny beside her. The child, though still with a tear-streaked, grubby face, had lifted her fork and was trying the food in front of her. She chewed it and then nodded across the table at Billy. 'It's nice, Billy. Give it a try.'

Billy Harrington wrinkled his nose but did as she suggested. After a moment, he, too, nodded. ''S'all right, is this. Ta very much, missis.'

The large lady, who seemed to be in charge of the others, laughed and nodded, her several chins wobbling. 'Ya welcome, duck, I'm sure.'

When they'd finished eating, Mr Tomkins stood at the end of the room. 'It's too late now to get you to your billets, so your foster parents will come for you in the morning. You'll stay here tonight. We have mattresses and blankets for you to sleep on the floor and Mrs Clark' – he gestured towards the large friendly woman – 'is the caretaker at this school. She'll show you where the toilets and washbasins are. Perhaps' – he looked towards Miss Chisholm for her help – 'some of the older boys would help Mrs Clark move the trestle tables out of the way. Then in the morning . . .'

His words were lost as Billy leapt up from his seat and began directing his classmates to move the forms they'd been sitting on and to fold up the tables. There was a lot of noise – chatter and scraping of furniture – but soon Mrs Clark, still beaming, led them to the next room where there was a pile of straw mattresses and grey blankets.

'The girls will sleep in here and the boys in the other room. Now, lads, tek a mattress and a blanket each.'

It took an hour or more before the children began to settle down, tiredness and the emotion of the day catching up with them. Jenny lay on the scratchy straw palliasse, snuggling beneath the coarse blanket and clutching Bert tightly. She lay there listening to the sounds of the other sleeping children and her heavy eyelids began to close. It had been a long and traumatic day for all of them, but for no one more so than Jenny, who'd not only left the only home she knew, but also had been dragged away from her friend. 'I wonder where Bobby is now' was her last thought as she fell into a troubled sleep.

Heavy-eyed and feeling as if she'd only been asleep for a few minutes, Jenny woke to the sound of Miss Chisholm's voice and her clapping hands. 'Rise and shine. Come along, children. Time to get up.'

The children washed hurriedly in the school's cloakroom and Mrs Clark and two other ladies served them porridge and a drink of weak tea on the tables the boys had set up again. When they'd all finished, the long trestle tables were set to one side of the hall and the children stood in rows facing Mr Tomkins. The three ladies, who had served breakfast, went down the line handing a paper bag to each child.

'These are provisions for you to give to your foster mother,' Mrs Clark explained. Inside each bag was a tin of meat, a bottle of milk, some biscuits and a bar of chocolate. One or two of the children grinned cheekily; the bar of chocolate would never reach their foster parents. Mrs Clark, intercepting some of the glances between the children, merely smiled to herself and made no attempt to remind them that the goodies were not for them. Poor little mites, she was thinking.

When all the bags had been handed out, Mr Tomkins cleared his throat. 'Now, children, you are to be billeted with people in the town. We'll try to keep families together where possible, so if you'd stand in rows on either side of the hall, the people who've volunteered to take you in will be here at ten o'clock and will make their choices.'

'You mean we're going to be picked?' Billy piped up. 'Like at the Battersea Dogs Home when folks choose a stray?'

Mr Tomkins blinked. 'Er, well, not quite like that, I hope. You'll find that the local farmers will want strong lads like you, young man,' he added with a smile. 'And the girls will be able to help in the house. Now, I'm sure you'll all be good children and grateful to the people who are going to take you into their homes.'

'Huh!' Billy muttered, so that only those closest to him could hear. 'Sounds like cheap labour for 'em to me. Bed and board and a lot of hard work, that's what we're in for.'

'But you'll be going to school too, of course,' Mr Tomkins went on a little nervously. He and his wife had no children and confronted with these raggedy, solemn-faced youngsters, poor Mr Tomkins was out of his depth. He turned towards Miss Chisholm. 'Will you be staying to take your own class?'

'Only for a day or so to see them settled in. We have to return home. Not all the children in our school have been evacuated and those left behind still need teaching.'

Mr Tomkins nodded. 'I just wondered. I've been told we're to expect a further batch of children tomorrow, so the school won't be able to cope with such a number all attending at the same time. We'll have to work out some sort of rota for attendance.'

At his words, Jenny pushed her way to the front. 'Another train coming tomorrow? Will it be Bobby's train, Miss? Will Bobby be coming here?'

Miss Chisholm looked down at the grubby little girl with pity. Gently, she said, 'I don't expect so, Jenny.

Bobby and the rest will already have arrived wherever they're going.'

Jenny's face fell.

The children stood waiting, not knowing quite what was expected of them and wondering what was going to happen next.

Five

At three minute past ten the first of the locals arrived. A farmer followed by his wife strode into the hall and down the length of the lines of children. Billy was the first to be picked.

'You look a good, strong lad.' The farmer smiled. 'A' ya coming to work for me? You'll be well fed.' He jerked his thumb over his shoulder. 'My missis is a good cook and there'll be plenty of food on my farm, no matter what shortages are going to happen. What d'ya say, lad?'

Billy blinked. He couldn't understand every word the man had said. The farmer's accent was unfamiliar, but he caught the gist of the man's meaning. 'Just me?' he asked.

'Ah well, now, I could do wi' two, 'cos one of my lads ses he'll be volunteering for the army if there is a war. And if there isn't, well, you lot'll all be going back home, won't you? So no harm done, eh?'

He seemed a chatty, friendly man, dressed in sturdy hobnailed boots, corduroy trousers with his shirtsleeves rolled up under a black, unbuttoned waistcoat. His cap, which he'd removed on entering the room, was now twirling between his work-callused fingers. Behind him his plump wife with brown curly hair, liberally flecked with grey, smiled kindly. Billy took a step towards him, emboldened to ask, 'You won't beat us, will yer, mister?'

A silence fell over the room as the man and the young boy regarded each other. Billy saw a friendly man, jovial at the moment, but the boy's eyes had alighted on the wide leather belt around the man's waist. The farmer saw a tall lad, too thin for his height. Good food and a healthy, outdoor life would soon build the youngster up, he thought. But the boy's question had startled him and now he looked closer he could see that though the lad gave an outward show of bravado, there was something in his eyes that belied the swagger. There was a fear and an experience of things that a youngster of his age should not have known.

Miss Chisholm held her breath and Mr Tomkins frowned. She was about to step forward when the farmer held out his hand and said, more gently now, 'Me name's Joe Warren of Purslane Farm, young 'un, and this is my wife, Peggy. And no, I don't beat my workers or guests in my home. In fact, I don't reckon I've ever beaten anyone in me life, not even me own lads. Mebbe the odd smack on the back of the legs when they was young. Scallywags, they were, at times.' He'd seen Billy's gaze on his belt and now Joe forced a laugh as he touched it and added, 'But this is just to hold me trousers up.'

The tension in the room eased and one or two children giggled nervously. They'd never have dared to voice such a question, yet it had been in the back of some of their minds. Just how were these strangers going to treat them?

Now, without any hesitation, Billy put his hand into the farmer's and said, 'Billy Harrington. I'd be pleased to come with yer, guv'nor.'

Miss Chisholm sighed with relief. Billy was a ringleader amongst his peers and if he led the way with his polite acceptance of the man's offer, then others would follow his example.

'A' ya got a brother to come wi' ya?' Joe Warren asked.

Billy blinked, trying to work out what the man had asked. 'No, I've no brothers or sisters. There's only — only Dad and me. Me muvver's dead.'

Joe nodded. 'I'm sorry, lad. Yar dad'll likely miss ya.'

Billy shrugged dismissively and the farmer could see that whatever the father was feeling, the son certainly wasn't going to miss his home. Joe turned and raised his eyebrows to his wife. She gave a little nod and moved forward. 'We can take two, Joe.' Peggy Warren spoke in a soft, gentle voice. 'Perhaps Billy would like a friend — someone he knows — to come along with him.'

'My best friend's Frankie Mills.' Billy pointed to a boy standing at the back of the group of children. 'But he's lame, guv'nor. He had polio when he was little and he has to wear a leg iron.' He beckoned to the boy. 'Come and meet Mr Warren, Frankie.'

The farmer looked down doubtfully as the children parted to let Frankie through to the front. He limped forward, his leg iron clanking on the wooden floor. Peggy touched her husband's arm and whispered, 'We'll take him, Joe. We'll look after him. There'll be little jobs he can do. Best to let friends stay together. They'll likely settle better.'

'Aye, aye, you're right, Peg. We'll look after 'em both. Come along, you two. Let's get you home.'

He put his arm around Billy's shoulders and held out his hand to Frankie. He glanced across the room at Mr Tomkins, who was busily writing down the details of the first placement on his clipboard. 'Thank'ee, Mester Tomkins.'

Mr Tomkins looked up and nodded. 'I'll be along in a day or so to see how things are.'

'You'll be welcome any time, Mr Tomkins, but you've no need to worry about these two. They'll be fine with me and the missis.'

Lucky Billy, Jenny thought, as she watched the two boys leaving with the farmer and his wife. Bet I don't get anyone as nice as them.

More folk were coming into the hall and moving down the lines of children. More choices were made and soon there were only three left without a billet. Jenny was one of them. She was standing alone now. The other children had moved away from the girl whose coat still reeked of vomit, whose hair was lank and greasy and who kept scratching her head every so often.

The other two were picked and led away and now there was only Jenny left. Mr Tomkins conferred with Miss Chisholm in whispers, but Jenny's sharp ears picked up every word.

'I've only one place left for yesterday's arrivals,' Mr Tomkins said. 'The two Miss Listers,' he glanced worriedly at Jenny, 'but I don't think . . .'

'She's a good child really, given a bit of understanding. Nothing that a good bath and a change of clothes won't sort out.'

'Mm.' Mr Tomkins was still doubtful. 'Well, it'll just have to do. There's nowhere else at the moment and with another batch due tomorrow . . .'

The three of them walked along the street. Jenny slipped her hand into Miss Chisholm's. It wasn't something she'd normally do. You just didn't hold your teacher's hand, but the girl couldn't remember ever feeling so fearful. She'd never felt so lost and alone in her life; not even when she'd been shut in her bedroom

for hours on end away from her mother and whatever
'uncle' was visiting. She'd always known that Aunty
Elsie and Bobby were just next door. But now . . .

'Here we are.' Mr Tomkins stopped in front of a
small cottage with a thatched roof. The door opened
straight on to the road and white net curtains veiled the
front windows. Dark green ivy covered most of the wall.
It was very quiet, with no sign of life except for a tiny
wisp of smoke curling up from one of the chimneys.
They seemed to wait an age before anyone came in
answer to his knock. Then they heard a shuffling behind
the door and it creaked a little way open.

'We don't use this door, Mr Tomkins. Please go
round to the back. My sister is waiting for you.'

'I'm sorry, Miss Lister. Of course. I do beg your
pardon.'

The door closed and Mr Tomkins cast his eyes
heavenwards before gesturing them to follow him down
the side of the house, through a dilapidated gate and
into a backyard, beyond which was a small, badly
overgrown garden, the flowers choked with weeds.

'What a shame!' Miss Chisholm murmured.

'The Miss Listers are too old now to manage gar-
dening.'

'Are you sure they'll be able to manage a child?'

Doubt crossed Mr Tomkins's face. 'I hope so. They
want to "do their bit", as they've put it. They lost two
nephews – young men who were very dear to them – in
the last war and they're appalled that it's all going to
start again. They do have a young girl living with them
– a maid. No doubt she'll look after, er – ' He consulted
his clipboard.

'Jenny Mercer,' Miss Chisholm reminded him.

'Yes, yes, quite so. I'm sure she'll be all right and my

35

wife, Mabel, will call in often just to see . . . And you'll be staying for a day or two, you said, so . . .'

They had arrived at the back door and an elderly woman stood there dressed from head to toe in black. She stooped a little and her small face was covered with lines and wrinkles. Her white hair was a wispy cloud around her head. She did not smile a welcome, but held the door open for them to step inside.

They crowded into the small sitting room, the three visitors and the two Miss Listers. It was dingy and uninviting, the only natural lighting coming from one of the small front windows.

'So, this is the girl you want us to house,' the elder of the two women – the one who had opened the back door and ushered them in – began. They saw now the other sister for the first time. She was taller than her sister, thin and straight-backed. Her grey hair was scraped back from her face into a bun. She, too, was dressed completely in black.

'Yes, Miss Lister.' Mr Tomkins almost bowed with respect. 'Her name is Jenny Mercer and she's – er –' Again he consulted his clipboard. 'Ten years old.'

The taller of the two sisters – Miss Agnes – looked the girl up and down. 'Rather young. We were hoping for someone older, Mr Tomkins. Someone who could help Christine about the house.' She sniffed. 'This child is going to be more of a hindrance than a help.'

'Jenny's a very willing girl,' Miss Chisholm put in. 'I'm sure she'll help with whatever jobs she can.'

Jenny was growing more anxious by the minute. She didn't like the look of these two old women. The house was dingy, the room cluttered with ornaments and the horsehair sofa, she knew, would scratch the back of her bare legs.

She tugged on Miss Chisholm's hand. 'I don't want to stay here. I don't like—'

'Hush, Jenny, there's a dear.'

Mr Tomkins cleared his throat. 'I'm afraid there are no other billets left. If you could just—'

'I see,' Miss Agnes said primly, her mouth pursed. Although the younger of the two sisters, she now seemed to speak for both of them. 'We've been given the dregs. The child no one else wants, have we?'

'Miss Agnes—' the hapless man began, but the woman's tirade was not finished yet. She held up her hand. 'My sister and I take it very personally, Mr Tomkins, that you did not see fit to choose a more suitable evacuee for us to welcome into our home. I doubt this little – ' she paused, searching for the appropriate word – 'urchin even knows the meaning of the word "gentility". Still, perhaps whilst she is with us, we may be able to instil into her a modicum of respectability. Never let it be said that the Miss Listers shirk what they know to be their duty, however – ' again there was a pause – 'arduous that duty might be.'

Jenny didn't understand all the words the woman was using, but she felt the animosity, the disgust in the woman's tone and in her manner.

'Miss Chisholm – ' Again she tugged at her teacher's hand. 'Please . . .'

Miss Chisholm bent down and whispered in the girl's ear. 'Now, you must be a good girl and do exactly what you're told. I'll come again in the morning and see how you are. I promise.'

And that was all that the teacher could offer. She was helpless to question Mr Tomkins's authority, though once outside, she promised herself silently, he would certainly hear her thoughts on the suitability of handing over a city streetwise kid into the care – if it could be called that – of two prim spinsters.

Once Mr Tomkins and her teacher had gone, Jenny felt bereft of all that had once been familiar. She'd been plunged into an alien world. In her own environment, she was a feisty, spirited little girl, who would fight her own corner with her fists if necessary. But here, she was lost. She had no idea how to behave or what was expected of her.

For the first time in her short life, Jenny was afraid of another human being. No one had ever made her feel like this before. Not her mother nor any of the 'uncles' who had passed through her life. But as she stood in front of this tall, thin, imposing woman who was backed by her witch-like, wispy-haired sister, Jenny began to shake with fear.

Six

Jenny felt a little better when Miss Agnes pulled on a
cord at the side of the fireplace and a young girl came
scurrying into the room. She was round faced with shiny
red cheeks. She wore a spotless white apron and a mob
cap. When she entered the room she bobbed a curtsy.
Jenny stared in astonishment. Who were these 'Miss
Listers'? Royalty?

'Christine, *this* is our evacuee. Take charge of the bag
of provisions she's been given.' The old woman's eyes
gleamed for a brief moment. 'They'll come in very
handy. Now, take her into the kitchen and fetch the tin
bath out of the shed.'

The maid's eyes widened. 'The bath, Miss Agnes? But
it isn't Friday.'

'I know that, but the girl needs a bath. And a bath
she's going to have. And mind you wash her hair –
thoroughly.' Miss Agnes glanced down at Jenny's strag-
gly locks with distaste. 'You, girl,' she went on, addressing Jenny directly for the first time. 'Go with Christine
and mind you do as she tells you.' She turned back to
her maid. 'You can give her something to eat – *when*
she has bathed.'

In the kitchen, Jenny watched with mounting horror
as Christine tugged the zinc bath into place on the
hearthrug in front of the range. Then, taking up a jug,

39

the maid began to draw water from a tap at the side of the range and tip it into the bath.

'I'm not getting in there,' Jenny muttered.

'Won't hurt ya,' the girl smiled, 'we'll get you looking all clean an' pretty and then . . .' she paused, watching as Jenny scratched vigorously at her head.

''A you got nits?' Christine asked bluntly. She set down the jug on the hearth. 'Come here. Let's have a look.'

'Nah . . .' Jenny moved backwards until she was pressed up against the dresser. Christine, strong from her daily work, grabbed the younger girl by the shoulders and turned her round. Still holding Jenny fast with her left hand, she parted the child's hair at the nape of her neck. There was a moment's silence before Christine released her hold suddenly and leapt back. 'Ugh! You dirty little tyke. You have got nits.'

Jenny turned slowly to look at her, noting the expression of horror on the maid's face. Jenny grinned happily, suddenly seeing her way out of this austere and miserable household. The red-cheeked country girl might like it here, but the city child most certainly did not. 'Oh aye, I often get 'em. Half my class at school have got 'em.'

Christine's mouth dropped open. 'You mean – you mean, all those kids that've come here, they've all got nits?'

Jenny pretended to think, wrinkling her forehead. 'Not all of 'em, but a few.'

'Ugh!' Christine said again and pulled a face. Then she pointed her finger at Jenny. 'Stay there and don't move. I'll have to fetch Miss Agnes.' She left the kitchen but not many seconds had passed before she returned, both the Miss Listers following her. They stood facing

Jenny, accusing and disgusted. 'Is this right? Have you got head lice?'

Deliberately now, Jenny scratched her head.

'Stop that at once. Turn round and bend forward.'

Jenny stopped scratching and stared at the woman. 'What you gonna do? Hit me?'

'Of course not, child. I – I just want to see for myself.'

'Oh Agnes, dear. D'you think you should?' Miss Lister said, her voice quavering. 'Ought we to get Dr Bennet to look at her?'

'There's nothing the matter with her that a good bathing and hair washing won't put right, Hetty. But her hair's too long. It needs cutting short.'

'You ain't touching my hair,' Jenny shouted, growing red in the face.

'If you want to stay in this house, then—'

'I don't want to stay here. I don't like it and I don't like you. None of you.'

'Now, now, I won't have such rudeness—' Agnes began but Jenny opened her mouth and screamed, the sound rending the air and startling the elderly women and even making Christine jump.

Hetty clutched her sister's arm. 'Send her back, Agnes. We can't cope with her. Send her back to Mr Tomkins. He'll have to find her somewhere else.'

Miss Agnes seemed to ponder for a brief moment before saying loudly above the noise Jenny was still making: 'Christine, fetch her suitcase from the sitting room and take her round to Mr Tomkins's house. I'm afraid my sister's right. We cannot cope with such a child. As billeting officer, he should have known better.'

Jenny stopped screaming abruptly now that she had got her way. She stood staring at the two women whilst Christine fetched her case and held it out towards her, distaste written on her face. 'Here, you can carry it yarsen. Come on, I'll take you back.' She turned to her mistress. 'I'll try not to be long, Miss Agnes.'

The woman merely nodded, not caring for once what time the girl took just so long as she got this dirty little urchin out of their home.

'She's got head lice, Mrs Tomkins,' Christine explained when her loud knocking on the door of the Tomkins's home was answered. 'And when Miss Agnes said she'd have to have her hair cut off, she threw a right old tantrum, I can tell you.'

'Oh dear. What are we to do? Mr Tomkins isn't in and I understand there's no other place for her at the moment. And we're expecting more children to arrive some time today. My husband's out now trying to find billets for them.' Mabel Tomkins bit her lip and then sighed. 'Well, there's nothing for it. We'll just have to have her here for the time being.' She forced a smile at the young girl, trying not to show revulsion at the stained coat and the greasy hair that evidently housed creepy crawlies. 'Come along in, dear.' She reached out her hand to take Jenny's case but the child held on to it.

'Are you goin' ter make me 'ave a bath?'

'It would be best, dear. We ought to try to – to try to get rid of your – er – of what's troubling you.'

Jenny scowled.

'I'll leave you to it, then,' Christine said, backing away thankfully.

Mabel sighed as she was left alone with the child, wishing heartily that her husband would hurry home.

The argument raged for the rest of the morning. Whilst Mabel Tomkins gave her milk and biscuits and began to prepare lunch, the child flatly refused even to wash her face. She sat at the table, drinking the milk and leaving a white 'moustache' on her upper lip. She munched on the biscuits and scratched her head often. Mabel shuddered inwardly, but tried to keep a bright smile on her face. She avoided broaching the delicate subject of the girl's hygiene. She was waiting until her husband came home.

'Hello.' Len Tomkins stopped in surprise as he entered the back door and saw Jenny sitting at the kitchen table. 'What're you doing here?'

Mabel, her eyes anxious, beckoned him towards the door leading further into the house.

'You needn't whisper. I know what you're goin' ter say,' Jenny piped up. 'Them 'orrible old women say I've got head lice and they don't want me staying wiv 'em.'

'Oh dear.' Mr Tomkins glanced helplessly at his wife. 'I haven't another place for her. I'm already having a job finding billets for the next lot of arrivals. I'm sorry, love, but we'll just have to keep her here for a day or two until—'

Jenny sprang up from the table. 'I ain't having a bath or my hair washed.'

Len held out his hand, palm outwards, placatingly. 'No – no, all right.'

'But—' Mabel began, but Len shook his head. 'I'll find her somewhere,' he promised and then lowered his voice, 'And they can deal with the – er – problem.'

Behind her glass of milk, Jenny smiled.

Seven

Two days passed before Len had an idea. Two days that passed so slowly for Mabel. The child ate heartily – that was no problem. But getting her to wash even just her face was a battleground. 'I don't reckon even an army drill sergeant could deal with this one.'

'Maybe we should send her to the front,' Len joked. 'She'd likely repel the enemy better than our lads.'

Mabel couldn't see the funny side but glared at him as she delivered her ultimatum. 'You'd better find a place for that child and be quick about it. How I'm ever going to fumigate that bed after she's gone – the whole room, if it comes to that – I just don't know. Maybe even the whole house. Ugh!' She shuddered.

'Mabel, love, don't be so hard on the poor kid. It's not her fault.'

'What sort of parents has she got? That's what I'd like to know.'

'According to Miss Chisholm—'

Mabel looked puzzled.

'Her teacher,' Len explained. 'She's only got a mother and – well – not to put too fine a point on it, the child has to put up with a succession of "uncles", if you get my meaning.'

Mabel stared at him, appalled, before saying, 'Well, it's still no reason for her to be so dirty.' But her tone had softened and she was beginning to understand her husband's reasoning. It wasn't the poor child's fault. She sighed. 'I suppose we'd better resign ourselves to keeping her, then. But if we do, Len, somehow we're going to get her into a bath.'

'I've been thinking,' he said slowly. 'I saw Miles Thornton on Sunday. He and his family had listened to Mr Chamberlain's declaration of war on the wireless.'

'Him at Ravensfleet Manor? Charlotte's husband?'

'The very same.'

'And?'

'He and Charlotte are offering to take an evacuee.'

'Why didn't you say so before? Let's get her bag packed and on her way.'

'Whoa, there. Hold your horses, love,' Len laughed. 'We ought to think this through. This is the manor we're talking about. Miles Thornton became the local "squire" when he came here in – when was it?'

Mabel wrinkled her brow thoughtfully. 'It must be twelve or thirteen years ago.' Her expression softened. 'Do you remember when they arrived? How little Georgie – he must have been about six – marched up the aisle of the church and announced to the congregation who he was.' She was smiling fondly now. ' "I'm Georgie," he said. "I'm six and we've come to live at the manor." I'll never forget it. Such an adorable little boy. A blond, blue-eyed little cherub. We all fell in love with him and Charlotte most of all. She adored him. Still does.'

Len nodded and his voice was husky. 'Yes, and he's grown into a fine young man and now' – he paused and met his wife's gaze – 'he's in the RAF. And it'll be in the hands of young men like him that our salvation lies.'

Mabel wiped her eyes with the corner of her apron. 'Poor Charlotte and poor Miles. What if all Miles's boys go to war? Philip and Ben too.' Philip, the eldest Thornton boy, was a solicitor with a law firm in London. Ben, the middle son, now ran the Ravensfleet estate and, in particular, Home Farm. 'What if—?'

'Don't, Mabel. Don't even think about it.' There was a pause before Len cleared his throat and said more briskly, 'But I think Miles and Charlotte are looking for something to take their minds off what their sons might do.'

'They're not Charlotte's sons, though, are they?' Mabel murmured.

Miles Thornton had been a widower with three young sons when he'd bought the Ravensfleet estate and moved into the manor thirteen years earlier. Two years later he'd married Charlotte Crawford, the only child of an embittered man who resented her for being a daughter and not the son he'd craved.

'But she loves them all like they're her own,' Mabel said softly now. 'And they're all she's likely to have. After eleven years of marriage, there's still no sign of a child. I don't suppose there ever will be now.'

Len sighed. 'Aye, poor lass, tied for years to that miserable tyrant of a father, but at least she's found happiness with Miles.'

'But we all know that they'd love more children.'

Len laughed. 'And Miles has made no secret of the fact that he's always longed for a daughter. Ironic, isn't it, that old man Crawford made poor Charlotte's life a misery because she wasn't a boy and then Miles, with his three sons, wanted a daughter. Well, now he can have one. Jenny Mercer.'

Mabel gave a wry laugh. 'I don't think she's exactly what he had in mind.'

'I'm going to telephone him anyway. They don't have to have her.'

Mabel closed her eyes as if in fervent prayer. 'Oh, but please God, they do.'

When Len told her that the Thorntons had agreed to take the girl, Mabel began to feel guilty that she was handing over such a problem child to Charlotte.

'I've grown up with Charlotte. I can't do that to her. I'll have one more go to get Jenny to have a bath before they collect her.'

'You'll have to be quick about it. They're coming for her straight away. Can't wait, by the sound of the excitement in Miles's voice.'

Mabel pulled a face. 'Maybe they won't be so keen when they see her. Anyway, I'll see what I can do.'

The Tomkinses had a proper bathroom, not just a zinc bath in front of the fire on a Friday night. Mabel filled the bath with warm water and then went downstairs.

'Jenny,' she began, 'you're going to stay with some lovely people at a big house with a big garden where you'll be able to play. They're coming to pick you up very soon. Now, don't you think it would be nice if you looked your best?'

Jenny, guessing what was coming, put on her most innocent look. 'You've sponged me coat. It doesn't smell any more.'

'But your hair would look so much prettier if you washed it and—' Mabel got no further as Jenny opened her mouth and began to scream. 'I ain't 'aving a barf.' Then she picked up the unfinished bowl of cereal and threw it on the floor. The bowl smashed, the cereal and milk spilling on to the tiles.

Len poked his head round the kitchen door. 'They're here. Can't you stop her making that awful noise?' He glanced at the mess on the floor, then at the child. Above the noise he shouted. 'You mentioned a bath, I suppose?'

Mabel nodded helplessly and, as Len disappeared to answer the knock at the front door, Jenny shot after him. As he opened the door, she pushed past him and between the two people standing there. She ran out of the gate and into the road. She paused briefly to shout over her shoulder. 'I ain't stayin' here no longer. I'm going 'ome. I'd sooner face old 'Itler's bombs than stay here anuvver minute.'

Jenny ran a short distance and then slowed to a walking pace, realizing she wasn't sure that she was going in the right direction for the station. She heard footsteps and glanced behind her to see that the man who'd come to fetch her was following her. He was tall and broad shouldered and his long strides were catching her up easily. As he neared her, she could see that he was very smartly dressed, but not in a flashy way like Arthur. He was wearing a grey suit with a waistcoat. He looked a right toff, yet he was bothering to chase after *her*. His dark brown hair, flecked with grey, was brushed back smoothly from his face. To the young girl, he looked old, but a little voice inside her whispered: *He does look nice.* Nevertheless, he'd more than likely want her to take a bath, so she made herself scowl and set her little mouth in a grim, determined line.

Jenny had reached a corner in the road and didn't know which way to go. She stopped and waited for him to approach her. He stood for a moment, about a yard away, looking down at her and smiling. 'Hello, there.' His voice was deep and gentle. 'You're Jenny, aren't you?'

He squatted down on his haunches, so that his face was level – perhaps even a little lower – than hers. It made her feel safer, as if he was really trying not to frighten her by looming over her. But Jenny had met men like him before amongst the 'uncles'. All sweetness and light one minute and bringing presents and the next giving her a cuff round the ear if she was in the way. She didn't trust any of their smarmy ways.

Beyond him, she saw the woman who'd come with him walking towards them. With a sudden movement, Jenny turned away and stepped into the road but the man caught hold of her arm and even though she screamed loudly and kicked out at his shins, he refused to let go.

'You'll get run over, love. Calm down. I'm not going to hurt you. But you must look where you're going.'

Now the woman had reached them. She was smiling, yet the girl could see the worry in her eyes. Dark, violet eyes. Jenny had never seen anyone with eyes that colour. They were beautiful and her shining black hair was drawn back into a chignon at the back of her head and yet a profusion of curls and waves surrounded her face. Her clothes, too, were perhaps not fashionable – not like the ones Dot wore – but they were well cut and looked expensive. She'd been right; these folks were toffs.

'Jenny, if you're going back to London,' the woman was saying in a soft voice, 'haven't you forgotten a couple of things?'

Jenny stopped struggling and stared up at her. 'What?'

'For one thing, you must take your gas mask and for another – what about Teddy? You surely weren't going to leave him, were you?'

Jenny stood very still. Bert. How could she have forgotten Bert? And her clothes. Her mum'd tan the hide off her if she arrived back home with none of her belongings and besides, they didn't want her there. They wouldn't be pleased to see her back. Not like Aunty Elsie if Bobby and Sammy went back home . . .

The man's voice interrupted her thoughts. 'If you promise me not to run into the road without looking both ways, I'll let go.'

Jenny nodded. Then she looked up into the kind face of the woman. Against her will, she was intrigued by these two people. Why on earth did toffs like them want to take in a dirty little urchin like her?

'His name's Bert,' Jenny muttered in answer to the woman's question. 'I'd better get him. And me gas mask.'

'And what about the train fare? Have you any money?'

'Don't need no money. We come on the train an' didn't 'ave ter pay.'

'I think that was special, because the train was bringing you all to the country. But if you choose to go back without the others, you'll have to pay.'

Jenny felt tears prickle her eyelids and, against her will, her lower lip trembled. She dropped her head so that they wouldn't see how lost and afraid she felt. There was no one she could turn to. Even Miss Chisholm had gone back to London the previous day. How she wished she'd known; she'd have gone with her. Though she doubted the teacher would have allowed it.

The woman was squatting down in front of her now

and speaking in a soft voice. 'Tell you what, how about you come home with us for a day or two? If you really don't like it, then we'll pay for your train fare back home.'

Jenny looked up, meeting the dark eyes. 'Promise?'

'Well, I don't think your mum'll want you to go back to the city when she's sent you here to be safe, but if you're really so unhappy, then—'

'Don't think mi mum'd be bothered. She's got a fancy man an' I was in the way.'

'Oh – oh, I see.' After a moment, the woman stood up and held out her hand. 'You come with us, Jenny. Give us a try, eh? Maybe you'd like to stay with us for a little while and then we'll see, eh?'

Jenny thought for a moment. She realized now escape was impossible, at least for the moment. She wasn't going to be able to get home. She couldn't run away and – worst of all – she wasn't going to escape having the bath and hair washing they all seemed to want her to have. But at least if she went with this couple, she wouldn't be sent back to those dreadful old women or anyone like them. 'All right, missis. I'll give it a go, but if I don't like it . . .'

'Then I promise we'll take you back to London ourselves and talk to your mum. All right?'

Jenny nodded and put her grubby paw into the woman's outstretched hand.

Eight

They walked through the streets of the little market town, Jenny still holding the woman's hand and clutching Bert to her chest. The man carried Jenny's meagre possessions.

'My name's Charlotte and this is Miles.'

Jenny twisted her head to look up at the woman walking beside her. 'Don't I call you Mr and Mrs something?'

The woman chuckled. 'No, Charlotte and Miles will be fine.'

'Not even Aunty or Uncle? I've had lots of uncles,' Jenny confided. 'That's what I 'ave to call me muvver's fancy men.'

Jenny felt Charlotte's hand tremble slightly in hers and she looked up sharply to see if the woman was laughing at her. But Charlotte was biting her lip and there were tears in her eyes. 'No,' her voice was husky, 'just – just Charlotte and Miles.'

They were walking away from the town centre now along a road where the houses were not built so close together. Jenny glanced around her nervously. She was used to narrow streets and row after row of terraced houses, not the wide open spaces of the countryside. The sky looked huge and it frightened her. They reached some gates leading up a driveway to a large house with smooth lawns in front of it. Beyond the house the flat land stretched towards a line of low hills. And she could hear a strange rushing sound that ebbed and flowed, but she had no idea what it was. Jenny stared at the huge house in front of her. For a moment, she forgot her fears. 'Cor! Is this where you live?'

'Yes,' Miles said, coming to stand beside her. 'Welcome to Ravensfleet Manor, Jenny. We do want you to stay with us and we'll do everything we can to make you happy.'

The girl glanced about her and then pulled her hand away from Charlotte's. Still clutching her teddy, she ran towards the steps leading up to the front door. She climbed them and then stood close to the front door until they reached her.

'Here we are, then,' Miles said, opening the door and ushering her inside.

Jenny had never been inside such a big house. The front door opened into a large hallway with rooms leading off on each side. Directly in front of them was a wide staircase.

'Now, I'll take you up to your room,' Charlotte said. 'It's right next door to our bedroom, so if you want anything in the night, you only have to shout. All right?'

Jenny nodded, her blue eyes wide with wonderment as she gazed around her. She felt a little safer indoors, but it was still very big. Paintings lined the walls of the hall and there were even more on the landing. There were several landscapes, but the ones which intrigued Jenny were portraits. She stopped in front of one. 'That's 'im, ain't it?'

'Miles? Yes.'

Jenny stared at it, studying it carefully. Even her young and inexperienced eye could see that the painting was magnificent. She moved away slowly, but the picture still held her gaze.

'This is your bedroom while you're with us,' Charlotte said encouragingly as she opened the door into a room decorated in pink with flowered curtains and a bedspread to match. 'Shall we hang your clothes in the wardrobe?'

'I'll do it,' Jenny said quickly. She didn't want this nice woman turning her nose up at the tatty clothes.

Charlotte nodded. 'All right. Come downstairs when you're ready. Oh, let me show you the bathroom.'

Jenny stood by the bed and hugged Bert even closer. 'I don't want a barf.'

'Oh, not just now, but I thought you might need to know where everything is. Come along.'

The girl followed Charlotte reluctantly and eyed the deep, white bath with apprehension. In a small voice she said, 'I s'pose I'll have to 'ave a barf, won't I?'

'I'd like you to, Jenny. But don't worry about it. Maybe tonight, eh, just before you go to bed?'

Jenny didn't answer; she just frowned and her little face hardened as she schemed how she could avoid it. The water would be so deep in that big bath, she'd drown. She knew she would. And nobody would care. Not her mum, not Arthur. Maybe Bobby, but there was no one else she could think of who would miss her that much.

'Now, we'll go down and get you some lunch. Are you hungry?'

Jenny nodded, bringing Charlotte's attention to the child's dirty hair and the woman hid a shudder as she imagined what lurked beneath those greasy curls.

Downstairs, Charlotte went towards a door leading

off the hall near the front door and opened it. 'Miles, we're just going to have lunch. I thought we'd have it in the kitchen.'

'Ah, yes,' Jenny heard the man say, 'I'll come too.'

He emerged from the room and smiled down at her. 'How are you settling in? Do you like your bedroom?'

Jenny nodded again and, still clutching Bert, she followed them through another door that led from the hall towards the kitchen.

'Mrs Beddows – this is our house guest for the next few weeks.' Miles made the introductions. 'At least, we hope she's going to stay with us. Mrs Beddows is our cook, Jenny. And Kitty over there near the range is our maid. And the tall gentleman over there in the dark suit is Wilkins. I'm not quite sure what his title is, but he's an invaluable member of the household.' Wilkins looked very sedate and rather worried, Jenny thought. 'And then there's Brewster who is the chauffeur – '

The child looked up at him with innocent eyes. 'You've got servants? Like the King 'as?'

There was a brief silence and then everyone laughed. 'No, no,' Miles said. 'They work for us, yes, just like the men on the estate do too, but we don't call them servants. They're our friends' – he chuckled – 'at least, I hope they are.'

'What's a 'state?'

'The Ravensfleet Estate is most of the land around here. We have three tenant farmers and then there's Home Farm, which I run. Well, Ben does now. And then there's Buckthorn Farm on the flat land between Ravensfleet and the sea. But that's not part of my estate. Mr Crawford, Charlotte's father, owns that.'

'Who's Ben?'

'My son. My middle son. I've got three. Philip – he's the eldest. He's a lawyer in London. Then there's Ben, and Georgie's the youngest.'

'Will Georgie play wiv me?'

Miles laughed. 'He might, but he's a bit older than you.'

'How old?'

'He's nineteen.'

Jenny wrinkled her nose in disgust. 'Oh, that's old. He won't want to play with the likes of me.'

'He might,' Charlotte said softly. 'You'll like Georgie, Jenny. He's—'

Jenny glanced up at her. Charlotte had a catch in her voice and though she couldn't understand it, couldn't have rationalized it and put it into words, even the young child understood that there was something very special about this woman's youngest son. 'He's very kind and great fun.'

She saw the man and the woman exchange a glance and wondered at the concern that showed plainly in both their faces.

'Kitty'll serve lunch in the dining room,' the cook was saying. 'It's all ready.'

'No, no, we'll have it in here, if that's all right with you, Mrs Beddows.'

Mrs Beddows's face showed her surprise, but she merely nodded and began to clear the kitchen table.

'I'll set it, Mrs Beddows,' Charlotte said, going to a dresser at the side of the kitchen and pulling out a white tablecloth. The three women, Charlotte, Mrs Beddows and Kitty, bustled about the kitchen setting the table and dishing up the food. But in only a few minutes they were all sitting around the table. Miles carved the joint of meat and Mrs Beddows served the vegetables, pouring rich, thick gravy over it all before setting a plateful in front of Jenny.

'I haven't given you too much, lovey, until we find out what your appetite's like,' she said. 'But you can always ask for seconds in this house.'

Jenny blinked and gazed up at the woman. 'What we 'avin' Sunday dinner today for? It's Tuesday.'

'Well,' the cook explained as she sat down in her own chair and picked up her knife and fork, 'we usually have a light lunch. But today – when Mrs Thornton told me you were coming – well, I thought I'd do a nice hot meal for you. Make you feel welcome. Usually, we have dinner in the evening. And that's a cooked meal like this.'

Jenny picked up her knife and fork and stabbed at the piece of meat and then sawed at it with her knife, expecting it to be tough to cut through. But her knife slid easily through the thin slice of beef and when she chewed it, it seemed almost to melt in her mouth.

'Actually, don't Lincolnshire folk call their midday meal dinner, and it's tea in the late afternoon, isn't it?' Miles said.

'That's right, sir,' Kitty, who was Lincolnshire born and bred, agreed. 'And then it's supper if you want a snack just 'afore bedtime.'

'You don't arf talk funny,' Jenny said.

'So do you,' Kitty countered, but she was smiling as she said it.

Jenny giggled and said in her cockney accent, 'You're 'avin' a giraffe.'

'A what?'

'A giraffe. A laugh.'

57

Kitty laughed too and answered in broad Lincolnshire dialect. 'Aye, an' I reckon you'm as wakken as a rat, young 'un.'

Jenny's smile disappeared. 'You callin' me a rat?' she accused.

'No, no.' Kitty flushed with embarrassment. 'I'd never do that, duck. No, it's one of our sayings. It means you're as sharp as a rat. You know, clever. I'm sorry, I didn't mean to—'

''Ave you got rats here? In the house?'

'Not here,' Miles said gently. 'On the farm, yes. But Ben has a little dog that's a very good little ratter. He catches them.'

'We could do wi' 'im at home. We've got two in our roof. I 'ate 'em.' As she stuffed more food into her mouth, she was aware of the grown-ups exchanging glances.

As they were finishing the first course and Mrs Beddows was serving the pudding, the back door opened and a young man stepped into the kitchen.

'Leave your boots outside, Master Ben, if you don't mind.'

Ben – with dark brown hair and soft brown eyes – smiled sheepishly and disappeared for a moment, returning wearing just his thick socks. He padded to the kitchen sink and washed his hands before sitting down at the table. He glanced across at Jenny and smiled. 'Hello.'

Jenny didn't answer but just stared at him.

'This is Jenny. She's come to stay with us for a while,' Charlotte explained. 'She's from London.'

'Oh yes. I heard about children coming here from the cities.'

'Jenny – this is Ben.'

'I'll show you around the farm sometime, if you'd like,' he offered, but still there was no response.

Jenny dropped her eyes lest the young man – in fact, all of them – should see in them that she had no idea what a farm was. She'd seen pictures, but she'd never visited a real farm. And, so far, she wasn't sure she wanted to go outside any more. The flat landscape and the huge skies were scary for the city child.

During the afternoon, Charlotte showed Jenny the nursery on the first floor next door to the room where she was to sleep.

The girl gazed wide-eyed at the toys, books and games on the shelves and in the cupboards. In the centre of the room stood a rocking horse and in one corner stood a beautiful doll's house. The whole front opened in two doors, revealing tiny furniture and the family of dolls looking rather as if they were just waiting for someone to play with them.

'You can play with all the toys and if there's anything you need, Jenny, you only have to say.'

The girl looked up at her sceptically. 'What do I have to do for it?'

Charlotte blinked and looked puzzled. 'I don't understand.'

'At home, if I gets a treat – sweets or anything – I have to stay in me room or go to the pictures with Bobby. You know, stay out o' the way.'

Charlotte stared at the child and shook her head slowly. Huskily, she said, 'You don't have to do any-thing. We just want you to be happy here and if there's something you want, we'll do our best to get it for you.'

Jenny's chin trembled. 'I want to know where Bobby and Sammy've gone.'

'Who are they?' Charlotte asked gently.

'Me friends. They live next door to us. Me an' Bobby play together.'

'Did they come on the train with you?'

'Yeah, but we got to a station and we all had to get off, but then they got back on the train and we got on another one that brought us here. I – I don't know where they went.'

'I'll ask Mr Tomkins for you. He might know.'

'Will yer?'

'Of course. I'll see what I can find out for you.'

'Ta, missis.'

'Charlotte . . .' the woman reminded her gently.

Nine

But the tentative steps towards understanding were shattered when, after dinner or tea or supper, or whatever anyone in the household now wished to call the evening meal, Charlotte insisted on Jenny having a bath.

'Can't you leave it for tonight?' Miles whispered. 'Let her settle in a bit first. Get to trust us.'

'Miles, the child is filthy. I really can't.'

Miles sighed and shrugged.

'Come along, Jenny,' Charlotte said kindly, but there was a note of firmness in her tone now. 'Time to get ready for bed.'

The girl followed her, dragging her feet, but when Charlotte headed for the bathroom Jenny stood at the top of the stairs, hanging on to the banister.

Charlotte ran the bath water until it was about twelve inches deep. She turned off the water and came out on to the landing, holding a large jar in her hand. Jenny was still standing where she'd left her. 'You can have some of my special bath salts. They smell lovely.'

'Don't want to.'

Charlotte continued as if the girl had not spoken. 'And I've some lovely shampoo that will make your hair shine.'

Jenny's glance took in Charlotte's black hair that looked so sleek and well cared for. It was very different from her mum's brassy, dyed hair with its dark roots.

She took a step towards the bathroom and then another. Charlotte waited patiently until Jenny was in the room.

'Would you like me to help you undress?'

Jenny hesitated. Her cold heart melted a little under Charlotte's gentleness. All the jibes about her dirtiness that she'd suffered at school, about her ragged clothes, about the livestock in her hair, even about her mother and the uncles began to fade. She stared at Charlotte and decided to succumb to whatever the next few minutes held. She nodded.

'Right, let's take your plimsolls off first.'

Jenny held up her feet one after the other and then raised her arms as Charlotte peeled off the thin, faded cotton dress and lastly her knickers.

'Missis,' Jenny whispered.

'Charlotte,' she was reminded.

'Charlotte,' the child repeated after her, feeling shy at using the Christian name of a grown-up.

'Yes, dear?'

'I – I think I've got – things – in me hair.'

'Not to worry,' Charlotte said cheerfully. 'We'll give your hair a good wash in the bath and get rid of them all, shall we? And then perhaps if I comb your hair with a special comb—'

'You mean a nit comb?'

'Er – well – yes, but that would do the trick. Anyway, let's wash it first and see how we get on.'

Jenny blinked. This woman – a real lady in the young girl's eyes – wasn't throwing up her hands in horror or treating her as if she was something untouchable. Her puzzlement must have shown in her face for Charlotte smiled and said, 'I was brought up on a farm, Jenny. A few nits don't bother me, I promise you. In fact, my father still lives at Buckthorn Farm. Maybe we can go there one day and I'll show you all the animals.'

'Have you got pigs and hens?'

'Yes,' Charlotte put out her hand to help the girl into the bath, 'and cows. You can watch them being milked, if you like.'

Forgetting just what was happening as she chattered about the animals, Jenny put her hand into Charlotte's and climbed into the warm water. 'I ain't never seen a cow. Only in pictures.'

Charlotte began to soap the child's body, wondering at the bruises she saw on the girl's arm, but she knew better than to ask. Jenny submitted to the washing with good grace. In fact, she revelled in the smell of the soap and the bath salts. But when Charlotte asked her to lie back and have her hair washed, Jenny began to scream and thrash about in the water, sloshing it over the side of the bath on to the floor.

But Charlotte pressed on, talking soothingly to her all the time.

'I'll drown,' the girl screamed.

'I won't let your head go under the water, I promise. But don't wriggle so. I'll get shampoo in your eyes.'

Charlotte was stronger than the girl had bargained for and though she was getting soaked too, she lathered Jenny's hair and rinsed the shampoo off three times. Then she combed it with a fine-toothed comb, struggling to pull it through the tangled locks without hurting the child. But all the time, Jenny screamed and splashed.

The bathroom door opened and a merry voice called, 'Need any help, Charlotte?'

'Georgie!' Charlotte exclaimed. 'What a lovely surprise.'

At the sound of the man's voice, Jenny stopped shrieking and stared up at him. He was tall with fair, curly hair and blue eyes that sparkled with fun and laughter. He stepped through the water flooding the floor and squatted down beside the bath, holding out his hand. 'Hello, I'm Georgie. I'm very pleased to meet you. Would you like me to dry your hair for you, while Charlotte clears up all this mess?'

Jenny considered for a long moment then she smiled suddenly, quite unaware of the difference her smile made. It was like the sun appearing from behind a stormy sky. It transformed her mutinous little face, turning her into a pretty child in the blink of an eye. She nodded and then clambered to stand up.

Charlotte wrapped the huge white towel round her. 'Take her to the nursery. Kitty's been busy all morning cleaning it and lighting a fire in there. It should be cosy by now.'

As Georgie picked her up and carried her from the bathroom, Jenny wound her arms around his neck and clung to him. He carried her into the room Charlotte had shown her earlier – the one with all the toys that she'd been given permission to play with. The little girl from the poorest streets in the city could hardly believe her good fortune. The only thing she hadn't liked in this household so far had been the bath. But now, as the handsome young man sat down on the hearth rug beside her in front of the fire, she had to admit – though only to herself – that it was nice to feel clean, and so cosy and warm too.

'Now,' Georgie was saying, 'let's get that hair dry.'

Jenny sat patiently whilst he rubbed her hair with a warm, dry towel.

'My, what pretty blond curls you've got,' Georgie murmured.

Jenny giggled. 'You sound like the big, bad wolf in "Little Red Riding Hood".'

Georgie laughed too – a deep chuckle that made Jenny smile all the more. 'Oh dear, do I? Well, I promise you I'm not a big, bad wolf.'

Jenny twisted her head round to look at him. No, she thought, he doesn't look like a wolf. She liked the way his eyes crinkled up when he smiled – a smile that seemed to light up the whole of his face.

'There, I think that'll do,' he said, giving her hair a final rub. 'Now, have you got a nightie and dressing gown?'

Jenny shook her head.

'Oh – er – right, then I'll fetch a blanket to wrap you in. I won't be a minute.'

Georgie left the room and returned almost at once carrying a blanket from his own room. When she was snugly wrapped in it he asked, 'Shall I read you my favourite story? One that Charlotte used to read to me when I was little?'

Jenny stared at him without answering immediately. Then she asked, 'Why d'you call 'er Charlotte and not Mum?'

'Because she's not my mother. My mother died when I was born and my father married Charlotte – ooh, let me think—' he wrinkled his forehead – 'about eleven years ago now.'

'Is she your wicked step-muvver?'

Georgie threw back his head and laughed. 'Heavens, no. Charlotte is the sweetest, kindest woman you could ever meet.'

'Has she got any children, then?'

Georgie's face sobered and he whispered sadly, 'No. She and my father would love to have children, especially' – now he smiled wistfully – 'a little girl. My father always wanted a little girl, but he only got three boys.'

'Didn't he want you, then?'

For a moment Georgie looked shocked at her question. 'Oh yes, of course he did. He's never, ever made any of us feel unwanted.' Just in time, Georgie stopped himself from saying, 'Not even me when my poor mother died giving birth to me.' The girl was too young to be burdened with such thoughts. But Jenny was a lot more streetwise and knowledgeable than he gave her credit for and she tugged the young man's heartstrings when she said, in a matter-of-fact manner, 'I haven't got a dad and my mum didn't want me. She ses I'm her little mistake.'

Georgie didn't know what to say, but his arm tightened involuntarily around her. After a few moments, he cleared his throat and said, 'Now shall we find that book and I'll read to you?'

Jenny scrambled up. 'I'll get it. What's it called?'

'*The Wind in the Willows*. It's over there on the bookshelf. That one right at the end. That's it. You've got it.'

Jenny picked it off the shelf and carried it carefully back to Georgie. Then she sat down on the rug beside him.

'Have you read this before?' he asked.

Jenny shook her now-drying curls and Georgie paused to marvel at their silky softness and at her bright blue eyes. And when she smiled her cheeks dimpled prettily. She was going to be a beauty when she grew up.

'Nah, Mum never reads to me. Miss Chisholm does, though.'

'Who's Miss Chisholm?' Georgie asked, visualizing a kindly, elderly neighbour who took pity on the child. The young man could sense her loneliness even without being told details of her home life.

'My teacher. She brought us here on the train, but she's gone back to London now.'

'Really?' Georgie was surprised. 'I'd heard that teachers were staying to help out at the schools.'

Jenny shrugged. 'Well, Miss Chisholm isn't.'

She looked down at the book expectantly and so Georgie opened it and began to read. Jenny snuggled closer to him, resting her head on his chest and putting her thumb in her mouth.

His voice was deep and soothing and soon Jenny was drowsy. Georgie stopped reading the story and looked towards the door. Beneath her drooping eyelids, Jenny saw Charlotte and Miles standing there.

'We're reading,' Georgie said.

'So we see.'

They came into the room and stood looking down at Jenny and Georgie sitting on the rug.

'I think it's time she went to bed,' Jenny heard Charlotte say and though she would have liked to have argued to stay up a little longer, she really hadn't the energy to resist.

'Right, little one,' Georgie said. 'Time for beddibyes.' He picked her up and Jenny wound her arms round his neck and laid her head against his shoulder.

'Poor little scrap,' she heard Miles murmur and felt

his gentle touch on her curls as Georgie carried her out of the nursery and into the bedroom next door to it. He tucked her into bed and Jenny heard him say, 'Charlotte and Miles are right next door and I'm just down the corridor. If you want anything, you only have to shout and we'll come running. All right?'

'Mm.' She was very tired but there was one more thing she needed before she could go to sleep. 'Bert?'

She heard them speaking to each other, asking what it was she wanted. And then Charlotte must have realized for, after a moment, she was tucking the shabby teddy bear in beside her. And then, to Jenny's astonishment, Charlotte bent to kiss her forehead.

As the three grown-ups moved away, Jenny drifted into sleep, comforted and reassured by the night light left burning on the mantelpiece and still with the feeling of the gentle kiss on her forehead.

Ten

By the time Jenny stirred the following morning, the sunshine was streaming in through the gap in the curtains. She stretched, luxuriating in the softness of the bed. She opened her eyes and looked around the room at the pretty wallpaper and the white furniture. Her fingers touched the crisp cotton sheet and the soft blanket covering her. She sat up slowly, still staring about her. Then she remembered: she'd been evacuated with her schoolmates. Into her mind came the picture of Bobby and Sammy's train departing without her. Her heart contracted at the loss of her friends. Now she was amongst strangers and she had no idea what to expect. Remembering the trauma of the two disgusted spinsters throwing up their hands in horror at the sight of the head lice made her shudder again. She touched her hair. It felt soft and silky and her head no longer itched.

She sat up in the bed, clutching Bert, and wondered what she ought to do. She could hear no sounds from below and didn't know what time it was. Should she get up now or wait until someone called her?

Perhaps the maid, Kitty, would come or maybe the lady called Charlotte. Or better still, perhaps Georgie would come to wake her. But the minutes passed and no one came. Jenny grew restless and, at last, still clutching Bert, she scrambled out of the big bed and went to the window. She pulled the curtains open and looked out. The view from the bedroom window was over the flat land towards the sea and seemed, to the city child, to stretch for miles. The sky overhead was a cloudless bright blue and so vast that Jenny shrank back from the window. She'd never seen such space, such emptiness, nor experienced a place that was so quiet. Always, in the city, there seemed to be noise. Shouting, laughter, doors banging, the sounds of footsteps in the street and the rattle of wheels – even, now and then, the sound of a motor.

She padded to the door, opened it and peered out up and down the landing. Kitty was emerging from the room next door; the one Jenny had been told was where Charlotte and Miles slept.

'Oh!' Kitty was startled by the girl standing there completely naked and even more surprised that the child showed no embarrassment.

The maid blinked and then said kindly, ''Mornin', duck. Did ya sleep all right?'

Jenny nodded. Kitty came towards her. 'Let's help you get dressed and then I'll take you down for your breakfast. The other's have all finished theirs, but Cook says you can sit in her kitchen to have yours.'

'Where's Georgie?'

'Master Georgie? Oh, he's around somewhere.'

Jenny could see Kitty's look of disgust as she picked up the girl's clothes. The thin cotton dress was second-hand – maybe even third-hand – and washed so many times that even by the time Jenny got it, the pattern had faded. But now the pattern was even further obscured by dirt.

'This could do with a wash, duck,' Kitty said, but not unkindly. 'Have you got another frock?'

Jenny shook her head. She didn't want Kitty, who

was dressed so neatly in a clean, white apron, to see her only other dress, which was even dirtier than the one she was wearing.

'We'll have to put this 'un on for the minute, then. I'll tell madam and see if we can get you summat else. Where's your socks?'

'Ain't got none,' Jenny said, pulling on her plimsolls. They seemed too tight for her and already her big toe had worn a hole in the right one.

'Right, you'll have to do, then.'

Kitty had not troubled the child to wash; she'd heard the commotion in the bathroom the previous night and didn't want to spark another rumpus. Instead, she led the child down the wide staircase and through the door from the hallway that led to the kitchen.

'Here she is,' Kitty announced to Mrs Beddows.

The cook looked up from peeling apples and smiled a welcome. 'Come in, lovey. I bet you're hungry, aren't you?'

Jenny merely nodded and climbed on to the chair at one end of the table. Kitty set a bowl of cereal in front of her and poured creamy milk over it. 'There now, you get that down ya an' then I'll make you some toast.'

'I'll just go and find madam,' Jenny heard Kitty murmur to Cook. 'Tell her little 'un's up.'

But a few moments later, not only Charlotte but Miles, too, came into the kitchen as Jenny was finishing her breakfast.

'Hello,' Charlotte said softly. 'Did you sleep well?'

Jenny nodded.

'Cat's got her tongue, I reckon,' Kitty laughed.

Jenny gazed up at Charlotte and Miles, her glance going from one to the other. 'Where's Georgie?'

'He's outside. Would you like to go and find him?'

Jenny glanced towards the big kitchen window and shook her head. But as she slid off the chair, she looked up at Mrs Beddows and said politely, 'Thank you for my breakfast.'

'You're welcome, lovey.'

Charlotte held out her hand. 'Let's ask Georgie to come indoors, then, shall we?'

For the first time that morning, Jenny smiled.

Georgie played with her for the rest of the day. He showed her how to climb on the big rocking horse in the nursery and how to play several of the games stacked on the shelves; Snap, Draughts and even Happy Families, when they roped in Miles and Charlotte to play too. But the little girl's favourite time was after she'd succumbed to another bath and hair wash and was wrapped up snugly in a brand new nightdress and dressing gown and was sitting on Georgie's knee reading more chapters of *The Wind in the Willows*.

If she had to suffer a bath to be able to sit on Georgie's knee each night, Jenny decided, then it was a small price to pay.

When Charlotte had come home in the afternoon loaded with parcels, Jenny's eyes had been round with wonder as the garments spilled from the wrappings and the bags.

'A' they all for me?' she whispered.

Georgie laughed. 'Well, they're too small for Charlotte and I'd look silly in a girl's dress, now wouldn't I? How about you try them on and show us how pretty you look?'

With Kitty's help in her bedroom, Jenny had tried on everything, each time running downstairs to the morning room to show them. She stood before Charlotte, Miles and Georgie, twirling round.

'They fit nicely,' Charlotte smiled, 'but you'll have to come with me when we buy you some shoes. You'll need to have your feet measured properly.'

Jenny stared at her. 'Yer mean I'll 'ave to go outside?'

'Yes. Perhaps, Miles will take us in the motor car. Would you like that?'

Jenny didn't answer but none of them could miss the look of fear in her eyes. Over the next three days, they found out the cause of the child's apprehension. Used to the city back streets amidst tight-knit row upon row of houses and buildings, Jenny found the vastness of the sky and the flat, far-reaching landscape frightening.

Gently, Miles introduced her to the world outside the window as Georgie brought one of the horses from the stables on to the lawn for her to see. Then Miles took her to the front door and out on to the steps. They stood there for several minutes until she got used to the lawn stretching smoothly before them. Then, still holding her hand, he led her down the steps and on to the grass.

'Look what I found,' Georgie said, grinning as he returned from taking the horse back to the stable. He came towards them, bouncing a football.

By lunchtime, Jenny was happily kicking the ball backwards and forwards to Georgie on the front lawn.

Charlotte and Miles stood watching them.

'She seems to be settling in,' Miles said.

'Mm. But what's going to happen when Georgie has to go back the day after tomorrow?'

Eleven

What happened was a tantrum; a proper, full-blown tantrum.

When Georgie insisted on saying goodbye to Jenny, refusing to sneak off without telling her, Charlotte had warned him there'd be trouble. And trouble there certainly was. Jenny lay on the hall floor, screaming and kicking out at anyone who tried to get near her.

'That's just temper, that is,' Kitty remarked sagely. 'There's no tears.' She had a younger brother who displayed the same anger occasionally. She recognized the tantrum for exactly what it was.

Georgie, Miles and even Charlotte stood helplessly by, not knowing what to do. Georgie squatted down beside her and shouted above the noise. 'I've got to go now, Jen. Won't you come and wave me off?'

But the screams only grew louder.

He stood up, shook his father's hand and kissed Charlotte's cheek. And then he was gone.

At last, when she could see her efforts were in vain, Jenny stopped squealing. She rolled over on the floor and drew her knees up into a tight ball, tensing herself against the smack she was sure was coming. But instead she heard Miles's deep voice saying gently, 'Shall we go and see if we can find Ben and help feed the chickens? It's about time they were having their tea. Perhaps we could help feed the pigs too.'

Slowly Jenny twisted her head to look up at him. Miles was standing over her, with Charlotte just behind him. They didn't look angry, only worried. And Miles was holding out his hand to her and smiling. Slowly, Jenny stood up and picked up Bert from the floor. Then she marched towards the front door, knowing instinctively that Miles would follow.

'Will Ben play wiv me while Georgie's away?' Jenny asked as they walked towards the land and buildings closest to the manor known as Home Farm.

The Ravensfleet Estate, which Miles had bought in the mid-1920s, had three farms occupied by tenant farmers, but Home Farm had always, by tradition, been run by the man who owned the whole estate and lived in the manor. Miles, however, was no farmer and as soon as he was old enough, Ben had attended agricultural college and had then taken over the running of Home Farm, and attended to estate matters, 'like a duck to water', as the locals said. He loved the life and wanted no other.

'He might,' Miles said in answer to Jenny's question. 'But he works long hours on the farm.'

'What about the other one?'

'Philip? Oh, he's a bit of an old sobersides.'

Jenny twisted her head to look up at him.

'You didn't have no girls, then?'

Miles shook his head and Jenny, child though she still was, could see the sadness in his eyes. 'We were never – blessed with a daughter.'

'Georgie told me his muvver died when he was born.' She knew all about mothers dying in childbirth. It happened often where she lived. And most times the baby died too. 'But Georgie didn't die, did he? And mebbe Charlotte could still have a baby girl for you.'

75

Miles's voice trembled a little as he said, 'Maybe.' But the sorrow in his voice told the young girl that he'd given up hope.

She stepped closer to him and squeezed his hand as they walked on in silence.

At first, Jenny was afraid of the animals, but Ben, the quiet one of the family, introduced her gently to the most docile of the creatures first and gradually Jenny grew more confident in the outside world of the countryside.

On her first visit to the Sunday service at church with the family, Jenny met some of the other villagers including Charlotte's father, Osbert Crawford, a grumpy, nasty old man who looked down his nose at her. And she saw some of the other children she'd travelled here with. After the service, Billy Harrington came up to her. 'We've got to go to school here. Did yer know?'

Jenny nodded. 'Yeah. Charlotte told me yesterday.'

'Who's Charlotte?'

'Mrs Thornton.' Jenny nodded her head towards Charlotte, who was helping her father into his pony and trap.

The boy's eyes widened. 'You're allowed to call 'er "Charlotte"?'

Jenny nodded. 'Yeah. An' I call 'im "Miles".'

'Cor! But he's the squire – whatever that is. Everyone calls him Mester Thornton.'

Jenny shrugged. 'Well, I don't.'

'Don't they mind? Don't they tell you off?'

'They're nice,' Jenny murmured, realizing that this was the truth. 'They told me to call them that.' She turned to Billy. 'What about the folks you're with?'

'Yeah, they're all right, an' all. The Warrens. They're

76

tenant farmers of your Mr Thornton. That's them over there.' Billy pointed and Jenny saw the man and woman who'd come to the school to pick out Billy and his friend. With them were two younger men and a young woman.

'Who are the others talkin' to Mr and Mrs Warren?'

'That's their sons. John and Jackson. John's married. That's his trouble and strife with her arm through his.'

'How's Frankie getting' on?'

'Great. They're really kind to 'im. The missis gets him to collect eggs and feed the hens. He's started helping get the pigswill ready. The mester ses he'll let him 'ave a go at feeding 'em soon.'

Jenny didn't know what pigswill was, but she wasn't going to show her ignorance to Billy by asking. 'You like it here, then?'

Billy thrust out his chest. 'Yeah. I don't ever want to go back home, Jen. I hope this war lasts for ever.'

Jenny said nothing. Anyone overhearing what the boy had said would think it dreadful, but she understood exactly what Billy meant. He didn't want to go home to a father who beat him and kept him half-starved. Here he was being treated kindly and in the short time they'd been here, he already looked fitter and healthier.

'So,' Billy interrupted her thoughts, 'a' yer going to school termorrer?'

Jenny grimaced. 'S'pose I'll have to.'

It could have been worse, Jenny supposed, but not much.

The evacuees were all herded together to sit at the back of the room.

'Turn round and face the front,' the harassed teacher

77

snapped at her class, but heads continued to twist round to gawp at the newcomers. Eventually, the resident children settled to their work and the teacher – a grey-haired, thin woman called Miss Newton – came to the back of the room. 'Now,' she said sternly. 'We'd better see what level you're at.'

She handed them sheets of paper and pencils. 'Write me an essay about yourselves. Where you live, your families and so on.'

The newcomers stared at her; it was the worst possible thing she could have asked them to do. Two of the girls started to cry at once at the thought of their parents and the home they'd left behind. But Jenny's dilemma was different; she didn't want to tell anyone about her home life. What could she put about a mother who left her alone at night, who brought a succession of men back to the house and who banished her daughter to her bedroom while they were there? A mother who was handy with her slaps, but sparing with her hugs? How could she talk about the head lice, the dirty clothes she'd worn and the even dirtier home she lived in and how their neighbours, proud East Enders to the core, despaired of Dot Mercer's slovenly ways? If it hadn't been for Elsie Hutton and her family, Jenny would have gone hungry many a time.

And then the girl began to smile as an idea formed in her mind. She picked up her pencil and began to write. Whilst the other evacuees chewed their pencils and struggled to write even a few sentences, Jenny's words flowed on as she described life in the Hutton household with her mum and dad and her three brothers, Ronnie, Sammy and Bobby.

*

In the playground, the newcomers congregated together seeking comfort from the staring eyes and pointing fingers.

'Dun't go near them vaccies,' one local boy shouted. 'They've got nits.'

'Well, if we 'ave,' Billy shouted back, 'we've caught 'em off you.'

The jeering and the name-calling went on, until Jenny turned and marched towards the school gate, pulled it open and stepped into the road.

At that moment, Miss Newton appeared. 'You, girl, where do you think you're going? Come back here this instant.'

But Jenny marched on away from the school and towards the manor. She wasn't going to stay there another minute. Her curly hair was clean and shining and she was dressed in lovely new clothes, which Charlotte had bought for her. She even had proper shoes and white socks. The local children had no need to call any of them names. She'd been proud to walk to school that morning, to meet up with the other evacuee children and see the surprise on their faces at her transformation.

'Cor, Jen, you look a real toff. You must have got some good foster parents an' all, then,' Billy had greeted her. 'I thought, when I saw you yesterday at the church, they'd just got you some Sunday-best clothes.'

Jenny shook her head and smiled. 'Charlotte and Miles are ever so nice. All of 'em at the manor are. They've bought me loads of things.' She shuddered. 'But the first billet that Mr Tomkins took me to was awful. A couple of horrible old women.'

Billy's grin widened. 'Never mind, Jen. You've landed on yer feet now.'

And until this morning, she really thought she had,

but she wasn't going to put up with being called such names; especially now it wasn't true. When she'd been dirty and scruffy, there was nothing she could do about it, but now it was undeserved. She walked on, ignoring the questioning glances of the villagers she passed on the way.

'You all right, duck?' a woman asked her, but Jenny passed by without answering.

'Hello, lovey,' Mrs Beddows greeted her kindly as she entered by the back door. 'Come home for lunch, have you?'

Jenny nodded and climbed into a chair at the kitchen table.

'Maybe Mr and Mrs Thornton would like you to have lunch with them. Kitty's just about to serve it upstairs. Kitty—' she began, but Jenny cut her short.

'No, I'll stay here.'

'Perhaps it'd be best. You'll have to get back for afternoon school, won't you? Here, I'll serve you first before Kitty takes it up. Just sandwiches for lunch today and then it'll be pork chops and apple sauce for dinner tonight. You'll like that, won't you?'

Jenny smiled and nodded. For a moment, the cook's words made her think of home, of 'Mr Chops' and his butcher's shop. But the thought didn't make her feel homesick – not for a moment. She wanted to stay here now with Charlotte and Miles and the hope of Georgie coming home again on leave. But she expected to be in serious trouble for having left the school when she was supposed to stay there for her dinner. There'd surely be a punishment. Maybe they'd banish her to her bedroom and feed her on bread and water for several days. So, she'd make the most of the food before that happened, though she hoped she'd get to eat dinner tonight. But just in case she didn't, she ate all the sandwiches and the cheese and biscuits that followed.

'My, you've got a good appetite, lass, I'll say that. We'll soon feed you up a bit, lovey.' Mrs Beddows beamed at the empty plates that the child had actually licked clean of all the crumbs, much to Kitty's amusement. As she was about to climb down and make a pretence of returning to school, Ben entered by the back door.

'Hello,' he said in surprise at seeing her there. 'How did it go this morning?'

'Now, Master Ben, sit down. Your lunch is all ready.' Mrs Beddows bustled about the kitchen serving the young man. 'Master Ben always has his lunch with us down here on a weekday,' she explained to Jenny and laughed as she added, 'Mrs Thornton doesn't want him in her dining room with his muddy boots.'

Ben chuckled softly. 'Knowing Charlotte, I don't expect she'd mind, but it's easier when I'm working.' He stuck out his feet. 'But, see, today I've remembered to take my boots off to come into Mrs Beddow's spotless kitchen.'

Jenny stared at Ben as began to eat. He'd been kind to her, showing her the animals and telling her she needn't be afraid of them. But he was too busy to play with her. He didn't laugh and joke and tease her gently.

He was nice, she decided, but he wasn't Georgie.

Twelve

'I'm not going back there,' Jenny said obstinately when Mrs Beddows, glancing at the kitchen clock, reminded her she'd be late for afternoon school, if she didn't 'get a move on'.

The cook blinked. 'Why?'

The girl's chin was sticking out stubbornly and Mrs Beddows feared another outburst like the one the child had displayed on the day Georgie had gone back to camp.

'They call us "vaccies",' Jenny muttered, 'and they're – they're not nice to us.'

'Well, if you stay away, lovey, Mr and Mrs Thornton'll likely be in trouble for you not going to school. Now, you wouldn't like that, would you?'

Jenny hesitated. Everyone in this house had been kind to her, she couldn't deny that. She didn't *want* to deny it and, most of all, she didn't want to be sent away from here in disgrace. She knew instinctively that she'd landed on her 'plates of meat', as Arthur Osborne would have said.

She stood still, biting her lower lip until Mrs Beddows said, 'I think we'd better tell the master.'

Jenny didn't mean to be a cry-baby, but at the cook's words tears started in her eyes.

'Aw, lovey,' the woman bustled round the table and bent down to put her arms around her shoulders, hug-

82

ging her to her white apron. 'Don't cry. Mr Thornton'll sort it.'

'Will they send me away?'

'Send you away?' Mrs Beddows sounded shocked. 'Of course not. Fancy you thinking that. They love having you here.' She bent forward as if sharing a secret. 'The master's always longed for a little girl and now he's got you, so no, I don't reckon they'll send you away. But it would be nice of you to try to be a good girl for them, now wouldn't it?'

Jenny nodded vigorously until her blond curls shook, but she still declared, 'But I ain't going back to that school.'

'We'll see, we'll see,' was all Mrs Beddows said as she ushered her out of the kitchen and through the hall. She paused outside the morning room and then tapped on the door.

Hearing Charlotte say, 'Come in', the cook opened the door and was about to step into the room when Jenny broke free of her grasp and headed for the stairs, shouting back over her shoulder, 'They'll make me go. I know they will.'

Jenny ran swiftly up the stairs and into her bedroom, slamming the door so hard that Miles and Charlotte heard it downstairs. Miles threw down his newspaper and leapt to his feet as Mrs Beddows entered the room. 'Whatever's going on?'

The cook explained swiftly and Miles ran upstairs at once taking the steps two at a time.

'He won't be angry with the little lass, will he, Mrs Thornton? 'Cos she's frightened, that's what.'

'No, no, of course he won't.' Despite her concern over Jenny, Charlotte chuckled. 'Have you ever known the master get angry?'

Mrs Beddows laughed, 'Well, now you mention it, madam, no, I haven't. A nicer man never walked God's earth, as they say.'

Charlotte smiled but murmured, 'Nevertheless, I'd better go and see what's happening. It'll probably be Miles wanting some help.'

'I hope you don't think I was telling tales on her, madam, but there'll likely be trouble all round if she plays truant.'

'No, no, you were quite right to bring her to us and I'll make sure she understands you only have her best interests at heart.'

Mrs Beddows pulled a face. 'I doubt she'll see it that way. I reckon I'd best make her a chocolate cake. At least, whilst I can. I reckon there's going to be shortages and rationing soon enough.'

The sound of crying that had not yet escalated into screaming met Charlotte as she entered Jenny's bedroom. The child was sitting on her bed, clutching Bert. Miles was kneeling in front of her. He glanced round helplessly.

'There's been name-calling and the teacher – would you believe it, Charlotte? – set them all to write an essay about themselves. About their home life. I call that cruelty, don't you?'

'Tactless, to say the least,' Charlotte agreed.

Miles rose. 'I ought to speak to the teacher, but Jenny feels it will only make matters worse. I think she should stay away for a day or so.'

'Well.' Charlotte hesitated, glancing between the two of them. 'If you stay off school, Jenny, won't it make matters worse? The other evacuees will get settled in and you might feel even more left out.'

'Doesn't sound as if any of them will "settle in", as you put it,' Miles muttered, 'but I see what you mean.'

But neither Miles nor Charlotte could bring themselves to drag the little girl kicking and screaming to the school, because they knew that was what would happen if they tried.

'We're giving in to her,' Charlotte said worriedly as they got ready for bed that night. 'If only Georgie were here, I think she'd go to school for him.'

Miles chuckled softly, aware that the child was sleeping right next door. 'Georgie would have gone to the school like a knight in shining armour and played with all the children until he got them – what's the word I'm looking for?'

'Integrated?'

'Something like that. At least he'd have had them all playing together in no time.'

Charlotte sighed. 'But he's not here.'

They lay in bed side by side, but sleep evaded them and they continued to whisper far into the night, trying to think of a way to resolve the problem.

'Poor little scrap,' Charlotte said. 'Mrs Beddows told me that Jenny thought we'd send her away.'

Miles snorted. 'Well, she needn't worry about that. I'd never send her away.'

'No,' Charlotte murmured pensively. 'That's what Mrs Beddows told her.'

At last the loving couple fell asleep in each other's arms, still worrying about how to help the little girl who they now felt was their responsibility. Sending her away would never have crossed either of their minds.

*

Three days later, Mr Tomkins rode his bicycle up the drive of the Manor, dismounted and leaned it against the stone wall. Then, solemnly and not relishing his task, he climbed the steps and rang the door bell.

'Ah, Mr Tomkins,' Miles greeted him as he was shown into the study. He stood up and moved round the desk to shake the man's hand and bid him sit down. 'I was half expecting a visit from you. May I offer you tea or coffee? At least I can still offer you some at the moment.'

'No, no, thank you,' Mr Tomkins said, not wanting to delay the reason for his visit any longer than necessary. 'The thing is, Mr Thornton, I understand Jenny has not been to school for the last three days since walking out of the playground at lunchtime on Monday.'

'That's correct.'

'Is she ill? Only, it's usual to let the school know why a child is not attending and her teacher tells me there has been no word from you.'

'No, she's not ill, but she is very distressed at the treatment meted out to her and her fellow evacuees by the local children. And, I might add, the teacher is hardly to be commended for setting these poor children an essay to write about their homes, when they've been dragged away from them and must be feeling desperately lost and lonely. How thoughtless can the woman be?'

Mr Tomkins wriggled his shoulders in embarrassment. 'Well, yes, I grant you that was a little – inappropriate. But to get back to Jenny. It's our responsibility. She must go. Unless, of course . . .' He hesitated before outlining a plan that might solve not only Jenny's problem, but also alleviate the strain put on the local school by the sudden influx of evacuee children.

He left an hour and a half later with the task of getting in touch with the Education Authority to put the idea to them.

Meanwhile, with a beaming smile, Miles went in search of Charlotte. 'Not a word to Jenny yet,' he warned. 'It might not be approved.'

'Oh Miles, but wouldn't it be wonderful if it was?'

Thirteen

Charlotte and Miles waited in a state of excited antici-
pation tinged with anxiety for several days until Mr
Tomkins once again appeared at their door. They'd
longed to tell Jenny of their plan, but dared not do so in
case nothing came of it.

But when Miles himself opened the front door to the
ringing doorbell, Mr Tomkins was smiling. 'They've
agreed to a temporary trial, Mr Thornton and – if it
works and their inspectors are happy with the arrange-
ments – then they'll allow it to carry on.'

'Let's go and find Jenny,' Miles said happily, leading
the way up to the nursery. 'Come along, Mr Tomkins.'

Jenny was sitting on the floor playing a noisy game
of Snap with Charlotte. As the two men entered the
nursery, the girl glanced up, saw Mr Tomkins and
scrambled to her feet, ready to run. But Miles held out
his hands. 'Don't worry, Jenny. You're not going to
have to go to that school again.' His smile widened.
'School is coming to you. Here.'

The girl was puzzled and glanced from one to the
other. Then her face cleared. 'You mean I'm to be like a
toff's kid and have a governess?'

Miles laughed. 'Not exactly. We hadn't thought of
that, had we, Charlotte? No, what's going to happen
is this. The school is very overcrowded because of all
the children who came here at the same time as you.'

Another batch of evacuees had arrived only two days after Jenny and to accommodate all the children, both locals and the evacuees, the school had to divide the day. Some children – the younger ones – attended in the mornings, the older ones in the afternoon. 'And because we've plenty of room here,' Miles went on, 'we're going to hold classes here. A teacher will come and everyone will have their lunch here.' His smile widened. 'Mrs Beddows will be in her element cooking for so many.'

'Will it just be us vaccies?'

'That I can't say,' Mr Tomkins put in. 'It depends how the head teacher decides to divide the children up. I'm guessing they'll send children of a similar age, so it would be locals as well.'

Jenny grimaced and hung her head. Charlotte touched her shoulder and said softly, 'But Miles and I will be around to see there's no bullying or name-calling.'

'Will they be sending one of the teachers from the school?' Miles asked Mr Tomkins.

Mr Tomkins shrugged. 'I really don't know.'

Jenny's head shot up. 'Miss Chisholm could come back.'

Now no one answered, unable to find the words to explain to the child that her teacher was needed in London. Already, there was talk of the evacuees going home because the expected bombing attacks had not started.

Miles and Charlotte threw themselves into the preparations.

'We'll use the dining room as their classroom and they can have their lunch served there too,' Miles suggested.

'I think it would be better for Mrs Beddows and Kitty

if they were to eat in the kitchen. Not so much fetching and carrying.'

'Wouldn't they be in Mrs Beddows's way?'

Charlotte shook her head. 'She says not. We've talked about the possibility already and she plans to move the big kitchen table a little. They'll all be able to sit around that and then she'll have a smaller one to work on.'

'Well, if she's sure. It would be easier than the children having to clear away their books at lunchtime every day, I grant you.'

With Wilkins's help, although not, it seemed from the anxious expression on his face, with his complete approval, a blackboard and easel was set up at one end of the room and places set around Charlotte's long dining table. Books were brought from the school, but Miles went into the nearby town of Lynthorpe and bought a stack of writing paper, drawing paper, pencils and crayons. He bought storybooks and he and Wilkins moved a small bookcase from Miles's own study into the dining room for the children to use. Jenny watched in wonderment. She'd never met a man like Miles Thornton, nor a woman like Charlotte either, if it came to that. She couldn't believe they were going to so much trouble to help other people, strangers in their midst.

On the Sunday evening before lessons were due to start at the manor the following morning, Miles took Jenny's hand and led her into the dining room with Charlotte following.

'Now, I need your help, Jenny,' he said. 'Have we missed anything? Is there something – anything – you'll need that we've forgotten?'

Jenny walked all round the table, looking at the place settings, six down each side of the table and one at the end, with the teacher's place at the head. Exercise books and writing paper were neatly stacked and a storybook was set beside each place. Jenny ran her finger along the gleaming polished mahogany surface of the table. She looked up at Miles with worried eyes. 'What if they scratch your table? They – they might even carve their names. Some of our lot might—'

To the young girl's surprise, Miles was chuckling. 'Just like I did when I was at school.' He laughed even louder as he added, 'But no one will get the cane here like I did. Don't worry, Jenny. A table's just a table. Your happiness – and those of your fellow evacuees – is far more important than any old table.'

Jenny was still running her fingers gently up and down the surface. 'But it's lovely. It shines so.' She breathed in. 'And it smells so nice.'

'Kitty's been giving it an extra polish.'

Jenny glanced at Charlotte. Maybe Miles didn't mind about his table, but his wife might. But she was smiling too.

'I'll watch 'em,' Jenny promised.

The next morning, twelve children arrived at the manor just before nine o'clock. Most of them were evacuees, but there were one or two locals too.

'Hello, Alfie,' Charlotte greeted one of the boys. She turned to Jenny. 'Jenny, this is Alfie Norton. He lives in one of the cottages on the way to Buckthorn Farm. Do you remember me telling you that Mr and Mrs Norton and their three children lived there?'

Jenny had been to Buckthorn Farm with Charlotte once. It was where Charlotte's father, Osbert Crawford, lived on his own with only a housekeeper and her husband to help him. And no wonder, Jenny had thought. Who'd want to live with that grumpy old man? She could hardly believe that such a horrible man was Charlotte's father.

'Alfie's father,' Charlotte was explaining, 'manages Buckthorn Farm now.'

Alfie grinned. 'That's what you say, miss, but we all know it's still you what runs things. Me dad only does what you tell him, he'd be the first to say that.'

'Now, now, Alfie, I couldn't manage without your father.'

'You did for years, miss, so me grandad ses when he was your foreman.' Alfie grinned at Jenny. 'As good as any man at running a farm was Miss Charlotte. That's what me grandad always ses.'

'Who's your grandad?' Jenny asked.

'Mr Warren at Purslane Farm. He's Mester Thornton's tenant now, but he used to live in the cottage where we live and he worked for Miss Charlotte when she ran Buckthorn Farm afore she got married.'

'That's where Billy is,' Jenny smiled, 'at Purslane Farm. And Frankie. They really like your grandad and your grandma. Is Billy coming here for lessons? Oh I do hope so . . .'

Her wish was answered immediately as she looked beyond the front door to see Billy helping Frankie down from the back of a farm cart, driven by the very man they'd been talking about – Joe Warren. He climbed down and came up the front steps, pulling his cap off his head as he did so.

''Morning, Miss Charlotte. Hello, Alfie lad. You coming here an' all? We've brought Billy and Frankie. Teacher thought it best. Little lad gets teased because of his leg iron and then Billy sticks up for him and it ends up in a fight.'

'We'll watch out for them both, Joe,' Charlotte promised. 'Don't you worry.'

'Oh, I won't. Not now they're both here with you. I heard as how they'll all be staying here for dinner, miss, is that right?' When Charlotte nodded, Joe added, 'Then I'll fetch 'em home in the cart about four.'

'Perfect, Joe, though I think Mr Thornton wants to play games on the lawn with them after school when it's fine. You know, let them run some of their energy off and get a bit of fresh air too. So make it half past, would you?'

Joe's face sobered. 'Frankie won't be able to play with them.'

'No, I realize that, but I can always be on hand to do something with him. Read or play cards or board games or do a jigsaw – whatever he wants to do.'

Joe's face cleared and he pulled on his cap, nodded to them all and went back down the steps to his horse and cart.

At first the new arrivals were nervous and subdued. Even the locals, who knew Miles and Charlotte Thornton, were in awe of being in the 'squire's house'. But that afternoon when the teacher, Miss Parker, ended lessons for the day, Miles was waiting in the hall with a football in his hand.

'Now,' he said, raising his voice as the children tumbled out of the dining room in their haste to end the school day. As they saw Miles, they stopped and huddled together, shuffling their feet. Were they in trouble? They glanced at each other, wondering what they had done wrong during the day. But Miles was smiling.

'Now, if any of you don't have to get home immediately – by that I mean, as long as your mothers or the

93

people you're staying with won't worry where you are – how about a game of football on the front lawn?'

The hall echoed with the shouts of 'Yes, yes,' and twelve of the thirteen children ran out of the front door, down the steps and capered about on the lawn whilst Charlotte appeared with an armful of books and games.

'We'll go into the morning room, Frankie. What would you like us to do?'

The boy's face brightened and he limped after Charlotte as Miles began to follow the children outside. But as he moved to the front door, Miles saw his manservant, Wilkins, lurking near the stairs.

'Would you like to act as linesman, Wilkins?'

The dour, strait-laced man who'd been trained as a butler and valet looked horror-struck as if his employer had asked him to jump naked into the cold North Sea. 'I – er – um – would rather not, sir. If you don't mind.'

'Not at all, Wilkins. Perhaps you could bring out some of Mrs Beddows's home-made lemonade at half-time. We'll play for about fifteen minutes each way. So in about a quarter of an hour . . . ?'

Wilkins, manfully hiding his disapproval, gave a little bow and murmured, 'Very good, sir.'

But down in the kitchen Wilkins gave vent to his feelings. 'Well, I've seen it all now. Scruffy little urchins sitting round the dining table and running riot through the house. And now the garden's going to be a muddy football pitch in no time. I've never seen the like in all my born days, I haven't.'

'Now just you listen to me, Mr Wilkins.' Mrs Beddows waved her wooden spoon at him. 'Ever since this war started you've been moaning because you're too old to volunteer. We've told you and told you to join the local volunteers for some sort of war work—'

'Air raid precautions warden,' Wilkins murmured. 'That's what I was thinking of doing.'

'Yes, that, but you reckon you can't do that because the master needs you here at his beck and call, even though he's told you it's fine with him for you to join. But no, you know best. But you're still feeling guilty because you're not "doing your bit", aren't you?' Wilkins opened his mouth but Mrs Beddows was not about to let him get a word in. 'Well, this is the way we can all do our bit. Look after these poor bairns who've been sent miles from their homes into the hands of strangers. They had no idea where they were going – I expect half of them still don't know exactly where they are – and probably their parents don't know either.'

Now Wilkins was staring at her and when at last she paused for breath, he said hesitantly, 'So – so you think this is worthwhile war work?'

'Of course it is, you silly man. The authorities thought it necessary to send these children to safety and if we're that "safety", then it's our duty and our privilege' – again the wooden spoon was waved in the air – 'to look after them. They're the next generation, Mr Wilkins. They're the future and we've got to make sure it's not under Hitler's jackboot. And if it means a bit of mud on the floor and a scratch or two on the dining table, then it's a small price to pay.' Her voice dropped and she lifted the corner of her apron to her eye. 'And if you can't think of any other good reason, then do it for Master Georgie. Just think of him flying up there over the Channel in his plane.'

Solemnly and somewhat abashed, Wilkins murmured,

'You're right, Mrs Beddows. And thank you. Now,' he went on briskly, squaring his shoulders, 'Mr Thornton wants some of your home-made lemonade for everyone at half-time.'

Mrs Beddows beamed.

For the first few weeks of the war – indeed for the first few months – nothing much seemed to be happening. Several evacuees went home. Parents, missing their children and heartened by the lack of the expected bombing, sent for them. The numbers at the temporary school dwindled and now there were only nine children coming each day to the manor. Once more, Mr Tomkins rode up the drive on his bicycle.

'The head says they could manage at the school now, if you'd prefer it.'

'I wouldn't,' Miles said shortly. 'Jenny is settling nicely now. We're not getting so many tantrums and she smiles now more than she frowns.'

'She looks a different child, Mr Thornton. You've done wonders. You and Mrs Thornton. When I think about the short time she was with us – when the Miss Listers sent her back—' He shuddered. 'My poor Mabel didn't know how to handle her either.'

Miles said nothing, but he was thinking plenty. How could people be so hard-hearted? Could they really not see beyond the outward dirty appearance to the small, frightened little girl who obviously didn't have much of a home life to start with? Obviously not, he thought grimly. But he smiled at Mr Tomkins.

'Well, she's much better now and I don't want anything to disrupt that.'

'You do realize that if her mother sends for her to go

back home,' Mr Tomkins explained carefully, 'we'll have no choice but to—'

'We'll worry about that when it happens. In the meantime, I want the children to carry on having their lessons here. I'll even pay their teacher out of my own pocket, if it means—'

'Oh, that won't be necessary, I can assure you. The head would actually be very grateful if the arrangement could continue, but she felt it only fair to let you know that—'

'Quite,' Miles said tersely. 'But please tell her we enjoy having them here. Besides, we've got Christmas coming up and the children are getting excited about everything we've got planned for the end of term.'

Mr Tomkins was still shaking his head in disbelief as he mounted his bicycle once more and rode off to impart the good news to the headmistress. He'd never met anyone quite like Miles Thornton.

When yet another child announced excitedly that she was going home, Miles began to fear that Jenny's mother, too, would send for her, but the days went by and no word came. And strangely, Jenny never asked about when she might go back to London. Her only question – much to the amusement of Miles and Charlotte – was, 'When's Georgie coming home again?'

Fourteen

'Sir – Madam – might I have a word?'

Mrs Beddows knocked on the door of the morning room just after lunch one rainy November day. The children were having their afternoon lessons and Miles was watching for a break in the weather so that he could take them into the garden for a game of football that would leave them pink-cheeked and breathless as soon as lessons ended for the day.

'Of course, Mrs Beddows,' he said, moving away from the window. 'Come in. Do sit down.'

'It'll not take long, Mr Thornton.' Her glance shifted towards Charlotte. 'It's really madam I ought to be asking, I suppose.' Charlotte retrieved her knitting from beneath a cushion where she'd hidden it quickly when the knock had sounded on the door.

'I'm knitting dolls' clothes for Jenny's Christmas present,' she explained. 'I've bought a doll, but it needs dressing. I thought it might be her coming in.'

Miles chuckled. 'Jenny wouldn't knock, my love. You'll have to be more careful than that.'

'I've been thinking,' Mrs Beddows said. 'I'm about to make my Christmas puddings and I wondered – if their teacher agrees, of course – if the children would like to help me.'

Charlotte stared at her for a moment. 'I'm sure they'd

love it, Mrs Beddows, but wouldn't they make an awful mess?'

Mrs Beddows smiled. 'I'm sure they would, madam, but the kitchen'll clean. And Kitty's up for it. I thought we could let them all make a little pudding each to take home – I mean, to where they're staying. That's if you wouldn't mind the cost, madam.'

'It's not that, Mrs Beddows, but what about all the ingredients? We're starting to get shortages now and I read in the papers yesterday that butter, bacon and sugar are going to be rationed very soon.'

Mrs Beddows flapped her hand and laughed. 'Oh, I've had all the dry ingredients put away in the pantry since the summer. And what I haven't got, I know I can get. Master Ben'll let me have eggs, I don't doubt. And I'm sure there'll be carrots.'

'What about sugar?' Charlotte was well aware of the recipe Mrs Beddows used.

'I've plenty.'

'We could let them make a pudding to send home – to their real homes, I mean,' Miles put in excitedly. 'They must be feeling the pinch in London by now. What d'you think, Charlotte?'

'That's a lovely idea, but we should talk to their teacher first. She'll have to agree.'

Miss Parker was only too happy. 'It'll be a cookery lesson combined with learning about Christmas traditions. I'd already planned a lesson about why we have a Christmas tree and so on. That'll be perfect.' She beamed. 'I'll bring my apron.'

The following afternoon the kitchen at the manor had never seen such fun and laughter. Even Wilkins stood near the dresser, well out of the way, but smiling benignly at the 'goings on'. Now nothing shocked the man and to his surprise he was enjoying having the children in the house. Despite the extra work, he marvelled at the change not only in Jenny but also in the faces of all the evacuees since they'd first arrived. The skinny, pale-faced children now glowed with health, and laughter and running footsteps rang through the once-quiet house. It reminded him – and he was sure it did the same for the Thorntons – of the time when the three boys – Philip, Ben and Georgie – had been youngsters.

'Now,' Mrs Beddows began, taking charge. The children stood around the table, covered with aprons or with tea towels tied around their waists. The boys had removed their jackets and rolled up their shirt sleeves. Miss Parker, Miles and Charlotte, suitably dressed in aprons too, stood with them, quite prepared to be part of the class.

'Have you all washed your hands thoroughly?'

'Yes, Mrs Beddows,' came the chorus.

'Today we'll be preparing the first stage of making the puddings. There are four ingredients, which have to be mixed together and left overnight.'

Around the table, faces fell.

'But,' the cook went on, 'there's plenty to prepare for tomorrow afternoon when you can all come back again.'

'When do we get a pudding to eat?' Billy piped up.

'Not until Christmas Day,' Mrs Beddows said firmly.

'But some of us might 'ave gone home by then.'

A look of longing crossed some of their faces, but Jenny said, 'I ain't goin' home. I'm staying here.'

'Yer'll 'ave ter go if yer mam sends for yer.' Billy prodded her in the ribs. 'Even I'll 'ave ter go if the ol' man wants me back.' He dropped his voice as he added, 'I'm just hoping 'ee won't.'

'Well, my mum won't neither, so there. She doesn't want me back.'

'Now, now,' Mrs Beddows chided. 'Let's get started. Some of you can grate the carrot. Be careful not to catch your fingers on the grater and the rest of you can crumble the bread into crumbs and then there's the suet to prepare . . .'

By home time, several large bowls of breadcrumbs, mixed in equal measure with grated carrot, suet and sugar, were set on the side and covered over with a damp teacloth for the next twenty-four hours.

It was already dusk by the time they washed their hands at the deep white sink in the scullery and trooped outside.

'It's got a bit late today,' Miles announced. 'But a quick game – five minutes each way – and then it'll be time you were going home.'

As they trooped out of the back door and ran around the house to the front lawn, which was already beginning to look like the muddy football pitch that Wilkins had gloomily predicted, Charlotte and Mrs Beddows exchanged an amused glance.

'Doesn't want to miss his game of football, does he?' the cook murmured.

Charlotte shook her head. 'No. He loves having them all here and tries to put off them leaving for as long as possible.'

'Well, you've got Jenny.'

A cloud of anxiety crossed Charlotte's face. 'Yes, but I'm so afraid that he – both of us, I suppose, if I'm honest – we're getting too attached to her. When she has to go home . . .' Her voice faded away and there was already a stricken look in her eyes at the anticipated loss.

'By the sounds of it, madam,' Mrs Beddows said briskly, 'that won't be happening yet. You've had no word from her mother, have you?'

Charlotte shook her head. 'No. Jenny's not even had a letter and we made sure she sent a postcard home when she first came here to let her mother know the address. I can't understand it.'

Mrs Beddows sniffed. 'By the look of the poor mite when she got here, mebbe the mother doesn't care. And Jenny doesn't seem to be homesick. Not in the slightest.' The cook nodded towards the place where Jenny had stood at the table. 'You heard what she said this afternoon.'

'Yes,' Charlotte's voice was husky. 'Yes, I did. Poor little girl.'

But at that moment the 'poor little girl' was capering on the lawn, squealing with joy in the noisy game of football. She couldn't remember ever having enjoyed herself so much or being so happy. If only Bobby could have been here to join in the fun. She hoped the Huttons were all right; Charlotte still hadn't been able to find out where they were now.

And if Georgie would come home too, then her life would be perfect.

The puddings had been finished, steamed for two hours and carried carefully home or back to their billets by the other children. Jenny's was safely in Mrs Beddows's pantry to be served to the family on Christmas Day.

But Georgie was still not home.

He came at last, on the day before Christmas Eve, staggering in through the front door beneath an armful of presents for everyone.

Jenny danced around the hall, clapping her hands. 'He's home. Georgie's home and he looks like Father Christmas.'

Georgie stopped and cast a horrified glance at Charlotte. 'Oh lor',' he muttered. 'I never thought.'

Calmly, Charlotte moved forward to help him. 'It's all right. All under control. Don't worry. Jenny – come and help put all these in a pile near the stairs.'

The girl ran forward eagerly to take the parcels from Georgie.

'They've all got to be wrapped up and put under the tree for Christmas morning.'

'But we haven't got a tree.' Jenny looked up at Georgie. 'Have you brought a tree an' all?'

Before he could answer, Miles appeared from his study. 'Not yet, but Ben is bringing one home tonight.' He clasped his son's hand warmly as he said, 'Good to see you, Georgie. Everyone's home now. Philip arrived a couple of hours ago on the lunchtime train.'

It was the first time Jenny had met Miles's eldest son. When he'd walked in through the front door, she'd stood on the bottom step of the stairs eyeing him warily as Miles and Charlotte greeted him. He was tall and slim and, like Georgie, fair haired. In fact, his hair, straight and smoothed back from his forehead, was so blond it was almost white. He had blue eyes too, but whereas Georgie's were merry Philip's were rather cold.

'Who's this?' he'd asked, catching sight of Jenny.

Charlotte had made the introductions, but instead of picking her up and swinging her round as Georgie might have done, he gave her a curt nod as he passed her on the stairs on the way to take his bags up to his room. He didn't even smile at her.

But Georgie's arrival a little later was very different.

At once, fun and laughter pervaded the house as he asked, 'I haven't missed the tree decorating, then?'

'No, we waited for you especially,' Charlotte said.

So, the whole family was together when Ben struggled in with a huge tree that he then stood in the corner near the stairs. There was much laughter as the men tried to get the tree to stand up straight in the wooden barrel, sawn in half and filled with earth to plant the tree in.

'Is it straight yet, Jen?' Georgie asked, panting as he straightened up. 'We're relying on you to tell us.'

Charlotte and Jenny stood back from the tree. 'A bit to the left, I think,' Charlotte said. 'What do you say, Jenny?'

'That way,' Jenny said, flinging out her left arm.

'Right, chaps, let's give it another go.'

At last the tree was positioned to everyone's satisfaction and the decorating began.

'Now, Father, you must put the fairy on the top – just like you always have.'

After all the laughter and chatter and gentle arguing where the baubles should hang, where the paper streamers should go, there was a quieter moment when Miles climbed up the stairs and leaned over the banister to attach the fairy to the top of the tree.

'And now,' Philip said languidly, 'do you think we could have dinner? I'm starving.'

Jenny monopolized Georgie. She was in awe of Philip, who, of all the family, kept himself aloof from the jollity, though he had joined in with decorating the tree. She liked Ben; he was kind, but quieter than the ebullient Georgie. But she couldn't weigh Philip up. He was something grand – a lawyer – in the city and she felt he looked down on her. She was thankful he'd not seen her when she first arrived. Though she stared at Philip, she slipped her hand into Georgie's.

'Will you read to me tonight?' she whispered.

'Of course. How far have you got with *The Wind in the Willows*?'

She smiled up at him, her cheeks dimpling prettily, her shining blond curls dancing. 'We haven't read any more. That's *your* book. Charlotte reads *The Swiss Family Robinson* but I wouldn't want to be a castaway, would you?'

'But they're very enterprising, aren't they?'

The child looked puzzled.

'I mean, they make the best of it and build a shelter and find food, don't they?'

She nodded. 'They're all together. A family. A real family . . .' Her tone was wistful and Georgie wondered, not for the first time, just what this poor kid's home life was really like. 'But if you were on your own . . .'

'Yes, that would be a bit tough, wouldn't it?' He squeezed her hand. 'But you're part of our family now, aren't you?'

She looked up at him and he was staggered by the hope in her eyes. 'For always?'

'Well, for a while. Until it's safe for you to go back home.'

'They don't want me back,' she said in a small voice. 'Mum's got this new feller. Well, I suppose he's not that new now. She met him last New Year's Eve. He's all right but I know they'd rather be just on their own.'

Georgie – the brave young flight lieutenant who flew his Hurricane several times a week over the Channel – felt as if his heart might break.

Fifteen

No present, not even a card or a letter, arrived for Jenny and though no one referred to it, the whole family tried to compensate for the child's mother's lack of interest.

'Not one word from her mother,' Miles raged when they were sitting together round the fire late on Christmas Eve after Jenny was in bed and asleep. 'No card, no present – nothing!'

'Not everyone's as big on "family" as you and Charlotte,' Philip drawled. When his father had first married Charlotte, Philip had resented the woman he saw as trying to take his mother's place. Now there was a truce between them, uneasy though it still sometimes was. 'And of course,' he added with a touch of sarcasm, 'Jenny's a girl. The daughter you always wanted, Father.'

He was touching on a delicate subject – the secret sorrow that Miles and Charlotte had to live with – that she'd not been able to give him more children and especially the daughter he'd always longed for.

'Well, I've offered to wear a wig and dress up in a skirt,' Georgie joked, 'but I'm not really the girlie type.'

Everyone laughed – they couldn't help it – as the image of the tall, broad-shouldered, handsome young man in a dress and blond wig entered their minds.

'Heaven forbid!' Miles muttered, but his mood lightened. No one could stay miserable or angry for long when Georgie was around. He'd always been greatly loved by all his family and Miles had never allowed him to bear any feelings of guilt because his birth had caused Louisa's death. He'd even been forgiven, as Georgie himself would say, for not being a girl. And it was Georgie who, over the next two days, made everyone forget the war; Georgie who arranged the noisy games and even managed to involve Philip, much to everyone's surprise, in a hilarious game of charades. And it was Georgie who focused all his attention on the little girl far from home and her own family. He longed to ask her about them, but knew he'd be treading on feelings that the young girl was perhaps trying to keep hidden. But Jenny displayed no sign of homesickness, no sign of missing her mother, though she did refer once to her friends, the Hutton family.

It was while they were eating Christmas dinner that she suddenly said, 'I hope Bobby's getting a dinner as good as this.'

There was silence round the table until Georgie asked gently, 'Who's Bobby?'

'My friend. He lives next door.' She laid her knife and fork neatly on the empty plate as Charlotte had taught her to do and began to tick the members of the Hutton family off on her fingers. 'There's Bobby. He's a year older than me. Then there's Sammy – ' she wrinkled her forehead. 'I think he's twelve and then Ronnie. He's the oldest. He's left school an' goes to work. That's why he wasn't 'vacuated.'

'And their mother?' Georgie was the only one who dared ask and even then his tone was tentative.

Jenny's face brightened. 'Aunty Elsie? She's nice. I go to their house a lot when Mum's out.'

Now, even Georgie couldn't voice the questions that were tumbling around in his head, but Jenny carried on.

'And then there's Uncle Sid – their dad. He works on the docks now but he used to be in the navy. Aunty Elsie said he'd be going back in if there was a war.' Her face clouded. 'I wonder if he has.'

'Charlotte told me that you came on the train with Bobby and Sammy but they went on somewhere else,' Miles put in. 'I did ask Mr Tomkins, Jen, but he didn't know anything. Would you like me to try and find out? If they're not too far away, maybe we could take you to see them.'

Jenny's face brightened. 'Would you?'

'Of course.'

'It seems', Philip drawled, glancing at Georgie, 'that we have another golden-haired cherub in our midst, now you're too old to lay claim to the title.'

Georgie only grinned, but Jenny, though not understanding the reference to the description that folk had given Georgie as an impish though adorable youngster, nevertheless instinctively recognized the sarcasm in Philip's tone.

She frowned and her blue eyes glittered as she glared at him.

The day after Boxing Day, Georgie was obliged to return to camp.

There was no tantrum this time, but Jenny clung to him.

'I'll be home again as soon as I can,' he promised. 'And next time, if the weather's better, I'll take you down to the beach. You've not been yet, have you?'

Jenny shook her head.

'Now be a brave girl, because I want you to look

after Miles and Charlotte and old Ben here for me. Will you do that?'

Now she nodded and tried valiantly to stem the tears. But as she stood on the top step, waving goodbye to him as he walked away down the drive on his way to the railway station, she could no longer hold back the heart-wrenching sobs.

But Georgie was unable to keep his promise to her. The weeks turned into months and still he didn't come home. Miles and Charlotte did not discuss war news in front of Jenny. In fact, they deliberately protected her from it. But she wanted to know what was happening to Georgie and, just as she had at home, Jenny began to eavesdrop. It hadn't been difficult at home; the walls were thin and Dot and Arthur made no attempt to keep their voices low. At the manor it was more difficult for if she listened outside Miles's study or the door of the morning room, Wilkins was likely to creep up and catch her.

But just before Easter, Georgie arrived unexpectedly late one afternoon just as the children were leaving the manor.

'Hey,' he grinned as he came into the hall and dropped his kitbag, 'am I just in time for a game of footie?'

'Georgie!' Jenny squealed and flung herself into his arms. He swung her round and then set her down again. 'My, you're growing.' He looked round at all the other children. 'All of you are. Now, let me get changed out of my uniform and I'll be with you. My father is already waiting on the lawn, kicking the football up and down . . .'

Gales of laughter rang through the grounds of the manor for the next half an hour and when it was time for the other children to go home, Miles, Georgie and Jenny came into the house.

'Oh my – I must be getting old,' Georgie declared, flopping into an armchair in Charlotte's morning room.

'How long have you got?' Charlotte asked as she poured tea.

Georgie pulled a face. 'Only two days, I'm afraid. The powers that be think things are hotting up across the Channel and all leave might be cancelled, so I thought I'd better get a quick visit in before it does.'

Jenny scrambled on to the broad arm of his chair and put her arm round his neck. 'You promised to take me to the beach when you came home again. Can we go tomorrow?'

'What about school?'

'We could go after.'

'What about the football?'

'After that.'

Georgie chuckled. 'I'm not going to get out of it, am I?'

Jenny grinned and shook her blond curls.

'What about the other children? Do you want them to come with us?'

'No. Just you an' me,' the girl said firmly. Charlotte and Miles hid their smiles.

'Now,' Georgie said in a serious voice as they tramped down the long straight lane leading from the manor to the seashore. 'There are one or two things you must remember if you ever come to the beach on your own. One, you must always watch out for the tide coming in. On this part of the coast, the waves swirl round and form big pools called creeks. You can easily get cut off.'

As they crested the top of the dunes, Jenny said, 'I'd never seen the sea before I came here. Now I love it, but it is big, isn't it?'

Georgie nodded as his glance scanned the shore. 'We can't get right to the water's edge, by the look of it. They've put rolls of barbed wire everywhere. Charlotte said they had but I hadn't seen it for myself.' He gave a heavy sigh. 'You're not seeing it at its best, Jen. I am sorry.'

With her hand tucked into his warm grasp, Jenny didn't care.

'Tell you what, we'll walk across this bit of marshy ground and I'll show you where the samphire grows. It's not ready for picking until June but I'll show you what we do. Now, there's a box somewhere here where we leave pegs and rags to mark the path.'

'Why?'

'Because if a sea mist comes in – and they do some-times very quickly – you have to be able to find your way back. It's very easy to lose your sense of direction in a fog and you might walk out towards the sea instead of away from it. Ah yes, here it is.'

For the next hour, Georgie painstakingly marked a path through the marsh towards where the samphire grew.

'What's samphire?' the city child wanted to know.

'It's a dark green marsh plant that you can boil and eat as a vegetable. You must come with Charlotte or Miles when it's in season and take it home for Mrs Bed-dows to cook for you. She used to do that for me when I first came here and Charlotte brought me to gather it.

And she showed me how to mark the path sticks and tie the white rags on, just like I'm showing you.' Suddenly, his voice sounded wistful.

'Charlotte's not your mum, is she, but you love her, don't you?'

Softly, Georgie said, 'Yes, I do.'

Jenny dropped her head and whispered, 'I wish she was my mum. I wish I could stay here for ever and ever.'

Georgie couldn't answer her for the lump in his throat for he knew that both Charlotte and Miles wished exactly the same thing. But sadly, he couldn't tell Jenny so.

Whatever her own mother was like, however she treated this lovely girl whom she didn't deserve, she was still her mother and, one day, she'd want her daughter back.

It was a couple of weeks or so after Georgie had gone back that Jenny watched Miles reading his morning paper with a solemn face. Although he folded it up and tucked it under his arm to carry it to his study, she overheard him telling Charlotte later that Hitler had invaded Denmark and Norway. Jenny wasn't sure exactly what this meant, but from the seriousness of his tone she knew it was bad news.

What about Georgie? she wanted to shout, but she couldn't. She couldn't let them know she'd heard or they'd be more careful in future and she'd learn nothing.

But by the beginning of June, even Miles and Charlotte could not keep the news of the evacuation of the British Expeditionary Force from Dunkirk from Jenny. Everyone was talking about it, even the children who still came to the manor. They plied their teacher with so many questions that, in the end, Miss Parker was obliged to tell them a little about what was happening.

'But it's the army, isn't it, Miss?' Jenny said. 'Not the RAF. It's not Georgie, is it?'

Miss Parker forced a smile. 'No, dear,' she was able to say quite truthfully. But what she didn't explain to the children was that now Britain stood alone and only the RAF could protect its shores and its people.

Sixteen

After school that same day, Miles had to go into town and Charlotte was visiting her father at Buckthorn Farm. The other children and Miss Parker had left and Jenny was on her own. She wandered through the house, upstairs to the nursery, but today the toys didn't interest her. She picked up the battered copy of *The Wind in the Willows*, but she had no heart to try to read it herself when Georgie wasn't there. She went into his bedroom, but everything was so neat and tidy. Nothing was set out on the dressing table; no clothes lying on the bed ready for him to put on. She ran her fingers along the dressing table and touched the pillow where his head had lain, even though she knew the bedding had all been changed since he'd left. Clean sheets and pillow-cases awaited his return. She glanced round the walls at the pictures. Opposite the end of the bed was a painting of the village school where she'd been so unhappy. Perhaps Georgie had gone there as a little boy. He must have liked it there or he wouldn't have wanted a reminder on his wall staring down at him. She smiled as she realized who'd painted the picture for him. She'd seen the paintings on the landing, and downstairs in Miles's study hung several more portraits. Miles had told her all about them. One was of his first wife, Louisa, painted a long time ago, but more recent pictures were there too. One of each of Miles's sons: Philip,

114

dressed in his robes at his graduation at university, Ben standing against a tree with the land stretching away towards a vibrant sunset and then Georgie, resplendent in his RAF uniform.

'Charlotte painted all these later ones,' Miles had told her proudly. 'She's a very clever artist.'

'There isn't one of her.'

Miles had chuckled. 'She could have done one, but Charlotte is too modest to paint a self-portrait.'

Now Jenny turned away from the picture on Georgie's wall. She missed his merry laughter, the way he swung her round until she shrieked for him to stop, the way he devoted his time to playing games. Listlessly, she climbed the next flight of stairs to the upper landing. She hadn't been up here before; it was where Mrs Beddows, Kitty and Wilkins all slept. She peeped into each of their bedrooms but did not go in. They might be cross if anyone caught her and she didn't want to make them angry; they'd all been so nice to her.

She walked the length of the corridor and opened the door of the room at the end. Then she gazed around the room in wonderment. It was an artist's studio. This must be where Charlotte did all her paintings. Jenny stepped inside, closing the door behind her. Canvases were stacked on the floor leaning against the wall. An easel stood near the window with a half-finished painting of a church on it. It was the one in Ravensfleet – the one they took her to every Sunday.

On a table nearby were tubes of oil paint, tiny square pans of watercolour paints and a pad of thick paper with brushes in a jar close by. Jenny wandered round the room. There was even a little sink with taps in the corner for clean water. She picked up a bottle that read 'linseed oil' and another that just had 'turps' scribbled on a label. There were pencils and pens with different-sized nibs, a bottle of black ink, pastels and charcoal. Intrigued, Jenny fingered everything. Miss Chisholm had once asked a friend of hers who was an artist to visit the school and talk to the class about all the materials an artist could use, although the children had not been allowed to touch them. But here, in the quietness of Charlotte's room, Jenny revelled in the feel of the brushes. Some were soft, others spiky and stiff.

Then she inspected Charlotte's paintings. There were portraits, painted in oils like the ones on the landing, of people she recognized. There was one of Charlotte's father. Jenny giggled aloud. Charlotte had caught the grumpy old man's expression perfectly. She'd been to the farm several times with Charlotte now. Sometimes Alfie was there and they played hide and seek, hiding in the barn and even climbing up to the hayloft. As they'd walked home after one such visit, Charlotte had confided, 'I used to hide in the hayloft when I was a little girl when I didn't want to be found.'

Jenny continued to wander around the room, looking at all the pictures. There were lots of portraits of people who lived nearby. She didn't know all their names but she recognized them as people who greeted Charlotte and Miles every week at church. And there were landscape pictures painted in softer colours.

A copious apron, covered with paint splashes, lay across a chair. Jenny picked it up and wrapped it around herself. She squeezed some thick yellow paint from a tube on to a palette. Then she tipped the brushes out of the jar and filled it with water from the tap. Carrying it back to the table, she picked up a brush, dipped it in the water and then into the yellow paint and daubed it across the bottom across a clean sheet of paper. But the thick paint didn't seem to spread very well on the paper. So she picked up one of the soft brushes and dipped that in the water. Then she scrubbed at one of the little pans of yellow paint and swept it across another sheet of paper. This worked much better.

'That's the beach,' she murmured. 'Georgie'll take me again when he comes home. He promised. Maybe next time the samphire will be ready to pick. I'll put it in my picture for Georgie. Dark green, he said it was . . .'

Jenny had found something that fascinated her. She loved the feel of the paints on the brush, of sweeping vibrant colours across a page, of trying to get the shape of a tree just right. But she couldn't find the exact green she wanted for the leaves on the trees or the grass or for the samphire on the beach. She tried mixing colours, wrinkling her brow in concentration as she tried to remember what Miss Chisholm's friend had told them, but nothing came out right. She used several pieces of paper trying to work it out for herself and threw them on the floor in disgust when the picture didn't come out like she imagined in her head.

After a while, she heard voices below. She removed the apron and washed her hands in the sink, then she skipped back to the nursery just in time before Charlotte came looking for her. But whenever the house was quiet and she thought she wouldn't be missed, Jenny went back to the studio. Charlotte didn't seem to go up there very often at the moment, and the girl had the room to herself.

One Saturday morning when Miles was outside with

Ben discussing farming matters and Charlotte was in the kitchen with Mrs Beddows, Jenny crept upstairs and shut herself in the room.

She wrapped herself in the apron that was now liberally stained with paint, fetched water from the tap and picked up the brush she'd been using. It had dried to a stiff point and the paint in the little pans had dried too. But she'd learned that if she stabbed the brush into the jar of water and wet the paint again, all was well. She wrinkled her nose as she looked around for a fresh piece of paper, but she'd used them all. She pulled out one of the canvases and squeezed the thicker paint from a tube labelled 'oil paint'. She didn't understand the difference, only that it was thicker than the watercolour paints and daubed very satisfyingly on to the canvas. Paint had splashed on to the linoleum and even on to the wall, but she knew it didn't matter. This was an artist's studio and she was now an artist, painting picture after picture for Georgie.

She heard voices downstairs calling, but she was so engrossed on trying yet another picture of the beach that she took no notice and carried on splashing the paint on to the canvas with sweeping, unrestricted strokes.

The door opened and Kitty peered round the door. 'Oh my, what have you done?'

Jenny glanced up but the maid had disappeared and she heard her shouting, 'Sir – madam, she's up here.'

She heard the murmur of conversation on the landing and then Miles and Charlotte were standing in the doorway, gazing round the room. Jenny glanced around her too, seeing for the first time the state of the room through their eyes. Now she'd be in trouble. Perhaps they'd send her away for making such a mess, for using

Charlotte's paper and paints without permission. She took a deep breath and said the only words she thought would save her.

'Hello, I'm painting a picture for Georgie.' She held her breath, waiting for Miles to stride across the room and raise his hand to smack her, but he was standing in the doorway still looking about him. The look on his face was more anxious than angry and it was Charlotte who made the first move.

For a brief moment Jenny cringed, but Charlotte was smiling and coming towards her saying, 'How nice, darling. May I see?'

She stood beside Jenny and studied the picture carefully. 'Why, it's the beach.'

Jenny smiled her most winning smile. 'I want some green for that spiky grass, but I can't remember what to mix.'

'Blue and yellow. Here, let me show you.'

Jenny spent the next hour happily, with Charlotte showing her how to mix the different colours and by the end of that time, with Charlotte's guidance, Jenny had produced a picture that was almost like the one in her head. The beach now had little white shells and brown pebbles. The sea was blue with white tips to the waves and the grass at the bottom of the picture was just the right colour. There was even a patch of dark green samphire.

'Now, I think we'd better tidy up a bit, don't you?' Charlotte said gently when the picture was finished. 'But I tell you what we'll do. We'll find a table for you and put it in the corner over there. Then you can have your own paints and brushes.'

'And paper?'

'And paper,' Charlotte promised. 'You can have your very own space in the studio. And you can come up here any time you like. How would that be?'

The child didn't answer. Instead, she flung her arms around Charlotte's waist and buried her face against her. Charlotte stroked her hair, feeling a lump in her throat as she remembered her own happiness when Miles had fitted out the studio as his wedding gift to her.

Seventeen

Georgie came home the following week. He arrived whilst the children were still having lessons, but he was waiting for her in the hallway when they skipped out of the dining room. Jenny's eyes shone and her mouth formed an 'Oh!' of delight. 'I've got a present for you,' she said, when at last she found her voice. 'Wait there.'

She skidded across the hall and tore up the stairs, returning only minutes later with her precious painting. Miles had had it framed for her in readiness for Georgie's return.

'That's wonderful, Jen. My favourite place – the beach. We'll go there whilst I'm home, if it's fine.'

Later, he insisted that the picture should hang on the wall in his bedroom next to the one of the school in Ravensfleet, which Charlotte had painted, but the moment was spoilt by the arrival home of Philip.

Now Jenny would not have Georgie all to herself.

Over dinner, there was a strange tension between the family members that the child could not understand. All three brothers were at home and she'd heard both Ben and Philip admit that they'd joined up. This news had upset both Charlotte and Miles; only Georgie seemed pleased, slapping his brothers on the back and declaring that the war would soon be over now.

Jenny glanced from one to the other, aware of the atmosphere, yet too young to understand. But to her delight, Georgie was true to his promise. He had three days' leave and he spent most of his time with her. He taught her to ride the second-hand bicycle that Miles had bought for her and even managed to persuade her to ride a little pony.

'Don't let go,' she cried, clinging to him. 'He might gallop off with me.'

'No, he won't.' Georgie laughed. 'He's getting old now. His galloping days are over. But he likes to feel useful. He loves giving you a ride.'

When they arrived back home, Jenny asked, 'Can we go to the beach tomorrow? Just the two of us.'

Playfully, Georgie tweaked her nose. 'As long as it's not raining.'

But when Jenny drew back her bedroom curtains her bedroom was flooded with sunlight and after breakfast, they set off.

'Let's see if the samphire is ready,' he said as they mounted the hill, their feet sinking into the soft sand. He stood on the top and shaded his eyes. 'The tide's a good way out, that's good. We'll try over there. Now, we'd better take our shoes and socks off. We'll leave them here in the sandhills.'

'Won't they get nicked?'

He glanced at her in surprise. 'Eh? Oh no, they'll be safe enough.'

'I don't want to lose my best shoes,' she warned. 'Charlotte bought me these and I've never had a brand new pair all of my own before.' Her tone was quite matter-of-fact and she was quite unaware of the pathos in her words that made the brave fighter pilot swallow hard.

They collected the pegs and the white rags from the box hidden in the sandhills and then Jenny skipped beside him, holding his hand, across the sand and the mud to where the samphire grew on the salty marsh.

When they reached the place, Jenny asked, 'Is that it? That green stuff.'

'Yes, we'll take some home and Mrs Beddows will show you how to cook it. But first, do you remember everything I told you last time about the tides? Charlotte taught me when we first came to live here, Jenny, and it's very important.'

Jenny repeated everything he'd told her.

'And promise me you'll always be careful when you come to the beach?'

She looked up at him, still and quiet, aware of the seriousness in his tone. Jenny nodded solemnly. She would promise Georgie anything, but even the city child realized the importance of what he was telling her.

For half an hour they picked the fleshy plant, placing it in a basket to carry home. Georgie stood up and eased his aching back. 'Come on, Jen. Time to go home, the tide's coming in.'

But the promised cookery lesson with Georgie and Mrs Beddows was cancelled. When they arrived back home, there was an urgent message for him that all leave was cancelled.

'I have to go back to camp now,' he told Jenny as he packed his things into his kitbag. She stood in the doorway of his bedroom watching him. 'Why?'

He came and squatted down in front of her. 'Because I have to go and fly my plane.'

Jenny stared at him. Even she, young as she was, could see the haunted look in his eyes, the kind of fear that she'd felt when she'd first arrived here at the emptiness of the flat land and the wide open spaces, the huge sky above her head. She put her arms around his neck and her cheek close to his to whisper. 'You will come back, won't you?'

There was a moment's hesitation before he said brightly, 'Of course. Just try and keep me away.' But it was a forced gaiety; even Jenny could recognize it.

Downstairs he said goodbye to the rest of the family. He picked Jenny up and swung her round before setting her down again. He ruffled her hair. 'Be a good girl, won't you?'

She nodded, unable to speak for the lump in her throat as she watched him hug Charlotte and then he was gone.

As the door closed behind him, Charlotte, her voice unsteady, held out her hand to Jenny. 'Come, let's go and cook that samphire.'

Britain and the Commonwealth now stood alone and whilst the Battle of Britain was being fought by the RAF over the south of England, Philip and Ben completed their basic training and managed to come home on leave before they were posted abroad. Miles had taken over the running of the farm and the estate during Ben's absence but he was a reluctant farmer and happily handed back the reins, even though it would only be for a short time. Philip didn't seem to want to do anything. He sat on the terrace reading the newspapers or just gazing into space, avoiding anyone's company.

Jenny stood for several minutes watching him from behind a pillar on the terrace. She'd sensed – though at her tender age she was unable to put it into words – that Philip somehow didn't fit in with the rest of the family. He seemed aloof and there was a definite constraint between Charlotte and him. Jenny knew only too well what it was like to feel lonely, to be the odd one out. She'd never felt as if she belonged anywhere. She was a misfit. At least, she had been until she'd come here, to the manor. Miles and Charlotte and Georgie – oh especially Georgie – had made her so welcome. Even Ben, in his quiet way, leading her around the farm, showing her the animals and how, if she always treated them with respect, there was no need to be afraid of any of them. Not even the big, lumping cows.

'They're gentle creatures, really, as long as you don't startle them,' he'd said in his soft voice. She couldn't imagine Ben becoming a soldier and having to shoot the enemy. But Philip – she could imagine him being a major or something and leading others into battle. He was the sort who won medals. But today Philip looked lonely. Suddenly, she felt sorry for him. After all, he was Georgie's brother and Georgie was fond of him, she knew.

Jenny had an idea. She crept away and ran up to the nursery, picked up a book and returned to her position behind the pillar. She stood again for several moments until the man became aware that he was being watched.

'What d'you want?'

'Georgie's not here.'

'No-o,' Philip said slowly as she moved nearer.

'And Charlotte's gone to see that grumpy old man.'

'Ye-es.'

'And the mister's busy, so – '

'So?'

Jenny tweaked the newspaper from his grasp and dropped it on the floor.

'Will you read to me?' She held out the book. 'It's

the one Georgie gived me.' She clambered on to his knee. 'We've got to Chapter Eight where Mr Toad's just been put in a dinjun.'

'A dungeon,' Philip said mildly.

'That's what I said – a dinjun.' With Bert clutched under one arm, she put her thumb in her mouth, curled up on his lap and, resting her head against his shoulder, waited for him to begin.

Philip opened the book. 'My mother used to read this to me.'

'Your real mum? Not Charlotte.'

'Mm.' He was fingering the pages gently as if reliving memories from his own childhood. Then, slowly, he began to read.

'You have to do the funny voices like Georgie does,' Jenny ordered.

'Ah yes. Sorry. I'll try to do better.' But his words were sincere. For once, there was no sarcasm in his tone.

Until his leave ended, Jenny monopolized Philip, who laughingly allowed himself to be commandeered into all sorts of escapades. He even joined in the rowdy games of football on the lawn after lessons finished.

But at the end of a week both he and Ben had to go too.

Eighteen

There were no lessons at the manor during the summer holidays, but by now Jenny had made one or two friends amongst the local children as well as her fellow evacuees. And she was more confident out of doors.

'Can I come to Buckthorn Farm with you today, Charlotte? Alfie might be there.' The two had become firm friends. The boy had almost replaced Bobby in Jenny's affections. Almost, but not quite. Jenny still wondered where her best friend was. Despite Miles's efforts, they hadn't been able to find out where Bobby and Sammy had gone.

'Of course, dear,' Charlotte said.

'I won't have to see the grumpy old man, will I? He always frowns at me and tells me I should have been a boy.'

Charlotte laughed out loud. 'He always told me that too.'

'Why's he always so grumpy?' the child remarked but before Charlotte could think of a suitable reply, Jenny added, 'I 'spect it's 'cos he lives on his own.'

'Maybe, but he's got Mr and Mrs Morgan to look after him.'

'I like Mrs Morgan. Do you think she'll have any scones and jam and cream today?'

'I'm sure she will. You can sit and talk to Mary whilst I see the – ' Charlotte chuckled – 'the grumpy old man.'

Mary Morgan was always as kind and as welcoming as Mrs Beddows and Jenny was soon seated at her scrubbed kitchen table, munching scones, the cream and jam spreading around her mouth. 'Have you worked here long, Mrs Morgan?'

'Years and years.' Mary smiled as she beat a cake mixture with a wooden spoon. 'I came here when Miss Charlotte's mother was first married and I've looked after Miss Charlotte ever since.'

'Is her mother here, then?'

Mary pursed her lips and shook her head.

'So, I haven't got a dad and Charlotte hasn't got a mum.'

Mary Morgan didn't answer but concentrated on beating margarine and sugar together until it was a thick, smooth cream.

Jenny watched for a moment and then asked, 'What happened to her mum? Did she die?'

'I – you'd better ask Miss Charlotte about that, love.'

'Don't you know?' The candid blue eyes stared at Mary.

'Well – er – yes, but it's not my place to be gossiping.'

'Oh!' There was a pause and then, 'Why do you call her *Miss* Charlotte?' Jenny had noticed that a lot of people called her that instead of the expected 'Mrs Thornton'.

Mary laughed with relief as the child's attention turned to an easier question. 'I've always called her that and old habits die hard.'

At that moment, Charlotte appeared back in the kitchen. 'Better in health than temper, as usual,' she laughed, sharing the joke with Mary. Then she held out her hand to Jenny. 'Let's go outside and see if Alfie's around. Maybe he'll play with you while I have a talk to Eddie.' As Jenny scrambled down from her chair and took Charlotte's hand, she said politely, 'Thank you for the scones, Mrs Morgan. They were lovely.'

'You're welcome. Come and see us again soon, won't you?'

Outside, they turned towards the outbuilding that had been converted years earlier into a farm office. As they entered, the man sitting behind the desk looked up and smiled. 'Miss Charlotte, just the person I need to speak to. Can you spare a few minutes?' His glance flickered to Jenny. 'Hello, there, Jenny. Alfie's cleaning out the hen house, if you want to go and find him.' He glanced at Charlotte. 'Alfie helps out now and again.'

Charlotte raised her eyebrows. 'You mean he *works* here? On Buckthorn Farm?'

'Yes. I didn't think you'd mind.'

'Of course I don't mind, Eddie. But I haven't seen his name on the wages' sheets.'

Eddie Norton laughed. 'Oh, I don't pay him.'

Quite seriously, Charlotte said, 'Then you should. Or rather, we should.'

Eddie smiled. 'Well, if you're sure. He's a big lad now and he is very useful about the place.'

'Then all the more reason for him to have a wage.'

'But your father—'

'Never mind my father. What the eye doesn't see . . .' The words were lost on the young girl, but Charlotte and Eddie exchanged a look of understanding, of conspiracy almost. 'Does he want to go into farming when he leaves school?'

'I think he'd like to do what Master Ben did. Go to agricultural college.' Eddie grinned ruefully. 'He's the clever one of the family.' His voice was only a whisper as he added. 'Must tek after his dad.'

'Now, now, Eddie,' Charlotte said quietly and, again, another look of a shared secret passed between them.

Eddie shuffled the papers on his desk and stood up. 'Off you go, then, young 'un. Alfie'll show you around Miss Charlotte's farm.'

Jenny twisted her head to look up at Charlotte. 'Is this *your* farm? I thought it was your dad's.'

Before Charlotte could answer, Eddie said, 'Miss Charlotte's been running Buckthorn Farm since she was not much older than you.'

Jenny's mouth dropped open as Charlotte began to laugh. 'There you go, exaggerating again, Eddie. I was a bit older than ten.'

'Eleven,' Jenny put in. 'I was eleven last week.'

Charlotte stared down at her. 'It was your birthday? Last week?'

Jenny nodded.

'Oh Jen, why didn't you say? We would have had a party.'

The girl blinked. 'A party? For – for me?'

'Of course. A birthday party. Miles is going to be so upset we didn't know. And Mrs Beddows too. She'd have made you a cake.'

'Mum always gets cross if I remind her that my birthday's coming up,' Jenny said in a small voice. 'She says it looks as if I'm asking for presents.'

'We'd never think that of you.' Charlotte squeezed her hand. 'Tell you what, we'll still have that party and you can invite all your friends.'

'Right,' Eddie said with a broad wink at Jenny. 'A quick look around the farm and then I'll find you some eggs and butter to take back to Mrs Beddows if she's going to be busy baking a birthday cake.'

As they walked home, Jenny asked tentatively, 'Char-

130

lotte, you know I've got a mum but I haven't got a dad. Not a real dad.' Charlotte waited, wondering what was coming. 'Well, you've got a dad, but – but you haven't got a mum, have you?'

There was a short silence until Charlotte said softly, 'I have. She lives in Lincoln. I go there sometimes to see her.'

'Oh, is that where you go when you're away for a whole day and Miles fetches you home from the station just before dinner?'

'That's right.'

'Why don't your mum and dad live together? Did they fall out.'

For a moment Charlotte's face was bleak. 'Yes. A long time ago. I was only small. I think my father blamed my mother because I wasn't the son he wanted and he was unkind to her. So she – she went away.'

Jenny was thoughtful for a moment before she said, with a child's frankness, 'You can't blame her then, can you?' With her curiosity satisfied, she skipped ahead to tell Miles about the promised belated birthday party, leaving Charlotte staring after her and murmuring, 'No, I don't suppose you can.'

As Charlotte had predicted, Miles was mortified when he heard that they'd missed Jenny's birthday. 'And not a card or a letter from her mother – *again*,' he muttered angrily.

'We'll make up for it,' Charlotte tried to placate him. 'We'll give her the best birthday party she's ever had.'

But Miles was not to be comforted. 'From what she says, it'll be the *only* party she's ever had.'

'Well, maybe it's the first, but as long as she's with us,' Charlotte said, 'it'll not be the last.'

It wasn't quite the right thing to say for the bleak look on Miles's face told her that her words had reminded him that Jenny wasn't theirs and that one day she would have to go back home.

'Will Georgie be able to come home for my party?' Jenny asked, and then, as if afraid she might offend them if they were not included, added, 'And Philip and Ben too?'

'I don't think Philip and Ben will be able to come home; they've only just gone. But I'll telephone Georgie's camp and see if I can speak to him.'

Jenny's eyes widened. ''Ave you got a telephone?'

Miles smiled. 'Yes, it's in my study. Why, is there anyone you'd like to telephone?'

Jenny was thoughtful and Miles waited, fully expecting that she would say she'd like to speak to her mother, but instead she said, 'Could we telephone Mr Tomkins and see if he's heard where Bobby is yet?'

'Of course we can.'

But Mr Tomkins still had no idea where the other children had gone. 'But I'll keep trying,' he promised Miles.

Two days later, the day before the party, Mr Tomkins rode up the drive on his bicycle.

'I've found out at last that they went further north. Somewhere in north Lincolnshire, but I understand that they've gone home – back to London. I think they went back before Christmas. As you know, the expected bombing never happened.'

Miles held his breath. He was sure now that Jenny

would say, 'Then I want to go home too.' But instead, she just looked anxious and her voice trembled as she looked up at him and asked, 'Have I got to go back too?'

'No, no, of course not,' he reassured her swiftly, relief flooding through him that she didn't seem to want to go. 'You can stay with us as long as you want to, but I'm sorry we can't invite your friends to your party.' The girl shrugged no longer too upset now that she'd been told she could stay at the manor.

The party was a huge success; the table was loaded with all the food that children love. Mary Morgan had contributed and she and her husband, Edward, who was Mr Crawford's manservant at Buckthorn Farm, came to help. Mary was welcomed into the kitchen by a flustered Mrs Beddows and Wilkins looked as if he was about to hug Edward Morgan. 'Am I glad to see you! Having them here for lessons is bad enough, but they're going to go wild at a party.'

But Wilkins's doleful predictions were unfounded. True, there was a lot of noise, shouting and laughter as they played the various party games and, outside on the lawn, they ran riot. But sitting around the dining table, instead of the kitchen table, they were all remarkably well behaved.

As Miles, Charlotte and Jenny stood on the steps to wave them goodbye, Jenny sighed with happiness. 'Thank you for my lovely party,' she murmured. 'I just wish Georgie could have been here too.' But when she felt Charlotte squeeze her hand and Miles touch her shoulder, though neither of them said a word, the child knew they were both feeling exactly the same.

Nineteen

There was something wrong; Jenny could feel it.

Charlotte had been away all day in Lincoln. 'That's a big city about forty miles away,' Kitty told her. 'She's gone on the train.'

'She'll have gone to see her mum.' Jenny nodded wisely. Kitty's eyes widened but she said nothing.

Jenny was playing in the garden, kicking the football and waiting for Miles to join her as he had promised when she saw a boy in a kind of uniform ride up the drive to the front door. He jumped off the bicycle and leaned it against the pillar at the foot of the front steps. Absently, Jenny nudged the ball with her foot, but her gaze was on the boy as he climbed to the front door and rang the bell. When Wilkins opened the door, she saw, from where she stood, the boy hand him what looked like a letter. The door closed and the boy ran back down the steps, mounted his bike and pedalled away, much faster than he had arrived.

Jenny waited but Miles did not come out to play with her.

In the middle of the afternoon, Kitty said, 'I'll take you to Buckthorn Farm.'

'But Charlotte will be home soon and then we'll have dinner.'

'You go with Kitty, lovey, there's a good girl,' Mrs Beddows said and turned away, but not before Jenny had seen the woman's face crumple in distress.

Jenny glanced from one to the other. Kitty had never taken her anywhere or played with her; she was always too busy. But today she'd taken her apron off and had put on her afternoon dress, as she called it, and made Jenny wash her face and brush her hair. And now she was hustling the young girl out of the back door and towards the long pathway through the fields that led to Buckthorn Farm.

Jenny didn't feel like skipping alongside Kitty. Something had happened and no one was telling her.

Was she to be sent home? Had that boy brought a message from Mr Tomkins that all the evacuees had to go home, like Bobby and the others had already done?

She could bear it no longer. 'Why're we going to Buckthorn Farm? Are they cross with me? Have I done something wrong?'

'No, no, lovey, nothing like that. The master, he – he just needs a bit of time alone with madam when she gets home.'

Jenny was silent. At least, she thought, they haven't shut me in my bedroom like Mum does when she wants me out of the way.

Arriving at Buckthorn Farm, Kitty exchanged hurried, whispered words with Mary. The older woman's eyes widened and then she whispered, 'Oh no! NO!'

Jenny saw Mary gesture towards her and then Kitty shook her head. What was going on? There was definitely something wrong. Jenny sighed and shrugged her shoulders. Grown-up stuff, she supposed. Obviously, they weren't going to tell her.

'I'll go and find Alfie,' she said in a loud voice. The

135

two women, still whispering together, looked startled. They both turned to stare at her as if they'd forgotten she was there.

'You do that, lovey. Tell him – tell him there'll be a cuppa and a scone for him in a little while.'

Jenny grinned. 'And for me?'

'Of course.'

But as Jenny went to the back door to go out into the yard, she glanced back to see the two women still talking, their faces so serious that she knew the last things on their minds were cups of tea and buttered scones.

' 'Lo, Alfie, can you play?'

The boy turned and grinned at her. 'I've got to feed the hens, but you can help me, if you like.'

For the next hour, Jenny followed Alfie around the outbuildings, helping him to throw corn to the hens, watching him carry the heavy buckets of pigswill to the sties and giggling as the pigs, grunting loudly, pushed each other out of the way to be first to the trough. But her laughter soon died when Kitty came to collect her for going home. She could see the maid had been crying. The promised scones seemed to have been forgotten as she'd guessed they might be.

'What's up with her?' Alfie whispered.

'I don't know. They're all like it at home, but no one will tell me why.'

'Oh,' was all Alfie said, but a worried frown now wrinkled his forehead and, as he waved goodbye, she saw him hurry towards the farm office, no doubt in search of his father, Eddie.

*

They arrived back at the manor at about five o'clock, Kitty leading her round to the back door and into the kitchen. As they entered, the maid asked in a low voice, 'Is madam home yet?'

Mrs Beddows shook her head. 'The master will be going to fetch her from the station soon.' She turned to Jenny. 'You go and play in the nursery like a good girl, will you?'

Jenny glanced from one to the other and asked again, 'Am I in trouble? Are they sending me away?'

'No, lovey. It's got nothing at all to do with you. It's – it's just – ' Mrs Beddows glanced up at Kitty helplessly as if seeking help, but the maid turned away, her shoulders shaking. Jenny knew she was crying again. The cook took a deep breath. 'It's just that the master and the mistress will need to talk about – about something when she gets back, but it has nothing to do with you, I promise. But just you be a good girl for us, will you?'

Jenny nodded and left the kitchen. She glanced at the door of Miles's study. It was firmly closed and there was no sound from inside.

Slowly, she climbed the stairs to the playroom. She touched the toys there, but nothing interested her today. She could feel the tension and sadness permeating through the house. Without consciously making the decision, her footsteps took her up to the next floor and along to the studio she now shared with Charlotte. As she sat down at the little table, picked up her brush and began to paint, she forgot about everything else. Just so long as they weren't going to send her home, she'd keep out of their way until they'd sorted out whatever it was that was bothering everybody.

Some time later – she wasn't sure how long she'd been sitting there – the door opened and Charlotte was standing there.

'I'm painting another picture for Georgie,' Jenny told her. 'He'll be home again soon. That's samphire, that is. We picked it together – me an' Georgie.'

Charlotte turned away with what sounded suspiciously like a sob and went out again, closing the door quietly behind her.

With her paintbrush suspended in mid-air, Jenny stared at the closed door and listened to the footsteps hurrying away along the landing.

They were all subdued at dinner. Charlotte was red-eyed and Miles was quiet, but they were trying valiantly to act as if nothing was wrong.

They've had a row, Jenny thought, and don't want me to know. They're not like Mum and her fellers. If they have a row, she thought, they don't care if the whole street hears and especially they don't hide it from me, shut away in my bedroom with my hands over my ears. Mind you, the girl had to admit, there hadn't been so many quarrels since Arthur had arrived. If Dot got on her high horse, he just laughed, left by the front door, sprang into his sports car and roared off up the street with Dot waving her fist at him. It was difficult to carry on a row with someone who wasn't there any more. Then, having given her enough time to calm down, Arthur would reappear bringing little gifts for both Dot and Jenny and everything carried on as if the fight had never happened.

But that wasn't what was happening at the manor. Miles was solemn and hardly eating the meal Wilkins had placed in front of him. Charlotte, too, was merely picking at her food. Only Jenny cleared her plate. Rows didn't faze her; she was used to them. It'd soon blow over.

But Jenny was wrong; whatever the problem was, it seemed to be affecting the whole household. Even the children and Miss Parker, who arrived at the manor the following morning for the start of the new autumn term, were subdued. It took the whole day for Miss Parker to get everyone settled back into their lessons after the long summer break. At the end of the afternoon, the children filed quietly out of the dining room, reached for their coats, headed towards the front door and ran down the steps. A few were already walking away down the drive.

'Aren't you going to play football?' Jenny shouted after them, standing at the top of the steps with the ball in her hands.

They turned and stared up at her, then Billy, the self-appointed spokesman, stepped forward. 'We're going straight home. We don't reckon we should stay. Not today. Not after what's happened.'

'What d'you mean?'

'Yer know.'

'No, I don't know.'

The children glanced awkwardly at each other, whispering.

Jenny ran down the steps and grasped Billy's arm. 'Tell me.'

He nodded towards the house behind them. 'They're all upset. 'Course they are. We thought you'd be an' all.'

'How can I be when I don't know what you're talking about?'

Billy looked at her and then blurted out, 'He's missing – their son. The fighter pilot. He'll've been killed.'

Jenny stared at him, the shock hitting her like a physical blow. For a moment, she was rigid with grief. She stared around at the solemn faces. Then she dropped the ball and began to run. Down the drive, across the main road and down the lane that led to the beach, sobs bursting from her as she ran. 'Georgie, oh Georgie. No. No! NO!'

She ran and ran until she came to the sandhills, where she fell to her knees, threw back her head and howled like an animal in pain. But there was no one to hear her. No one to comfort her. She cried and screamed aloud until there were no more tears to shed.

At last, Jenny stood up, scrubbed the tears from her face with the back of her hand and set off towards the place in the sandhills where they'd left the box containing the pegs and the white rags. Carrying the bundle, she headed towards the place where the samphire grew. And as she went, she planted the pegs in the sand and the mud, just as Georgie had taught her. Sobs filled her throat and tears that she thought were all cried out welled again in her eyes.

With the path marked, she reached the plants and began to pull at them savagely, grief and rage filling her heart. Never again would Georgie come with her to collect it, but she'd collect it for him. He wouldn't ever see the new picture she'd painted for him, but she'd carry on, just as before, painting for him. She'd never forget him; she'd never stop thinking about him and if, by the sheer force of her will, she could bring him back to life, she would do so.

His words filtered into her grief-stricken mind. 'Remember the tide, Jenny.' It was as if he was speaking to her; she could hear his voice, feel him standing beside her. She stood up and gazed around her, but the water was far out. She was quite safe. She squatted down again and carried on picking samphire. After several minutes, she stood up and checked again. The water was definitely nearer this time; the tide was coming in, but she was still safe for the moment.

The third time she stood up, she saw them. Miles and Charlotte were walking towards her and behind them, their horses were tethered on the dunes. She waited, holding her breath. She'd be in real trouble for coming here on her own, without their knowledge or per-mission. Now they'd really send her home. To have worried them and caused them to come looking for her was unforgivable. Especially when they were grieving for Georgie just as much as she was. She steeled herself against the onslaught of anger, but all Miles said was, 'My, you've collected a lot. Mrs Beddows will be pleased. But the tide's coming in now, love. Time we were heading back. Come on. We've got the horses on the sea bank. You can ride in front of me.'

As they rode home, Jenny buried her face against Miles's chest, her tears falling once more. Georgie had taught her how to set the pegs and the white, fluttering rags, and to watch for the incoming tide. He had kept her safe even though he was no longer here with her and never would be again.

Twenty

By October, the games of football after lessons had to stop. Parents and the guardians of the evacuees wanted the children at home before dark. So Jenny was alone in the nursery, playing with the doll's house tucked away in one corner.

'Such a shame,' Kitty had whispered to Jenny when she'd dusted it so that the young girl could play with it soon after she'd first arrived at the manor. 'The master bought it when his wife – his first wife, that is – was expecting Master Georgie. They were so sure he was going to be a girl. The master's always wanted a daughter.' The housemaid had turned and smiled down at Jenny. 'That's why he's making such a fuss of you, lovey. He's enjoying having a little girl to spoil, even though we all know one day you'll go back home to your mum.'

Jenny had said nothing but gently had touched all the miniature furniture in the doll's house and the two little porcelain dolls – a mother and baby – who lived in the house. Since that day, she'd played with the little house often, but this was the first time she'd touched it since they'd heard the news about Georgie being posted missing. On that dreadful day when Miles and Charlotte had found her at the beach and taken her home, Miles had taken her into his study and sat her on his knee. Then, very gently, he'd explained what they knew.

142

'Georgie's been what they call posted missing, but presumed killed. One of his friends saw his plane go down into the sea near the French coast.'

'So they don't know that he's – he's – ' She hadn't been able to finish the sentence; the thought was so awful.

'No – they don't know for certain that he's been killed, but we have to be very brave and understand that it is possible. In fact, it's more than likely that he has.'

'Well, I don't think he has,' the girl said stoutly, though her voice trembled. 'And I won't believe it.' She jutted out her jaw, slid off his knee and marched towards the door where she paused briefly to say, 'I'll carry on painting pictures for him. And he *will* see them. One day, he *will* come back and he'll see all the pictures I've painted for him.'

With that she turned, ran across the hall and stamped up the stairs, ignoring the worried eyes of Wilkins as he watched her go. Only in the solitude of the studio, did Jenny allow fresh tears to fall and blotch the picture she had been painting for Georgie so carefully.

Since then, Jenny had painted many more pictures, all for Georgie, she told Charlotte as she piled them in a corner of the studio. 'There they are, all ready for when he comes home.' But today as dusk gathered and the light from the window faded, Jenny was about to turn on the light so she could carry on painting when there was a loud banging and the house seemed to shake. She pulled open the door and fled along the landing, down the stairs and into the morning room. With a flying leap she landed on the sofa beside Charlotte, snuggled up to her and put her thumb in her mouth.

Miles hurried to the window as they heard the planes, sounding as if they were flying overhead. Jenny screamed and buried her head against Charlotte as dull thuds sounded in the distance. 'It's 'Itler. He's coming.'

Only a few days earlier, Miles had gently explained to her that London was being heavily bombed almost every night. 'But your mum and Arthur will be all right. They'll go to the shelters.'

'And Bobby too, 'cos he's back there now, ain't he?'

'Of course he will,' Miles had reassured her. 'And the rest of his family.'

And now the enemy was dropping bombs on Lynthorpe, the town just up the coast from Ravensfleet, but it didn't go on for very long, not like the poor Londoners were suffering in Hitler's promised Blitz.

A month later, however, several incendiaries fell even closer to Ravensfleet and the manor in a field belonging to one of Miles's tenant farmers. No one was hurt but Frankie, who was still staying with the Warrens, wrote home to his parents telling them with great excitement how they'd heard and seen the bombs falling.

When Arthur Osborne heard the news in the pub one evening, he narrowed his eyes against the smoke from the cigarette he was smoking and listened to the comments going on around him.

'No safer in the country than they are here now, mate,' the barman said.

'Well, all I hope is,' Arthur said, draining his beer glass, 'the ol' gel don't get to hear about it. She might start wanting the kid to come home. And me an' Dot are doing very nicely on our own, ta very much.' He'd winked at the barman and changed the subject. 'Now, about that whisky you asked me to get . . .'

But Dot did get to hear. 'We're fetching her home,

Arfer, so you'd better get some petrol. We'll go termorrer. I don't want folks thinking I don't want me own
daughter back.' Dot knew her neighbours gossiped
about her – had done for years – and the last thing she
wanted was to give them any more ammunition to look
down their noses at her.

'But the Blitz ain't over yet, darlin'.' Arthur tried one
last argument. 'We're still getting bombed nearly every
night.'

'Elsie's lads've been home months,' Dot argued.
'They're safe enough.'

'Only 'cos Elsie takes them up the underground
whether the planes come or not.'

Dot's eyes narrowed. 'Arfer, we're going. Now,
where did I put that postcard she sent?'

'I ain't coming.' Jenny stood in the driveway at the
manor glaring at her mother and Arthur. 'Not if *he*'s
still there.'

It was the only excuse she could think of and she
knew she was being unfair. Arthur had been good to her
and he said as much now. She felt guilty about using
him, implying something to make Miles and Charlotte
believe Arthur treated her badly, but it was all she could
think of; she could hardly say that she didn't want to go
back with either of them, not even her own mother.
Charlotte – kind and loving Charlotte – would never
believe that a mother, any mother, could treat her daughter so off-handedly as Dot did. But she knew they'd
believe her about Arthur. In his flash clothes and his
jovial manner towards people he'd only just met, he was
the exact opposite of the reserved and well-mannered
Miles Thornton. Oh, they'd believe her all right. To

exaggerate her tale, Jenny pretended to cower behind Miles as if she was physically frightened of the man.

Miles tried to be polite, extending his hand in welcome, offering them tea. But the invitation was refused and Dot was adamant that they had to get back to London but that they weren't leaving without Jenny.

The wrangling went on, but at last Miles persuaded them to go indoors. Dot gave in grudgingly. 'Just a cuppa while she gets her things together.'

But Jenny had other ideas. As they began to move towards the house, she turned in the opposite direction and began to run. Although she heard them shouting, she ran on. Down the drive, across the road and down the lane. She knew just where she could hide. She'd remembered what Charlotte had told her she used to do when she didn't want anyone to find her. They'd never find her in the hayloft at Buckthorn Farm.

Jenny reached the farmyard and paused briefly, but there was no one about as she headed to the barn and climbed the ladder to the hayloft, where she buried herself in a mound of hay and waited. Gradually her breathing settled. Despite the cool November day, it was warm and cosy in the loft and the girl drifted into sleep.

It was dusk before she woke to the sound of someone climbing the steps to the hayloft. She held her breath.

'Jenny,' came Charlotte's soft voice through the gloom. 'Are you here?'

Jenny lay perfectly still, not answering, until Charlotte had climbed up into the hayloft too. She didn't move a muscle; the hay would rustle if she did. But Charlotte came and sat down beside her. She didn't say anything, just sat waiting. Realizing she couldn't stay here for ever, Jenny sighed and sat up. 'Have they gone?'

'Yes.'

Charlotte wouldn't lie to her, would she? Was it really safe? Well, she couldn't stay here all night. With a sigh, she pushed her way out from under the hay.

They sat close together with Charlotte's arm around her whilst she explained to the girl that although, for the moment, her mother and Arthur had gone, Dot was adamant that she wanted her daughter back and there was nothing they'd be able to do to stop it. 'Miles and I would like you to stay for ever, and that's the truth, but your mum loves you. She wants you to go home.'

As they walked back to the manor, Jenny said in a small voice, 'Charlotte, you won't be cross with me if I tell you something, will you?'

'No.'

'I was a bit naughty about – about Uncle Arfer.'

'Oh, why?'

'We-ell, I sort of made you think I'm frightened of him.'

'It did seem as if he was the reason you didn't want to go home, yes.'

Jenny sighed. 'He's all right, really. I feel bad about doing that. He's tried to be nice to me, bringing me stuff, presents, you know.'

Charlotte didn't really but she said nothing, allowing the girl to explain at her own pace. 'But Mum always gets mad if he buys me things. *She* likes to be the one he spoils.'

'So – why didn't you want to go home?'

Jenny was silent for a few moments as they continued walking back towards the manor. 'I – like it here. You're both so kind – everybody is. At home – ' And then it all spilled out. About being shut in her bedroom when Arthur visited, even about being left in the house alone at night when her mother went out. 'And she pretties herself up all the time. Buys herself new clothes and has her hair done at a hairdresser every week, but – ' she bit her lip, even now not wanting to be disloyal to her mother – 'she never buys me nice clothes. But you did. And you taught me that it was good to have a bath and wash my hair. I'm not the mucky kid I was when I first came here, am I? But if I go home . . .'

She didn't need to say any more; Charlotte understood. But there was something Charlotte felt obliged to tell her. As they walked home through the darkness, Charlotte held her hand and said gently, 'More than anything, Jenny, we want you to stay with us. We love having you here and – and we've both come to love you, but your mother has threatened to go to the authorities and demand that we send you back. If she does that, there'll be nothing we can do. You – you do understand that, don't you?'

'We could run away.'

'We could – but they'd find us and then Mr Thornton would be in terrible trouble. You wouldn't want that, would you?

'No,' came the swift answer. 'No, I wouldn't.'

Charlotte squeezed her hand. 'Let's hope the red tape takes a long, long time to unravel.'

Jenny wasn't sure what Charlotte meant by 'red tape'. She had visions of someone sitting in an office somewhere untying lots of knots in a length of red ribbon. But whatever it was, as long as it meant she could stay here – at least for the time being – then she didn't care.

Twenty-One

Jenny had always looked forward to Christmas, even at home. Each year she'd hoped that things might be different, might be better. They never were, but with childlike optimism she'd always hoped. Last year, with the Thorntons, had been the best Christmas she'd ever known, but this year she wasn't looking forward to it because Georgie wasn't going to be there. There had been no further news and with each day that passed the family had to accept that their beloved Georgie was dead. Everyone, that is, except Jenny. She flatly refused to believe that he would not come back and when she talked about him it was always as if he was still alive and would come bounding up the front steps and in at the door at any moment.

But everyone made a supreme effort to make this Christmas extra special, especially as it might be the last one that Jenny would spend with them. And no one made more effort than Philip, who came home on a special five-day leave. Ben hadn't been able to get home, so it fell to Philip to help decorate the house and the Christmas tree. He suggested that Jenny should leave a mince pie for Father Christmas and a carrot for his reindeers near the huge tree in the hall and then he piggy-backed her upstairs to bed and helped her hang her stocking on the end of her bed.

'This isn't nearly big enough,' he said, holding up her

stocking, 'for all the presents he's bound to bring you. Let's find a pillowcase.'

And the following morning he was the first one kneeling on the bedroom floor helping Jenny open her presents – just as Georgie would have done.

Later they played noisy games and ate until they felt they might burst. But on the morning after Boxing Day, Philip had to go and suddenly the house was very quiet once more.

School began again, though now the number of evacuees had dwindled so that there was no reason for classes to be held at the manor any longer. But by this time Jenny had got to know the local children and she settled in quite happily at the school in Ravensfleet.

'Just so long as you come and meet me every day after school,' Jenny instructed Miles, who acquiesced gladly.

Two air raids over Lynthorpe during the first months of 1941 killed at least two people and Jenny knew that Frankie would again write and tell his mother. Kind though the Warrens had been to him, Frankie, unlike both Billy and Jenny, wanted to go home, back to London, and he would use any means he could to get his way.

'Mum'll get to know,' Jenny said in a small voice as she walked home through the dusk of the winter's evening with Miles. He squeezed her hand but could think of nothing to say to comfort her or reassure her. He knew she was right and, at the end of March, it fell to Mr Tomkins once more to deliver the news that this time Jenny really would have to go home.

'We'll have another party,' Charlotte said. 'And we'll invite all your friends and even your teachers from school.'

'And I,' Miles said in a tone that brooked no argument, 'am taking you home myself.'

'All the way to London?' Jenny's eyes were round.

'All the way. I want to see you safely back home.'

The party would have been a huge success if it hadn't been for the thought that it would be her last at the manor. Everyone came; all the friends that Jenny had made and the grown-ups, who were friends of Miles and Charlotte.

But the day came early in April when Jenny had to return to London.

'I just wish Georgie could have been at the party,' Jenny said as she helped Charlotte pack all the clothes, shoes, books and toys that she'd been given into a brand new suitcase that Miles had bought for her. 'But you'll tell him all about it when he comes home, won't you, Charlotte?'

Charlotte stood very still, one of Jenny's summer dresses in her hands. 'Jenny, dear – '

'He will come home,' Jenny insisted. She touched Charlotte's arm as she added softly, 'He's alive. Somewhere he's still alive. I just know he is.'

Charlotte looked down at her and tried to smile through her tears. How she wished she had this child's faith. And how she wished this little girl, whom they'd come to regard as a daughter, didn't have to leave. The house would seem empty without her and how lonely both she and Miles would be.

*

The morning Jenny and Miles left the manor was heart-breaking. Everyone hugged her; even Wilkins. Jenny sobbed as she clung to Charlotte.

'Promise you'll write to us, Jenny.'

Jenny nodded and then, reluctantly, she stepped back and reached for Miles's hand as they left the house and walked down the long drive. Miles carried her suitcase and a bag with gifts of eggs, butter and a joint of pork, bacon and sausages from a pig that had been killed recently. At the end of the driveway, Jenny turned and waved to Charlotte standing on the steps, looking as lost and lonely as the little girl was feeling inside.

It wasn't far to the station and they reached it all too soon. They were both quiet, hardly speaking; they didn't know what to say. When the train puffed in, Miles found a carriage and lifted Jenny into it. He stowed her suitcase on the luggage rack and sat beside her.

'Here,' he said. 'I bought you some comics to read.'

'Ta,' Jenny said and took them, but she couldn't concentrate and the words kept blurring in front of her tear-filled eyes. Instead she gazed out of the window at the countryside flashing past. Flat and uninteresting to most, Jenny had grown to love it. The sea and the sky and the way you could see for miles and miles. She was no longer afraid of the open spaces; she wanted to live here for ever.

And most of all, she wanted to be here when Georgie came home.

It took them nearly all day to reach Jenny's home in the streets near the docks. Miles was appalled by the bomb damage. All around them there were piles of rubble and huge craters where a building had received a direct hit.

He was bringing the girl back into danger. He knew he was, but there wasn't a thing he could do about it. And the way she was clinging to his hand, Miles knew that Jenny was as apprehensive as he was. Strangely, it was now the bustling, dirty streets that frightened her. The place where she'd grown up and had known no other life was now alien to her. She gripped Miles's hand as they walked along the street and at last turned the corner. Miles stood a moment, looking about him at the dirty, smoke-encrusted row of houses, the children playing in the street, and the mothers with arms folded standing in their doorways on their freshly scrubbed front steps, gossiping.

'This is our street,' Jenny said at last in a small voice. There was no rejoicing, no slipping from his grasp and running ahead to find her mother. 'Our house is about halfway down on the left.'

'Right,' Miles murmured, but his face was grim.

'No, left,' Jenny said with a half-hearted attempt at humour. But it fell flat for both of them.

They walked down the street and came to the house where the paint was peeling and the curtains at the window were grey with dirt. There was no clean front doorstep at this house. Jenny glanced up at Miles, silent apology in her eyes. He squeezed her shoulder in a gesture of understanding, but he could think of nothing to say.

Jenny took a deep breath and opened the door. 'Mum,' she called tentatively. 'Are you home?'

''Course we are.' Dot came hurrying through from the back room and made a great display of hugging Jenny. Arthur, too, stood grinning in the doorway leading to the back room. 'Come on in. We've got the kettle on. 'Spect you'd like a cuppa, guv'nor.'

'Thank you. That would be nice. Where would you like me to put Jenny's case?'

Dot's eyes gleamed as they alighted on the brand new suitcase. 'Oh my, is that all her stuff? You have been spoiling her.' She laughed, a high-pitched affected sound that seemed insincere. 'And you've grown, Jen,' she said. 'I don't know if the new clothes I've bought you will fit.'

Jenny stared at her. 'New clothes? You've got me some *new* clothes?' Her tone was incredulous.

'Well, Arfer did, didn't you, Arfer? They're not new, exactly, but then times is hard down here. Good to you, Arfer is, Jen, and don't you forget it.'

They moved through into the back room – a small, cramped kitchen with a scullery beyond.

'Now, sit down, mister. I'll pour tea.'

Arthur ruffed Jenny's hair and said, 'Nice to have you home, Tich. I got you a toy or two and some books.' He grimaced. 'They're not new either, love, but you know how it is.' He glanced at Miles for understanding.

Miles nodded. He realized how hard it must be for Londoners with all the bombing. He cleared his throat. 'I – we just want you to know, Mrs Mercer, that if things get worse here, Jenny can come back to us any time you like. You've only to say the word. In fact,' he hesitated fractionally, but he was willing to offer anything if it meant they could have Jenny back, 'you'd all be welcome.'

'That's good of you, but now we're all together again, I reckon we'll stay that way. All the other kids in the street are home now and I wouldn't want Jen to be the odd one out.'

'I don't mind,' Jenny said at once but the remark earned her a glare from her mother.

'I was just thinking of her safety, that's all,' Miles said. 'And yours too, of course.'

Dot pushed a cup of tea towards him with an angry movement, slopping the liquid into the cracked saucer. 'She'll be safe enough here. We've got a Morrison shelter in the front room and there's always the underground.' Dot smiled. 'It's quite a lark going there. We have a right old sing-song. Oh no, mister, you needn't worry your head any more about our Jen. Not now she's back with her mum.'

Miles smiled weakly. He couldn't stop the feeling that that was exactly why he was worried about the girl.

A little later, he was obliged to say goodbye to her. Jenny clung to him and wept openly, not even trying to stem her tears. She stood outside the front door and waved until he reached the corner of the street. He turned and waved too and hesitated for a long moment. Jenny held her breath. She thought he was going to come back, sweep her into his arms and carry her back home. Back to Ravensfleet. But slowly, with obvious reluctance, he gave a last wave, turned and disappeared round the corner, leaving Jenny staring at the empty street.

Twenty-Two

'Now, Miss High-an'-Mighty – '

Dot was standing near the table when Jenny went slowly back into the house, and Arthur was standing with his back to the fire. Dot folded her arms and Jenny shuddered inwardly. It was a stance she remembered only too well.

'You can forget all about your fancy friends. You're back home now and you'll do what I say. You can unpack all the stuff they've given you – '

Jenny turned to see her suitcase open on a chair, the new clothes and shoes spilling out of it.

' – and leave it all in a pile on that chair.'

'I'll take it upstairs.'

'No need. Most of it'll be going to the pop shop. I'll get a few bob for it. It's all good stuff. They've not been mean wiv you, I'll give 'em that.'

Jenny stared at her mother in horror. 'They're *my* things. They bought 'em for *me*. You're not takin' anything to the pop shop.'

Dot moved swiftly and grabbed Jenny's arm, her fingers digging into her. 'Now, look 'ere, you'll do as you're told. Times is hard down here. We don't live on no fancy farm wiv plenty to eat. Queuing for hours, I am, to get a measly bit o' sausage—'

'They've sent you some sausage and bacon and eggs.'

'Where?'

'In that bag.'

Dot released her grip and Jenny rubbed her arm where her mother's nails had dug into her flesh. She watched as Dot picked up the bag and pulled out the packages, her mouth curving in a smile.

'Can I keep my things now, then?'

'What?' Dot looked up and her eyes narrowed. 'I'll think about it. See how good you are.'

'Aw, let 'er keep 'em, Dot,' Arthur said, giving Jenny a sly wink.

'I said "I'll see", didn't I? Besides, it ain't for you to say. She's *my* daughter. You keep out of it, Arfer, if you know what's good for you. I never wanted 'er back, you know that. She could 'ave stayed there for ever for all I care.'

Jenny gasped and stared at her mother. She was hurt. Her mother didn't even want her but, more than that, she was angry – uncontrollably angry. And it made her tongue unguarded. 'Then why did you send for me? I wanted to stay there. I didn't want to come back here. So why?'

Dot's hand smacked Jenny's cheek before the girl could dodge out of the way. She rubbed her face ruefully. Her reactions had slowed. Before she'd gone away, swift though Dot's slaps always were, she'd rarely landed a blow. Jenny had always been quicker to duck.

There was a malicious smile on her mother's mouth. 'Gotcher! Not so quick now, are yer? See, you've been spoiled in more ways than one. Well, I'll soon have you back in line, miss. And don't you ever – ever let me hear you say again that you didn't want to come back home, else I'll tan the 'ide orf of yer.'

Greatly daring, Jenny said, 'But you said *you* didn't want *me* back, so why?'

'What I say and what you can say are two different things,' Dot said irrationally. 'No, I didn't want you back. I never wanted you in the first place. I tried to get rid of you. Nearly killed me, it did, going to a woman in the next street. Sitting in a hot bath and drinking gin and then her poking about at me, but you still clung on.' Dot's face twisted into a wry smile. 'Still, did me one favour. Left me not able to 'ave any more brats, so I suppose I've got that to be grateful for. I can 'ave me fun and not worry about bringing another mistake into the world.'

'Steady on, Dot,' Arthur said quietly. 'Little lass won't understand what you're on about.'

Dot's eyes narrowed. 'She knows all right. And there's something else she'd better know. And it's never too early to learn it.' She reached out and nipped Jenny's ear, twisting it painfully. 'If you ever come home with your belly full, you're out on your ear. And see if your precious fancy friends'd want you then, eh?'

Jenny said nothing. Her anger dissolved, over-whelmed by her mother's hurtful words. But she wasn't stupid; she wasn't going to tell Dot any more about her time in Lincolnshire. She'd keep her mouth shut; not another word would pass her lips about Charlotte and Miles and never, ever, would she even breathe Georgie's name in Dot's hearing. She couldn't bear to have her mother spoil her memories. Only in the loneliness of her bedroom would she relive those happy times.

'Get that stuff upstairs, then. You can keep it for now, but if I get short of money . . .' Dot left the threat hanging in the air, but Jenny knew that it would only be a matter of time before all her nice new clothes started disappearing one by one.

'The stuff I bought for you is on your bed, but I 'spect that won't be good enough now.'

'Course it will, Mum.' Jenny forced herself to sound grateful, trying to mend fences.

She went upstairs to the cramped bedroom at the back of the house. How small it seemed after the big bedroom at the manor. She glanced round at the dirty wallpaper and peeling paint and then moved towards the bed, where two dresses and a coat lay. The cotton dresses, as she'd known they would be, were faded and mended. The blue coat looked a little better but there was a strip of darker material where the hem had been let down. Some other girl had worn the coat until she could wear it no more. The cuffs were frayed, the elbows shiny. Jenny smiled sadly, realizing that before she'd gone away, the sight of such clothes would have thrilled her. Maybe her mother was right; Charlotte and Miles had spoiled her.

She tipped everything out of her suitcase on to the bed and began to hang her new clothes in the wardrobe. There was no use trying to hide anything; her mother would find it and she'd get a slap into the bargain. She sighed.

She came to the bottom of the pile and found the drawing book, the pencils and the box of paints that Charlotte had given her. She chewed her bottom lip, glancing round the sparsely furnished bedroom. Now she really didn't want to lose these. Where could she hide them? The only place she could think of was on top of the wardrobe. Maybe Dot wouldn't think of climbing up to look there. Quietly, Jenny pulled the chair near to the wardrobe, climbed on to it and tried to push the drawing book, pencils and paints as far back as she could out of sight. But they wouldn't slide any further than about halfway. Jenny wasn't tall enough to see from the chair she was balancing on what was in the way. She'd never put anything up there. She stretched out her fingers and touched something hard and round. Scrabbling at it till it came nearer the front, her hand closed around it and she pulled it down. It was a tin of peaches. Jenny stared at it in amazement, before understanding dawned. Her mother was hoarding food in case they ran short. She reached up and put the tin back where she'd found it, pushing it as far back as she could. It clinked against other tins. Jenny climbed down. The only place now to hide her paints was under the bed. She knelt on the floor began to push her belongings far underneath but again there was no room there. The whole area beneath her iron bedstead was taken up with boxes and packages. She pulled one out and opened the lid. It was full of more tinned fruit. She opened another to find bottles of whisky.

'Jen, are you going to stop up there for ever?' Her mother's strident voice drifted up the stairs. 'Yer tea's ready. Look sharp, me an' Arfer's going out.'

Jenny pulled a face. 'Fancy that,' she muttered sarcastically. In her normal voice she called back. 'Coming.'

Hastily, she pushed all the stuff back under her bed, but she was still faced with the problem of where to hide her paints. She'd have to leave them in the bottom drawer of the chest of drawers for the moment. Maybe she'd think of a better place later . . .

As they were finishing tea, a loud knock came at the front door. Jenny saw Arthur and Dot glance at each other in alarm. Jenny began to get up from the table to go to the door, but Dot grabbed her arm. 'You sit there. Keep quiet and don't move.'

'Why?'

'Ssh, I said,' Dot hissed, her eyes round with fear. 'Arfer, is the door locked?'

Arthur shrugged. 'Jenny came in last, I . . .'

Dot's grip tightened on Jenny's arm. 'Did you lock the door?'

'No, I—'

'Ssh.'

'We never lock the door,' Jenny whispered, catching some of her mother's fear. 'Why?'

'We do now. Just sit tight. Mebbe they'll go away if—'

But at that moment they all heard the front door rattle and open. Dot drew in her breath sharply, her eyes widened as she stared, terror-struck, at Arthur.

Then a cheery voice called out, 'Jen, are you 'ere?'

Jenny leapt to her feet and dragged herself out of her mother's grasp. 'It's Bobby! Bobby!'

Dot relaxed as she muttered, 'Silly little bugger, frightening us like that.'

But Jenny was gone, out of the room and rushing through the front room to the door. She didn't see the look of relief that passed between Arthur and Dot. 'Just make sure she knows to keep the doors locked now, eh?'

'I will,' Dot muttered grimly. 'Don't want no more scares like that.'

Twenty-Three

The boy was standing in the doorway grinning. 'Thought it was you. I saw you walking down the street with a posh gent. Who was he, then?'

'Miles. I've been staying with them in the country. Oh Bobby, it was awful when you went off on that train.'

His face was bleak for a moment. 'I know. And it were no better when we got where we was going.'

'Didn't you like it?'

'Like it?' Bobby was scornful. 'You kidding? We went to a farm – right out in the middle of nowhere, it were. Mind you, they did keep me an' Sammy together. But work. Cor! Up at five to do the milking before we went to school and then the same when we got home at night. And talk about the cold. It was freezing in winter. Mind you, we came home just before that first Christmas. We wrote home soon after we got there saying how awful it was, but we reckon the farmer's wife must've opened our letters and burnt 'em, cos Mam never got 'em.'

'So, how did you get home, then?'

Bobby grinned. 'Sammy ran away. Came all the way back home hitching lifts and he told Mam and she sent for me.'

'You could have come to where I was. It was great, it—' She stopped and glanced over her shoulder, fearful

162

that her mother might be listening. 'I'll tell you sometime. So, your mam hasn't sent you anywhere else.'

Bobby shook his head. 'She wants us with her, specially now Dad's gone.'

Jenny gasped. 'Gone?'

'Oh, not that. At least – ' Bobby grimaced and his
eyes were suddenly fearful – 'not yet.'

'What d'you mean?' Jenny whispered.

'He's gone back in the navy.'

'You said he might.'

Bobby nodded. 'Volunteered, he did. He used to be
in the merchant navy, yer know, but he came out when
Mam had our Ronnie and got a job on the docks so's
he could be at home with his family. Fat lot o' good
that did, didn't it? Now there's a war, he's gone back
anyway.'

Jenny didn't often read the newspapers or listen to
the wireless, but she'd heard snippets about ships being
attacked in the Channel by the Luftwaffe. Bobby's dad
would be in constant danger. She didn't know what to
say, didn't know how to comfort her friend. She wanted
to tell him about her own loss, how Georgie had been
posted missing, presumed killed. Even though she had
stoutly declared to anyone who would listen that he was
still alive and would come back one day, secretly deep
in her heart she knew that there was always the possibility that . . . no, no, she wouldn't believe it, she
couldn't believe it.

She had to believe that somewhere he was safe.

Now she squeezed Bobby's arm. 'He'll be all right,'
she said huskily.

Bobby made a valiant effort to smile and say cheerfully, 'Come round whenever you want. Mam'll be
pleased to see you.'

'I will.' She leaned forward conspiratorially. 'I might nip in later. Mum and Arfer are going out.'

'Nothin' new there, then.' Bobby chuckled and cast her a sympathetic glance. 'Just mind they show you how to get into the Morrison before they go out, in case we have an air raid. We get 'em all the time.'

Jenny's eyes widened. 'All the—?'

'S'all right. We're safe as houses, specially if we go down the underground.' Now he laughed. 'Actually, we're safer than houses 'cos that's what's getting bombed.'

'Oh Bobby!' Jenny could think of nothing else to say.

Later, after Dot and Arthur had roared off in his sports car, Jenny went next door.

'Jen – ' Elsie Hutton greeted her with open arms. 'It's good to have you back, darlin', but I'd rather you'd stayed safely in the country. Didn't you like it?'

Unbidden and before she could stop them, tears sprang to Jenny's eyes. 'I loved it, Aunty Elsie, but Mum sent for me to come home.'

Elsie's mouth was a hard line as she nodded grimly. 'I thought as much. Never stopped going on about how she was the only one whose kid hadn't come back and she didn't want anyone to think she'd sent you away to get rid of you.' Elsie snorted derisively. 'But she should have left you there. London's been taking a battering for months now an' it's not over yet.'

Jenny nodded, accepting the truth even though it hurt. 'She only sent for me 'cos everyone else has come home and she didn't want to be the odd one out. I know that. She didn't really *want* me back. Not like you wanted your boys.'

Elsie put her arms around Jenny. 'Aw, don't you worry. You're welcome here any time. An' when we go down the shelter or the tube, we'll send our Bobby round for you an' you can come with us.'

Jenny hugged her in return, thankful to have this family who she knew really did care for her.

'Now,' Elsie said briskly, 'come an' have a bite of tea with us.'

'Oh, I don't want to take your food. 'Sides, I've already had tea.'

'Then come and sit with us while we have ours and then you and Bobby can have a game of Ludo.'

The evening passed pleasantly enough and though part of Jenny was pleased to see her old friends again, the other part of her yearned to be back at the manor, playing with the doll's house, out on the lawn playing football with Miles or painting in the quietness of Charlotte's studio.

Or on the beach with Georgie.

'What's all that stuff under my bed?'

As soon as the words left her lips, Jenny knew she shouldn't have asked. Dot gasped and lashed out at her. But Jenny, quicker once more in her reflexes, ducked. 'Don't you poke your nose into what doesn't concern you.' Dot tapped her own nose. 'Keep it out. You hear?'

Jenny glared at her. 'It's in my bedroom.'

'*Your* bedroom.' Dot laughed nastily. 'Since when did you contribute to the rent for this place? If it's anybody's now, it's Arfer's. He's moved in an' he pays the rent.'

Jenny had guessed as much.

When they'd arrived back the previous night, or rather early this morning, laughing and staggering up the stairs, she'd heard her mother's bedroom door bang and, through the thin walls, other noises that a young girl should not be subjected to. In the morning, Arthur had still been there, sitting at the breakfast table, smoking, as if he did indeed own the place.

And now it seemed, in a manner of speaking, he did. He paid the rent.

'And don't you go telling folks about what's under your bed, neither.'

Jenny said no more but she counted the boxes under her bed from time to time and noticed that sometimes there were more, sometimes less. And yet they never had tinned peaches for tea, nor did she see Dot and Arthur drinking whisky. There was no one she could ask, but gradually even she began to understand that with all the rationing and the shortages, people would pay a little bit extra to someone who could supply what they wanted. And Arthur, it seemed, was that 'supply'. But she was careful never to ask questions, never to tell anyone – not even Bobby – about what she'd found.

Jenny had been home two weeks. She was back at school, back in Miss Chisholm's class, and she was reasonably happy at home. Dot was better tempered when Arthur was around and, if Jenny kept out of their way, life was bearable. Though she still longed to be back at Ravensfleet Manor and to make matters worse, as she had threatened, Dot began to take the fine clothes that Jenny had been given to the pawnbrokers. She spent the money she got on new clothes for herself. A skirt and two blouses had already disappeared by the time Arthur noticed what was happening and said, 'Yer don't need to take the kid's stuff, Dot. I give you enough to buy whatever you want.'

'She don't need posh clothes. She'll only get 'em dirty. She's a scruffy little urchin.'

Arthur winked at Jenny, who was watching sullenly as her mother folded two of the dresses that Charlotte had bought her ready to pawn.

'Not so scruffy now. She keeps her hair ever so nice and—'

Dot rounded on him. 'Are you sayin' she didn't before she went away? Are you saying I can't look after me own kid? She's always had a bath once a week and washed her hair, so don't you go sayin'—'

'No, 'course I'm not, Dot, but she's growing up. Why don't you let her keep the things she's been given?' Craftily, he added, 'There's a lot of wear in them and it'd save you having to buy more for her.'

Dot paused, undecided now. To press home his point, Arthur threw two pound notes on the table. 'There, that's more than you'd get up the pop shop, darlin'. Let her keep her stuff. I'll see you right, you know I will.'

Grudgingly, Dot muttered, 'All right, then, but she'd better look after 'em.' Then she wagged her forefinger in Jenny's face. 'You'd better say "thank you" to your uncle Arfer. He's very good to you, he is.'

Jenny grinned at Arthur as she scooped up the dresses from the table before her mother could change her mind and scuttled upstairs to hang them back in her wardrobe. Just as she was closing the wardrobe door, the now familiar sound of the wailing air-raid sirens began and she heard Arthur shouting up the stairs.

'Look sharp, Jen. Get down here.'

'Let's go to the underground. It'll be safer,' Dot was saying as Jenny burst into the kitchen.

'No time,' Arthur said, pushing them both towards

the front room where the Morrison shelter had been constructed. 'I can hear the planes . . .'

The roaring and the thud of bombs dropping went on for what seemed hours. Squashed into the oblong metal box-like shelter with its steel-plate top and wire-mesh sides beside Dot and Arthur, Jenny clutched Bert closely and covered her ears. It had never been as bad as this in the country. Just a few noises in the distance, but this was right overhead. Any minute a bomb might fall on their house . . .

Dot lay with her head buried against Arthur's chest.

'We'll go down the underground another night before it starts,' he promised.

Dot raised her head to say accusingly, as if it was all Arthur's fault, '*If* we get through this one.' At that moment there was a loud whistling and a tremendous crash and the sound of breaking glass. The whole house, even the ground beneath them, shook. Dot screamed and clung to Arthur, whilst Jenny curled herself into a round ball. Dust choked her and she began to cough.

They emerged unscathed into the cold light of dawn, but when Arthur opened the front door it was to see that a house on the opposite side of the street had taken a direct hit.

'Is Bobby's house all right?' Jenny asked fearfully, pushing her way out beneath Arthur's arm.

'Yeah. 'Sides, I reckon they went down the underground. I saw 'em setting off with blankets and pillows before the air raid started.'

'And that's what we'll be doing in future,' Dot said firmly. 'I ain't standing another night like that.'

It seemed as if Hitler was determined to break the spirit of the Londoners. But if he could have seen them lying in rows on the station platform, sharing their food, joining in a sing-song and playing games with the children, he might have realized it was going to be a much harder task than he'd envisaged.

Elsie greeted them the following night when they arrived on the underground platform. 'Come on, you lot, make room for Jenny and her mam. Ronnie, help Arthur spread the blankets out. There we are, all nice and cosy.'

Dot glanced around her and turned up her nose. 'Is this where we sleep? On the draughty platform?'

''Fraid so,' Elsie laughed and eyed her neighbour done up in her best clothes, full make-up on, her brassy hair piled up on top of her head and wearing high heels and silk stockings. Now I wonder how she's come by them? Elsie Hutton thought. But she had no need to wonder for long; Arthur. He was a wide boy right enough. A spiv, as his sort were being called. She glanced down the lines of makeshift beds to see Arthur had settled himself at the very end, next to Ronnie, Elsie's eldest boy. She frowned, worried to see that Arthur Osborne was engaging her son in whispered conversation.

'Come on,' she raised her voice, trying to break up the cosy chat. 'Let's 'ave a sing-song. "My Ol' Man . . ."' Her voice was tuneless, but soon she had the whole crowd joining in and, to her delight, she saw Arthur shrug and abandon trying to talk to Ronnie above the noise. The boy turned and saw his mother watching them even whilst she was leading the singing. To her relief, Ronnie winked and grinned at her.

That's my boy, she thought. He'll have none of Arthur's goings on.

They sang raucously, trying to drown out the sound of the dull thuds from above ground, trying desperately not to think of the damage being caused to their homes and, maybe, even the loss of life. Dot moved her position to sit next to Arthur, clinging on to him and making a great show of being frightened.

Someone handed them mugs of tea; others were giving out sandwiches, sharing their precious food with anyone who needed it, but all the time they kept singing. It went on until the small hours when the grown-ups realized that it was time the children settled down to sleep, if any sleep were possible.

Jenny, Bobby and the other youngsters, wrapped warmly in blankets, fell asleep but for some of the adults the night was long and restless. When they emerged into the daylight at the sound of the all-clear it was to see devastation all around them.

'Let's get home, Arfer,' Dot said, suddenly subdued. 'That's if we've still got a home to go to.'

Twenty-Four

Their street was just as they'd left it. The house further down that had been hit the previous night was still in a state of collapse, but no other damage had been done.

'Thank Gawd for that,' Dot said, opening her front door. 'Hello, door's not locked. Didn't you lock it, Arfer?'

''Course I did,' he said irritably, then a look of fear crossed his face. He pushed past Dot and Jenny and hurried upstairs. He came down with a face like thunder. 'Me stuff's gone.'

Dot gasped. 'All of it?'

'Yeah. If I catch up with whoever's—' He frowned and murmured, 'I wonder.'

He strode out of the house and banged on the Huttons' door. Dot and Jenny stood watching.

'What's goin' on, Mum?' But Dot didn't answer.

'Ronnie – Ronnie, come on out here,' Arthur shouted. Families, trooping back cold and tired after their night in the underground, glanced at him curiously.

The door flew open and Elsie Hutton stood there. She was not her usual warm-hearted, friendly self. Jenny was shocked as Elsie folded her arms across her chest and said harshly, 'What d'you want?'

'Your son, that's who!'

'Which one? I've got three.'

'Ronnie.'

171

'He's not 'ere.'

'Yes, he is. He was coming along the road just after us, his arms full of blankets, so where else would he be going?'

'Work. He's gone to work. Got a job on the docks now, he has.'

Arthur grunted. 'I know that.' He glared at Elsie. But the woman returned the scowl in equal measure and thrust her face close to Arthur's with such menace that he took a step backwards. 'You stay away from me an' mine, Arthur Osborne. I know what your little game is. Black market, ain't it? Now you listen to me a minute. 'Cos you're shacked up wiv Dot now, you're one of us. More's the pity. And we don't grass on our own even though the whole street knows what you're up to.'

'Then where's me stuff, I'd like to know?'

Elsie blinked. 'What stuff?'

'Stuff I'd got hidden in the house, in the girl's bedroom.'

'In Jen's—' Elsie gaped at him, robbed of speech for a brief moment before she spat, 'You've been hiding your ill-gotten gains in that little lass's bedroom? Is there no depths you lot won't sink to? I suppose you thought no one'd look in a kiddie's bedroom.'

Jenny glanced at her mother, but Dot had disappeared back into their house.

'It's not nicked, if that's what you're thinking. I'm no thief,' Arthur added indignantly.

'As good as,' Elsie muttered. 'Wheeling and dealing in black-market goods, I know. But I 'spect you get others to do your dirty work for yer, so you can come up smellin' of roses. And I saw you talking to my Ronnie down the shelter. Trying to get him to nick stuff off the docks, were yer?'

Arthur didn't deny Elsie's accusation. Instead, he changed tack as his voice softened. 'Now listen, Elsie. Any time you want a bit of extra food for that growing family of yours, you just say the word.' He tapped the side of his nose. 'Know what I mean?'

'Oh I know what you mean, all right, and I wouldn't touch it wiv a barge pole.'

'Where's the harm? It's all bought and paid for, Elsie.'

Grimly, Elsie nodded. 'Aye, and well above the going rate an' all, I 'spect.'

There was silence until Jenny heard Arthur say in the tone of voice she'd heard him use so many times to Dot, 'Aw, now come on, Elsie. I can put a bit of money your boy's way if he'll do me a few favours now and again—'

He got no further for Elsie gave him a violent shove in the chest that sent him reeling backwards. He almost lost his balance but managed not to fall as she yelled, 'You keep away from my lad, Arthur Osborne, if you know what's good for yer, or I'll tell my Sid when he comes 'ome on leave.' Then she slammed the door with such finality that even Arthur, frantic to find where his 'stuff' had gone, dared not knock at her door again. And the thought of her burly husband, strong from years of work as a docker, coming after him with flying fists made him think more than twice.

As he turned, he saw Jenny standing against the wall. He crossed the space between them and stood over her. Though she was quaking inside, fearing that somehow she was going to get the blame for his belongings having disappeared, Jenny faced up to him squarely. But he was not angry with her; instead it seemed he needed her help. 'You're mates with those lads, aren't you?'

'Ye-es,' Jenny admitted.

He squatted down in front of her, bringing his face down to her level. 'Then do your uncle Arthur a favour, will you? Ask 'em if young Ronnie took my stuff, will yer?'

Jenny stared at him. 'It was still there when we went to the underground shelter.'

'How d'you know that?'

'Because I wanted to take Bert with me and he was on the floor, half under the bed, and when I fished him out I saw all the boxes still stacked there.'

'You sure?'

Jenny nodded vigorously.

'You wouldn't tell your uncle Arthur porkies, would you?'

Now she shook her head just as vehemently. 'Cross me heart ... And,' she went on, 'Ronnie was in the shelter with us. The whole family was there when we got there and they were walking home behind us when we came home, so he couldn't have nicked your stuff, Uncle Arthur, could he?'

'Mm. It was a long night, Jen. He could have slipped out when we was asleep.'

Jen laughed. 'He wouldn't have dared. His mam would have leathered him up and down the street if he'd so much as poked his nose above ground during an air raid.'

'We-ell,' Arthur said slowly, 'you could be right.'

''Sides, you know what Aunty Elsie's like? Where would Ronnie hide it away from her beady eyes?'

'That's true. Now that is true. I can see that.' He grinned suddenly. 'Fiery piece, ain't she?'

'Aunty Elsie?' Jenny smiled too. 'She can be, but she's lovely really. She's—' Jenny stopped, afraid that what she'd been going to say would sound very disloyal to her own mother. But it seemed Arthur understood, for he squeezed her shoulder and said softly, 'I know, I know. Elsie's good to you, ain't she?'

Jenny nodded. 'I really don't think she'd have any truck with her lads being involved in – well – anything,' she added lamely, not quite sure exactly what it was that Arthur did. She'd no idea what the term 'black market', which she'd heard Elsie use, meant. But from the tone of the woman's voice and the accusation in it, it didn't sound good. To the young girl, it sounded next door to stealing.

Arthur was thoughtful. 'If it weren't him, then who was it?'

Jenny shrugged. 'It could have been anybody. Aunty Elsie said everybody in the street knows.'

Arthur looked grim as he patted her curls and said, 'Well, you just keep your ears open for yer uncle Arthur and if you hear anything, you let me know and I'll buy you a nice present. How'd that be?'

Jenny smiled thinly. Though she didn't dislike Arthur now, she really didn't want him buying her presents; it always made her mum resentful and Dot took it out on her.

Arthur and Dot were twitchy; that was the only word Jenny could think of to describe how they were acting. Both the front and the back doors were securely locked day and night, even though East Enders never normally locked their doors. Warm-hearted and friendly and secure in their own community, there'd never been the need. But now Dot and Arthur were decidedly nervous about something. They were forever looking out of the front windows. They jumped physically if a knock came at the door and they wouldn't even answer it until they knew who was there.

'Don't you go opening the door to anyone, Jen. You tell me, see?'

'Yes, Mum.' She paused and added, 'But it's all right if it's someone I know, isn't it?'

'No, it ain't. Aren't you listening to what I say?' Dot raised her hand and Jenny said swiftly, 'Yes, Mum.'

This state of affairs carried on for the next two days. Arthur stayed in the house the whole time, peering out of the front windows yet keeping well back so that he could not be seen. The slightest sound made him jumpy and even Dot got irritated with him.

'I'm going shopping,' she announced.

'No, yer not,' Arthur snapped. 'Yer not leaving this house.'

'But we've no food and—'

'Send the kid. No one'll bother her.'

'She doesn't know how to shop. Yer 'ave to queue for hours just to get a bit of scrag end. They'll do 'er.'

'Jen's got more nous than you give 'er credit for,' Arthur said, turning away from the window. 'Let her go this once and see how she gets on. You never know.' He grinned. 'If Jen puts on her pathetic look and smiles nicely, they might take pity on her.'

Dot regarded her daughter steadily. 'It might work, I suppose.'

Arthur laughed – the first time he'd done so since he'd discovered that his hoard had gone missing. 'I know she can't flash her tits at 'em like you do, Dot, but she's got a cheeky little smile that might work just as well.'

Dot's eyes narrowed. 'You saying I can't work me magic any longer?'

'Nah, Dot, would I?' He put his arm around her shoulders and gave her a squeeze. He put his mouth to her ear and whispered, 'And while she's out . . .'

Dot hurried to find her handbag.

Twenty-Five

Jenny joined the long queue of women outside the butcher's shop. After a few moments, someone else came up behind her.

'Hello, darlin'. Where's yer mum?'

Jenny turned to smile up at Elsie Hutton. 'At home.'

'Is she poorly?'

'No.'

Elsie's face darkened. 'Then, why . . . ?' She stopped and her mouth tightened in fury. Had Dot Mercer no shame? Sending a young girl to queue for hours to get a tiny piece of meat? But, no, she hadn't, Elsie thought, else she wouldn't have shacked up with that rascal, Arthur Osborne. She forced a smile on to her face for Jenny's sake and tried to think of something they could talk about, anything to steer the conversation away from Jenny's home life. 'Have you heard from those folks you were staying with in the country?'

Jenny bit her lip and shook her head.

'Have you written to them?'

The girl nodded and whispered, 'Three times. Mum said she'd put stamps on them and post them, but they've never written back.' From the tone of Jenny's voice, it was obvious to Elsie that the girl was deeply hurt and her next words tugged at Elsie's heartstrings. 'I thought they'd have written to me.'

'I'm sure they will, love. You just keep writing to them.'

'Mum ses it's a waste of paper and her money buying stamps. She – she ses they must've been glad to get rid of me.'

Was there nothing Dot wouldn't stoop to? Elsie had to clamp her lips together to stop herself from saying exactly what she thought. Forcing her tone to sound casual, she said, 'I'm sure that's not true, Jen. I bet they loved having you.'

'They were very kind and Georgie . . .' Her voice broke and she stopped.

'Who's Georgie?' Elsie asked gently, noticing the catch in the girl's voice.

'He – he was – is – a fighter pilot. He was posted missing.' Her head shot up as she met Elsie's sympathetic eyes. 'But he's coming back. I know he is.'

Elsie could think of nothing to say, so she just squeezed the girl's shoulder. Instead, she changed the subject to the matter uppermost in their thoughts. 'Now, when you get to the counter – *if* we ever get to the counter – don't you let Mr Chops diddle you.'

Jenny's eyes widened and she giggled, her thoughts turned away – as Elsie had hoped they would be – from sadness. 'Is that his name? Is it really "Mr Chops"?'

Elsie chuckled. 'No, but it's what we all call him. He's always saying "'Ow abart a nice pawk chop?' Elsie broadened her own cockney accent even more to imitate their local butcher. Then she pulled a face. 'But I don't reckon there'll be many pork chops left by the time we get to the front, Jen.'

At last, Jenny was standing in front of the rotund figure of Mr Chops.

'Good morning, madam,' he said, his eyes twinkling

behind his round spectacles. He was a big man, rotund and jovial. 'And what can I get for you today?'

'A nice piece of brisket, if you please, Mr Chops,' Jenny said in her best, grown-up voice.

There was a ripple of laughter amongst those in the queue just behind her, who had heard her words. Elsie nudged her and whispered, hardly able to keep the laughter from her voice. 'His real name's Mr Bartholomew.'

But the butcher was laughing uproariously, his great belly shaking. Jenny smiled up at him, her cheeks dimpling prettily, her blue eyes dancing. She could see that he hadn't taken offence in the slightest. 'I ain't got no brisket today, but you give me your ration books and I'll see what I can find for yer.' As he placed the ration of meat for three people into a newspaper parcel, he reached beneath the counter and winked at her. Then he slapped three sausages on top of the portions of meat and wrapped it up swiftly. Only Elsie, standing close behind Jenny, saw his actions. He leaned forward and whispered, 'Tell yer mam, them's for you. Nobody else, just you.' He winked again, straightened up to take her money and then glanced at the loose coupons Jenny had shaken out of an envelope on to the counter. For a moment his smile faded. 'Ain't you brought your ration books, love?'

'Mum said I might lose them, so she cut them out,' Jenny said innocently. It was what Dot had told her to say, although the girl hadn't actually seen her do it.

'Mm.' The butcher was frowning worriedly. He picked up the coupons and scrutinized them carefully. 'All right. I'll take 'em just this once, but you tell yer mam to sent the books next time, eh?'

Above her head, he exchanged a glance with Elsie,

raising his eyebrows in a question. He knew Mrs Hutton lived next door to Dot Mercer. But Elsie shrugged, thankful that she didn't know whether the coupons were forgeries or not.

'Thank you, Mr Ch— Mr Bartholomew,' Jenny said politely.

'Oh, Mr Chops to you, darlin',' the man said kindly, fully aware that if there was anything dodgy about the coupons she'd handed over, it wasn't the little lass's fault. 'We're mates now, ain't we?'

Again, Jenny gave him her most winning smile as she turned and wove her way amongst the lengthening queue out of the shop. Outside, she waited until Elsie joined her so that they could walk home together.

The house was quiet when she let herself in by the front door and Jenny knew better than to disturb Dot and Arthur, so she put her bag of shopping on the table and slipped out again to the Huttons' house, remembering to lock the door carefully behind her.

'You playing out, Bobby?' she asked her friend, who was lounging against the front door frame of their house.

'Nah. I'm waiting for Sammy. He reckons he can get me a job as a delivery boy for the butcher.'

'Mr Chops?'

Bobby blinked. 'Eh?'

'I mean – Mr Bartholomew?'

Bobby grinned. 'Yeah, that's him.'

'Me an' yer mam have just been up there. He gave me three sausages, he did.'

'Aren't you the lucky one?'

But she didn't feel so lucky when she returned home

181

later to find Arthur sitting at the table and tucking into her sausages.

'They were for me,' she said, standing beside the table, eyeing the disappearing sausages enviously. 'Mr Chops said so.'

Dot tweaked her ear painfully. 'We share in this house, young lady, and don't you forget it.'

But Arthur looked up with an apologetic smile. 'Sorry, Tich. I didn't know. Look, there's one left. You have that.'

'Arthur . . .' Dot began warningly, but he pushed the plate towards Jenny and insisted she should eat the last one. Dot, pursing her mouth in disapproval, turned away. For once, there was nothing she could do.

There was no air raid that evening and some families stayed in their own homes, thankful for the respite and the chance to spend just one night in their own beds, though Jenny saw the Huttons setting off as usual to the underground armed with food and blankets.

'I ain't goin',' Dot declared. 'I could do with one night's proper sleep.'

But in the middle of the night, there came such a banging on the front door that Jenny woke up, startled by the sudden noise. She sat up in bed, her heart thudding, her whole body shaking.

Dot rushed into the room, her hair tousled, her eyes wide. 'Don't go down, Jen. Arthur ses not to answer it.'

'But—'

'Do as 'ee ses.'

'Who is it?' Jenny whispered, catching her mother's fear.

'The coppers.'

Jenny gasped. 'The – the – why?'

'Why d'yer think?' Dot snapped.

Jenny blinked in the darkness, her mind working rapidly. 'Is it about the stuff that was under my bed? Has Uncle Arthur told the police that it's been nicked and—'

Dot stared at her. 'A' yer stupid, or what? 'Course he's not reported it. Haven't you heard of the black market? It were stolen goods. Oh, I don't mean he stole the stuff,' her mother added swiftly, realizing that in her agitation she was saying too much. 'He was keepin' it for a mate.'

Jenny stared at her. She didn't believe Dot. If all those tins and bottles that had been under her bed had been stolen goods, then Arthur Osborne had done the stealing or had at least organized it.

They stayed quietly in Jenny's bedroom until Arthur crept in. 'They've gone, but they've shouted through the letter box that they'll be back. We'll have to go, Dot. Right now.'

For a moment Dot stared at him and then got up, muttering, 'Why the hell I ever got myself mixed up with a wide boy, I don't know.'

Even amidst their anxiety, Arthur grinned and tweaked her nose. 'Cos you can't resist me, that's why. An' I'm good to yer, aren't I?'

But Dot wasn't in a playful mood and she slapped his hand away. 'I'll not deny that.' She glared at him as she added, 'But I'm good to you an' all, ain't I?'

He seemed about to take her in his arms but she shoved him away. 'We'd better get going. Jen, pack yer stuff. We're getting out.'

Jenny bounced up and down on her bed. 'Back to Lincolnshire? You're taking me back to Ravensfleet?'

Dot rounded on her, her face twisted into a sneer. 'No, we're not. And you can forget all about the posh folk you stayed with. They don't want yer no more. A dirty little tyke like you. Now get dressed and put yer clothes into that suitcase they gave you. Least they were useful for something.'

Jenny sat very still, staring after her mother as she hurried from the room.

Arthur touched her shoulder. 'Come on, darlin'. It'll be all right. I'll look after you.'

Jenny tried to smile weakly. She knew he meant well, but it wasn't how she thought a man should take care of his family. Doing a moonlight. It wasn't what Miles or Charlotte or Georgie would have done. But then, she reasoned, they wouldn't have been on the wrong side of the law in the first place.

But just as they were about to collect their belongings together, the sirens began to wail.

Twenty-Six

They huddled together for the rest of the night in the Morrison shelter in the front room.

'I reckon it's stopping,' Arthur whispered after they'd listened to wave after wave of bombers flying overhead and heard the thud of bombs falling. Luckily, nothing fell very close.

'I ain't heard the all-clear,' Dot muttered.

'We'll have to risk it. We must be gone before the neighbours get back.'

'I want to say 'bye to Bobby and Aunty Elsie,' Jenny said, sitting up suddenly and banging her head on the top of the shelter. 'Ouch!'

'Serves yer right,' Dot muttered. 'And no, you can't say goodbye to nobody. No one must know we're going.'

Arthur eased himself out of the confined space and stood up, turning to help Dot out. 'Come on, Jen. Look lively.'

'But they might still be bombing.'

'He said,' Dot snarled, reaching in to grab the girl's arm, 'come *on*.'

Jenny scrambled out and headed for the stairs. She threw her best clothes – the ones that Charlotte had bought her – into the suitcase Charlotte had given her and put her precious drawing book and paints on the top. She closed the lid and, clutching Bert firmly, bumped it down the stairs.

'Don't make such a racket,' Dot hissed. 'We don't want nobody hearing us.'

In the murky early morning light of a city still under the threat of attack – still the All Clear hadn't sounded – Arthur pushed their belongings into a van.

When she saw it, Dot turned up her nose. 'Where's yer nice car?'

'Done a good deal on it.' Arthur winked at her. 'This'll be far more useful.' He turned to Jenny. 'You get in the back, darlin'. I've put a rug for you to sit on. And don't make a noise if we're stopped, will yer?'

Shivering, Jenny scrambled in and pulled the rug around her, still clutching Bert tightly against her. She wrinkled her nose. There was a funny smell. Beside her were more boxes – Jenny presumed them to be more tinned peaches or bottles of whisky – but the smell seemed to be coming from an oddly shaped parcel wrapped in cheesecloth.

Dot and Arthur climbed into the front of the van and Arthur started the engine. It echoed loudly in the still air and, catching the grown-ups' tension, Jenny didn't breathe easily until they were well away from their street and on their way north out of the city. There were two small windows in the rear doors of the van and for a while, she peered out. They passed through the bombed-out streets where disconsolate residents were already climbing over mounds of rubble attempting to salvage whatever belongings they could find. Tears prickled Jenny's eyes. She hadn't many belongings in the world – not that amounted to much – but she'd had to leave most of what she did possess behind. And she knew nothing would remain by the time they returned – if they ever did. Everything would have been either blown to smithereens in the bombing or taken by unscrupulous looters.

And, with every day that passed, Jenny was beginning to understand that she was in the clutches of just such a person.

By the time they'd left the London suburbs behind and were heading north, the day was fully light. Jenny was buffeted and bounced around in the back of the van, the petrol fumes from the dilapidated vehicle making her feel sick. And the feeling was not helped by the strange smell permeating the whole van. She wanted to knock on the thin partition between the back of the van and the front seats, but she dared not do so. She could clearly hear Arthur and her mother arguing almost as soon as they'd set out.

'Slow down, Arthur.'

'Got to get a move on, Dot. Can't risk getting stopped.'

'You will be, if you go at this speed in the blackout. I'm warning you, Arthur, if you don't drive at a sensible pace, I'm out of here. And Jenny too. And then where would you be?' Her tone had taken on a sarcastic note. 'Without your nice little family as a cover?'

Arthur had growled a reply that Jenny hadn't been able to hear, but he'd slowed the pace a little.

A little later, she banged on the partition. 'Mum, I need to *go!*'

But it was Arthur who shouted back. 'I can't stop yet. You'll have to wait.'

It wasn't until several miles further on when Arthur considered they'd reached a safe distance from the city that he pulled in at a roadside café.

Jenny clambered out of the back, feeling bruised and battered. 'I feel sick!'

'Why I have to be saddled with a nuisance like you, I don't know,' Dot said irritably, feeling none too comfortable herself. 'I should have left you in the country, then I wouldn't be having all this palaver.'

'I wish you had,' Jenny muttered.

'What did you say?'

But Jenny didn't answer, she was running towards the café, desperate to find the toilets.

When she came back, Dot was sitting at a table in the café watching with narrowed eyes as Arthur leaned across the counter towards a buxom waitress taking his order. Dot was glaring at them both.

Jenny sat down at the table beside her mother and followed her gaze. 'What's he up to?'

Dot sniffed. 'You might well ask. Up to his usual tricks, I 'spect. Flirting with anything in a skirt.'

But Arthur sauntered towards the table with a satisfied smile on his lips. 'Done a nice bit o' business there.'

Dot's frown deepened. 'What are you on about?'

Arthur nodded towards the van parked outside. 'The stuff in the back of the van. I've managed to shift some of it for a nice bit of profit. She's in charge while the owner's away and she's running short of things with all the rationing. Very glad to take some of it off me hands, you might say.'

Jenny put on her most innocent expression. 'What is it, Uncle Arthur?'

'Oh, you know, just a side of bacon and a few tins of fruit.'

'You'd have done better to hang on to it,' Dot put in. 'We might need it to find ourselves a place. Wherever it is we're going.'

'Where are we going, Uncle Arthur?'

'Up north somewhere.' Arthur replied.

'Can't we go to Ravensfleet? They'd take us in, I know they—'

Before Jenny had realized what was happening, she felt Dot's hand strike the back of her head. 'I've told you not to keep on about them. They don't want you – they don't want any of us – else they wouldn't have sent you back.'

Jenny, her eyes smarting, rubbed her head. 'They didn't send me back. You sent for me through the authorities.'

'I did no such thing. What would I want you back for? I'd've left you there for ever, if I could've done.'

'Now, now, Dot,' Arthur chided, sticking up for the girl. To his mind, the child was no trouble and, as Dot had rightly said, she was proving to be a useful cover for him. Arthur Osborne was becoming known as a black marketer, but he was also known to be unmarried. Moving in with Dot and her kid had been a smart move on his part. At first he hadn't wanted the child back either. He and Dot had been enjoying the high life together without the encumbrance of a child, but now she was with them, he'd realized that Jenny could be very useful to him. The police were on to him, he was sure, but they'd be looking for Arthur Osborne, the bachelor spiv, not a family man tucked away in the heart of the country. And he had other plans for Jenny too. No one would suspect the innocent-looking girl of being involved in black market racketeering.

When he'd carried the boxes of tinned fruit and the flitch of bacon into the café from the back of the van and received a fistful of money in return, they set off again. They drove for most of the day, stopping every so often for food and to stretch their legs. It was late afternoon as they drove through Chesterfield and into the hills and dales of Derbyshire.

'You got enough petrol to be coming all this way, Arfer?'

189

'Plenty in the back in cans, Dot. An' I've got coupons.'

'Where'd you get *them* from?'

'Ask no questions, darlin'.'

Dot sniffed, but wisely changed the subject. 'So, just where are we going, Arfer? Cos I 'aven't got a clue where we are.'

'We'll find a nice little country pub for tonight and then tomorrow we'll start looking for somewhere to rent.'

They found a village pub with a room to let. 'I've only one room,' the landlord said, smiling benignly at them, 'but t'little lass can sleep on a put-you-up.'

'Oh great,' Dot muttered under her breath but she smiled winningly at the man and simpered, 'so kind.'

'And you'll be wanting a meal, I spect? Come far, have you?'

Dot hesitated and glanced at Arthur. Leaving in such a hurry, they hadn't had time to concoct a story together, or rather, she hadn't had time to hear what the story was. He'd have one ready, she was sure. He should have been a writer, Dot thought morosely, the stories he could come up with.

'We're from London. Bombing's terrible there.' Arthur gave an exaggerated sigh and nodded towards Dot and Jenny. 'And I had to get the missis and my kid out of there.' He closed his eyes and shook his head in a fair impression of a concerned husband and father.

The landlord eyed Arthur shrewdly. 'Been called up, then, have you? Brought 'em to safety before you have to go?'

Jenny held her breath, wondering how Arthur was going to get out of that. But he was pulling a wry, almost apologetic face. 'I've got a heart complaint.

190

Doesn't show, but – ' he patted his breast pocket and his tone took on a slightly belligerent note – 'I've got the medical papers to prove it, if anyone doubts my word.'

Jenny gaped at him. It was the first time she'd heard this.

'Watch it, Jen,' Dot hissed quietly and the girl dipped her head before her look of incredulity should give Arthur away.

But the landlord didn't appear to have noticed as he said in more a friendly tone, 'Sorry to hear that. No offence intended.'

'None taken, mate,' Arthur said, all smiles again.

They ate in a small dining room, served by the landlord's wife. 'Steak and kidney pie, but not a lot of steak, I'm afraid. It's the rationing, you know.'

'I'd've thought you'd've been all right in the country,' Arthur said. 'Plenty of food about.'

'Oh we have to stick to the regulations just like anybody else. Mind you, I suppose we have better access to food that isn't on ration.' She laughed. 'And there's always ways and means to get around the rules, if you get my meaning.'

Arthur – sitting in the country pub looking every inch the London spiv – put on his most innocent expression. 'Really,' he murmured, 'we must have a little chat sometime.'

As they finished their meal and prepared to go upstairs to the bedroom. Arthur asked the landlord casually, 'I don't suppose you know of anywhere to rent around here, do you?'

'As a matter of fact I do. 'Tis a bit remote, mind. 'Tis in the next dale. A little cottage that was a farm labourer's. 'Tis on a farmer's land. Mr Fenton comes in here most evenings. Come down to the bar later on, when you've got the young 'un to bed, and I'll introduce you.'

Arthur's gratitude was genuine. It sounded just the sort of place he was looking for. Well off the beaten track and yet in the heart of the countryside where he might be able to carry on his nefarious business. Jenny saw her mother shiver at the bleak prospect, but the girl smiled inwardly. Living on or near a farm might be almost as good as living back at the manor.

Almost, but not quite.

Twenty-Seven

Jenny lay in bed listening to the rise and fall of conversation, punctuated by the occasional burst of laughter, drifting up from the bar below. She fell asleep wondering if Arthur and her mother had already met the farmer and if they'd be moving into the cottage tomorrow. She slept so soundly that she didn't hear her mother and Arthur come to bed shortly after eleven, or Arthur's gentle snoring through the night. She awoke suddenly as Dot shook her.

'Get up. Mrs Pearson's making breakfast. Smells good, doesn't it? And then we're moving into our new home.' Dot didn't sound exactly enthusiastic, but Jenny shot off the put-you-up bed and scrabbled for her clothes. Only minutes later, she was sitting down at the table whilst Mrs Pearson, the landlord's wife, placed a mouth-watering breakfast of eggs, bacon and fried bread in front of her.

'There you are, love. You look as if you could do with a bit of feeding up.'

Jenny smiled her most winning smile and picked up her knife and fork. She didn't – though the question was in her mind – ask how the landlady had come by all this delicious food. But she knew herself, after living in the countryside, that it was very different in the country to London, where they had to queue for hours to get a scrap of meat.

After they'd all eaten, Arthur paid the landlord and listened whilst Mr Pearson, with many gesticulations, explained the way to the cottage. Obviously, last night's negotiations with the farmer had gone well and Arthur had struck one of his famous 'deals'. Jenny just hoped this time it was all above board.

As they climbed into the van, Arthur laughed saying, 'I hope that geezer never loses his arms, he'd never be able to tell anyone anything.'

The cottage was set on a sloping hill amidst the farmer's land, a short distance from the farmhouse and the buildings surrounding it. The front windows overlooked the dale below where, beyond the river, rows of houses nestled beside the road that wound through the valley.

Dot wrinkled her nose. 'This place is filthy.'

But Arthur was undeterred; he was feeling safer already. The London police would never think of looking for Arthur Osborne, the flashy dresser, in a place like this and dressed in country clothes. 'I'll get our stuff out of the van. A bit of elbow grease, Dot, and the place will be like a little palace. There's a school down there somewhere,' he went on, speaking to Jenny now as he gestured out of the front room window, 'we'll get you booked in.'

Jenny said nothing. She hated starting a new school. Everyone stared at her and when she opened her mouth to speak, they all laughed at her accent or pretended they couldn't understand her. That's what had happened in Ravensfleet until Miles had set up schooling for some of the evacuees at the manor.

'You needn't bother, Arthur,' Dot snapped, bringing Jenny's thoughts back to the present. 'I ain't stopping here long in this godforsaken dump. You can find us a nice little flat in Sheffield or Manchester or somewhere—'

To Jenny's surprise, Arthur gripped Dot's arm. 'We're staying here. 'Tain't safe in the cities. Too many coppers about.'

Dot stared at him, his rough handling as much of a shock to her as it was to Jenny. Dot's eyes widened in fear as she whispered, 'I knew we had to do a runner from home, but – but you don't mean they'll come after us' – her voice rose – 'that they'll find us?'

'Not if you do as I say, Dot, there's a good girl. They're looking for Arthur Osborne, *bachelor*. Now look . . .' He loosened his hold on her and turned to include Jenny. He gestured towards the sofa. 'Sit down and let's sort this out now.'

Still a little shaken, Dot sat down obediently and pulled Jenny down beside her. Silently, they looked up at Arthur and waited for him to explain.

He sat in the armchair at the side of the hearth. 'You know I'd got a bit of trouble back home and that's why we had to leave.'

'What sort of trouble?' Jenny piped up.

'Shut up, Jen,' her mother muttered. 'Go on, Arfer.'

'It was getting a bit hot, that's all, but we'll be fine here. Besides,' he grinned, 'there'll be richer pickings here, I reckon.'

Jenny's heart sank. It didn't sound as if the scare he'd had had made Arthur want to give up his way of life. It had just prompted him to move somewhere else and start again.

'But we've got to get our story straight.' He glanced at Jenny. 'It's important. So here's what we tell folks. We're a family called Mercer. That'll be easier for you to remember, won't it, Jen? If we use Osborne, you might slip up. Besides, they're not looking for an Arthur Mercer, now are they?'

'Go on,' Dot said grimly. 'So, we're married, are we?'

Arthur grinned. 'S'what you wanted, ain't it, Dot?'

Dot made a noise in her throat like a low growl, but Arthur ignored it. 'We've come from London – no use trying to hide the accent, is there? We've brought our kid out of the bombing.'

'And what are you going to do, now that you've failed your medical so convincingly?' Dot asked sarcastically. 'By the way, *have* you got a heart condition?'

Arthur laughed loudly. 'Course I ain't, but there's several geezers on a nice little earner impersonating men who've been called up and don't want to go. Cost me about two hundred nicker but it was worth it.'

Jenny felt sick. She thought back to the Thornton family; how they'd all gone willingly into the services and Georgie had perhaps given his life in the service of his country. Even the young girl could see the difference between Arthur and the Thornton brothers. They were fervently patriotic; Arthur was not. He was only concerned with preserving his own skin and making money out of adversity. She bit her lip to stop herself from saying something she shouldn't, but even that did not stop the words bursting out. 'That's cheating.'

For once her mother did not smack her across the back of the head and Arthur only smirked and said, 'You have to do a bit of duckin' and divin', darlin', now don't you?'

'So, how are you going to earn an *honest* living here?' Dot asked, her question heavy with sarcasm.

'You mean *work*?' Arthur looked scandalized, as if he'd allowed a dirty word to pass his lips. He stared at Dot and when she didn't answer but merely stared back at him, he said shortly, 'I'll make contacts, don't you worry. If I get into the cities, I'll soon—'

'Then why can't we live in a city, Arthur? Why – ?'

'I shan't tell you again. It's safer out here in the middle of nowhere. Besides,' he smirked, 'where d'you think I'm going to get the goods from if not from the country? Plenty of "deals" to be done with the farmers, I reckon.' He winked. 'I've got a few documents they might be interested in. For a price, of course.'

'What sort of documents?'

'Never you mind, Dot.' He tapped the side of his nose. 'What the eye doesn't see, an' all that.'

Dot frowned but she asked no more questions, but Jenny had no such compunction. 'You could always work on the farm, Uncle Arthur. They're always looking for hands, now such a lot of the men have gone to war.'

Arthur looked askance. 'You expect me to get togged up in wellies and a smock and milk cows and feed the pigs? With my heart condition?'

'You just said—' she began, but Dot snapped, 'Shut it, Jen. Don't start interferin' in what you don't understand.'

Jenny turned away before they should see. She was grinning quietly to herself. She knew exactly what they were talking about. Uncle Arthur no more had a heart condition than she did and he didn't earn his money honestly, either. Her smile faded. What was going to happen to all of them if he got caught? She shuddered and tried not to think about it.

Twenty-Eight

To her surprise, Jenny settled in very well at the village school. The local children had already become used to evacuees arriving, to their strange accents and different ways. They'd got over that first curiosity and the teasing stage, so Jenny found herself accepted almost at once. In fact, two girls took her under their wing.

'My name's Beryl Fenton,' the dark haired one of the two said on Jenny's first morning. 'You've come to live on our farm in one of Dad's cottages. This is my best friend, Susan Gordon. Her dad's a farmer too. She lives on the next farm on the other side of the hill from us.' Beryl had linked her arm through Jenny's. 'You can be friends with us, if you like. We'll call for you every morning and walk home together at night and teacher says you can sit with us.' She beamed. 'I've already asked her.'

So Jenny allowed herself to be taken in hand by the friendly girls. Beryl was the chatty, more open one of the two. Susan was quieter but none the less friendly. Soon, the three were such firm friends that they whispered and giggled together in class and were often in trouble as a trio. Their class teacher was a young married woman whose husband was in the RAF. She was slim and pretty and kindly. All her pupils adored her and so behaved reasonably well for her. Mrs Matthews only had to adopt a disappointed expression for her pupils to feel ashamed of themselves.

Each afternoon, after classes had finished, the three girls walked home together from the village school by the river, over the bridge and up the long lane towards Mr Fenton's farm. The lane wound up the hill past a big house standing in it's own grounds. The three girls paused at the gate and stared up the driveway.

'What's that place?' Jenny asked.

'Our landlord lives there. Dad's only a tenant farmer.'

'He's ours too,' Susan put in. 'Mr Forester's a big landowner round here.'

It sounded just like Miles Thornton and his estate only perhaps on a much grander scale, Jenny thought. A wave of homesickness for Ravensfleet overwhelmed her. And for the people too. What were they all doing now? she wondered. And was Georgie home yet?

As they walked, Beryl continued to chatter. 'Dad farms all these fields. We keep cows mainly, 'cos the land is too stony to plough, specially up near the quarry.'

'We've got a few fields where we grow crops,' Susan put in. 'But we've got cows and a few sheep too.'

When they arrived at Wisteria Cottage, they found it locked up and no sign of Arthur's van parked outside.

'Why hasn't your dad been called up?' Susan asked suddenly.

Jenny ran her tongue around lips that were suddenly dry. Not only must she try to think of him as her father, but she must also tell lies to her new-found friends. Both actions went against the grain for Jenny. 'He's – he's got a bad heart. He failed his medical.'

The girls were at once sympathetic and Jenny felt even worse. One on either side of her, they linked their arms through hers.

'Come on,' Beryl said kindly. 'Let's go to my house. Mum'll've been baking today. There's always something good to eat on baking day.'

Jenny was just about to ask how Beryl's mother managed to find all the ingredients to bake cakes and such, when she remembered. They were on a farm. Of course Mrs Fenton had ready access to eggs, milk and butter. With one accord the three hungry girls quickened their steps.

As she stepped into the farmhouse kitchen, Jenny's eyes widened. Every spare surface seemed to be filled with cakes and pastries and pies. And the aroma that filled the kitchen was mouth-watering on its own without the sight of all the goodies.

Beryl's mother was round all over; she had a round face and a round little body covered with a copious white apron. And she was so kind and jolly as she bustled about her kitchen making her daughter's friends welcome by placing a slice of cake in front of them and a glass of home-made lemonade. Jenny was reminded of how Mrs Beddows had always made her so welcome in the kitchen. Tears welled in her eyes at the thought of her life at the manor. It wasn't only Georgie she missed, though he was top of the list. She missed Charlotte's gentle kindness, the way Miles was forever thinking up things to do, not only with her but with all the evacuee children. She missed the cook and Kitty – and the solemn Wilkins. And Ben, even though he'd been so quiet, he'd been kind to her, showing her all the animals and taking her all round the farm. She even missed Philip; he'd been kind to her after Georgie . . .

'So, lovey, what brings you to Derbyshire, then?' Mrs Fenton asked.

Jenny stopped munching and stared at the woman, feeling a sudden jolt of fear. She swallowed the mouthful of cake and then realized that the farmer's wife was only making polite conversation; she wasn't trying to catch the girl out.

'Just – just to get away from the bombing. A house in our street took a direct hit last week.'

The woman and the two girls stared at her in horror. 'Was anybody – hurt?'

Jenny shook her head. 'No. We were all down the underground.' She saw them glance at one another, a mystified expression on their faces. 'We all go down the underground and sleep on the platforms when there's an air raid.' She pulled a face. 'And that is most nights. It's safe down there, but we have to take blankets to sleep on and we all lie in rows on the platforms. It's a bit draughty, but it's better than bein' bombed.'

'How awful!' Beryl murmured and Mrs Fenton cut another huge slice of cake and slipped it on to Jenny's plate.

'Thank you.' Jenny dimpled prettily at her. 'It's not so bad, really,' she went on, still referring to their nights spent in the underground. 'We have a sing-song so we can't hear the planes and the bombs dropping. I s'pose the worst is when the all-clear sounds and we go home to see what's happened. That's if we've still got a home to go to.'

'Have you left a lot of your stuff at home?' Susan asked. 'Clothes and toys?'

Jenny bit her lip and avoided meeting their gaze as she nodded. But the girls and Mrs Fenton took it that the mention of the belongings she'd been obliged to leave behind was upsetting her. But the truth was that

Jenny was ashamed to be implying that their flight from home was anything to do with the bombing and that she'd had to leave a stack of clothes and toys behind.

'You can play with our toys,' Beryl offered generously and her mother added, 'And I might have some bits and pieces that Beryl's grown out of. You're a bit smaller than her.'

Tears prickled Jenny's eyes at their kindness. Suddenly, she felt the overwhelming urge to confide a little of the truth – or as much of it as she dared.

'I was 'vacuated when the war started. I went to a place in Lincolnshire near the sea. They were farmers too. It – it was nice,' she finished lamely, unable to say just how wonderful it had been and how she wished she was back there. It would sound very ungrateful to these people who were being so kind to her now.

'Why did you have to go back to the city, then?' Susan asked. Jenny glanced at her. She was beginning to think that Susan, though the quieter of her two new friends, was a mite more shrewd than Beryl. She didn't say a lot but when she did, her questions were probing.

Jenny shrugged, trying to avoid answering. She didn't really know what the truth was herself. Miles and Charlotte had said they didn't want her to go, that her mother had sent for her and there was nothing they could do about it, but Dot had said she hadn't wanted Jenny back – that it was the Thorntons who didn't want her. Jenny sighed. Maybe the truth was that none of them wanted her.

Seeing the girl's hesitation, though not understanding the reason for it, Mrs Fenton said, 'Maybe you could lend Jenny some of your books, Beryl.'

Beryl, plump like her mother, bounced up from the

table. 'That's a good idea, Mum. D'you like reading, Jen?'

All at once she was back in the nursery at the manor, curled up on Georgie's knee and listening to his deep voice reading to her.

Jenny nodded and in a husky voice asked, 'You don't happen to have *The Wind in the Willows*, do you?'

Twenty-Nine

'So, what have they got up at the farm? Lots of pigs and chickens?' Arthur questioned Jenny when she went back to the cottage, her arms full of books and jigsaw puzzles.

'I didn't see the animals. Not today,' Jenny chattered innocently, still revelling in the kindness of her two new friends and of the farmer's wife. 'But Beryl says I can go up there on Saturday for my tea and we can watch the cows being milked. Mrs Fenton was ever so kind. We had lemonade and two huge pieces of cake. Can I go, Mum?'

Dot opened her mouth and Jenny was sure she'd been going to say 'no', but before she could utter a word, Arthur said, ''Course, you can go, Tich. Only you mustn't ask anyone back here, you understand?'

Jenny turned her blue eyes on Arthur. 'Why?'

''Cos we say not, that's why,' Dot snapped.

'You take your things upstairs to your bedroom,' Arthur said softly, 'there's a good girl. I'll call you down when tea's ready.'

'She won't need no tea if she's been scoffin' cakes all afternoon,' Dot muttered. 'The old bat might have sent some down for us.'

Jenny scooped up the books and fled upstairs.

The friendship between the three girls continued and deepened. It helped to lessen Jenny's heartache over

204

Georgie and her homesickness for Ravensfleet Manor. But life at home – which had never been easy – was even more difficult. Dot hated the countryside with a passion and her feelings were made worse by the fact that both Jenny and Arthur seemed to revel in it. Arthur abandoned his flash city suits for country clothes.

'I'll not stick out like a sore thumb,' he told them when Dot and Jenny stared at him.

'You've shaved your moustache off,' Jenny remarked.

'Yeah. Time for a change.'

'Well, you needn't think I'm going to start dressing like a frumpish farmer's wife,' Dot said nastily. She fluffed her hair and smoothed her dress down over her hips.

'We'd not be so noticeable, Dot,' Arthur pleaded. 'We'd fit in better.'

'Oh yeah? Till we open our mouths.' She turned away. 'You do what you like, Arthur. But I'm a Londoner, a cockney, and proud of it, so there.'

'It's nothing to do with that,' Arthur frowned and his voice rose a little, 'it's common sense. We don't want to draw attention to ourselves.'

Dot's eyes narrowed and she turned on him. 'If you hadn't got the coppers after you, we wouldn't have had to do a moonlight and bury ourselves in this godforsaken place.'

'It's not so bad, Mum,' Jenny put in unwisely. 'The people are real friendly when you get to know them.'

Dot rounded on her. 'I'll have less of your lip, miss, else you'll feel the back of my hand.'

'You're a mite too handy with your slaps,' Arthur growled. 'Leave the kid alone.'

'And you can mind yer own business, Arfer Osborne. I'll bring my kid up how I like. T'ain't none of your business.'

Arthur laughed. 'But I'm not Arthur Osborne any more, am I, Dot? I'm Arthur Mercer. Your husband. And Jenny's father.'

They glared at each other, but for once it was Dot who gave way first. She turned away, muttering, ''Owever did I get myself into this?'

On the Saturday afternoon, Jenny walked up the lane to the farm. Beryl and Susan ran to greet her.

'Have you brought your wellies?'

Jenny looked down at her stout school shoes. Arthur had bought them for her when she'd started at the village school and they were the only decent pair, though second-hand, she possessed now, having grown out of the others.

'I haven't got any,' she murmured, remembering the pair of rubber boots that Charlotte had bought for her; the ones she'd worn about the farm and to go to the beach in with Georgie. She'd not taken them home with her. There was no need for wellies in London.

'I've got a pair that are too small for me now,' Beryl said. 'I don't think Mum's thrown them out yet. They'll be in the washhouse. Come on.'

The wellington boots were still there, standing neatly beside the bigger ones belonging to Beryl's father and mother. They fitted Jenny perfectly.

'You can keep them, if you want. They're no good to me.'

'Thanks,' Jenny said and felt her cheeks colouring. She felt like a charity case, but she did need boots like these for living in the country and Dot would never buy her any.

Beryl and Susan took her all over the farm. She saw the pigs in the sties in the farmyard, peeped into the byre where later the cows would be brought in from the sloping hillside fields. Hens and ducks wandered freely in the field nearest to the house and, tethered nearby, were four goats – a billy and three nannies.

'They're for our use,' Beryl said. 'We get a lot of milk from the nanny goats.'

'But don't you get enough from the cows?'

'Oh yeah, but that has to be sold. It's all to do with the wartime regulations. I don't understand it all and poor old Dad scratches his head every time more paperwork comes from the Ministry.' She laughed. 'And that's nearly every day. No wonder he's going bald.'

Jenny smiled. She hadn't met Mr Fenton properly yet, she'd only seen him in the distance when Beryl had been showing her around the farmyard. And since he'd been wearing a cap, she hadn't seen his hair.

'Let's go and have tea,' Beryl said, 'and then we can help fetch the cows in from the field to be milked.'

They'd washed their hands at the kitchen sink and were sitting down at the large kitchen table when Mr Fenton came in from the yard. He took off his boots, his cap and jacket, washed his hands and came to the table.

'How do, girls. You must be Jenny.' He held out a huge, callused paw and Jenny put her hand into his. His grasp was firm and warm but gentle.

Mrs Fenton sat down too and she and her husband chatted to the three girls as if they were equals. Jenny felt their friendliness envelop her. She was going to like it here. It was not as wonderful as Ravensfleet had been; nothing ever could be, but Honeysuckle Farm on the Derbyshire hillside was going to be the next best thing, she was sure.

If only she could write to Charlotte and tell her, but Arthur had impressed upon her that she mustn't write

to any of her friends, not even to Bobby back home.
'No one must know where we are, darlin'. You understand, don't you?' His voice had hardened and she'd felt
the veiled threat. His words had filled her with forebod-
ing, but here in the warmth of the Fentons' kitchen, she
pushed her anxieties aside.

Now they were in the country amongst these kind,
friendly people and Arthur had left his shady dealings
far behind, everything would be all right.

Thirty

Not long after they'd settled into their cottage – if settled was the right word for what Dot felt and frequently said about the accommodation – Arthur brought a newspaper home that told of the dreadful night of bombing in London on 11 May. It was as if the enemy was having one final fling; from then onwards the bombing became less frequent and the papers were reporting that Hitler had turned his attention away from London. By the end of June the startling news came through that he had invaded Russia.

'He'll not bother with us any more. Can't we go home, Arfer?' Dot pleaded.

''Itler weren't the reason we left,' Arthur reminded her.

'But we could go to another part of the city, couldn't we? I don't like it here.' But Dot's whining had no effect on Arthur. He did like it here.

Jenny was happy at school and her weekends were spent on the Fentons' farm with Beryl. During the hay harvest, they were enlisted to help rake the cut grass. Most of the time, Susan was with them too, but occasionally it was just Beryl and Jenny. Jenny liked these times the best when there was just the two of them. She liked Susan, but she was sure that the girl felt that the newcomer was encroaching on her longstanding friendship with Beryl. And one day it became obvious that this was indeed the problem.

'My mam says the papers reckon the bombing's finished in London, so you'll be going home soon, then?' Susan couldn't disguise the hope in her tone when Beryl was out of earshot.

'Maybe.' Jenny stared at Susan. 'Don't you like me, Susan?' she asked bluntly.

Susan shrugged. 'You're all right. It's just . . .'

'It's just you don't like me being friends with Beryl, do you? She's your best friend. And you think I might be trying to take her away from you.'

Susan turned a little pink and said hastily, 'No, no, I—'

'Oh yes, yes,' Jenny countered, but she was smiling. 'Look, I know you and Beryl are best friends and I'm not trying to break you up, but I want to be friends with both of you. And, like you say, I won't be here for ever, but whilst I am, I promise I'm not trying to come between you. Okay?'

Susan nodded and smiled. 'Okay.'

After that, things were better and when Jenny spent time with Beryl on her own, Susan no longer seemed to mind. But she hardy ever asked Jenny to go to her home. But then, Jenny thought, I don't ask them back to the cottage. Arthur had made it very clear: No Visitors. But he, too, seemed to have taken to country life. He chatted to all the locals, even visited one or two farms asking if they had any light jobs he could do.

'I've got a heart condition, mate,' Jenny heard him say to Jack Fenton one Saturday morning when she was playing with Beryl and Arthur arrived. He fished out the piece of paper from his inside pocket. 'That's why I can't go and join up. I'd go like a flash if I could, but I failed the medical. But if you've any little jobs I could help out with, then I'd feel I was doing my bit.'

Jack Fenton had pulled off his cap and scratched his head. 'Farming's heavy work, Mester. I don't rightly know what I could find you to do, but I'll keep you in mind.'

'Thank you,' Arthur held out his hand, 'I appreciate it, mate.'

From the other side of the yard, Jenny watched as Arthur strolled away, but it was the look on Jack Fenton's face as he too watched the other man that disturbed her. It was a puzzled look, but mingled with suspicion. Had the farmer seen right through Arthur Osborne – or Mercer, as she must remember to call him now?

Dot had no intention of even trying to settle in. 'These women have no interest in fashion or make-up or *anything*,' she grumbled. 'They dress like scarecrows and hardly ever go out. The highlight of their week is the Women's Institute meeting. They don't even go to the pub with their husbands. They just sit at home knitting and listening to the wireless. And have you seen the size of that woman – the farmer's wife? She's like a little barrel on legs.'

'I'll get you a wireless, Dot, if that's what you want.'

She glared at him. 'Yeah, all right. That'd be nice, but don't you dare buy me any knitting needles.'

'It'd help with the war effort.' Arthur chuckled and was rewarded by a wet dishcloth being thrown in his face.

If things had continued in this way, their stay in the country might have been all right, but when the days

grew shorter and the dark nights longer, Arthur began
to go out late, not returning until the afternoon of the
following day.

'Where's he going, Mum?' Jenny asked.

'Never you mind,' Dot answered, her mouth tight
and her eyes unusually anxious. Dot rarely worried
about anything. Even the bombing hadn't really frightened her – just annoyed her that the war had interrupted
her life and deprived her of the things she wanted. She
couldn't always buy the make-up she wanted and only
Arthur could come by silk stockings for her.

'But . . .'

'Stop asking questions, yer nosy little bleeder.'

Jenny gasped and stared at her mother. Dot was
certainly rattled. The girl turned away and asked no
more, but from her bedroom window she watched
Arthur creep out into the night dressed in a black
sweater and trousers. He was also wearing a cap pulled
low over his forehead. To her surprise he didn't get into
the van, but disappeared into the darkness on foot.

Whatever was he doing?

Three nights later, Jenny found out and then wished
she'd stayed in blissful ignorance.

'I need you both to come with me tonight,' Arthur
announced at teatime.

Dot stared at him. 'Me?'

'Both of you.'

Jenny quivered inside. Instinct told her that creeping
out in the blackout couldn't be innocent. Arthur was up
to something.

'I need you to help me, Dot, and the kid can keep
watch.'

Dot glanced at Jenny and then back at Arthur. 'I don't think we should involve her.'

Jenny held her breath. Was her mother – for the first time that she could ever remember – actually thinking of her daughter's welfare? But the brief thought was dashed in a moment as Dot added, 'She might blab.'

'No, she won't.' Arthur turned his winning smile on Jenny. 'You wouldn't tell on your *dad*, would yer, Tich?' He reached out and grasped her arm with a firm squeeze that was perhaps meant to be friendly. But Jenny felt it was a threat.

She glanced at her mother for help, but Dot was avoiding her gaze.

'What do you want us to do?' Dot whispered.

'I can get a good price for chickens and ducks in Sheffield. I've made one or two good contacts there and a couple in Manchester too. Butchers who don't ask too many questions but are glad of anything they can get their hands on. Now, there's a farm about five miles away in the next dale where the chickens are in a field a good distance from the house. And there's ducks too. Ducks fetch a really good price.'

Jenny was glancing helplessly between Arthur and her mother. Surely, Dot was going to put a stop to this. It was stealing; there was no other word for it.

But Dot was nodding. 'We'd better get some dark clothes like—'

'For you, yes, you're coming to help me, but it doesn't matter about Jen. She's going to be keeping watch near the farm.'

Already Jenny was shaking inside.

'What if someone sees her? A kid of her age shouldn't be out late at night.'

Arthur grinned, obviously pleased with himself.

'Exactly. So if someone does see her, she starts to cry – loudly, mind, so we'll hear her,' He nodded towards her, now including Jenny in explaining the part she was to play. 'It's obvious she's a stranger here, an' when they get talking to her she can tell 'em she's an evacuee and she's got lost coming home in the dark from a friend's house. You'll have to take your time with the story, Jen, to give us time to get away and get home in the van. Then you can tell 'em where you live but take a long time about it. Make out you're not really sure where it is. They'll be a while bringing you here and that should give us plenty of time.'

'What if they call the police to deal with her?' Dot said. 'They might.'

'It's possible but most folks don't involve the police, specially now, if they can sort things out themselves.'

Dot sniffed as she muttered, 'Law-abiding citizens might. They're not all like you who wouldn't call a copper if you were dying.'

Arthur ignored the barb. 'So, you go and have a nice kip, Jen, and we'll wake you up when we're ready to go.'

Jenny went up the narrow staircase to her bedroom at the back of the cottage. They weren't even asking her if she agreed to help them. She was being given no choice in the matter.

Sleep was impossible; she lay on her bed, racking her brain as to how she could get out of this. But there wasn't anything she could do, short of packing her belongings and running away. And where could she run to? She had no idea really where they were. She had a vague picture in her head of where Derbyshire was. She remembered it from the atlas at school. Somewhere in the middle of England, a long, long way from London.

Lincolnshire was nearer, but she couldn't go there. Dot had said the Thorntons had sent her back because they no longer wanted her. And besides – she buried her head in her pillow and beat it with her fist – they certainly wouldn't want her now she was about to become a thief.

Thirty-One

As Jenny climbed into the back of the van she was shivering with cold and fear. Thrown from side to side as the vehicle bounced over the rough track, she was still trying to think of a way to escape. Arthur drove slowly through the blackout, anxious not to draw attention to himself and it seemed an age until the vehicle stopped. There was a pause whilst Arthur got out of the front and opened the back door for Jenny.

'Be very quiet, Tich,' Arthur whispered. 'The farm gate's up the lane there. Go and stand by it, but don't go into the yard. They've got a dog and if you start it barking the farmer'll likely come out to see what's going on.'

'Where – where are you and Mum going?'

'We'll be in the field further down the lane. Don't worry if you hear a lot of squawking and quacking. You've only got to worry if the lights go on in the house and someone comes out.'

'How – how do I warn you?'

'First of all, you wave this torch. Yer mum's going to keep watch for it. Then, if they come out, you start to cry like I told you.'

'But – but you're going to leave me here. You're going to drive off and leave me here on my own.'

'They'll look after you.'

'You know them?'

216

'No, 'course I don't, but folks aren't going to leave a kid wandering about in the dark on her own, now are they?'

'I – suppose not.'

'Good girl. Now, off you go. Give us a wave with the torch when you get to the gate and then I'll be moving the van a bit further along the road. When we've done, I'll signal you with my torch and you come to us. Aw' right?'

'Aw' right,' Jenny said in a trembling voice. There was nothing else she could say, but it was very far from 'all right'. She stood near the gate, every limb trembling. She glanced at the farmhouse. The windows were all in darkness, but that, of course, could be because of the blackout curtains. She couldn't tell if anyone was still up or awake. But there was no noise from a dog. At least – not yet. She strained her eyes and her ears in the darkness, trying to see down the lane to where Arthur and her mother were. Faintly, she could hear the vehicle moving but then it stopped again. She thought she heard the door of the van shut, but after that she could see and hear nothing, for there was no moon and a light breeze carried any sounds in the opposite direction. Besides, Arthur would be minding they didn't make any noise. She shivered and her teeth began to chatter.

After what seemed ages to the frightened girl, but was, in fact, only a few minutes, she heard squawking from the hen huts in the field. Jenny glanced towards the farmhouse and held her breath. Surely, the dog would hear and would begin barking. Animals had even better hearing than humans, she'd been told, and even she could hear the scuffling and cackling getting louder and echoing through the night air.

Suddenly, she heard the welcome sound of the van's

door being shut. Jenny peered into the darkness and saw the thin beam of a torch being waved. She ran down the lane, tripping and stumbling in her haste to reach them.

'Ssh,' came Arthur's whisper through the darkness. 'Don't make such a noise. Quick, get in the front with yer mam.'

Jenny scrambled in, squeezing in beside Dot. 'Mind where yer putting yer elbows,' Dot hissed as Arthur got into the driver's seat and started the engine.

Slowly he drew away, but the hens and ducks in the back started to squawk again.

'Gawd, I hope we're not stopped by a copper,' Dot moaned. 'There's no hiding what's in the back now.'

But they reached the cottage safely and took the three hens and two ducks into the shed at the back of the house. Arthur threw down some corn and the birds soon quietened.

'I reckon what I ought to do,' Arthur mused when they were safely back in the house and Dot had made them all a mug of hot cocoa, 'is to get a few hens and ducks all above board, like, and—'

'Then we wouldn't have to steal any,' Jenny said before she stopped to think.

Arthur glared at her, but he couldn't argue with what she'd said. What they'd done this night was stealing and there was no getting away from it.

Except that they had got away with it. This time.

'It'd hide the ones I – acquire.'

'Why can't you get rid of 'em straight away and why do you have to keep 'em alive?' Dot wanted to know. 'If you'd wrung their necks, we wouldn't have had all that racket.'

'Two reasons,' Arthur answered sharply. 'One, I can't be running backwards and forwards to the city with three chickens and a couple of ducks. 'Tain't worth the petrol and besides,' he admitted sheepishly, 'I don't know how to kill 'em.'

Dot and Jenny stared at him. 'Then you'd better learn pretty quick, hadn't you?'

Arthur looked at Jenny. 'Maybe you could ask your friends at the farm how I'd go about getting some chickens and that. Tell 'em we're trying to do our bit for the war effort.'

Jenny stared at him and her insides quaked. The last thing she wanted to do was to ask such questions.

'Don't you have to have permission from the authorities?' Dot put in. 'There's that many rules and regulations these days.'

'To keep a few chickens?' Arthur laughed. 'Nah.' He paused, was thoughtful for a moment before adding, 'Do you?'

Dot put her mug on the table and got up. 'Anyway, I've had enough for one night. I'm off to bed. You too, Jen. You'll never be up for school in the morning.'

Jenny dragged herself wearily up the stairs, but she slept fitfully, waking every so often in the middle of a nightmare where she was surrounded by huge cackling hens pecking her.

'I'll come up to the farm with you, Jen,' Arthur said on the Saturday morning. 'I want to talk to Mr Fenton.'

The stolen chickens and ducks were still shut in the shed at the back of the cottage. Arthur fed them every day from a sack of grain that had suddenly materialized.

'Oh Uncle Arthur, I don't—'

'Dad! You must call me "Dad".'

Jenny bit her lip. She'd never had anyone to call

'Dad' and the name didn't come easily. She was much more used to 'Uncle'. 'Won't he think it funny we've suddenly got chickens?'

'I'm not going to tell him we've already got some, silly. I want to find out about getting some. What I have to do.'

'Build a hen house and feed 'em,' Dot put in rationally. 'What more can there be to it than that?'

'He might be willing to sell me a few and – he might teach me how to kill them.'

Jenny shuddered, but there seemed no way she could get out of Arthur going with her to the farm.

'Morning, guv'nor,' Arthur greeted Mr Fenton jovially. The big man glanced at Jenny and smiled, but the look he cast at Arthur was wary and certainly not so friendly. 'I wonder if you could give me a bit of advice. Now we're living in the country, we'd like to do our bit – '

Jenny scuttled away towards the back door of the farmhouse; she didn't want to hear any more. But even when she found Beryl and they began to play Ludo, her mind was still on what was going on between Arthur and Jack Fenton in the farmyard.

Thirty-Two

Jenny's fears were unfounded. To her surprise, Jack Fenton was only too willing to help. But then, she thought, Uncle Arthur could be very charming and persuasive when he wanted to be. And he'd have laboured the point about wanting to do his bit, she knew.

'He's told me where to buy what I need to build a hen hut,' Arthur told Dot and Jenny later. 'There's an old wood yard not far away. I don't have to use new wood, he said. And he's agreed to sell me a few chickens and a couple of ducks to start us off. He wasn't sure about regulations for someone starting out to keep livestock, though he did say there were definite regulations about keeping a pig. You have to have a licence to kill a pig.' Arthur grinned and patted his pocket. 'As if I didn't know that. Already got one or two of the very documents.'

Dot blinked. 'Whatever for? And however did you come by them?'

'They're forgeries, yer daft mare. I thought they might come in handy if we ever moved to the country.'

Dot's eyes narrowed. ''Ave you been *planning* leaving London for a while, Arfer?'

Arthur shrugged. 'Just bein' prepared, Dot. Like a good boy scout.'

'You – a boy scout? Don't make me larf!'

Mildly, and with a wistful note in his voice, Arthur

221

said, 'Actually, I was once.' Then he cleared his throat and said briskly, 'But as far as the chickens and that are concerned, Fenton just said I'd better inform the Ministry.' Now Arthur laughed uproariously. 'Just to keep on the right side of the law, he said.'

'And shall you?'

'What?'

'Inform the authorities.'

'Nah, 'course I won't. I don't want officials coming round here poking their noses in.'

Yet again, Jenny shuddered.

So life fell into a pattern, but it was a pattern that Jenny didn't like. She had to hand it to Arthur that he was resourceful. He built a chicken hut and actually *bought* some feed for his hens and ducks so that at least part of his operation was legitimate. He learned from Jack Fenton how to kill the hens by wringing their necks. Jenny hated to see the poor things hanging limply by their legs and still flapping their wings even though they were dead.

Soon their livestock increased. Every week they went out at least one night, and 'collected' another hen or two, never taking any more so that the farmer was unlikely to notice the reduction in his numbers. Hens were notoriously difficult to count and as long as there was not a noticeable difference, Arthur seemed to be getting away with it. He always chose a different farm and never visited the same one again for several weeks. Their number of hens grew and lessened as more came and then more were killed and taken to the city.

But Arthur never took Dot or Jenny to Sheffield or Manchester or wherever it was he went, though Dot begged to be taken into the shops. 'I'll die if I don't get to go shopping soon,' she wailed.

'How do you think I can get the petrol to go gallivanting into town?'

'You can get it to do your dirty business,' Dot snapped back.

'That's different and it's at night. Petrol's rationed and you have to have a good reason to be travelling about. If I get stopped . . .' He didn't need to say any more but Dot cast him a baleful look. 'And that reminds me, I'm getting low on petrol. I need to get some. Jen, I'll need you to come with me tonight and be ready to do your bit of play-acting if necessary.'

'I'll come with you,' Dot offered, but Arthur shook his head. 'You can't act that you're lost. Besides,' he added with a smirk, 'if they see you hanging about on street corners, they might think you're up to something very different.'

Dot gasped and slapped his face, but it was done playfully, almost coquettishly, and Jenny turned away, feeling sick.

If only she knew they wanted her back at Ravensfleet, she'd run away. But Dot had been adamant that the Thorntons had sent her back, that they didn't want her there. And they hadn't written to her – not once – since she'd left, even though she'd written to them three times while she'd been back in London. She was sure her mother would have posted her letters and, even allowing for wartime postal delays, they'd had time to write back. So maybe Dot was right; the Thorntons really didn't want her. And now Jenny couldn't write to them and she daren't go back to London either. Dot and Arthur would soon come after her and besides, Aunty Elsie would ask too many awkward questions.

The summer school holidays dragged. Jenny saw Beryl and Susan occasionally but both girls were busy helping with the harvest and she felt excluded. So she spent the long days on her own. The only time she was truly happy was when Arthur took Dot out and Jenny could bring her drawing book and paints down to the kitchen. But before long she'd used up all the paper which Charlotte had given her. And there was no hope of being given a new supply for her birthday, which, as usual, passed by without any comment from Dot. No card, no 'Happy Birthday' and certainly no present. She remembered the belated party the Thorntons had given her. How she wished she could go back there, but she couldn't. She was trapped here, being led into a life of crime and there was nothing she could do about it.

The days were much shorter and the nights darker towards the end of the year and late one November night, Jenny was out in the van with Arthur. He parked down a side road and then crept towards a fenced yard next to a large barn. This was more dangerous; it was not in the open countryside, but on the outskirts of the village where Jenny went to school and there were houses just across the road. They got out of the van and Arthur removed a petrol can and a long piece of rubber tubing from the back.

They began to walk up the road towards the yard.

'What – what are you going to do, Uncle – Dad?'

'Syphon petrol,' he muttered.

'Where from?'

'Those vehicles in that yard.'

'But there's a big fence and the gates are padlocked. I can see it from here.'

Arthur's chuckle came out of the darkness. 'Never you mind what your dad's doing, you just keep watch and be sure to tell me if you see anybody coming.'

'Won't there be guard dogs or – or a night watchman at a place like this?'

'Nah – I've already checked. And once everybody's nicely tucked up in their homes with the blackout curtains drawn, nobody comes out much. I've been watching this place for several nights now. Right, you stand just there and keep yer eyes skinned.'

'Uncle – Dad, I really don't want to—' she began but his hand was heavy on her shoulder as he murmured, 'Be a good girl now.'

Jenny sighed and pulled her coat around her. The night was cold and fear was making her shiver. She stepped close to the fence and glanced up and down the street. All was quiet and the faint rattle as Arthur tried to open the padlock with a bunch of keys seemed to echo loudly in the night air.

'He'll never manage it,' Jenny muttered, but even as she said the words the gate swung open with a squeak that sounded even louder. Then she saw Arthur creep into the yard and disappear behind the line of six vehicles – two cars and four vans very much like the one he drove. Now he was out of sight, Jenny felt even more vulnerable.

He'd been gone what seemed like a long time, when the door of the house opposite opened and a man, briefly framed in the light from inside, came out. A small dog yapped and ran excitedly up and down the path. Jenny watched in horror as the man came down the path, opened the small gate and stepped out into the road. There was nowhere she could hide as she saw the man glance across the street and catch sight of her. She could see he was bending his head forward as if squinting through the darkness at her.

Jenny didn't have to feign the tears that Arthur had told her to shed if someone saw her; she was frightened enough for them to be real. She put her hand to her eyes and began to sob. The man came across the road, his little dog following him and bounding towards her.

'Hello, love. You all right?'

'No,' Jenny wailed loudly, hoping that Arthur would hear her and be warned. 'I'm lost.'

'Lost? How come at this time of night? Does your mother know you're out this late?'

Jenny hiccuped convincingly. 'I've been at a friend's and – and I said I'd be fine walking home, but I must have taken a wrong turn.'

'You're not a local, are you?' he said, coming closer. The little dog was jumping up at her, licking her hand.

'I'm a vaccie,' she wailed loudly again.

'A what, love?'

'A 'vacuee.'

'Oh, I see. Aye, we've got a lot o' them come. A' you staying round here, then?'

'Yes, but I don't know which way it is.'

'Well, you tell me and I'll walk along with you.'

Now a fresh fear flooded through her. Arthur would be dreadfully cross if this man took her all the way home.

'I – ' she began, not sure what to do or to say now. She wanted to glance behind her, into the yard to see if she could catch sight of Arthur, but knew she mustn't. Her action might give him away.

'Do you go to school here?' the man was asking again.

Relief flooded through her. 'Yes, yes,' she said in a loud voice, still trying to make sure that Arthur had heard her and knew there was a problem. She was sure now that he must have done, because the little dog suddenly began to bark and run a little way along the road towards the unlocked gate and then back again to them, as if asking them to follow him. But the man took no notice of his dog; he was more concerned with the lost girl.

'If you show me where the school is,' Jenny said, the relief in her voice genuine as she thought of a way to stop him accompanying her all the way to the cottage, 'I know the way home from there. I'll be fine.'

'If you're sure,' the man said worriedly. 'I'd walk with you all the way, but the wife isn't very well and I don't want to leave her for long, but Nipper here has to have his evening walk, haven't you, boy?'

Jenny was actually speaking the truth now. She didn't know where the school was from here, but once there, she knew the way back to the cottage up the long lane.

'Come on, then,' the man said, also sounding relieved at her suggestion. 'Best foot forward.'

They walked along, the man matching his strides to the girl's. Jenny dared not glance behind her and she crossed her fingers hoping that Arthur knew what was happening.

The little dog bounded ahead, running back to them every so often and barking excitedly. Surely, Arthur must have heard the dog if nothing else.

They passed by the van and Jenny's heart skipped a beat as the man paused and looked at the vehicle. 'Funny,' he murmured, 'I don't recognize that van. Wonder what it's doing here?'

Her heart pounding, Jenny walked on, trying to make out she was more interested in getting home than in a parked vehicle. The man shrugged and walked on, catching her up. It wasn't as far as she'd thought to the school and there she insisted she knew the way, that she'd be fine, and thanked him for his kindness. She bent and patted the dog and then hurried away from them both and was soon swallowed up in the darkness. As she walked on, she began to breathe more evenly, but now a new anxiety crept into her mind.

What if Arthur hadn't heard the commotion? What if he was still blithely unaware that she was no longer standing outside the fence on guard? What if . . . ?

At that moment, she heard the chugging sound of a vehicle behind her and she stepped on to the grass verge. Arthur's van slowed and stopped near her. He pushed open the passenger door. 'Get in.'

She couldn't tell from his tone of voice if he was angry with her, but at least he was obviously safe or he wouldn't be here. She scrambled in and, as she settled herself in the seat beside him, he patted her knee. 'Well done, darlin', I heard you crying loud and clear and hid behind the vehicles. When you went I hopped it back to the gate, locked it up and got in the van.'

'That man remarked about your van,' she told him. 'He wondered what it was doing there.'

'Don't worry, I'll mind not to park there again. In fact, we'd better not use that place again. I only took a little out of each vehicle so that no one will notice. On this game, Jen, the thing is not to be greedy. If you take too much of anything, they'll notice and then you'll get caught. See?'

Jenny didn't answer. He talked as if it was quite all

228

right to steal just so long as you took only a little; just so long as you didn't get caught.

Not for the first time, Jenny wondered with a sinking heart what Georgie would think of the life she was leading now. And inwardly, she wept.

Thirty-Three

Life continued in much the same way for a while. Christmas came and went but just as she always had, Dot couldn't be bothered to try to make the occasion special. So long as Arthur loaded her with presents, she didn't give a thought to anyone else. But this year the weather was bad with snow drifting against their door. Arthur couldn't drive his van anywhere and only the farm tractors could get about, doing their best to move the snow from the local roads.

''Ow can yer make puddings and a cake' – Dot had excused her laziness, 'when you can't get hold of the stuff to make 'em?'

'Yer've got eggs and plenty of sugar.' The latter had come from a night raid on a local grocer's shop in the next village just before the bad weather had set in with a vengeance, when once again Arthur had picked the lock on the back door of the premises. Jenny had been terrified; the shop was in the centre of the village and she couldn't think of a plausible story if she was asked what she was doing hanging about outside a shop at midnight and a long way from home too.

'I took just one or two items from the back of the shelves,' Arthur said, pleased with his night's work. Sugar, butter, tea and other rationed items lay in the back of the van under a rug. But as they drove home,

Jenny was still quaking. If they were stopped, how could Arthur possibly explain away the goods in the back of the van?

He couldn't.

Only when they reached the cottage, had unloaded the goods and stacked them on the pantry shelves, did Jenny start to feel safer. Safer, but not safe. She doubted she would ever feel safe again, not while she was with Arthur Osborne – Mercer, as she must remember to call him now. If only . . .

Tears prickled her eyes as thoughts of Ravensfleet filtered unbidden into her mind, but resolutely she pushed them away. There was no way back. They didn't want her.

'I was so frightened,' she blurted out as she sat sipping the hot cocoa Arthur always insisted that Dot made for the girl when she'd been out at night helping him. 'I thought an ARP warden might come along at any minute.'

Arthur, drinking cocoa too, though his had a drop of whisky in it, stared at her above the rim of his mug.

'Air Raid Precautions Warden,' he murmured softly. 'Now there's a thought.'

'What is?' Dot snapped. She was rarely in a good mood these days and the winter weather in the cold, damp cottage was making her even more irritable. She missed the busy streets of London, the camaraderie as they all faced the wartime hardships together. She even missed the rows with her neighbours. She hated it here and couldn't understand why Jenny didn't too. Her daughter was a city child, like her, and yet Jenny had changed ever since she'd come back from Lincolnshire. How Dot wished she'd never sent her there. But now she was staring at Arthur. She knew that look he'd got on his face. He was up to something. 'What's a thought?' she snapped again.

'Becoming an ARP warden. They're out and about all night with never a question asked, now aren't they?'

Dot snorted. 'You? An ARP warden? A representative of law and order? Don't make me larf.'

Arthur's eyes gleamed. 'But think of the pickings. There's been a lot of bombing in Sheffield. If I could get taken on there.'

Dot's eyes widened. 'Why? Why would you want to go into danger deliberately? You're a fool if—'

He leaned towards her. 'Sheffield was very badly bombed in December 1940 for three or four days. I've seen it with me own eyes. Bomb-damaged houses, Dot. Just think of it. All that stuff just lying there, waiting to be picked up. And in uniform, no one would question why I was there. Why I was rooting through the rubble. And they still get the odd raid now and again. And if an enemy plane misses its primary target, say Manchester or Liverpool, then Sheffield cops it.'

Realization began to dawn on Dot's face and Jenny, too, understood what he was suggesting. Dot jabbed her finger towards Jenny. 'You couldn't take her as lookout.'

'Wouldn't need to,' Arthur said promptly and Jenny's heart lifted. 'I'd be there legitimately, wouldn't I?'

Dot laughed wryly. 'That'd make a change.'

Arthur stood up. 'I'll ask around as soon as the weather improves. Find out what I have to do. I'm sure they'll be glad to have a fit feller like me.'

Dot stared up at him. 'But you're not fit, a' yer? You've got a heart condition, so that bit o' paper in your pocket ses.'

Arthur winked at her. 'Oh aye, but they'll tek anyone

they can get in the ARP and the Home Guard or whatever they call themselves now.'

Dot snorted, huddling closer to the fire, which was burning a sack of coal that Arthur had brought home, taken, Jenny believed, from someone's backyard in the black of night.

'Three or four days of bombing!' Dot muttered, thinking about what Arthur had just said. 'When we had months. They don't know they're born.'

Jenny glanced at her mother, marvelling yet again at her selfishness. Could she never think of anyone else but herself? However long or short the bombing lasted, it was just as devastating for those caught up in it.

'Anyway,' Arthur was saying, his mind made up. 'It's the ARP for me. That way I'd get a chance to be on my own now and again patrolling the streets watching for folks showing lights and that. But there'd be no chance of that in the Home Guard. All that drilling and guarding stuff. I'd be unlikely to get the chance to be on my own.'

'Aye, guarding stuff from folks like you,' Dot said grimly. 'You want to watch yerself. One of these days—'

'Don't you worry, darlin', I'll be careful. They'll never catch Arthur Osborne. I promise you that.' Even he forgot for the moment that he was now supposed to be Arthur Mercer.

When the weather improved, Arthur travelled to Sheffield, joined the ARP in the city and was welcomed by those who thought he was really trying to 'do his bit'.

'He didn't need to join us,' the other wardens agreed. 'He's not from these parts. You can tell that by the way he talks and he's got that piece of paper that says he's got a bad heart. He doesn't have to do anything. He could sit out the war doing nowt. But no, he's volunteered. Good on 'im, I say.'

So Arthur set off in his van three or four nights a week, able to obtain and use petrol legitimately now. Jenny breathed a sigh of relief that he no longer needed her. But, contrary to what he'd said, Arthur's greed began to get the better of his common sense. Perhaps, if the pickings in the city had been better, Arthur might have been content. But he hadn't a ready market for the belongings of people who'd been bombed out.

'It's not as easy as I thought,' he grumbled to Dot, and Jenny felt a flicker of fear.

'Don't knock it,' Dot said, happily trying on dresses, coats and even shoes that Arthur had 'rescued' from bombed-out homes in the city. 'I can't think why all this stuff has still been left for folks to find. Why haven't the people who owned them come back for them?' Then the awful thought seemed to strike her – the reason that Jenny had already thought of. Maybe the folks who'd lived in the houses had been killed. Dot paused a moment, eyed herself in the mirror and then shrugged and carried on trying on yet another frock.

'I can't take all this stuff to a second-hand dealer or a pawnbroker's. I can't make money on it.'

Dot stared at him. 'Have you tried?'

Arthur looked suddenly shifty. 'Yeah, one, but he started asking awkward questions. How had I come by it? Was it mine to sell? That sort of stuff.'

'And what did you tell him?'

Arthur moved uncomfortably in his chair. 'I said we'd been bombed and that – that me wife had died. But he still didn't want to know.'

Dot blinked and then said sarcastically, 'Oh thanks,

I'm sure. Since I'm supposed to be your wife now, that was meant to be me, then, was it?'

'Don't be so touchy, Dot,' Arthur said testily. 'I had to think of something quick.'

'You'll wish it on me,' Dot said petulantly. 'If we get bombed and I'm—'

'Don't be daft. We don't get no bombs out here. Just be thankful I couldn't sell 'em. Least you've got some new clothes.'

Dot snorted. 'Hardly new.' Then she capitulated and smiled at him. 'But it's better than nothin'. Thanks, Arfer.' And she moved to kiss him. Then she turned to Jenny and pointed at another bundle lying on the floor. 'There you are, Jen. Your dad's brought something for you an' all. There's girl's dresses and shoes in there. An' about your size. Go and try them on.' When Jenny stared in horror at the sack, but didn't move, Dot gave her a push and said again, 'Go on.'

Reluctantly, Jenny moved and picked up the sack.

'And say "thank you" niccly to yer dad.'

Jenny smiled weakly. 'Thanks, Dad,' she said dutifully and turned away to take the bundle upstairs. She shut the door of her bedroom firmly and put the sack on the floor. She sat on the bed and stared at it, making no effort to open it. She shuddered. Whatever was in there – and she had no intention of looking – belonged to some poor girl who, at best, had had her home bombed out and who'd now lost her clothes or, at worst, was dead. Perhaps it would have been easier for Jenny if she'd known the girl was dead, but to think of the unknown girl weeping because her things were gone, brought Jenny close to tears. She jumped up suddenly from the bed and stuffed the offending sack into the back of the wardrobe and slammed the door. She'd never wear whatever was in there; she didn't even want to look at it.

She curled up on her bed and picked up her pencil and sketch pad, which Arthur had given her for Christmas. In a few moments, she was lost in her own world, drawing a picture of the beach at Ravensfleet – and walking along the sand was the figure of a tall man in RAF uniform and beside him skipped a young girl.

Thirty-Four

By the spring of 1942, Arthur was running short of money. Their only income was from the odd jobs he did for the local farmers, since his ARP work was still voluntary.

'I don't know why we can't move into Sheffield and you sign on as a full-time warden instead of just three or four nights a week. You'd get paid then.' Dot smiled wryly. 'Not like you, Arfer, to do something for nothing.'

Arthur glared at her but couldn't argue. 'I'll have to start getting stuff locally again. I've still got my contacts in the city.' Jenny's heart dropped at Arthur's words; she knew what was coming next. 'And I'll need you to come out with me, Tich.'

Dot glanced at the girl but said nothing. She doesn't even stick up for her own daughter being dragged into a life of crime, Jenny thought bitterly. Now, if it had been Charlotte . . . She turned her thoughts away. She mustn't think about them; it only made her sad.

Despite Dot's goading, Arthur still intended to keep on his duties as an ARP warden. 'You never know when somewhere useful might get bombed. Like a grocer's or a butcher's or . . .' The list went on and Jenny shuddered. He talked as if the enemy was dropping bombs on these poor folk purely for Arthur Osborne's benefit.

On his next night off, he came downstairs dressed in his balaclava and dark clothes.

'Ought she to be in something black?' Dot asked. Far from trying to stop Arthur taking the young girl with him, Dot was encouraging their escapades. The only thing that seemed to annoy her was that she was not needed too.

'Yeah, maybe so tonight. Go and get that black coat of yer mam's. You're growing so fast, it'll nearly fit yer.'

''Ere,' Dot protested half-heartedly. 'I don't want that ruining.' But then she relented. It was no use arguing with Arthur and anyway, she was running short of money too. 'Just you be careful with it, Jen.'

'Get a move on then, Tich.' He tweaked Jenny's nose playfully, but she only frowned at him. She did as she was told but she was still trying to think of a way out of all this. More than once, she'd packed her clothes, her sketch pad and pencils in readiness to run away. But at the last moment, common sense had prevailed. She'd only be found and brought back and then, not only would her Mum and Arthur be mad at her, but also the authorities might start asking awkward questions. Much as she wanted to be out of this, she didn't want to be the cause of trouble for Arthur. In a lot of ways, he was still kind to her and her mother was less handy with her slaps when he was around. Jenny sighed. If it wasn't for the thieving, she'd have been quite happy really. Well, as happy as she was ever going to be now that she knew she could never go back to Ravensfleet.

'Right, you ready?'

Jenny sighed. She hated doing this, but there was nothing she could do. She was too young to stand up to them. She pulled on her wellingtons and her mother's coat and followed him out into the yard. She turned towards where the van was parked, but Arthur called softly, 'We won't be needing that tonight. We're walking. Come on, best foot forward.' Arthur walked up the rough track leading from the cottage to the lane and turned towards the Fentons' farm. Jenny hurried after him. 'What are we going this way for? You're – you're not going to Honeysuckle Farm, are you?'

'The Fentons' place? Nah.'

'Then – then where? There's nothing up this way. After the Fentons', there's only the quarry.'

'But there's a farm on the other side of the hill.'

'That's Susan's dad's place – Meadowsweet Farm.'

'That's where we're going.'

'But – but you can't. *We* can't.'

When Arthur didn't answer her, but just kept walking up the track, Jenny took little running steps to keep up with his long strides. 'You – you can't mean you're going to – to steal off Mr Gordon. Oh Uncle Arthur – you can't.'

He stopped, turned to face her and gripped her shoulder. In the darkness, she couldn't see his face, but she could hear the anger in his tone. 'Now look, don't get sentimental on me. It's got to be done. I know it's a risk, but it's one worth taking. I can get a good price for a whole lamb. Look,' he added, his tone softening a little, 'it'll be all right, Tich, honest. The sheep are in the top field well away from the farmhouse, aren't they?'

'But they've got a dog.'

'Ah well, now, I've got a little present for him.'

'It's a she,' Jenny muttered. 'Her name's Peg.'

Peg was the Gordons' black and white sheepdog. 'The best sheepdog in the world,' Mr Gordon had said when he'd proudly shown Jenny all the prizes his dog had won at the local sheep trials on one of the few

239

occasions when Jenny and Beryl had been invited to Meadowsweet Farm.

'Knows you, does she?' Arthur asked, his question sounding innocent enough.

'She jumps up and tries to lick my face. She's ever so friendly.'

'So, if you go into the farmyard and give her this nice piece of meat I've got for her, you don't reckon she'll bark at you.'

Jenny's heart seemed to skip a beat. 'I – I can't go in there. What if Mr Gordon's about?'

'He won't be. Not at this time of night.' Arthur's chuckle came out of the darkness. He was so sure of himself. ' "Early to bed" and all that. Isn't that these country folks' motto?'

'They get up very early,' Jenny said in a small voice.

'There you are, then. They'll all be in bed and sound asleep. They'll not hear a thing.'

'I don't want to do it. I—'

'Now look 'ere, you don't want me to go back and tell yer mam yer wouldn't do what I told yer, do yer?'

The mere thought of Dot's anger made Jenny shudder. 'No,' she whispered, 'but—'

'There you are, then,' Arthur said, ignoring her misgivings.

Jenny felt as if she was in a nightmare, but she wasn't. It was all too real and there was no way out.

They walked along the lane towards Jack Fenton's farm, passing it quietly in the darkness.

'We'll go past the quarry,' Arthur whispered. 'And over the hill at the top before it starts to dip down again into the next village.'

He'd certainly done his reconnoitring. Jenny had

never been as far as this for Jack had warned, 'Don't be going near the quarry, love. Beryl and Susan aren't allowed to go up there. It's not used now, but it's dangerous. It's in the middle of nowhere and if you fell down, there'd be no one to hear you.'

'No, I won't, Mr Fenton,' Jenny had promised solemnly, but now Arthur was taking her there and in the dark too. He always refused to put the torch on unless it was an emergency. 'Yer eyes'll soon get used to the dark,' he'd tell Jenny.

But tonight there was no moon and, out here on the hillside, no lights of any kind. Jenny was terrified; fearful of what he was leading her into and yet too afraid to leave him and try to find her way back to the cottage on her own.

'I'm going,' she muttered to herself, stumbling over tufts of grass and twisting her ankle in the ruts on the rough track. 'Tomorrow – if we get through tonight – I'm going. I don't care any more. I'll run away.'

Arthur was ahead of her, pausing now and again to make sure she was still following him. 'Come on, Tich,' he hissed. 'Get a move on.'

He'd turned away again and taken a step sideways around a huge boulder sticking out over the edge of the track. She heard him slide on the grass, heard his cry of alarm followed by the sounds of him falling through bushes and undergrowth. Another cry, this time of pain rather than surprise. And then there was silence.

Jenny inched her way forward and, though disobeying his orders, she shone the torch. The ground in front of her disappeared over the edge of what she guessed to be the quarry Mr Fenton had warned her about. The torch beam wavered in her trembling hand as she shone it down into black nothingness, the light not even reaching the bottom.

'Uncle Arthur,' she called in a quavering voice. 'Where are you?'

But there was no reply.

Thirty-Five

It seemed an age that Jenny stood on the edge of the quarry, shivering with cold and fear, not knowing what to do. The trees rustled in the darkness and an owl hooted somewhere close by, making her jump. She was just about to turn away and try to find her way home when she heard a low moan from far below her.

'Uncle Arthur,' she said in a loud whisper, but doubted he could hear her. Should she fetch her mum? Or Mr Fenton? He'd be sure to help, but he'd then ask awkward questions about what they were doing out this late at night.

'Jen – are you there?'

'Yes, Uncle Arthur. Are you hurt?'

'I've twisted my ankle, but – ouch! Bloody nettles.'

'What shall I do? Shall I fetch someone?'

''Course not, you silly mare. Want the whole neighbourhood to know we're up to no good.'

Jenny shivered again.

'Can you climb down here and give me a hand?'

'I can't see you.'

'I can bloody well see you waving that torch all over the place.'

Now Jenny shone the torch at her own feet and began to climb down. There was a little path, twisting and turning down the steep sides of the quarry. If she was careful, maybe she could— her feet slipped on the grass and she felt herself falling. She flung her arm out and clawed at the ground. Her fingers felt the branch of a small tree and she hung on to it.

'I can't, Uncle Arthur. I'll fall.'

'No, you won't. Just take it steadily.'

Jenny bit her lip and pointed the torch downwards again. It seemed an awful long way down. If she were to lose her footing and roll all the way down, then they'd both be trapped at the bottom.

And, like Mr Fenton had said, there'd be no one to hear their cries for help. Certainly not at this time of night when all law-abiding citizens were in their beds. Grimly, knowing that they couldn't stay there all night and nor could she go and find help, Jenny dug her heels into the ground and eased herself down, little by little. Every so often she stopped, hung on to a nearby bush and shone the torch down.

'I can see you now, Uncle Arthur. Hang on.'

'I'm hardly going anywhere, am I?' he retorted, but now he knew she was really trying to help him and not scooting off and leaving him there, he tempered his tone. He knew she hated coming out with him and that it was only the threat of her mother's punishments that kept her in line – for now. But one day he was sure she'd rebel. And, really, he wouldn't blame her – just so long as she didn't decide to do it right now and leave him here.

At last she reached the bottom and knelt beside him.

'Don't shine that in my face. Here, help me up.'

'Can you stand?'

'Give us yer hand.' He grasped her outstretched hand and hauled himself up, almost pulling her over. He stood beside her and tested the ankle he'd twisted in his fall. 'Seems all right. It hurts a bit, but I don't think it's broken.'

'Can you climb, d'you think?'

'Gotta, 'aven't I? Can't stay here and can't call for help. Come on, give us a pull.'

Slowly they climbed back up the steep, slippery slope until they were crawling over the edge at the top and lying, breathless, on the path.

'Let's go home, Uncle Arthur. Please.'

'Not likely. I ain't going through all that just to go back empty handed. Just give us a minute an' I'll be as right as ninepence.'

Inwardly, Jenny groaned but there was nothing she could do. At least, not at this moment, but her resolve to run away hardened.

Arthur stood up, testing his ankle again and though he was limping quite heavily, he took the torch from her and began to walk up the track again towards the top of the hill, making sure to keep well away from the side of the quarry now.

When they reached the gate leading into the yard of Meadowsweet Farm, Arthur took a paper parcel from his pocket and pushed it into her hands. 'Here, take this to the dog and make sure she eats it.'

'I'm not *staying* there.'

'Yes, you are,' he said, squeezing her shoulder again warningly. 'I want you to make sure she eats it all up.'

'Why?'

'Don't ask questions,' he snapped, feeling confident once more. 'Just do as I tell you.'

Arthur opened the gate. It squeaked loudly and they both held their breath and stood very still waiting to see if anyone had heard. But even the dog didn't bark.

Maybe Peg was so familiar with the noise that she didn't think anything of it.

'Go on, then,' Arthur urged, giving her a little push. With every step across the yard Jenny's heart beat faster and faster, so loudly that she thought it would wake the family! She was being silly, of course, but her legs were trembling and she couldn't breathe properly. How had she ever got into this mess? Into this awful life where she'd been turned into a criminal? Stealthily, Jenny moved forward. She was almost at the back door of the house when the dog became aware of her. Peg came out of her kennel with a little bark and then a whine of welcome as she recognized the smell of the person coming towards her.

'Here, girl. Here, Peg,' Jenny whispered, feeling like the very worst kind of traitor. Arthur was going to steal one of Mr Gordon's lambs and there was nothing she could do to stop him. Why ever hadn't she run away weeks ago when all this had started?

Peg wolfed the meat hungrily. She didn't get given meat like this very often now; this was a rare treat for the dog. As the animal licked her lips around the last morsel, Jenny patted her head. The dog whined and wagged her tail. She crept back into her kennel and lay down, her nose on her paws. Jenny crept away, back to the gate where Arthur waited. They closed the gate and waited a moment, but all was still quiet.

'Right, come on now.'

They walked on further up the lane to the very end where it gave way to pasture on the steep slopes of the hillside. Shadowy shapes lay in the field.

'Won't they make an awful noise if we go in there?'

'Go very carefully and quietly,' Arthur whispered.

246

'I'm only taking one lamb. More might be missed. Like I said, it doesn't pay to be greedy.'

Jenny had always believed in the saying that it was crime that didn't pay, but it seemed to be doing so for Arthur. They moved into the field and amongst the sheep until Arthur bent and picked a lamb up from the ground where it lay cuddled against its mother. At once a loud bleating filled the night air and Jenny gasped in terror. Surely Peg would hear the noise, even from this distance, and would start barking.

'Come on.' Arthur had the lamb in his arms, his strong hand clamped over its mouth so that it could no longer make a loud noise. But the mother sheep had struggled to her feet and was now bleating too and following them.

'Run to the gate, Jen, and get ready to close it the minute I get through.' Jenny ran ahead on legs that trembled so much they would hardly carry her. She opened the gate a little and Arthur squeezed through, carrying the lamb. Just as the mother sheep was about to put her nose through the opening, Jenny shut the gate.

'Come on, we'd better hurry.'

'We're not going back past the farm, are we? What if Peg hears us?'

Arthur chuckled. 'Don't you worry your head any more about the dog. She'll be fast asleep by now.'

Arthur was struggling to carry the lamb and keep it quiet as they retraced their steps past the farm gate and on down the lane. 'I didn't realize it'd be so heavy,' he muttered, then added, cheerfully, 'Still, all the more meat.'

Jenny strained her eyes through the darkness, but she

could neither see nor hear anything. There was no barking, no movement. As Arthur had said, Peg must have fallen asleep after her nice meal.

The following morning, Jenny knew she wouldn't be able to concentrate on her schoolwork. Not only was she very tired after her late night, but she was also very worried that Susan might somehow know what they'd been up to the night before. But Beryl and Susan didn't seem to notice. They had other concerns on their minds. Susan came to school with red eyes. She'd obviously been crying. Beryl rushed up to her in the playground and put her arm around her shoulders. Jenny followed, feeling guilty. Her heart felt as if it was pounding in her chest. Susan must know that one of their lambs was missing.

'It's Peg,' Susan sniffled and broke into fresh tears.

'What's happened?' Beryl asked.

'She's – she's died.'

'Died!' Beryl was shocked and Jenny gasped and felt the blood drain from her face. Guilt shot through her like a knife.

'But she wasn't ill, was she?' Beryl was asking. 'You never said.'

Susan shook her head. 'Dad doesn't know why. She was fine yesterday, he said, and she's not old.'

'Is he going to take her to the vet? Get him to find out what's happened to her?' Beryl asked. Jenny felt a sliver of fear and held her breath, waiting for Susan's answer.

'No. Vets cost too much money. I bet your dad always says the same.'

Beryl pursed her lips, but nodded, forced to agree.

'But,' Susan went on, and her next words brought cold dread to Jenny's heart, 'he reckons she might have been poisoned.'

'Poisoned? How and – and why?'

Susan shrugged. 'You know there's a lot of thieving going on. Dad hears the other farmers talking at the market. Oh, nothing on a grand scale, they say, but pilfering. A few chickens, a duck or two. Eggs, even animal feed.'

Arthur. It was all Arthur's doing. Jenny felt herself growing hot with shame and fear as Susan went on, 'Dad reckons someone must have wanted to keep the dog quiet so they probably gave Peg some poisoned food.'

Beryl stared at her friend, shocked and upset. Tears welled in her eyes too now. Jenny didn't know what to say or do. She wanted to run, out of the playground, away from the school – as far away as possible. How could he? How could Arthur have done such a terrible thing as to poison the Gordons' dog?

At that moment, as Jenny stood by, watching her two friends who would no longer be her friends if they knew the truth, the bell went for the beginning of school. They trooped into the classroom and sat together in their usual places in the back row, Beryl in the middle with the other two on either side of her.

The lessons drifted over Jenny's head and several times the teacher spoke sharply to her, telling her to pay attention or to repeat something she'd just said. Jenny couldn't; she hadn't been listening because she was too busy with her own thoughts. The tiredness had left her but her powers of concentration, usually so good because she enjoyed school, had completely deserted her.

'Jenny Mercer, you will stay in detention after school tonight,' the teacher said at last, her patience exhausted. Beryl touched Jenny's arm sympathetically. 'We'll wait for you,' she whispered.

Jenny smiled thinly and tried to apply herself to the history lesson. It wouldn't do to get hauled out to the teacher's desk at the front of the class and to be asked awkward questions. If that happened, she'd cry, she knew she would.

They were still waiting for her when the teacher finally let her go with the warning that she'd better try harder the next day or she'd be sent to the headmaster.

Beryl linked her arm through Jenny's. 'Come on, let's go to mine. It's baking day.' It had become a regular routine that the three girls would go straight to the kitchen of Honeysuckle Farm after school on Mrs Fenton's baking day.

'No, sorry,' Jenny said. 'I'd best get home. Mum'll be wondering where I've got to.'

Both Beryl and Susan glanced at her. 'You don't normally worry about telling your mam where you are,' Beryl said, frowning. 'You stay ages at mine sometimes after school.'

Jenny bit her lip. She didn't want to go to Beryl's and certainly not to Susan's. She wanted to get home and run up to her bedroom and bury her face in her pillow. But she couldn't tell them that. Suddenly, she realized how weak she was becoming. She'd allowed Arthur and her mother to push her into crime. Young though she was, she should have fought them. She shouldn't have gone along with it. Georgie wouldn't recognize her now. At the thought of him, tears filled her eyes.

'What's up?' Beryl asked bluntly.

'I – I just feel for Susan, that's all.' It was the truth,

but the other two girls didn't understand the full story. Jenny hoped they'd never find out. 'I – I never had a pet. It's difficult, living in the city, you know. So I can only guess how you must feel losing Peg. She – she was a lovely dog.'

'She was more than a pet,' Susan said, 'she was a valuable working dog. My dad's going to be lost without her helping to round up the sheep. She'd won prizes, you know.'

Jenny had thought she couldn't feel much worse, but she did now.

The three girls walked along in silence until they came to the cottage. 'You coming then, or not?'

'No – not tonight. Thanks.' Jenny turned and ran through the open gate and down the grass track leading to the cottage. With a shrug Beryl linked her arm with Susan's and they walked on, their heads bent close together.

Jenny glanced back. She was sure they were talking about her. It was the first time she'd ever refused an invitation to go to the Fentons' farm, the first time she'd ever shown any anxiety to get home.

Had it been a mistake? Would the girls wonder why? But she had to get home. She had to talk to Arthur.

She burst into the cottage, but it was silent and empty. There was no one there. Only then did she realize that the van had not been parked in its usual place.

Jenny closed her eyes and groaned aloud.

Thirty-Six

Jenny ran upstairs. The decision she'd made last night up near the quarry came back to her. She was going. Running away. She wasn't going to stay with her mother and Arthur a moment longer. She refused to take part in any more thieving and creeping about in the dark poisoning dogs. She shuddered afresh as she thought that it was her fault that Peg was dead. She'd given the poor dog the meat – though, of course, she'd had no idea it had been poisoned. It had never even crossed her mind that it might have been drugged to put the animal to sleep – or worse. She'd just thought that Arthur was trying to keep the dog quiet by giving it a nice, satisfying meal.

She dragged the suitcase off the top of the wardrobe and flung her clothes off their hangers, bundling them into the case. Then her shoes and, on top of everything, her sketch pad and pencils. She wasn't going anywhere without those. Lastly, the ever-faithful Bert was squashed in. Just as she hauled the heavy case off the bed, she heard sounds from below. Arthur and Dot were back. Now, she'd have to wait until dark before she could sneak out. And if Arthur had other plans . . .

'Jenny, are you in? Come down here this minute,' Dot was shouting up the stairs. Jenny bit her lip. Her mother sounded angry. Now what was up? Had they seen her teacher and been told that she'd been inattentive in class and kept in detention? But she dismissed the thought almost as soon as it entered her head. Dot had never been bothered about her daughter's schooling and was never likely to be. If, somehow, the teacher had seen her, Dot would merely smile, shrug and fluff her blond hair. She wouldn't give a damn. No, this was something else. For a moment, Jenny stood still, thinking. She squared her jaw. She was going, she didn't care what they said. She wouldn't tell them, but the very first night when Arthur went on duty in the city as warden, she would be off.

She pushed the suitcase under the bed and hurried downstairs. Best not to annoy her mother any more.

Dot's first words surprised her so much, Jenny's mouth dropped open. 'Get yer case packed. We're leaving.'

'Wha – ? Why?'

'He's gone one step too far. Silly bugger. Not that I want to stay here, mind. I hate it, but Gawd knows where we'll go now.'

Jenny moved closed. 'What's happened?'

Dot sighed and sat down at the table, resting her elbows on its surface and dropping her head into her hands. At that moment, Arthur came into the room, his face grim and Jenny repeated her question, since her mother was making no effort to answer her.

'Nothin'. Yer mum's panicking over nothin'.'

Dot lifted her head. 'You call the gossip in the local market, nothin'?'

Arthur shrugged. 'No one can prove anything. I've got rid of everything.'

'Even the – the lamb?' Jenny stammered.

'Yeah. Took it to Sheffield to the butcher I know this morning. Very pleased, he was. Gave me a good price

an' all.' His grin widened as he winked at Jenny. 'We'll
have to try that again, Tich.'

'Oh no,' Jenny shouted, her vehemence surprising
even her. It was the first time she'd stood up to Arthur
and, despite the fear of what might follow, it felt good.
'I'm never going out thieving with you again.'

Arthur frowned and Dot raised her head and stared
at her daughter. Jenny glanced from one to the other as
she said slowly and deliberately, 'I didn't realize that
meat you gave me for Peg was poisoned. Susan's dog is
dead, *Uncle* Arthur.' She laid stress on the name to
emphasize that her acquiescence in all his schemes was
over. She would never call him 'Dad' again. He took a
step towards her and for a moment she felt a quiver of
fear, but she stood her ground and glared at him. She'd
thought he was about to strike her, he looked so angry,
his fists clenched at his sides, but suddenly his mood
changed and he tried to wheedle his way around her.
'Now look 'ere, Tich, you're a big help to me, you are.
Don't go all soft on me. Not now.'

'I'm not doing it any more,' Jenny shouted. 'I don't
kill dogs.'

Dot sprang up. 'Keep yer voice down. If someone
hears you . . .' She glanced at Arthur and took her cue
from him. Slaps and punishments weren't going to solve
this one. Jenny could be a hard little madam when she
wanted to be. No, Arthur was right. They'd have to
cajole her. But being nice didn't come naturally to Dot.

'Look, darlin'. Like I said, we're getting out of here.
Going somewhere new.'

'No, we're not, Dot,' Arthur snapped. 'Not yet. It'll
look suspicious. Jen's got to keep going to school and
we've got to carry on as normal.'

'Normal?' Jenny was still shouting at them both.

'You call the way we're living "normal"? Well, I don't. The way Charlotte and Miles live, that's normal. This isn't, this—'

She got no further for, unable to restrain her temper any longer, Dot raised her hand and slapped Jenny hard across the face. 'You cheeky little bugger. You'll do as you're told and don't you dare mention them folks again. You hear me? If they were so bloody wonderful, why didn't they keep you then? I'll tell you why. 'Cos they didn't want a dirty little thief like you, that's why.'

'I wasn't a thief. Not until he' – she jabbed her finger at Arthur – 'made me into one.'

Although her cheek was stinging and turning red, Jenny wasn't going to give her mother the satisfaction of knowing she'd hurt her. And she wasn't backing down either.

'Look,' Arthur said, trying to placate them, trying desperately to keep them both on his side. He couldn't lose Jenny's help; she was too valuable. 'It'll all be all right. I'm on duty tonight and tomorrow night in the city and—'

'Oh yes,' Jenny sneered, throwing all caution to the wind. 'And you'll come home with a van full of stuff you've looted from folks' bombed-out houses, I suppose.' Suddenly, she felt so much older than her years. Older and wiser even than the two adults standing before her. How could they be so stupid, so wicked? Well, she wasn't having any further part in it.

'No,' Arthur said quietly. Shouting and slapping wasn't going to win this stubborn kid over. As he gazed at her mutinous little face, he realized what a little beauty she was turning into. Despite the wartime rationing, which, thanks to him, hadn't affected them much, at almost thirteen Jenny was filling out in all the right places. In a year or two, she'd be a stunner. He shook the thoughts out of his head, bringing himself back to the present. 'I promise I won't do nothin' tonight.' He grinned. 'I'll be a good lad and then, in a day or two, or maybe a week or so, when all the hoohah has died down, we'll move on.'

'And what if it doesn't die down? What if the police or someone comes knocking? What about all the stuff you've got stacked in the barns? The petrol? And the extra food on Mum's pantry shelves? How are yer going to explain all that away, eh?'

Arthur's grin widened. 'All gone. Well, all that can't be explained anyway.'

'How?' Jenny demanded suspiciously. 'How've you got rid of everything?'

'Been running about all day like a couple of scalded cats,' Dot put in crossly. 'Backwards and forwards. It's a wonder we haven't got stopped and asked where we're getting all the petrol from. I'm shattered.'

'I'm an ARP warden, aren't I?' Arthur smirked. 'Doing valuable war work.'

'What about the chickens and the ducks?' Jenny was still worrying. There were now quite a few more in the pen in the back garden than ever Arthur had bought legitimately.

'When we're ready to go, I'll take them to the butcher in the city. We can start up again somewhere else.'

'Not with me, you won't.'

'Don't talk daft, Jenny. You've got to stay with us. Where do you think you're going to go?' Dot said and added with a sneer, 'Reckon you're going to run back to them marvellous Thorntons, do yer? Well, I wouldn't hold yer breath.' Her voice rose. 'I've told you till I'm blue in the face, they don't want yer.'

'Then I'll go back to London. I can stay with Aunty Elsie. She'll let me —'

'No, she won't. An' you're not going nowhere near London, so there. You'll have the coppers on to us in no time.'

'No, I won't, 'cos I won't know where you are, will I?'

'They'd wheedle it out of you that we was in Derbyshire. They'd soon come looking.'

The wrangling went on for an hour.

'Look, we've nothin' to worry about now. Even if anyone does come snooping round,' Arthur said again, 'they're not going to find anything. Like I say, Jen, you go to school for a few more days. Act normal and then by next week, we'll be off.'

Jenny glowered at him, more because she was feeling the trap closing in on her again. If only she'd made her escape before they'd come home. She had a little money saved up from whenever Arthur had been feeling generous, as he sometimes was when she'd been particularly helpful. She could have been on her way to the station by now and buying a ticket to London.

Now she closed her mind to hopes of ever going back to Lincolnshire. Dot was so vehement that the Thorntons didn't want her, it must be true.

But the final acceptance of her mother's words lay like a leaden weight in her chest.

Thirty-Seven

'One of our lambs has gone missing,' Susan announced at school the following morning. Jenny bit her lip, held her breath and waited. 'Dad reckons it happened the same night as Peg died. He's going to take her to the vet and get him to find out if she had been poisoned.'

Jenny tried to swallow the lump of fear rising in her throat.

'Yeah and we lost two chickens last week.' Bruce Porter lived at a farm on the opposite side of the village; the farm Arthur and Jenny had visited one night the previous week.

'We'd never have known,' the boy went on. 'Dad says they're crafty blighters, whoever's doing it, 'cos they only take one or two.'

'How did you know, then?' Beryl asked. ''Cos your dad's got thousands of chickens.'

Bruce grinned. 'Not quite. Hundreds, mebbe. Thing was, Dad's got a favourite speckled hen – the only one we'd got – and that's one of the ones they took. So when he saw she was missing, he counted 'em, and we've lost two.'

'Could've been a fox,' someone suggested but Bruce shook his head. 'No, you know what foxes is like. Kill half a dozen and then only take one away. And there's always feathers around and that. No, it wasn't a fox.'

'The grocer in the village reckons he's lost some sugar an' a lot of other stuff as well,' Rosie, Bruce's younger sister, put in. 'He was telling Mam the other day that there was several things gone from the back of his shelves in the storeroom. He reckons it's been gone for a bit, but he never noticed till he came to want it. And then he hadn't got as much as he thought he had – as much as he should have had. He checked his – what do they call them, Bruce?'

'His invoices.'

'That's it – his invoices and there was quite a lot of stuff missing. Just one or two of each item taken from the back of the shelf so they wouldn't be missed straight away.'

'Clever, whoever they are.'

Jenny knew she ought to say something. Her silence might be noticeable, but the other children were so intent on swapping the stories they'd heard that they didn't seem to realize she was taking no part in the conversation. Not even Beryl or Susan remarked on it. Perhaps, as she was fairly new to the area, they thought she didn't know the places they were talking about. But as they walked home together after school, it would become more obvious between just the three of them if she said nothing.

'How long will it be before they find out about Peg?' she asked tentatively.

'A day or two,' Susan said. 'The vet said he'd do it as soon as he could.'

'Let's go to mine,' Beryl said. 'You coming, Jenny?'

Jenny nodded. It would look odd if she refused two nights in a row, when usually she would do anything to avoid going home. Act normally, Arthur had said.

So for two agonizing hours longer, Jenny had to

endure the conversation being dominated by Peg's death and the loss of Mr Gordon's lamb.

'Can't say we've lost any livestock,' Beryl's dad said as he sat down at the tea table, 'but then it's not always easy to count chickens – or sheep, for that matter.'

'It was only because the mother sheep was making such a noise searching for her lamb that Dad realized,' Susan said, helping herself to Mrs Fenton's home-made jam and spreading it thinly on a piece of toast. Even the youngsters were conscious of the phrase 'there is a war on, you know' that was quoted so often by the grown-ups, and the children chanted it in the playground as part of a game they'd made up.

'You'll have to make sure you keep the pigs locked up, else one of them'll be disappearing,' Mrs Fenton said. 'Specially one of the little ones. Someone could take one of them, fatten them up and get a good price for it.'

'Aye, I'll make sure the dogs are loose in the yard,' Jack Fenton said grimly. 'And I've me shotgun ready at the side of the bed.'

Jenny choked on her piece of toast and had to be slapped hard on the back.

Jenny stood before Arthur and Dot later that night, her arms folded, her bright, blue eyes sparkling with anger. 'They're having Peg examined by a vet to see'f she'd been poisoned.' She leaned towards them to press home her point. 'Because Mr Gordon knows one of his lambs is missing.'

Arthur stared at her for a moment and then guffawed loudly. 'How can 'ee possibly know that amongst all them sheep he's got?'

'Because,' Jenny said slowly, as if explaining to a dimwit, 'the mother sheep was looking for it and making a right racket. Otherwise, I don't think he would've known, no.'

Arthur blinked, nonplussed for once. Dot punched his arm. 'There y'are, not so clever after all, are yer, Mr Big? We'll have to go now.'

'Wait a bit, wait a bit,' Arthur said, lighting a cigarette and puffing at it as if his life depended upon it. 'Let's not panic. Let's think this out. Even if they do find out the dog was poisoned, they still don't know who did it, do they?'

Dot and Jenny glanced at each other. Jenny had the feeling that Dot was beginning to think the same as her; the sooner they got away from here, the better.

'So, like I said, we stay put a bit. If we run now, it'd look suspicious.'

'But they're all on the lookout for us now,' Jenny persisted and shuddered afresh as she remembered Mr Fenton's words. 'And Beryl's dad's keeping his shotgun at the side of his bed. Just in case.'

'That does it, then. I'm not arguing with no shotgun.'

'So?' Dot said eagerly. 'We're going?'

But Arthur was still shaking his head. 'Not yet. But we just won't be going out at night any more.' Relief surged through Jenny, but it was short-lived as Arthur added, 'At least, not round here.'

The next few days were agony for Jenny. She tried to keep up the pretence at school, taking in all the gossip and reporting it every night to Dot and Arthur, hoping that eventually it would push Arthur into deciding to leave.

'The vet's told Mr Gordon that there was poison in the last piece of meat that Peg ate. He's reported it to the police and they're going to start making inquiries, he said.'

For once Arthur looked anxious. 'Then I'd better kill the extra chickens we've got. I thought I might be able to explain away what we've got left, but if they come asking . . .' He got up at once and moved towards the back door. 'I'll just leave the ones we bought off Fenton. I'll take the rest with me tonight when I go on duty.'

For the next half an hour there was a lot of scuffling and squawking and Arthur emerged from the hen house looking as if he'd gone ten rounds with Joe Louis. He put the dead birds under a rug in the van and drove off towards Sheffield.

'He'll be for it if he gets stopped and searched,' Dot muttered worriedly.

But it seemed that Arthur Osborne had the luck of the Devil for he arrived home the following morning grinning from ear to ear with a wad of cash in his pocket. Generously, he threw pound notes on the table for Dot and Jenny.

'There you are. Never let it be said that Arthur Mercer doesn't treat his girls right.'

Jenny grabbed hers and scurried up the stairs to hide the money. It was a little more towards her savings for running away. When she was going to do it, she didn't know, but her resolve was now unshakeable. One day – as soon as she could – she would run away.

Thirty-Eight

The days dragged on and Arthur still refused to budge. The only blessing as far as Jenny was concerned was that she no longer accompanied him on his nightly escapades. Arthur had given up stealing from the locals – at least for the time being, but he still brought home all sorts of things he'd looted in the city.

'I don't know how you're getting away with this, Arfer,' Dot said as she rifled through the clothes and belongings he'd taken from bombed-out houses.

Three weeks had passed since the incident of the lamb and Peg's death, but just when Arthur was beginning to feel safe again the police came to the cottage.

'We're making inquiries,' the sergeant said ponderously as the constable with him took out his notebook. 'About alleged thefts in the area.'

'Really,' Arthur said. He was feeling confident. It wouldn't matter if the police decided to search the cottage from attic to cellar; there was nothing there now that he or Dot couldn't explain away.

'Come in, do.' Dot smiled winningly at the sergeant. 'Would yer like a cup o' tea?' She giggled girlishly, 'But I hope you don't take sugar, 'cos we've only got our rations.'

'Don't push it, Dot,' Arthur muttered as the two policemen came into the small sitting room, seeming to fill it with their forbidding presence.

Jenny moved to the corner of the room. She was tempted to leave, to go upstairs to her bedroom, but she was compelled to stay. She had to hear what was being said; she had to know what was going on.

'You're not from these parts,' the sergeant began, sounding friendly enough.

'Nah. We lived in London but the bombing was that bad.' Arthur shook his head. 'We've our girl to think of. He gestured towards Jenny. 'Night after night spent in the shelter or in the underground was no life for her.'

The sergeant was staring at Arthur, assessing him. 'May I ask why you're not in the armed forces, sir?'

'Weak heart.' Arthur pulled a wry face. 'I volunteered, yer know. Didn't even wait to be called up' – that was a lie for a start, Jenny thought – 'but I failed the medical. I've got a paper here, if you want to see it.'

'So, er, what do you do now, sir?'

'I'm an ARP warden in Sheffield. Got me blue uniform and me tin hat with a big W on it.'

'You manage to get petrol all right to get there and back, do you, sir?' the sergeant said slowly, his keen gaze still on Arthur's face.

Dot moved between them, making a great play of handing round the tea. 'Sorry, I can't offer you any biscuits.' She giggled again. 'There is a war on, you know.'

The sergeant pursed his lips and glanced angrily at her. Her interruption – and he believed it to be deliberate – had disrupted his line of questioning. But Arthur answered nonchalantly enough. 'So far, I have.'

'Are you employed full time as a warden?'

'No – it's voluntary. Three or four nights a week usually. More, if I'm needed.'

'You have other employment?'

'I pick up a bit of temporary work here and there.'

'Do you indeed, sir. And what sort of *temporary* work might that be?'

There was silence in the room and Jenny shuddered.

'Oh, just labouring, you know,' Arthur said airily. 'On the farms mostly. They find me light jobs, yer know.' He tapped his chest again. ''Cos of me heart.'

The sergeant regarded him for a long moment before saying softly, 'I'll take your word for it, sir.'

To Jenny, it sounded as if the man was doing anything but believing Arthur.

Now the police officer turned to Dot. 'May I see your ration books, madam?'

Dot blinked. 'Er – er, yes. I'll – I'll just fetch them. They're in my handbag upstairs.'

Whilst Dot scurried upstairs, there was an awkward silence in the room. Jenny shifted uneasily from one foot to the other and avoided meeting the sergeant's gaze. She didn't want to be asked any difficult questions. She didn't want to be asked any questions at all.

Dot came back, glancing worriedly at Arthur as she handed the books over without a word. The sergeant flipped through the books, pausing over the one with the name Arthur Mercer on the front cover.

'Registered with the local shops, are you?'

'That's right,' Arthur said easily.

'The ones in the village?'

'That's right.'

'The grocer in the next village has lost a lot of his stock from his shelves at the back of the shop.'

There was a brief pause whilst Arthur thought quickly. 'Yes, we'd heard the talk.'

The sergeant was still holding Arthur's ration book in his hands. 'Seems you have a few unused coupons in this book, sir.' He rose slowly and handed the three books back to Dot. 'I'd get them used up, madam, before they go out of date. Precious things these days are coupons.'

'Yes – yes. Thank you.' Dot took the books back with fingers that shook slightly. The sergeant smiled at her, but he was watching her closely. 'Makes a lot of people nervous does a visit from the police.'

Dot smiled thinly and lifted her chin a little. 'More tea, officer, before you go?'

'No, thanks, madam. But that was very nice. We'd best be getting on. A lot more people to talk to if we're to get to the bottom of what's been going on round here.'

Arthur led the way to the front door.

'Oh just one more thing, sir. You've got a few chickens and ducks, I believe.'

'That's right. Care to see them? They're out the back.'

'Not just now, sir. I didn't bring my wellingtons today. Another time, perhaps. We'll no doubt be seeing you again.'

As Arthur closed the door behind them, the veiled threat was left hanging in the room.

'That's it, we're going.'

'Won't it look worse than before if we disappear straight after a visit from the police?' Dot asked. 'Specially as we never mentioned that we might be moving.' Her face brightened. 'We could always go back to the Smoke. Oh Arfer – ' she moved to him, resting her palms on his chest and gazing up at him – 'let's got back to London. Let's go home. Please.'

Impatiently, Arthur brushed her hands aside. 'No, we're staying in the country. We'll move but stay near enough to Sheffield so's I can carry on being an ARP warden.'

'They'll still find you if they want to. You told 'em you were a warden in Sheffield.'

Arthur glared at her, realizing that she was right. He had let that slip out. In trying to prove that he was a law-abiding citizen, determined to do his bit, he might have made the police look more closely at exactly what was happening in the city when Arthur Mercer was on duty.

'Sheffield's a big place,' he muttered, his mind working quickly. He lit another cigarette as he pondered. 'You're right, we'd better stick it out another day or two at least.'

Jenny spoke for the first time. 'But what if they come back?'

To that, neither Arthur nor Dot had an answer.

Thirty-Nine

'Get your stuff packed up. We're going termorrer night after Jen's school breaks up for the summer holidays.' He pointed at Jenny. 'And you mind you tell 'em all termorrer that we're going on holiday.'

'Holiday?' Dot frowned. 'Folks don't go gallivanting on holiday, Arfer. There's a war on.'

He pondered a moment. 'Then tell 'em – tell 'em yer granny's ill and we've had to go to London to see her.'

'I haven't got a granny,' Jenny said in a small voice. How she wished she had; it would have been somewhere to run away to.

Arthur was growing agitated. 'Then make one up. Draw a picture of an old woman in a rocking chair and show it to your mates. Tell 'em it's your granny. You like drawing. You can do that, can't you, for your *dad*? Yeah, that's a good idea,' he went on, nodding at his own ingenuity. 'And I'll tell 'em the same at the Wardens' Post – that Dot's mam's been taken ill.'

'What about the rest of the chickens and ducks?' Dot asked suddenly.

'I'll kill them all termorrer afternoon and we'll take them with us.'

'But if we're stopped . . .'

'We won't be. We'll set off just before six o'clock. That's when the local copper comes off his day shift.'

268

'How d'you know he's on his day shift now? He might be on nights and just starting.'

'Because I've been watching 'im for a while an' timing 'im, that's how. He's got two days left to do before he finishes his run of days.' Arthur smirked. 'Never think to alter their routine, do they?'

'Where are we going?'

'Don't know yet. We'll just set off and see where we land up.'

'But—'

'Just do it, Dot.'

Jenny didn't have much packing to do; it was already done in the suitcase still hiding under her bed. The following evening she sat on the edge of her bed, swinging her legs and biting her lip. If only she'd run away before now. The railway wasn't far away, but if she went with her mother and Arthur, they might really end up in the middle of nowhere and it might not be so easy to get to a train station.

She held her breath. Should she go now? Before they left. If she crept down the stairs with her case whilst her mother was banging about in her bedroom packing all her clothes and belongings, could she make it to the station before she was missed? Arthur was in the back garden killing the chickens; he wouldn't be in for a while.

Jenny pulled on her socks and shoes and reached for her coat. Thrusting her arms into the sleeves, she picked up her suitcase and had already begun to move towards the door when she heard her mother shouting. 'Jen – Jen. Come here. I need some help.'

Jenny stood for a moment, undecided. Should she make a dash for it? But if her mother came looking for her, she'd be missed straight away. Maybe Dot wouldn't come looking, maybe—

She heard her mother's bedroom door open and Dot's yell. '*Jen!* Where are you, you lazy little bugger? Come and give me a hand.'

With a sigh, Jenny put her case back on the bed and took off her coat.

'Coming, Mum,' she shouted back, resigned to being stuck with the two of them for a little while longer.

They set off a few minutes before six, Jenny sitting in the back huddled against a mound of dead chickens and ducks hidden beneath a blanket. The smell made her feel sick, but she dared not make any complaint; Dot was in a bad mood and there was a row erupting already in the front seats of the van as they drove away from the cottage.

'Where are we going, I'd like to know?'

'I told you, Dot, I don't know myself yet. Give it a rest, will yer?'

'Give it a rest, he says. Give it a rest. Dragged halfway round the country in the middle of the night.'

'Six o'clock's hardly the middle of the night. It's still light and we're meant to be off to see yer mam. Remember?'

'I meant when we left London.'

Arthur couldn't argue with that one.

As they reached the outskirts of Sheffield, Arthur said, 'I'm just going to drop these birds off at this butcher I've been dealing with.'

'He won't be open now, will he?'

'He lives above the shop.'

They pulled off the main road into a side road and then turned again into an alley that ran at the back of the row of shops and houses. Arthur stopped the vehicle and switched off the engine. 'Wait here. I won't be long.'

'You'd better not be,' Dot muttered.

Minutes later, the back doors of the van opened and a small, portly man stood beside Arthur. He looked shocked when he saw Jenny and took a step backwards. He recovered quickly to joke, 'I didn't think you meant that kind of a bird, Arthur.'

Arthur grinned and winked at Jenny. 'She's not for sale, mate. Far too valuable, is our Jen.'

He had an easy, bantering relationship with his partner in crime, but Jenny glared at the man as if he was personally responsible for Arthur's criminal ways. He was not, of course, but he was encouraging her so-called stepfather by being an outlet for stolen goods.

'We're having to move on, Jim. These'll likely be the last for a while. But I'll be in touch if things pick up again.'

'Where are you going?'

'Wherever we can find a place.'

'You can stay here for a night or two, if you like.'

Overhearing the man's offer, Dot was out of the front seat and moving round to the back of the van.

'That's real kind of you – Jim, is it?' She flashed her smile at him and fluffed her hair. The man blinked behind his round spectacles and turned pink. Dot was flirting with him. 'But won't your wife mind?'

'Er – I haven't got a wife,' he stammered. 'I live on my own. But there's a spare bed all made up. My brother comes down from York to see me now and again and stays the night.'

Dot linked her arm through his. 'What? A nice man like you not married? I can't believe it.'

Jenny sighed inwardly and closed her eyes momentarily. Dot's flirting always embarrassed her. Her mother hadn't been so bad just lately, since she'd been with Arthur. They'd been together for nearly four years now and that was a long time for Dot to stay with one man. Jenny glanced at Arthur, but he was just grinning, backing Dot in making up to Jim as it would earn them a bed for the night at least.

'That's very kind of you, mate, ain't it, Dot? We'll take you up on that offer. It's getting late for Jen, here.'

Jim peered into the van as if he'd forgotten Jenny's existence. 'Oh yes, well, I haven't actually got a bed for her.'

'She'll be all right on the floor. Couple of blankets and a pillow an' she'll be as right as nine pence.'

'I might be able to get a mattress from next door. It'll be uncomfortable on the floor for the little lass.' The man was considerate, Jenny thought. She'd give him that.

'No, no, don't put yourself out. It's only for one night till we can have a look around. She'll be fine,' Arthur insisted.

But the one night turned into two and then three and four. For once Dot discovered the shops in the city, she refused to leave. 'Just one more day, Arfer, there's a dear,' she wheedled. 'Jim doesn't mind, do you, Jim?'

And the portly little man turned pink once more.

A week to the day since they'd first arrived, Arthur finally persuaded Dot that they should move on.

'If one of me mates from the wardens' post sees me, they'll wonder what I'm still doing here when I'm supposed to be down south.'

They set off, leaving the outskirts of the city, and headed back into the Derbyshire countryside, but further north than where they'd been before. They'd travelled about ten miles when they came to a huge lake.

'What stunning views,' Arthur said as they all got out of the van and stood admiring the sun shimmering on the stretch of water. 'I'd love it if we could find a place somewhere round here.'

'But it's in the middle of nowhere,' Dot wailed. 'It was bad enough before, but here . . .'

Now she'd had a brief taste of city life once more, she couldn't bear to be buried alive in the dales again. 'No, Arthur, we're not stopping here.'

'We'll do as I say, Dot. It'd be safe here and it's still near enough to Sheffield for me to carry on with my warden's duties.'

Jenny glanced at her mother and caught the gleam in Dot's eyes. Now what's she planning? the girl wondered.

'Uncle Arthur—'

'Dad,' he reminded her. 'We're still the Mercer family and don't you forget it.' He tweaked her ear.

'What's those two towers at the end of the lake?'

Arthur squinted towards them. 'Oh, I know where we are. This must be the Derwent reservoir. And they're building another one somewhere near here and I seem to remember reading that they're going to drown a couple of villages.'

Jenny gasped. 'You mean, they're going to drown the people?'

'Don't be daft, Jen. 'Course they aren't. The folks'll have to move out.'

'Leave their homes?'

Arthur shrugged. It was no concern of his and he couldn't have cared less. 'That's progress, Jen. The big cities need a supply of water from somewhere.' But Jenny felt for the folks who were going to lose their homes. Maybe it was necessary to provide water for the big cities, but, nevertheless, it must be hard for the villagers.

'Now.' Arthur's eyes were gleaming as an idea came to him. Jenny's heart sank; she didn't like that look. 'If villagers are already leaving their homes, there'll be some empty houses maybe going cheap to rent.'

Dot stared at him and Jenny trembled inwardly. Whatever was he suggesting? It was Dot who voiced their fears. 'If they've gone, Arfer, then they've gone for a good reason. I'm not livin' in no cottage that's going to be flooded.'

Arthur laughed. 'Yer silly mare. They won't be flooding it yet. Work's going a lot more slowly now because of the war. They can't get the building materials so easily.' He nodded towards the wall of the dam and the towers, indicating that something similar must be under construction for the new reservoir. His grin broadened. 'In fact, I might see if there's any work going. They'll be short of labourers if a lot of the workers have been called up.'

'What?' Dot sneered. 'With your bad heart? Yer can't have it both ways, Arfer. Dodge the call-up and then get taken on to do heavy work.'

'I s'pose you're right. Anyway, ' Arthur turned away from the picturesque view, 'let's go house hunting.'

They found a small stone cottage to rent on the outskirts of one of the villages due for eventual destruction. Jenny shivered, her sensitive soul already feeling the air of desolation and sadness. Several of the houses were deserted and the word was that the coming Christmas of 1942 would be the last that the residents would spend in their old homes. But Dot had more personal problems on her mind than where strangers were going to live. The cottage Arthur found was even more primitive than the one on Jack Fenton's farm. There was an outside lavatory and no running water. It had to be carried from a well and heated in the range in the kitchen.

'I'm not standing this for long, Arthur, I'll tell you now.' Dot was adamant.

'You'll have to stick it for a bit. I've signed up with the owner for a month.'

'Well, you can unsign it, Arthur Osborne—'

'Mercer,' Arthur murmured automatically.

' – because me and Jen aren't stopping here.'

'Actually,' Arthur said, ignoring Dot's rant. 'It might be better if we used the name Osborne.' He turned to Jenny. 'Can you remember to call yourself Jennifer Osborne from now on?'

Jenny stared at him. 'When I start a new school, they sometimes ask to see my birth certificate.'

'Tell 'em it got lost in the Blitz.'

More lies, she thought, and dropped her gaze.

'What about the ration books,' Dot asked. 'They're all in the name of Mercer. Even yours.'

Arthur shrugged. 'It's no bother getting new ration books. You just tell 'em we were bombed out in London and they were lost.' He grinned. 'You might even get some money out of 'em if you tell 'em we lost everything.'

Dot sniffed. 'No doubt we have by now. Our old house will have been looted even if it hasn't been bombed.'

'There you are, then. It'll be the truth.'

Dot snorted and almost smiled. 'For once,' she muttered.

275

Forty

'She'll have to go to school. I don't want the attendance officer knocking on my door.'

'Shouldn't worry,' Arthur grinned, 'he'll have to find her first. And where's he going to look for Jennifer Osborne?'

Dot glared at him. 'I don't want her mooning about the place all day under my feet. Get her into a school.'

'I've no idea where the nearest one is.'

'Then ask the neighbours. Is there one in the village? They'll know.'

Arthur laughed. 'What neighbours? We're right on the edge of the village. The nearest house is at least half a mile up the road.'

Dot shuddered and muttered, 'And don't I know it.'

'Just like I like it,' Arthur murmured, ignoring her. 'Jen'll be all right. I'll get her some books and some paints. She loves drawing and painting. Encourage the kid, Dot, and she'll be fine. I don't want her going to school here, even if there is one.'

'Drawing, indeed. What good's that going to be? She'll never get a job *drawing*.'

'Maybe not, but if it keeps her happy and out of your hair . . . besides, she says she wants to go to art school when she's older.' Arthur knew more about Jenny's ambitions than her mother did.

'Art school? Whoever heard of her sort going to art

school? Oh that little madam's got ideas above her station and no mistake. I blame those folks she was with when she was 'vacuated. Far too la-di-dah for the likes of us.'

'They were good to her, Dot.'

'Yeah, too good. Gave her big ideas.'

'No harm in having a dream,' Arthur said and added wistfully. 'I had dreams once. I was going to be an engineer. All set to take up an apprenticeship, I was, and then my dad died and I had to get a job quick.'

'My heart bleeds,' Dot said sarcastically. 'And what sort of *job* did you get? Started the wheeling and dealing straight away, did yer?'

Arthur glared at her, but didn't answer and Dot knew she'd hit the proverbial nail on the head.

Jenny wasn't bothered about school either. Once Arthur had bought her paints and paper, she was quite happy drawing and painting to her heart's content. The only drawback was that no one was interested in her efforts. Arthur merely glanced at them and said, 'Very nice, Tich,' whilst Dot's lips curled in disapproval. His pet name had stuck even though now she was nearly as tall as her mother.

How she missed Charlotte's smile and her constructive comments on her work, leaning over to show her with a swift and expert dash of the paintbrush how she could improve. If Jenny closed her eyes, she fancied she could smell Charlotte's perfume close by. And then there'd been Georgie who'd hung her paintings on the wall in his room.

She hoped they were still there, waiting for him to come back.

*

Jenny was left alone at the cottage a lot. Whilst she missed the company of other children – she almost longed to be back with Beryl and Susan but for the trouble Arthur's thieving had caused – she could wander the fields and the woods and the lanes around the edge of the reservoir untroubled. She saw very few people. In fact, she avoided meeting anyone, afraid that they'd ask why she wasn't in school.

But maybe they wouldn't have asked; Jenny was growing fast, was tall and leggy and filling out in all the right places. With her naturally blond, curly hair and her brilliant blue eyes, she was startlingly pretty. She looked older than her thirteen years and easily could have passed for having left school already.

Where Arthur disappeared to, she had no idea and didn't ask. She didn't even ask if he'd found work at the building site. It was enough for her that he didn't involve her any more in whatever he was up to and for that she was thankful. As for Dot, Jenny knew exactly where she went; into the city, returning with items of clothing or shoes almost every time. Where on earth she got the money or the clothing coupons, only Jenny could guess: Arthur, of course. By this time, he'd built up a circle of mates in the city who were heavily into black market trading which included forging coupons and other documents.

Jenny sighed. They were all at it. Even that nice little man, Jim, the butcher, wasn't above taking stolen meat from Arthur. And if either of them were caught, Jenny knew they'd probably both end up in prison. She'd seen a newspaper recently that Arthur had left lying about and in it had been the court case of five men who'd been sentenced to hard labour by the magistrates for stealing food from the docks in Bristol. And she'd read about

278

two ten-year-old boys who'd carried out a smash-and-grab on a sweet shop. So, she wasn't the only youngster involved, though she was an unwilling one. And there were several reports of both men and women stealing rationed goods and the punishments they received if they were caught. She just hoped her mother hadn't resorted to shoplifting in the city to feed her obsession with clothes.

Dot never thought to bring anything for Jenny. The girl had grown out of the garments which Charlotte had bought for her and now she only had patched and mended dresses from second-hand clothes shops. Even her birthday in August had passed, yet again unremarked by Dot, and Arthur didn't seem to know the date. By happy coincidence, though, that very evening he'd brought home a new supply of paper and paints for her. So Jenny regarded it as a birthday gift. Goodness knows where he got them, she thought. I'm probably as guilty as the rest of them now – receiving stolen goods.

Jenny couldn't help thinking back to two years ago when Charlotte and Miles had been so upset to find out that her birthday had passed by without them knowing. She smiled pensively as she remembered the flurry of excitement, the party and the birthday cake.

She sighed. If only . . .

They stayed in the cottage near the reservoir through the winter and into the New Year of 1943 and still Jenny stayed away from school.

'She can help me about the house. Time she made 'erself useful.'

'I thought she already did,' Arthur remarked mildly.

'She washes up most nights after tea and I've seen her doing all the ironing. You want to watch she doesn't burn 'erself swapping irons on to the hob one after the other.' The ironing was done by spreading a blanket on the kitchen table and heating two flat irons on the hob on the range.

'She'll manage,' Dot said shortly.

Arthur winked at Jenny and produced some new watercolour paints from his pocket.

'Oh, thanks,' Jenny said eagerly. 'I can finish my picture of the lake now. I'd run out of blue paint.'

'Paints, paper, brushes,' Dot sneered. 'That's all you seem to bring home these days. For *her*. When are you going to bring me something nice, Arfer?'

Arthur's eyes hardened and he jabbed his finger at her. 'When you stop moaning, that's when. You've done nothin' but grumble lately. What's the matter wiv you?'

Dot glared back at him. ''Cos I can't get into town, that's why. It never stops raining!'

Although the weather wasn't as bad as it had been the previous winter, it was nevertheless very wet and cold. Dot hated it almost as much as she had done the snow. She became more and more irritable with both Jenny and Arthur too. Neither of them could do anything right for her. Even when spring arrived and she could get to the city more easily, she still came home in a bad mood, complaining that there was nothing in the clothes' shops, not even in the second-hand ones. 'Everyone's hanging on to what they've got now. And I've no coupons left.'

'Use mine,' Arthur offered. 'I don't need fancy clothes now I'm a country bumpkin. Besides, you've only got to say,' he added with a huge wink. 'I can get plenty of coupons.'

One evening in April, when they were just preparing to go upstairs to bed they heard a low droning noise that came nearer and nearer.

Dot screamed. 'They're back. The bombers are back. Quick, under the table.'

They had no air-raid shelter here; Arthur had deemed it unnecessary out in the middle of the countryside. 'Who's going to bomb us out here?' he'd said. 'It's the cities they're after.' And so no shelter of any kind had been constructed.

Dot was weeping with anger and fear and hitting out at Arthur as the three of them crouched beneath the table. 'I told you we should have had an Anderson. I told you.'

'Shut up, Dot, and listen.'

The noise grew louder and louder until it was shaking the china on the mantelpiece and rattling the doors and windows.

'I'm going out to see what's going on,' Arthur said, crawling out from beneath the table.

'No,' Dot shrieked. 'Don't leave us. What'll happen to us if you get killed?'

Arthur paused briefly. 'Oh, you're priceless, Dot. Ne'er mind what happens to me so long as you're all right, eh?'

He turned away, stood up and moved towards the back door. They heard him open it and close it again, going out into the darkness. The planes kept coming, one after the other, right above their cottage. It seemed to go on for hours and still Arthur didn't come back.

When at last the noise died away into the distance and Dot thought it safe to emerge from beneath the table, Jenny said, 'I didn't hear any bombs dropping, did you?'

'No. Mebbe they're just trying to frighten us to death. Well, they nearly succeeded,' she muttered morosely. 'And where's Arfer?'

The quiet that now followed the deafening noise was just as scary. Arthur came in about half an hour later. 'I've been watching them.'

'Watching them? Whatever for?'

'Because I wanted to know what was going on.'

'You didn't need to go outside to know. We could hear it in here. They've come back to bomb us all to kingdom come, that's what.'

'No, it ain't, Dot. Jen, make sure the blackout's tight shut and light a candle or two.'

'You needn't bother. I'm off to bed,' Dot muttered, getting up.

'Don't you want to hear what I saw?'

'If I must,' she said grudgingly, sitting down again. But Jenny could see that her mother's interest had been aroused. 'Go on, then.'

'They're our planes.'

'Our planes?' Dot and Jenny both spoke at once.

Arthur nodded. 'They're flying low over the reservoir and between the two towers where the water falls over the dam. One after the other, time and time again. I reckon they're training for something special.'

Dot's lip curled. 'Them RAF lads out joy-riding, that's what it'll be. Well, I won't put up with that night after night. Yer can write to somebody in the morning, Arfer.'

'Oh yeah. And let everybody know where we're living?'

Dot glared at him in the flickering candlelight and Jenny sensed a row brewing. 'Yer can send it anonymous.'

Arfer lit a cigarette and leaned back in his chair. 'Go to bed, Dot. Yer'll just have to put up with it.'

Dot – and everyone else in the area – had no choice. The RAF were indeed training for something very special and continued to fly low over the reservoir night after night. Some of the locals did write to the authorities to complain about the low-flying aircraft.

'My milk yield's down,' complained one farmer and another declared that his hens had stopped laying.

It wasn't until the middle of May when the papers were full of the raid that had been made on the German dams in the Ruhr valley that the locals realized just what had been going on. The aircrews of the Lancaster bombers, specially adapted to carry the 'bouncing bombs', had been practising low-level, night flying.

'Ah well, then, if that's what it was all about,' the local farmers who'd protested to the authorities when all the noise had been going on said to one another, 'in that case, I don't mind my livestock being frightened half to death. If only they'd told us . . .'

But of course the training had been done in strict secrecy, known only to a few – apart, that is, from the people living near the Derwent reservoir, though at the time even they hadn't known why.

Forty-One

'Jen, I've got something to tell you.'

Dot stood uncertainly in the doorway of Jenny's bedroom. Surprised, the girl looked up, her paintbrush suspended in mid-air. It wasn't often her mother sought her out and she hardly ever came to find her. Usually, it was a yell from downstairs. 'Jen, get yerself down here this minute.'

Dot came into the bedroom closing the door quietly behind her. That was something else that was different. Usually, Jenny thought, you could hear just where Dot was in the house by the noise; slamming doors, rattling pots and pans or the wireless blaring out the latest dance music. Dot loved the Glenn Miller band and was always begging Arthur to take her dancing. But now she perched on the end of Jenny's bed, twisting her fingers nervously. 'We're leaving.'

Jenny said nothing. This news was no surprise. Her mother hated the country, but she'd thought that at least here, where her mother was able to get into the city regularly, it had been better than at the first cottage. At least, for Dot. And for Jenny. Apart from not attending school, she was drawing and painting every day with Arthur's encouragement and even with Dot's tacit approval.

'I'm – leaving Arthur.'

Now Jenny was surprised, shocked even. 'Leaving

Uncle Arthur?' She regarded her mother steadily, but Dot was avoiding meeting her gaze.

'Has he got another woman?' Jenny asked bluntly.

Dot bit her lip and shook her head. 'No – no. It's – it's me. I – we're – going to live with Jim.'

'Jim? The butcher?'

Dot nodded.

Jenny was silent for several moments, digesting the news, taking it all in and its implications before she said, 'What about Arthur? Does he know?'

Dot nodded.

'So – was that what the row was about last night?'

It had been nothing unusual to hear the couple quarrelling. Jenny had hidden her head beneath the bedcovers, trying to block out the raised voices. But now she realized that the noise had gone on longer than usual and had ended with a slam of the back door and the sound of Arthur's van driving off.

She'd fallen asleep then and hadn't heard the van return. When he hadn't appeared at breakfast, she'd just thought Arthur had had another of his late nights on ARP duties. She hadn't realized that he and his van hadn't returned at all until Dot said now, 'He's gone.'

'Gone? Gone where?'

Dot shrugged. 'He'll have stayed with one of his mates in the city, I 'spect.'

Jenny paused a moment, staring at her mother, before she asked, 'Don't you care?'

'Not really. He was a bad lot. Getting you involved in his thieving.'

Jenny almost laughed aloud. It hadn't bothered Dot at the time and, young though she still was, Jenny knew her mother would bend the truth to fit her own needs. Whilst she'd been with Arthur and he'd been generous with money and had looked after her – looked after both of them – Dot had turned a blind eye to his bad ways. She'd said nothing at the time about Arthur using Jenny as his accomplice. Only now, when it suited her, was it a useful excuse to leave him.

'How long's this been going on? You and Jim, I mean?'

'Er – well – soon after we got here, really. When I went into town, I'd call and see him and we'd have a cuppa in the back when the shop wasn't busy. And we got to talking. You know how it is.'

Not really, Mum, Jenny wanted to say. I'm only thirteen. But she didn't say a word because, yes, in a way she did know how it was. At least, she knew what her mother was like.

Arthur Osborne had lasted longer than most of the previous 'uncles'. Some had lasted only a few weeks, others a few months. Only Arthur had lasted over four years. But now even his time was up.

'Are you sure about this, Mum? Uncle Arthur's been good to you. To both of us.'

'I know he has, Jen, in his own way. But he's going to get caught eventually. Oh, I know he thinks he's got the Devil's own luck, but one of these days – ' She broke off and then added, 'And I don't want either of us to be accused of being his accomplice.'

'I agree with you there, Mum, but is Jim any better? He's been taking the meat that Uncle Arthur's been supplying. Maybe he's not doing the actual stealing, but he's receiving stolen goods, isn't he? And that's a crime too.'

Dot looked uncomfortable. Her pathetic excuse for leaving Arthur was not standing up to Jenny's shrewd

286

assessment of both men. One was not much better than the other.

Dot stood up suddenly. 'Well, we're going and that's an end to it. We're moving in with Jim above the shop and you can go to school and help him in the shop when you come home and at weekends. And he says when you're old enough to leave school, there's a job for you with him.' She smiled brightly as if she was trying to convince herself as well as her daughter. 'Now what could be better than that, eh?'

Jenny's eyes narrowed. 'Staying on at school, passing my exams and getting into Sheffield School of Art, that's what.'

Dot stared at her for a moment and then burst out laughing. 'Well, you can forget about that, sunshine. You're not with them bloody Thorntons now.'

Jim came with his butcher's van and loaded all Dot's clothes and shoes together with Jenny's few belongings into the back.

'You can both squeeze into the front, girls,' he said, his round, florid face sweating, causing him to mop it with a handkerchief. 'Now then,' he said, climbing into the driver's seat, 'off we go.' Jenny saw him put out a podgy hand to touch Dot's knee. 'I can't tell you how happy you've made me, Dot love. It'll be wonderful to have you living with me. Both of you,' he added hastily. 'I've been very lonely since my wife died. And we weren't blessed with children, so there's been no one – only my brother, and I don't see him very often.'

Dot smiled and patted his knee and then left it resting there. Jenny looked out of the window, sickened by her mother's flirtatious ways and the string of men she'd had. She'd make sure she wasn't like that when she was older.

As she watched the houses flashing by, the truth hit her with a jolt. There'd only ever be one man that she'd truly love. Young though she still was – and she knew that if she were to confide in anyone, they'd only laugh at her – she already knew that she loved Georgie Thornton like she would never love anyone else. The realization brought tears to her eyes, for even though she stoutly believed that he was still alive, that one day he would come back, she very much doubted that he would ever want to see her again.

And even if he did, he would always view her as a scruffy little urchin. Jenny Mercer – as Dot had told her she must call herself again now – was not the sort of girl that Georgie Thornton would, or could, ever love and want to marry.

The knowledge caused her bitter pain.

Forty-Two

Jim Bradshaw was trying to impress them both.

'This is our room, Dot. I've had it all decorated specially.' The smell of fresh paint still hung in the air. 'I hope you like it. And then Jenny shall have the spare room. I'll get that done out for you too.'

'What about when your brother comes to stay?' Dot asked.

Jim shrugged. 'He doesn't come very often and if he does, he can sleep on the couch in the front room. Jenny,' he added firmly, 'must have the spare room.'

They unpacked, Dot taking three times as long as Jenny to arrange her clothes. She even commandeered half of the wardrobe in the spare room.

'Tea's ready when you are,' Jim called up the stairs and they went down to find a sumptuous meal on the table.

'I've not seen food like this since before the war,' Dot marvelled. 'Oh Jim, you are good to us.'

'So, what do you like to do, Jenny?' he asked as they tucked into the meal.

'Oh, don't ask her that. She'll bore you to death with all her talk of painting.'

'You like to paint?' Jim persisted.

Jenny glanced at her mother, who was pursing her lips in disapproval, but then she nodded in answer to Jim's question.

'We've got an art school in Sheffield, but it was badly damaged in the bombing at the end of 1940. I believe the students are housed in temporary accommodation, though, so it's still going. Have you left school yet, Jenny?'

Again Jenny glanced at her mother for guidance.

'She's not been able to go to school for a few weeks – '

Another lie, Jenny thought. She hadn't been to school for almost a full school year.

'And,' Dot was saying, 'she's fourteen in August so she should be able to leave then. I don't think there's any need for her to go back now, do you? She can start helping you in the shop right away, Jim.'

Jim blinked. 'Oh, I think she should go back even if only for a few weeks until she can leave legally.' He leaned towards Dot and lowered his voice, though Jenny heard him add, 'I don't want attendance officers and the like coming here.'

Dot stared at him for a moment and then smiled. She put her hand over his on the white tablecloth. 'Of course, you're right, Jim. Whatever you say.'

Jim smiled and glanced at Jenny. 'There's a school just round the corner from here. I'm sure they'll take you.'

Three days later, Jenny was enrolled at the school. She was apprehensive at first, worried in case she was asked too many questions about her previous school, but it seemed the headmaster and his staff were used to their pupils having varying abilities. Though she had missed months of schooling, Jenny found she was by no means the worst in the class. And there was another thing she hadn't expected; the city kids were more like the ones she'd known in London. True, they spoke funny, but then they said she did too. But there was a mutual respect. Sheffield had had its share of bombing so all the children could identify with Jenny and sympathize with the Blitz which Londoners had suffered.

'There're lots of kids still away,' they told her. 'Evacuated to the country when the bombing started here and they haven't come back yet.'

The ones that were left were tough kids, too, who stood no nonsense, and they soon recognized that same feistiness in Jenny. And there was something else that was similar to back home: the boys and girls mixed freely. True, there were the groups, gangs almost, she supposed, but they weren't enemies with others. Boys didn't jeer at the girls and pull their plaits and the girls joined in the games of playground football rather than sticking to the girlie games of skipping and hopscotch. At the last village school she'd attended, the girls and boys had been strictly segregated and had skirted around each other warily. If a boy was seen walking home with a girl, or even speaking to one, he was teased unmercifully by his peers. 'Is she your girlfriend?' And the boy would blush, hang his head and thrust his hands deep into his trouser pockets and walk away. And that had been the end of any blossoming friendship, nipped in the bud before it could even begin.

But here it was different. The school had separate playgrounds for boys and girls, but they never seemed to stay in them. Boys came into the girls' quadrangle and girls into the boys'. And no one seemed to bother to stop them. The teaching staff were conspicuous by their absence at break time and lunchtime, no doubt huddled in the staff rooms taking a well-earned respite.

Jenny now attended a secondary school. There were no primary school children there, only eleven-year-olds and upwards.

'I'm surprised you've been evacuated to us,' her form teacher reiterated the children's comments as Jenny answered her questions about her age and previous school. 'A lot of our children have been evacuated out of Sheffield, not into it.'

'Don't tell 'em we've been in Derbyshire,' Dot had warned her as she'd set off for school on the first morning. 'Make out you've just come from London.'

But the children who were still left in the city were friendly enough and soon Jenny was involved in their games and forming tentative new friendships. And the very best thing about the new school was the art teacher, Miss Wells – a perceptive, go-ahead young woman who spotted Jenny's natural talent at once and, without setting her apart from her peers, quietly encouraged the girl.

They settled in with Jim; he was an easy-going man who was pathetically grateful for their company and even more thrilled to have a woman like Dot sharing his bed. And he was kind and generous towards Jenny. As he had promised, he redecorated the small bedroom where she slept, bought new bedcovers and told her to tell him if there was anything she needed. 'Anything at all, Jenny, and I'll try to get it for you.'

Tears prickled her throat. They were the same words that Charlotte had used when Jenny had first arrived at the manor. Now she smiled at Jim and murmured, 'You're very kind.'

'Now don't you go spoiling her,' Dot simpered.

*

Jenny was surprisingly happy at the school and whilst she still missed Bobby and the rest of the Hutton family, most of all she yearned to go back to Lincolnshire. She knew she couldn't – they didn't want her – but it didn't stop the longing deep inside.

'You're leaving school at the end of term,' Dot announced one morning over breakfast. Jim was already at work in the shop, but Dot was still in her dressing gown, her hair done up in curlers, smoking her first cigarette of the day and drinking tea.

Jenny's chin stuck out stubbornly. 'I don't want to leave. I like it there. Miss Wells says—'

'Miss Wells, Miss Wells – that's all I seem to hear from you. And who's this famous Miss Wells, when she's at home?' Dot glanced at her daughter and her eyes narrowed spitefully. 'At least she seems to be taking the place of those bloody Thorntons.' She snorted. 'I s'pose that's something to be grateful for.' There was silence between them whilst Jenny gritted her teeth and glared defiantly at her mother.

'And you can take that look off your face. If I say yer leaving school, then yer leaving, ne'er mind what any teacher ses. Jim wants you to work in the shop and *I* want you to be earning yer keep, so there.'

Jenny turned away, her eyes filling with tears. She already helped Jim out in the shop after school and at weekends. It was all right, she supposed. He was nice to her and thoughtful, but it could be very cold standing behind the counter all day. The meat had to be kept as cool as possible and Jim insisted the shop door was left open at all times, even when there was a gale blowing or it was pelting with rain. And it was summer now. What on earth it would be like in the winter, Jenny dared not think.

'My customers'll think I'm closed if my door's not open,' Jim explained one particularly wet day. 'Can't have that, now can we? Now, love, would you like to check the coupons for me?' He bent towards her, leaning a little too close for Jenny's liking. 'You can sit in the back where it's warmer.'

And so when the holidays came, Jenny said a sorrowful farewell to her classmates and an even sadder goodbye to Miss Wells.

'Keep up your drawing and painting, Jenny. You've a real talent. If only . . .' The young woman had bitten her lip, not wanting to cause the young girl any more anguish. She knew of Jenny's hopes and dreams. But she'd met Dot once and knew without even being told that Jenny's chances of further education were nil. Jenny's mother wanted her working and the sooner the better.

It was not unusual for parents to want their children to leave school as soon as they were able, but it was such a shame in Jenny's case. She was only of average ability in other subjects but her artwork was outstanding. Miss Wells even enlisted the headmaster's help, but there was nothing either of them could do in the face of the mother's demands.

On the first morning of the summer holidays, Jenny started work full time in the butcher's shop. She'd wondered if she'd see Arthur bringing further supplies but it seemed he never came near the place now.

'Can't blame him, I suppose,' Jim had said when she'd feigned innocence and asked. 'After all, I've stolen his girls, haven't I?' But it seemed that Jim still had other black market suppliers and the 'under-the-counter' meat was still available for those who could afford to pay an extortionate price for it. The only wonder of it all was that no one ever reported Jim to the authorities, but she supposed most of them were only too glad to take advantage of a bit more meat now and again and purposely never asked questions. As for Dot, she went out into the centre of town every day, roaming around the shops, trying on all the latest fashions and coming home most days with something new. Jim spoiled her even more than Arthur had done, his gratitude for her presence in his life knowing no bounds.

Jim had always been very careful with whom he dealt for his black market supplies. He'd only trade with men he knew, with whom he'd built up a trust. And the same went for his customers; he knew them all, knew they lived in the area. But then, after several months of keeping Dot in the manner she demanded and having to find a small wage for Jenny each week, Jim began to feel the drain on his savings. He began to take risks in dealing with people he didn't know. He began to buy meat from anyone who came into his shop and offered it to him, when it had obviously been obtained dishonestly. And he was willing to sell his meat to complete strangers if they asked him, with a wink and a nod, if he had anything 'under the counter'. Jenny guessed that his recklessness was because he was trying to keep Dot happy, but Jenny knew her mother. The more anyone gave Dot, the more she would take and the more she would demand.

It was only a matter of time before something went wrong.

Forty-Three

They'd been with Jim almost a year. Jenny had been working in the shop since she'd left school. She enjoyed the work, chatting to the customers, serving them, taking their money and giving them their change. The only thing she'd hated was the cold winter weather blasting in through the ever-open door. But now it was spring again and the sun dappled the tiled floor in the shop and the gusts of wind blowing in were warmer. Jenny was a quick learner and Jim had come to rely on her. He also knew he could trust her and no longer sent her through to the back or upstairs when his black market suppliers appeared. She even tried to warn him of the risks he was taking.

'Did you know him?' she asked bluntly as a man who'd brought them some very nice cuts of steak left the shop.

Jim shrugged. 'I can't afford to be choosy these days, love. Stuff's getting harder to come by and— Ah, good morning, madam, and what can I get for you this fine day?'

Jim rested his hands flat on the counter and leaned towards a woman whom Jenny had only seen in the shop once before. She was dressed in a navy mackintosh with a felt hat pulled down low over her face. Outside a man hovered in front of the shop window, watching.

Jenny bit her lip and pulled at Jim's arm, trying to warn him, but it was too late.

'Like a nice bit of sausage, madam?' He leaned even closer to the woman and dropped his voice. 'Or a nice bit of steak?'

The man came into the shop and held out his identity card. Jim's usually florid face turned pale and he began to sweat.

'We've been watching your shop for some time. You're under arrest for trading in black market goods,' the man said.

Jenny thought Jim was going to faint. 'I – I –' he began to splutter. 'I can explain it. A friend of mine killed a pig. He has a proper licence and—'

'I'm sorry, Mr Bradshaw, we know this isn't just a one-off.' His glance rested on Jenny. 'Is she in on it too?'

'Good Heavens, no. She's only fourteen.'

'Hmm.' The man was thoughtful. 'Well, we won't take any action against a minor, not this time. But be warned, young lady, if you break the law, of what will happen to you, no matter what age you are. Now, you'll need to close your shop, Mr Bradshaw, and come with us.'

'Close the shop?' Jim was scandalized. 'I can't close the shop.'

'I'm afraid you'll have to. We'll be sending in our chaps to confiscate your meat.'

'Oh aye,' Jim laughed bitterly. 'And we all know what that means, don't we? You and your cronies will all be eating well tonight.'

'Now, now, Mr Bradshaw. Insulting us won't get you anywhere. In fact, it'll make things worse for you. We're only doing our job.'

'Well, it's a pity you haven't got owt better to do

than persecute folks who are only trying to help their neighbours get through this wretched war.'

'Breaking the regulations is a criminal offence. You could be facing a jail sentence.'

Jim's bluster died at once and he turned even paler. 'Jenny, lass, fetch yer mam down here, will yer?'

Jenny scuttled up the stairs. Luckily, Dot was home, cooking a nice piece of steak for their tea.

'Mum, Mum, come quick, Uncle Jim's being arrested!'

Dot's mouth dropped open and then, as she digested the news, her mouth tightened. 'Huh, I should have known. I should've stayed wiv Arfer. He knew 'ow to keep out of trouble.'

'He wants you to come down.'

'Not flippin' likely.'

'But you'll have to. They're taking him away.'

'I'll do no such thing.' She gripped Jenny's arm and held on to it. 'And neither will you. You stay up here. They can't come up here. Not unless they've got a warrant. Stay out of it.'

They could hear the commotion downstairs now, as Jim shouted for Dot. Dot dragged Jenny with her to the front window and they peered carefully through the curtains as Jim was dragged from the premises. He cast one last despairing glance up at the window, but Dot stepped smartly back. 'Don't let him see you.'

'But we've got to do something. We've got to help him.'

'Why?'

'He – he's been good to us.'

Dot's mouth twisted in a sneer. 'He got what he wanted. What all men want. Now, we've got to think about ourselves. We're out of here.'

'But, Mum—'

'No buts. We're going.'

'Where?'

Now Dot smiled broadly. 'Where d'yer think? Back to London, of course.'

'London? But – but we ran away from there. Won't we be in trouble if we go back?'

'Nah. It was Arfer they was after, not us. We're pure as the driven snow, Jen.'

Jenny cast a wry glance at her mother, but said no more.

'Get packing and be quick about it. We don't want to be here when that lot come back. They might arrest me as his accomplice. I can talk me way out of most things, but they might think they can pin something on me. Come on, get a move on.'

And they got a move on. Jenny's belongings were soon packed and ready, but Dot's took a little longer.

'Jen, climb up that ladder into the loft and see'f Jim's got any suitcases up there. I can't get all me stuff into just one.'

Jenny smiled wryly. There was no way her mother would get all the fancy clothes, shoes and handbags she'd acquired recently into one suitcase, nor even three or four.

Jenny climbed the ladder nimbly and poked her head into the dark space. She heard a rustling in the far corner. Mice, she thought, but the little creatures held no fear for her.

''Ave yer got a torch, Mum? I can't see a thing up here.'

Dot was gone a few moments before she came back with the torch that Jim had kept in the shop. She handed it up to Jenny. 'Look sharp, Jen. They'll be coming back any minute. Who were they? The police?'

'I don't know. They held out an identity card but I couldn't read it. They weren't in uniform, though.'

'Plain clothes. That's how they catch folk. Do hurry up, Jen.'

Jenny clambered up into the loft and shone the torch around. There was all sorts of clutter in the loft. How she would love to delve amongst it, if only there was more time. But her mother's insistent pleas to hurry kept reminding her that there was no time to dally.

After a moment or two, she called down: 'I can't see any suitcases, but there's a big trunk.'

'That'll do.'

'It'll be heavy.'

'We'll manage,' Dot called back, determined not to leave any of her belongings behind.

Luckily, the trunk wasn't locked, but Jenny struggled with the fastening.

'Come *on*, Jen.' Dot's impatient voice drifted up into the loft.

'It's full of stuff,' Jen shouted as she threw back the lid. 'Old clothes.'

'Anything decent?'

'Can't see, but it smells all fusty. Ugh. There's something furry.'

'Is it a fur coat?' Dot's tone was suddenly interested and eager, all thoughts of the time passing forgotten.

Jenny pulled it out. 'I can't see.'

'Let me have a look. Throw it down here.'

Jenny crawled back to the opening and threw the garment down. It landed on Dot's upturned face and Jenny smothered her giggles as she watched her mother fighting her way out from under it.

'Blimey, Jen,' came Dot's excited voice. 'It's a real fur coat. I could 'ave done with this in the winter.'

So could I, Jenny thought ruefully. I'd have worn it in the shop. Aloud she said, 'But it pongs to high heaven, Mum, of mothballs or something. You can't wear that.'

'When we get home, I can hang it in the yard – let the fresh air get to it. My, it's a nice one. I wonder whose it was.'

Jenny crawled back to the trunk and tipped the rest of the clothes on to the boarded floor of the loft, then dragged the trunk to the opening. It was heavy for the young girl, even without anything in it.

'I don't reckon it's going to come down through the hole, Mum.'

'Course it will.' Dot was determined. 'It must 'ave gone up in the first place, so it'll have to come down.'

Dot climbed up the ladder to help manoeuvre it from below and eventually, with much pulling and pushing and swearing from Dot, the trunk was tugged through the hole and slid down the ladder. Jenny scrambled down after it and they carried it into the bedroom Dot had shared with Jim.

Dot knelt in front of it and threw back the lid, smiling as she saw the vastness of the interior. 'Perfect,' she muttered. 'Now, Jen, pass me my clothes off the bed.'

'We'll never lift it,' Jenny muttered as the items began to fill the big trunk.

'Then we'll drag it,' Dot snapped. 'Now, is that everything?' Dot glanced around the room. There was nothing left to say that she had ever been there. 'Sit on the lid, Jen, while I fasten it. There. Now get hold of that end.' But there was no way the woman and the girl were ever going to lift it. 'Just push it, then, an' I'll pull.'

Somehow they got it to the top of the stairs and pushed it down. It slid, bumping on every step and crashing into the walls on either side as it went, landing with a thud at the bottom.

'I 'ope it hasn't smashed it open,' Dot said worriedly, ignoring the scratch marks and the torn wallpaper its rapid descent had caused. But the trunk was sturdy and intact.

'Right, 'ave we got everything?' Back in the bedroom, her greedy glance swept the room. 'Yer know, I quite fancy them vases on the mantelpiece – '

'Mum, it's—' Jenny had been about to say 'it's stealing', but she knew that wouldn't even prick Dot's conscience. She sometimes wondered if her mother had such a thing. She altered what she had been going to say to, 'We can't carry anything else,' and then added craftily, 'It'll hamper us.'

Jenny didn't want them taking anything that wasn't theirs. Jim had been good to them both and she didn't want to steal from him. The poor man was in enough trouble. The time they'd lived with Jim had been easier for her in some ways than things had been with Arthur. School had been fine; she'd felt more at home with the city kids. And when she'd left, she'd quite enjoyed working in the shop except when it had been so cold.

But now she was going home. Back to London. Back to the streets and the people she knew and Jenny felt happiness surge through her. And though, even then, to say that there was nowhere else she would rather be was not quite right, she had to accept that she could never again go back there.

Forty-Four

Within three hours of Jim's arrest, they'd locked the shop up, posted the key through the letter box and were on their way to the railway station, dragging the heavy trunk behind them and each carrying a suitcase. Every so often they kept stopping for a rest.

'We'll never manage this, Mum,' Jenny panted. 'Everyone's staring at us.'

'Let 'em,' Dot said through gritted teeth.

'Want any help, love?'

They both looked round to see a workman digging rubble on a bomb site at the side of the road. 'Catching a train, a' ya?'

Dot straightened up and smiled her most winning smile. 'That's right.'

'Long way to the station for you two lovely ladies to be dragging that thing.' He nodded towards the trunk. 'Got all ya wordly goods in there, 'ave ya?'

Dot moved closer to the man.

'Actually, we probably have.' Dot opened her hand-bag and fished out a handkerchief. Then she dabbed her eyes gently so as not to smudge her make-up, which had not been applied with her usual care this morning because of her haste to get away. 'We were bombed out in London and came here to escape. But – but – ' her voice quavered – 'it's not much better here, is it?' She nodded towards the buildings nearby, some left only half standing, their inner rooms open to the elements now. There were even pieces of furniture left standing precariously on shaky floors. And beneath the man's feet was a pile of bricks that had once been someone's home.

The man clambered over the debris and shook the dirt from his overalls. 'Aye, it's a right bugger, ain't it, missis? Now, let's see'f me and my mate can help you.' He raised his voice. 'Ron, 'ere a minute. We need your strong arms.'

A man digging on another bomb site on the other side of the road looked up. He flung down his shovel and crossed the road. 'What's up, Bert?' Jenny almost giggled aloud. The man had the same name as her faithful old teddy, who was once again squashed into the top of her suitcase.

'These two lovely ladies need an 'and. And I reckon we're just the fellers to do it, don't you?'

Ron now eyed Dot whilst she simpered and smiled up at him. Jenny groaned inwardly, but for once she appreciated her mother's flirting might get them some badly needed help. The two men, strong from their manual labour, lifted the trunk between them easily.

'Where a' we going, Bert?'

'Railway station, Ron. These ladies are going home to London. You ready?'

'Aye. Lead on.'

At the station the men carried the trunk on to the platform and set it down.

'Now, let's find you a porter, missis.'

'Oh please, don't trouble yourselves any further,' Dot said, and added enthusiastically, 'you've been *wonder-*

ful. Please, will you let me buy you both a cup of tea? It's the least I can do.'

'That'd be right nice, love. But it's no trouble for me to find you a porter to look after you.' He winked at Dot. 'Me brother-in-law works here. If I can find him . . .' The man looked about him. 'Ah, there 'ee is.' He raised his voice to a man in uniform trundling an upright barrow along the platform. Jenny had see something similar at Ravensfleet; Ben had called it a sack barrow.

'Walter, over here, lad. You're just the man we want.'

As the man called Walter approached, Dot turned her smile upon him too.

'These ladies are catching a train, but this trunk's a big 'un.'

Walter grinned and nodded at Dot. 'Leave it to me, Bert. I'll see 'em safely on to the train. Which one a' ya catching?'

'I'm not sure yet. I haven't got our tickets. But we want the next one to London.'

'Well now, you might 'ave a bit of a wait. Next one's not till half past two and it'll probably be running late. And you'll probably 'ave to change at Doncaster. An' it'll be crowded. A lot of troops on the move, ya know.'

'I didn't know, but I can believe it.'

Bert guffawed. 'They'll look after you, love.'

Jenny felt ashamed. Bert had obviously eyed her mother up and seen her for exactly what she was. But the girl swallowed her pride and tried to smile. At this moment, they needed the help of men like Bert, his mate and his brother-in-law and they might also be very glad of help from soldiers, too, heaving the massive trunk on and off the train.

*

The journey was surprisingly enjoyable, even though the train was packed with soldiers and airmen, travelling either back to camp or home on leave.

'You can sit on my knee, love,' one soldier, older than most of the others, said, winking at Dot.

'Ta very much, I'm sure.' Dot winked back at him and promptly sat on his knee. The astonished look on the soldier's face had the rest of the carriage laughing. He hadn't expected such a response but then he didn't know Dot. 'There's a lot of you. Where are you all going?'

'Back to camp,' the man on whose knee Dot was sitting said. 'All leave's been cancelled.'

'Watch it, mate,' one of the soldiers next to him muttered. 'Careless talk and all that.'

There was an awkward silence for a moment until Dot giggled and said, 'Do I look like a spy, then?'

'Actually, love, you do,' the soldier who'd given the warning said, but he was smiling. 'You're the sort of pretty lady that us poor mutts would tell anything to.'

Everyone who'd heard the exchange of conversation laughed and then, deftly changing the subject, a young, fresh-faced airman with fair hair asked Jenny, 'Are you going to sit on mine?' His eyes crinkled when he smiled and his blue eyes were friendly and honest. He reminded her sharply of Georgie. 'I don't bite. My name's Mike.' He held out his hand to shake hers.

'Now, you go carefully with the likes of 'im, love,' one of the soldiers put in. 'You know what these RAF types are like. You're safer with us squaddies.'

On and on the banter and the laughter went, but they shared food and drink with Dot and Jenny and even persuaded them to join in a game of cards. Jenny quickly grasped the rules.

'I reckon you've played before, Jenny,' Mike teased her as she won again. 'Good job we're not playing for money, I'd lose all me pay.'

It was almost eight o'clock by the time they arrived in London though it hadn't seemed to take that long with the cheerful company they'd had on the journey. There were plenty of willing hands to help them off the train with their luggage, but once on the platform, they were alone.

'Well, we're not going to lug that thing on the underground, Mum. We can manage our cases, but not the trunk.'

Dot glanced around her. 'We'll leave it in the left-luggage office and I'll get someone to fetch it tomorrow.'

Jenny was about to say 'Who? There's no Uncle Arthur around now.' But she bit back the words. Dot, she was sure, would soon find someone to take his place and run her little errands.

At last, they were turning into the street where they'd once lived.

Dot stopped and stared. 'Well, bugger me! It's gone.'

Jenny, struggling with her heavy suitcase, dumped it on to the ground and looked down the street.

Where their house had once stood was a gaping hole and a mound of rubble. Jenny didn't know how to feel. She was sad that their home had gone. Whilst she'd not expected any of the few belongings they'd left behind still to be there, there was no chance they'd find anything now. And yet her disappointment was mingled with relief; relief that they had not been here when the bomb had struck. She gasped as a sudden thought struck her. 'Mum – Aunty Elsie and the others? Their house has gone an' all. D'you reckon they're all right?'

''Ow should I know?' Dot snapped. 'Where are *we* goin' ter go? That's what I'd like to know.'

'Let's ask,' Jenny said, ignoring her mother's concerns. She was far more anxious about her friends than where they would sleep that night. There was always a shelter somewhere. 'There's still folks living here.' She picked up her suitcase and set off down the street towards a woman sweeping the pavement in front of her house. It seemed like a thankless task to Jenny, but she admired the woman's spirit; she wasn't going to let a few of Hitler's bombs stop her housewifely pride. She was still trying to keep up her standards even this late in the evening.

Grumbling, Dot teetered after her.

'Mrs Smart,' Jenny called and the woman glanced up and the puzzled look on her face told Jenny that their former neighbour didn't recognize her. She'd grown and filled out in the time they'd been away.

'It's me, Mrs Smart. Jenny.'

The woman's face broke into a beam. ''Ello, Jen. 'Ow are yer? My, you've grown into a pretty mare.'

Jenny giggled. It was good to hear Gladys Smart's raucous voice again. That was the only thing she'd really missed; the sound of Londoners' voices.

As Gladys glanced beyond Jenny to see Dot struggling down the street with her case, her voice hardened. 'I see you've brought her back, then.'

Jenny bit her lip. Her mother's 'carryings on' hadn't endeared her to their neighbours. Only Elsie had overlooked Dot's faults. As Dot neared them, Gladys sighed, giving in to her better nature. She leaned her broom against the wall. 'You'd best come in and have a cuppa whilst we put our thinking caps on.'

'Eh?'

'Where you're gonna go.' Gladys nodded her head towards the ruins of Jenny's former home.

'Oh, I see what you mean.' Jenny turned and called to her mother. 'Come on, Mum. Mrs Smart's goin' to make us a cuppa.'

Dot stopped in her tracks and it was her turn to let out a surprised 'Eh?' Gladys Smart had never had time for Dot, but it seemed that a shared adversity brought out the best in folk. At least, in some people. In others, it gave the darker side of their character the chance to emerge. Jenny shuddered when she thought just how close they'd both come to being in trouble with the police, first with Arthur and then with Jim.

Dot put on the smile she used to charm women; it was somewhat different to the flirtatious one she adopted around men.

'Come on in.' Gladys beckoned them both. 'We ain't got much, but what we've got, you're welcome to share. I'll get you something to eat. I bet you're both hungry, aren't you?'

Jenny smiled. It was good to be back amongst the warm-hearted East Enders. Resolutely, she pushed aside thoughts of Ravensfleet and everyone there.

Forty-Five

'Where've yer been then, all this time?' Gladys asked as she poured the tea and pushed the cups across the table towards Dot and Jenny.

Dot cast a warning glance at her daughter. Already she'd instructed her, 'Don't you go tellin' folks where we've been. Least said, an' all that, and what they don't know they can't go tittle-tattling about.'

'Up north,' Dot said blithely. 'All over the place.'

'And what about that spiv you was with? Where's 'ee then?'

Dot sniffed. 'Gawd knows, Glad. We split up a while back.'

'You're well shot of 'im, Dot. None of us liked what he was up to. Get us all a bad name, the likes of 'im would.'

Jenny kept her eyes down, biting her lip to stop herself saying anything. Dot obviously wasn't going to divulge details about her latest amour and *his* goings-on. She hoped, when she met up with Bobby again, he wouldn't ask too many questions. She wasn't good at telling lies, even though she'd had good training! Thinking of her own friends allowed her to open up a safer topic of conversation. 'Is Bobby all right? And all his family? D'you know?'

'Living in the next street,' Gladys said promptly, gesturing towards the street that ran parallel to theirs

310

beyond the back of her house. 'In fact, their yard backs on to mine. We often 'ave a chin wag, me an' Elsie.'

'Can I go round and see'f Bobby's there, Mum?'

'Not yet. We've got to find somewhere to go. Do yer know of anywhere, Glad?'

Gladys Smart frowned. 'There's a lot of places empty, Dot. 'Specially them what's been bombed, but I don't know of anywhere round here that's habitable.'

'Maybe Aunty Elsie will know,' Jenny put in eagerly. 'Do let me go and see her.'

'Go on, then. I can see I'm not going to get a minute's peace till you do.' Dot glanced at Gladys and muttered, 'Kids!'

But Dot Mercer wasn't going to get any sympathy from Gladys Smart. She'd brought up seven children, all grown up and flown now. Two of her sons were in the army and a daughter was in the Auxiliary Territorial Service, working as a driver, and Gladys would have really given her eye teeth to have them all safely at home with her again. Even her old man was still working on the docks, which were in ever-present danger from bombing.

Jenny jumped up and headed for the front door. 'Thanks for the tea, Mrs Smart.'

'Yer can go through the back. Their back gate's opposite ours.'

Jenny retraced her steps through the kitchen and then through the scullery and out into the backyard.

Gladys watched her go. 'Now, Dot,' she began firmly, 'let me give you a piece of advice. You may not want it, but you're goin' ter get it anyway. Watch that little lass of yours. She's growing into a real little beauty. You'll have the lads round her like bees round a honeypot before you know it.'

311

Dot sniffed derisively. 'I don't reckon she's interested in lads, Gladys. Not normal, if you ask me. At her age, I had a steady boyfriend.'

Gladys gestured again with her head after the disappearing girl. ''Er dad?'

Dot laughed. 'Nah. Don't be daft, Gladys. Me first was a spotty-faced lad who trembled when he so much as kissed me.'

'Who was 'er dad, Dot? You've never said.'

'No,' Dot said shortly. 'And I'm not going to now.' She felt like giving Gladys Smart a piece of her mind. Nosy old busybody! But Dot was sharp enough to realize that she needed the goodwill of all her former neighbours if she was going to get back on her feet and find a place for herself and her daughter to live. She hoped Jenny would have better luck at the Huttons.

But Gladys wasn't done with Dot Mercer yet. She'd waited years to get the young woman, who gave the impression she thought herself better than all her neighbours, in a metaphorical headlock.

Dot sighed. 'Jenny was a mistake, Gladys. I admit that.'

Gladys laughed wryly and there was sympathy in her tone when she said, 'Aye, an' you've never hidden the fact, have you, Dot? Not even from Jen.' The woman's sympathy was not for Dot, but for the young girl who'd grown up with the knowledge that she'd never been wanted. The mere thought saddened and angered Gladys.

''Ello, darlin'. It's good to see you,' Elsie Hutton said on opening her back door to Jenny's knock. The woman swept Jenny into her arms and gave her a bear hug. 'We 'aven't half missed yer. Come in, come in. Our Bobby'll be back soon. He's working now, of course. 'Spect you are too. Come in, do. Like a cuppa?'

'No, thank you, Aunty Elsie. We've just had one at Mrs Smart's. Mum's still there.'

Elsie's eyebrows shot up. 'Yer mam's at Gladys's? Well, wonders never cease.'

'I asked Mrs Smart if she knew where you were and she sent me through the back way.'

'It was all we could find. Not up to much. Not as nice as the houses we both had. But they're gone now and that's that. Got ter make the best of it, ain't we?'

'Do you know of anywhere that might be vacant to rent? We need somewhere to live.'

Elsie grimaced. 'I don't, love. Any building round here that's habitable is crowded out already. We were lucky to get somewhere close to where we used to live.' Elsie's face sagged. 'We lost ev'rything, Jen. Every blessed thing. You was lucky you got out when you did.' She laughed wryly. 'At least that Arfer were good for something. If it hadn't been for him having to scarper from the coppers, you might still have been here when we was bombed.'

'Did – did anyone get hurt?'

Elsie shook her head. 'No, thank God. We were all down the underground.' Now she stared at Jenny as if really seeing her for the first time and a slow smile spread across her kindly face. 'My, but you've grown up since we last saw yer. Our Bobby won't know yer.'

Jenny blushed and murmured, ''Spect he's grown too.'

And now Elsie asked the same question Gladys had. 'Where've yer been, then?'

'Up north,' Jenny muttered, following her mother's lead.

'Where you were before? When you was evacuated?'

Jenny shook her head as the familiar lump formed in her throat. Back home with Aunty Elsie, she was tempted to spill it all out. The hurt of being sent back home by the Thorntons, of not being wanted by anyone, of being dragged into thieving and deceit. And worst of all, not knowing – not really knowing – about Georgie. Perhaps she'd never know, since they didn't want to see her again. She felt the overwhelming urge to throw her arms around Elsie's waist and bury her head against her. The woman's voice pulled her back to the present. 'Tell you what, you and yer mam can stop here for a night or two till you find a place. No longer than that, mind.' Elsie wagged her finger. '*You* could stay here as long as you liked, Jen, but I can't be putting up with yer mam's goings on. Not under my roof.'

Jenny beamed as she jumped up. 'Thanks, Aunty Elsie. I'll go and tell her.'

Only moments later, Dot was tottering through the back door on her high heels. 'I knew you wouldn't let me down, Elsie. How've yer been?'

'Lucky, that's what we've been, Dot,' Elsie said grimly.

'Eh?' Dot blinked and glanced around her at the damp, peeling wallpaper, the old furniture – what little of it there was – and turned her nose up. 'You call this "luck"?'

Elsie laughed. 'Lucky not to have been killed, yer daft mare. And Sid's all right, far as I know. And all the boys. Yes, Dot, right now I count myself lucky.' Her glance ran up and down Dot, spotting the short skirt, the smart jacket and the new shoes. 'But you look as if you can't complain. Fallen on yer feet by lying on yer back, 'ave yer?'

'Elsie Hutton – mind what you're saying in front of my daughter.'

Elsie laughed even louder. 'I don't reckon there's much that little lass doesn't know.' She paused and then nodded towards Jenny. 'An' she's not so little now, is she?'

Dot turned her head and looked at her daughter as if really seeing her for the first time. 'You're right,' she murmured. 'Gladys – nosy old cow – was just saying the same thing.'

'Oh, so I'm a nosy old cow, an' all, am I?'

'No, no, Elsie, I didn't mean you. You're my friend – friend of the family. You can say what yer like, but 'er! She's always turned her nose up at us.'

Elsie chuckled to herself. She knew exactly what Dot was like and was still her friend, though, now they were back, she was determined to see that Jenny was treated a little better. 'Come on in, Dot. Make yourself at home. This all yer luggage?'

'There's a trunk at the station, Aunty Elsie. We'll have to get someone to fetch it.'

'Bobby might be able to help you there. He's working for a grocer who's bought a horse and cart 'cos of the petrol shortages. Bobby seems to get on all right with him so he might let Bobby fetch your trunk. Now, let's get you upstairs. You can 'ave Ronnie's room. He won't be home for a while. You don't mind sharing, do yer?'

For a moment, Dot looked as if she minded very much but a sharp nudge from her daughter reminded her that they had nowhere else to go.

'Why? Where is he?' Jenny asked.

Elsie turned slowly to look at her, her eyes suddenly full of the anxiety she carried every day. 'In the army, love.'

Jenny gasped. 'I hadn't realized he'd be old enough,'

she murmured, realizing that it was not only she who'd grown up in the time she'd been away.

And Bobby had grown and filled out too. When he came home just before nine after working late, his face split into a broad grin when he saw who was sitting at the table.

'My, you've grown,' he said, looking her up and down.

'So've you,' Jenny laughed.

'Yeah, but I ain't made as good a job of it as you, Jen.'

'Oh, I don't know,' Dot sidled up to him and put her arm round his shoulders, pulling him close to her, 'you're getting to be quite a handsome young feller.'

'Now, now, Dot, put him down, he's too young for you,' Elsie teased and laughed inwardly when she saw Dot's sulky pout. The woman never liked to be reminded how old she was getting. Deliberately, Elsie changed the subject. 'Dot and Jen are staying for a night or two until they can find somewhere to live. Can you ask around, Bobby?'

'No need,' Bobby said promptly. 'There's a place at the end of this street just come vacant. Folks have done a moonlight. I know, cos I've been knocking on their door for a week or more for the rent money they owe Mr Jenkins.'

'Who's Mr Jenkins when he's at home?' Dot asked.

'The bloke I work for. He owns quite a bit of property round here.' He pointed to the ground beneath his feet. 'He owns this one.'

Dot smiled and put her head on one side, her eyes sparkling as she looked at Bobby. 'Sounds like I should meet this nice Mr Jenkins. Where's he live? Above his shop?'

Bobby laughed. 'Nah. He's got a big house a few streets away.'

'Has he now?' Dot murmured and Elsie cast her eyes heavenwards. Dot Mercer would never change. She just hoped Jenny wasn't going to follow in her mother's footsteps.

Forty-Six

'Right, Bobby, are you going to take me to see this nice boss of yours?' Dot asked Bobby the following day when the boy came home at midday for his dinner. 'Jen, you help Elsie with the washing-up.'

Bobby glanced at his mother, who gave a little nod. 'Come on then, Aunty Dot.'

'Eh, none of this "Aunty" lark now. Not from a big lad like you.' Dot fluffed her hair. 'Let me just put a bit more lipstick on. I want to look my best.'

When they'd left the house and Elsie and Jenny had carried the dirty pots through to the scullery to begin the washing-up, Elsie asked quietly, 'How've you been, Jen? Really?'

It was tempting – very tempting – to tell the woman who'd always watched out for her, whose youngest son had always been her best friend, just what had been going on. But she couldn't do it. She couldn't let her mother down. For all she knew it might get them both into serious trouble with the police if it leaked out just what they had been up to in Derbyshire and Sheffield.

So Jenny shrugged and tried to act nonchalantly. 'It was all right. We moved around a bit.'

'And what about Arthur? What went wrong there?'

Jenny licked her lips nervously. She'd have to tell Elsie some of what had happened or she would begin to realize the girl was holding back. So Jenny smiled brightly and told as much of the truth as she dared. When you're telling lies, Arthur had always said, tell as much of the truth as you can. It's easier to remember. 'There was this bloke who was friendly with Uncle Arthur.'

'Oh aye.' Elsie's tone was sceptical. 'One of his spiv mates, I suppose.'

'No, no.' Jenny hesitated. Elsie was sharp. If she said too much the woman would guess exactly what sort of a 'friend' Jim had been.

'Anyway,' she ploughed on, 'to cut a long story short, Mum ended up moving in with Jim.'

'And what about you? Where were you when all this was going on?' Elsie was tight-lipped. Whatever had this poor girl been subjected to?

'Jim was very good to both of us. He even tried to get Mum to let me stay on at school and try for the art school in the city.'

'What city was that, then?'

Jenny bit her lip. She was such a truthful girl, she was finding it hard to tell a convincing story without telling deliberate lies. She took a deep breath. Surely there could be no harm in talking about Sheffield? It was such a big city, it would be safer than divulging exactly where they'd been in Derbyshire in much smaller communities.

'Sheffield.'

'So why're you here, then? Why've you come back?'

Now, Jenny couldn't meet Elsie's eyes. 'Oh, you know Mum. Doesn't stay with anyone for very long. We were with Jim a whole year and as for Arthur, well, he lasted over four.'

'Mm.' Elsie eyed her shrewdly. That was true enough though Elsie knew there was more than Jenny was telling her, but she decided not to press her. As long as it was nothing that had harmed Jenny, then Elsie wasn't worried. Dot could take care of herself, but the young girl was another matter and now they were back home Elsie meant to keep a sharp eye out for how Jenny was treated.

'Have you kept on with your drawing, then?' Elsie had known about Jenny's ability for years. On wet days, the children – Jenny amongst them – had sat at her kitchen table playing games or drawing pictures. Even then, Jenny's picture had always been the best and easily recognizable for whatever it was.

Now they were on safer ground, Jenny smiled easily, 'Oh yes. Uncle Arthur was very good about it. He used to bring me drawing paper and paints. I did loads of pictures, but – but I had to leave them behind.'

'Ne'er mind, darlin', you can soon do more.' There was a pause before Elsie asked gently, 'Your mam still not interested in your painting, then?'

Jenny shook her head. 'I've run out of a lot of my paints now and I've hardly any paper left.

Elsie squeezed her arm. 'I'll get our Sammy to see what he can do. He knows a lot of people. He works on the docks now. At least – ' Elsie bit her lip – 'at least until he's called up.'

Jenny's eyes widened. 'Sammy?'

Elsie nodded. 'He's eighteen next January.'

Jenny stared at her. Poor Aunty Elsie. She'd have three of her family in the forces then. 'Maybe it'll all be over before then.' She couldn't think of anything else to say but they both knew it was a vain hope.

'We met a lot of soldiers – and airmen – on the train when we were coming home. One of them said all their leave had been cancelled. He might have said more, but one of his mates shushed him.'

Elsie laughed. 'Quite right too, though we've heard rumours that there might be something going on. Evidently there's been a lot of movement of troops to the south coast. Sammy hears bits of gossip, y'know, from the dockers. Let's hope they're starting to get back at old 'Itler.'

'What a lovely man,' Dot enthused when she returned over an hour later. 'Donald says we can move in whenever we like. And he'll give us the first month free 'cos the place needs a bit of tarting up.'

Elsie raised her eyebrows and pursed her lips. She'd never heard of any landlord being quite so generous before. And already, it seemed, Dot was on first-name terms with him whereas Elsie had known him for years and still called him 'Mr Jenkins'.

'*And*,' Dot went on, 'he's letting Bobby borrow his horse and cart after work to fetch our trunk.'

'Bobby's always said he's all right, is Mr Jenkins,' Elsie said.

Dot's eyes sparkled with triumph as she waved a door key at them. 'He certainly is.'

Elsie sighed.

The house at the end of the street was habitable; just.

'It needs a lot of elbow grease,' Elsie remarked, wrinkling her nose. This was something Dot wasn't very good at, but Jenny's eyes were sparkling. 'It's bigger than our old place, Mum. There are *three* bedrooms.

Oh Mum, can I have the big one at the back? *Please*?' Jenny knew better than to ask to take possession of two of the rooms, but the one at the back had a bigger window than the other two. The natural lighting was good and there was room enough for her to set out her paints on a table under the window. She'd soon find another job, she was sure, and then she'd be able to buy paints and paper for herself.

'Yeah, course you can.' Dot was walking through the house with a smile on her face. True, it needed a lot of cleaning and a lick of paint wouldn't do it any harm. She was seeing herself nicely settled here, and entertaining her friends. And the room Jenny had set her heart on at the back was nicely out of the way. 'We'll get you some paint – a pretty pink – and you can decorate it.'

'You'll have to ask the landlord first, Dot,' Elsie warned. She was beginning to have misgivings about Dot being a tenant of Bobby's boss. She hoped it wasn't going to cause trouble for her son. He'd got a good job. It was close to home and Mr Jenkins was as generous as he could be with food items without actually breaking the law.

'I don't hold with all these black market goings on, Mrs Hutton,' he'd told her as he cut out the coupons from her ration book. Elsie was registered with him and did her weekly shopping there. 'I can't tell you the number of times I've been offered all sorts of stuff. I like to help my customers, 'course I do, but where'd they all be if I got myself locked up in prison? Besides, I've my reputation to think of. I've always been an honest trader, Mrs Hutton. I never give short weight nor charge more than I have to. None of this taking advantage of a bad situation to make an extra few shillings for myself.'

'I know that, Mr Jenkins. I wouldn't have let my lad come and work for you if I hadn't known you to be as honest as the day is long.'

'Mind you,' he confessed, 'I've been tempted now and again. When these 'ere spivs come along with their sugar and tins of fruit, it's very difficult to refuse when I know how much my customers would like an extra few ounces of sugar or a taste of fruit. But I couldn't let the wife down. She'd never forgive me. A very unforgiving woman, is Mrs Jenkins.' He sighed. 'It's a pity, ain't it, Mrs Hutton, that us honest folk are having the hardest time?'

'The law'll catch up with them that breaks it, Mr Jenkins. Some of the sentences the courts are handing out to those that get caught are quite severe.' She leaned closer. 'That butcher two streets away got sent to jail only last week.'

'Not Joe Robinson?'

Elsie nodded, her lips pursed. 'And he's got a wife and little girl. What's going to happen to them, I'd like to know? They've closed his shop, so I heard tell.'

Donald Jenkins stared at her, sighed and shook his head. 'Not worth it, is it, Mrs Hutton?'

'No, Mr Jenkins, it isn't,' she said quietly. She was thinking about Dot's fancy man, Arthur Osborne, and wondering what exactly had happened to bring Dot and Jen running back home without Arthur in tow, or even the new chap Jenny said her mother had been with for a year.

When her next shopping day came around, Mr Jenkins asked, 'And how's your friend settling into the house at the end of your street?'

'Very nicely, thank you, Mr Jenkins. She said you'd given permission for her to paint it up a bit.'

He nodded. 'She's a lovely woman. Very – what's the word – energetic?'

Elsie said nothing. That was one way of describing Dot, she thought, but it had nothing to do with painting and decorating, nor even with day-to-day housework. That was falling heavily on Jenny's shoulders.

'I'll have to call round to see if there's anything they need. There's a daughter, I understand, and they're all on their own. Such a shame. Where's her husband, d'you know? Oh,' his voice dropped to a whisper, 'he's not been killed, has he?'

Elsie was very tempted to tell this gullible man the truth as she knew it; that Dot Mercer had never had a husband. But then, weren't all men putty in the hands of women like Dot? Would he believe her anyway? Would he *want* to believe her? So Elsie sighed and said, 'I really don't know what happened to him, Mr Jenkins. I think she "lost" him before the war. I never knew him. Anyway, I'd best be getting back.'

'Give my regards to your friend. Tell her I'll pop by and see her when I can find a minute.'

Elsie gave him a thin smile as she picked up her shopping basket and left the shop, her shoulders stiff with anger. Dot, it seemed, had made yet another conquest and this time, it was a married man. Surely, she tried to tell herself, an upstanding man like Mr Jenkins wouldn't be so foolish? Elsie sighed as she walked back home. Yes, he would. Oh yes, he would.

Forty-Seven

Only a week after Dot and Jenny had moved into their new home, the papers were full of the news of the D-Day landings in Normandy. The whole street celebrated – everyone, that is, except Elsie, whose fears for her husband and eldest son intensified. She was glad that the Allies had landed back on the mainland of Europe and believed, as everyone else hoped, that this was the beginning of the end, but her overriding emotion was one of dread. And Jenny's thoughts, too, turned yet again to the Thornton family. Were Philip and Ben involved? she wondered. And what about Georgie?

'I thought I'd just pop round and see if you were settling in and if – if there was anything you needed.'

'Why, Mr Jenkins,' Dot purred, thankful that she'd just washed her hair and renewed her make-up. She'd been about to go out, but now the prospect of charming Mr Jenkins – the man with a big house and a grocery business that seemed to be thriving even in these hard times – was far more appealing than even the shops. 'How very kind of you. Do come in.'

Dot ushered him through the front room, where a Morrison shelter sat taking up a large space in the middle of the floor of what should have been Dot's best parlour. She pulled a face. 'Sorry about that contraption, but the folks that were here before us left it.'

Donald Jenkins smiled wryly. 'Ah yes. I expect it was too cumbersome to move in the middle of the night.'

'Dear me,' Dot simpered, 'the things some folks will do. I'm so sorry to hear you were treated so badly. Please come into the back room. We've made it quite comfy.'

And they had. Jenny had painted the walls. Rag rugs, bought from a market stall, covered the floor and freshly washed curtains covered the windows. Two armchairs, slightly the worse for wear but clean and comfortable, stood either side of the range. On the warm June day this was unlit, for there was a brand-new cooker, provided by Mr Jenkins for his new tenants, sitting in the scullery.

'Sit down. I'll make us a cuppa. You've time, I hope?' Dot, with pretended innocence, asked. 'You don't have to be rushing home, do you?'

'No,' Donald said flatly, thinking of the reception that awaited him in his own home; an empty house and a cold evening meal. His wife, Celia, had thrown herself into war work with a vengeance. She'd always flatly refused to help her husband in the shop, stating from the early days of their marriage that her place was at home caring for him and the family they'd have one day. But children had never come along and over the years the embittered, disappointed woman had lost interest in caring for just one man. She still refused to help in the shop but when war was declared she embraced the war effort with a passion, at last finding fulfilment. She'd joined the Women's Voluntary Service to help with the war effort and now Donald returned home most evenings to a cold, deserted house and a solitary evening meal.

But at least, he thought, I don't have to put up with

Celia's constant nagging and belittling accusations about what a failure of a husband I am. He sat down as Dot reached up to pull the blackout curtains, her already short skirt riding even higher up her shapely legs.

'Here, let me,' he offered, half rising again. He felt obliged to make the offer, but he'd much rather have sat and admired the bare legs with the stirring of long-denied feelings.

'No, no, I can manage. I've got the knack.' She gave the curtains a final twitch and turned. 'There, now we can put the light on.'

As she sashayed across the room in the half-light, Donald pulled in a deep breath, trying to quell his rising desire. He cleared his throat in embarrassment and tried to set his mind on something – anything – else. 'I understand you have a daughter. I'd like to meet her.'

'Yes. She's only young,' Dot emphasized, deliberately ignoring the fact that when the man saw Jenny for himself, as he was bound to do, he would see her as a blossoming young woman, not a child any more. 'She looks a lot older than she really is. The war's robbing our youngsters of their childhood.'

'Is she still at school?'

Dot gave a helpless shrug and the lie slipped easily from her lips. 'She should be, but as we've only just moved back here, she's refusing to go back, saying it's time she found a job.'

'I might be able to help you there. She'll have to register for work, of course, and might have to go where she's sent, but if I can help in any way . . .'

'Oh, Mr Jenkins,' Dot clasped her hands together, 'I don't want her to go anywhere unsuitable. She's such a little innocent.' She dabbed her eyes gently with a hand-kerchief, but was careful not to smudge her make-up.

Donald nodded. 'I understand, though, sadly, I've no children of my own. We – we were never blessed.'

'*Weren't* you? Oh, I am sorry. You'd have been a wonderful father, I'm sure. You seem such a kind and caring man.'

Donald smiled weakly, quite overcome by the warmth of her praise. It had been a long time since any woman, other than his customers, who he knew were only grateful to him for what he could offer in the way of extra rations – legitimately, of course – had made him feel worthwhile. He basked in the long-forgotten feeling.

'I'll get you that tea,' Dot said and, as she passed his chair, she patted his hand.

Only eight days after the euphoria surrounding the news of D-Day, a new and terrifying weapon was unleashed on the stoic Londoners. Warnings were soon issued to the public that should they hear the strange buzzing of the pilotless aircraft's engine suddenly cut out above them, they should seek shelter immediately, for at that point the weapon would dive towards the ground and explode on impact.

'As if we haven't had enough,' Dot grumbled. 'No time to get to the underground with these blessed doodlebugs.'

'At least we've got a Morrison in the front room, Mum,' Jenny said reasonably.

'If you think I'm sleeping in there, you've got another think coming.' She fluffed her hair as she added, 'I've got better things to do with my nights.'

Donald had begun calling two or three times a week

after he'd closed the shop. Gradually, the sad little story of his home life emerged.

'I don't want to malign my wife. She's a wonderful woman in many ways. She's very good at organizing and – and running things. I expect she's a great asset to the WVS. And she wasn't always so – so cold. When we were courting and even when we were first married, she was always busy and lively, but she's never been what you'd call an affectionate woman, not like – ' here, he'd paused and gazed into Dot's eyes. She leaned forward and gently kissed his lips. 'You're welcome here any time, Donald. You know that.'

And so the visits became even more frequent until the whole neighbourhood was aware of Donald Jenkins trotting down the street with a little parcel of goodies under his arm.

'I thought it wouldn't be long before that little mare had another feller in tow,' Gladys remarked to Elsie over the backyard wall.

'And he's a married man. She's never gone for a married man before.'

'As far as you know, Elsie. We didn't know a fat lot about that Arfer, now did we?'

'True, but I'm more worried about what effect it's having on young Jenny. She spends a lot of time at our house now. Keeping out of their way I suppose.'

'Best thing, as long as she's no trouble to you.'

'None at all. She's a real help about the place.' Elsie laughed wryly. 'Boys think housework's beneath them.'

'Shame she's not your daughter, Elsie, she'd've had a much better life than the one she's got with that mother of hers.'

Jenny saw little of Donald; she always made sure she

was in her bedroom or at the Huttons' house when he was due to call, which was most nights of the week now. But, inevitably, they were bound to meet now and again.

'Donald's coming for his tea on Sunday,' Dot told her. 'Now just you make sure you're nice to him. He was going to ask around about a job for you.'

'But I've registered for work. I've got to wait until—'

'No harm in seeing what he's got to say.' She gripped Jenny's arm tightly until the girl winced. 'You be nice to him, you hear me? We're in there, so you just do whatever he ses.'

Anger surged through Jenny as she thrust her face close to her mother's. 'And he's got a *wife* in the big house, so just how d'you intend to get rid of her, eh?'

'No need.' Dot smiled. 'I'm not anticipating marrying him. I just want what he can give us – for the moment.'

'But he worships you, Mum. I can see it in his eyes. More than any of the others. I – I think he really loves you.'

'There you are, then. Like I said, we're in there.'

'But—'

'No "buts", miss. Just do as I say. Be nice to him.'

Donald came with good news. 'I've talked to the authorities and they've agreed that I can take Jenny on to help out in the shop. There's such a lot of paperwork with all the rationing and the coupons. There, now what do you think to that?' He beamed at them both and Dot gave a little squeal of delight and flung her arms round his neck, pressing herself to him.

But Jenny was thinking, Oh no! Not again. Not working in a shop receiving stolen goods and serving

the customers with under-the-counter black market pro-
duce. I can't bear it. But her mother's words still rang in
her ears: *Be nice to Donald. You do whatever he asks
you to do.*

There was no escape for the young girl. If only she
could run away. But, now, there was nowhere for her
to run.

But Jenny had been wrong about one thing; Donald
Jenkins was not taking part in any black market
schemes. Even when Elsie had told her that he was an
honest trader, Jenny hadn't wholeheartedly believed her.
But now she saw it for herself. If anyone approached
him, they were sent packing, as Donald Jenkins said
himself, with a flea in their ear.

'I don't hold with it, Jenny,' he told her.

Jenny said a silent prayer of thanks that her new
employer was not like the last. She shuddered as she
realized just how close she and her mother had come to
being questioned by the police, if not worse. Perhaps
they might have ended up being arrested as accomplices.

Donald was like Jim in other ways, though; he was
kind to her mother and to her. He bought them little
treats and when Dot said that she would have to look
for work for Jenny's pay wouldn't pay the rent and all
the other household bills, he at once reduced the rent to
a mere pittance so that they could manage.

'I'm surprised you haven't been commandeered for
war work, my dear,' he said to Dot, but she merely
smiled and said, 'I don't expect they want someone like
me. I'm not much good at anything.'

'I'm sure you are. The very sight of you raises a man's
spirits,' Donald said gallantly. But it still puzzled him

why she was not gainfully employed in helping the war effort in some way. Whilst he deplored the way that his wife had rushed so enthusiastically into it, he nevertheless agreed that all able-bodied women who no longer had young children to care for should do something. But every time he broached the subject, Dot was evasive.

For several weeks, Jenny was happy in her work. The shop, though cool to help preserve the foodstuffs, was not freezing like the butcher's shop had been. And on cooler days, Donald let her work in the storeroom or in the office, checking the coupons and filling out the official forms. And there was the added bonus of seeing Bobby every day. The friendship the two had shared as youngsters was still as strong as ever.

In August, the day after Jenny's fifteenth birthday, the Allies marched into Paris and four long years of Nazi occupation for them was over. By September Belgium was free but, at the same time, London was faced with another, even more sophisticated weapon than the doodlebugs. These were Hitler's V-2s, long-range rockets that gave no warning sound. At first the Londoners thought the massive explosions were gasworks, but before long they realized they were yet again under bombardment.

In the view of many, the end of the war was in sight as German troops were pushed back, but the fighting was not over.

''Itler'll not give in,' Elsie said, still fretting over her boys. 'He'll fight to the death.' And in the January of 1945, Sammy, at just eighteen, was called up too.

'You won't have to go, Bobby, will you?'

'If it lasts another eighteen months, I will,' he said cheerfully, loading the boxes of groceries on to the back of the cart in the yard behind Donald's shop. 'In the meantime, I'd better get these deliveries taken out else I'll have all the customers gunning for me, ne'er mind 'Itler.'

'Watch out for the rockets,' she warned.

Bobby pulled a face. 'Least I won't know a lot about it, Jen.'

Jenny watched him manoeuvre the cart out of the yard and sent up a silent prayer for his safety.

Jenny turned to go back into the office with a sigh. There was a lot of paperwork awaiting her and she hoped that Donald would be kept busy in the shop. She enjoyed the work and being close to Bobby, but there was one thing that bothered her; sometimes Donald would come and stand close to her chair as she worked at the desk in the office. Then he would put his hand on her shoulder as he leaned over to explain something to her. It seemed innocent enough, but his closeness made Jenny's skin crawl. She settled herself in the room at the back of the shop and began to sort out the ration books. About mid-afternoon, she paused to rub her eyes and make a pot of tea, carrying a cup through to Donald in the shop.

'Ta, darlin'. Most welcome. How's the paperwork going?'

Jenny pulled a face. 'All right. Seems such a lot of it this month. I'd better get back to it.'

She was still working, checking the invoices against the deliveries, when closing time came and Donald came through to the back where Jenny was standing on a stepladder, piling boxes on to a high shelf. She could feel him watching her and she was about to step down, when she felt him touch her ankle and then slide his hand up the calf of her leg. She spun round, almost toppling off the stepladder. She regained her balance, climbed down quickly and turned to face him, her eyes blazing.

'How dare you?' she began, but he backed away, holding out his hands as if to ward off her attack.

'I'm sorry, Jenny. I didn't mean any harm. I thought you might fall, I—'

'You nearly *made* me fall,' she hissed.

'I'm so sorry,' he said again. 'It's just—'

'You're nothing but a dirty old man.'

'Jenny, please don't tell your mother. I beg you. It'll never happen again, I swear.'

'You're right there. It won't.'

Jenny moved towards the back door, snatching her jacket from the peg. She turned towards him briefly. 'You know what you can do with your job. And if you take my advice, you won't come round our house again.'

With that parting shot, she dragged open the door and hurried out, slamming it behind her with a finality that left Donald in no doubt as to what she intended to do.

Forty-Eight

'You stupid little bitch! What on earth have you done?'

Jenny gasped in the face of her mother's anger. 'What have *I* done? It's what he's done. Don't you understand?'

'Oh, I understand all right. You just might have scuppered the best thing we've ever had.'

'But – but he touched me. He stroked my leg. He—'

'For goodness' sake, girl. He's a *man*! It's what they do. And I told you to be nice to him.'

Jenny stared at her, wide-eyed with horror. 'You – you mean me to put up with – with that sort of thing?'

'Don't be such a stuck-up little prude, Jen. How d'yer think we're going to survive the war if we don't have help from the likes of Donald Jenkins? He's reduced our rent and he nearly keeps us in groceries. And—'

Jenny put her hands over her ears. 'I don't want to hear any more. I won't listen.'

'You bloody well will listen to me.' Dot grasped Jenny's wrists and pulled her hands down. She thrust her face close to her daughter's, her spittle raining on Jenny's face as she spat, 'You will go back this minute to the shop and you'll apologize. You'll say you didn't understand and—'

'I won't! I won't go back there. I don't want to see him again.'

'Well, I do.' Dot's grip tightened. 'So you'll do as I say, or else—'

Jenny wrenched herself free and headed for the front door. As she pulled it open she turned back and pointed a finger at her mother. 'Go yerself, 'cos I'm not going anywhere near that – that – ' She was stuck for a word to describe what she felt about Donald Jenkins, so she just ended her sentence with a low, menacing growl and slammed the door with such a force that it shuddered on its hinges.

By the time she arrived at Elsie's, Jenny was weeping tears of anger, frustration and fear.

'Aw, darlin', whatever's the matter? Come in, come in.'

Elsie's arm was comfortingly around her shoulders and she was leading her to the warmth of the fire. 'You're trembling, love. And you've come out without yer coat. What's happened?'

'Is Bobby in?'

'No. He's out with his mates. Is it him you want to see?'

Jenny shook her head. 'No – no, I'd rather he didn't know. At least, not yet. Oh Aunty Elsie, whatever am I to do?'

'Tell me what's the matter first, then we'll see, eh?' She stroked Jenny's hair back from her tear-stained face. 'Sit down and tell me all about it.'

'I can't stand it any longer. Today was the last straw . . .' She was tempted to tell Elsie everything, right from the time they'd left London sneaking away in the middle of the night in Arthur's van. All about their time in Derbyshire and how he'd involved her in his criminal activities. But she couldn't. Something was still holding her back from confiding in anyone about that. Instead, she concentrated on the recent months working for Donald Jenkins.

'He comes into the back office and leans over me. And sometimes, in the shop, in front of other people, he'll put his arm round me and squeeze me. It looks innocent enough. He's like an affectionate uncle.' She pulled a wry expression. '*Another* "uncle".'

Elsie smiled weakly but said nothing.

'But it isn't innocent, Aunty Elsie.' She gave a dramatic shudder. 'He's sort of – creepy. D'you know what I mean?'

Elsie nodded. 'Go on, darlin',' she said, encouraging the girl to tell her what had happened today to upset her so.

'Well, I never,' she said at last. 'I'd never have thought it of Mr Jenkins. He's always seemed such an upstanding man in the community. He's always refused to have any dealings with these spivs and their black market stuff.'

'You – you do believe me, don't you, Aunty Elsie?'

''Course I believe you. I know you wouldn't make up something like that and – ' her tone hardened – 'and you couldn't have mistaken what his intentions were, ne'er mind what yer mam ses. She's just trying to keep in with him. She'll be round there now, if I know Dot Mercer, trying to patch things up.'

'He'll have gone home by now. What if she goes round there? What if his wife's at home?'

'Then your mother, darlin', will get whatever's coming to her.' Elsie was immediately contrite. 'I'm sorry to speak of her like that to you.'

'It's all right, Aunty Elsie,' Jenny said, calmer now and wiping her eyes. 'I know exactly what she is. I've known for a long time, but she is my mother. I should've run away. I nearly did when we were in – when we were up north. I'd got my case all packed but then Arthur

337

came home and said we were moving again and I didn't
get the chance. Oh, if only I'd come back here then.'

'I wish you had.' Elsie didn't press the girl, but she
was shrewd enough to guess that there'd been more to
their life 'up north' than Jenny was telling her. There
was silence in the kitchen as they sat, still close together,
in the firelight. A sudden loud banging on the front door
made them both jump.

'Come out here, you little devil. I know you're in
there.'

They heard the door open and the next moment, Dot
was in the kitchen shaking her fist at them both. Elsie
stood up and turned to face her. 'Yer can stop that
racket right now, Dot. Calm yerself and let's talk this
through.'

'What's she been telling you, the little liar?'

'Jen's no liar,' Elsie said calmly, though she was
having difficulty in suppressing her own anger. 'Sit
down, I tell you, and we'll talk about it all.'

'She might've lost me the best thing that's ever happened to me in years.'

'Oh, so you don't mind an old feller like him making
advances to yer fifteen-year-old daughter, then?'

Dot's lip curled. 'What'd he want with her when he's
got me?'

Elsie leaned forward and said slowly and deliberately,
'Young, fresh meat, that's what.'

'Please – stop it,' Jenny begged.

Dot glared at them both and then sneered, 'Well, it
might surprise you to know that I've been round his
house just now and he's going to leave his wife and
move in with me.' She turned to Jenny. 'So you, me girl,
can sling yer hook. Yer stuff's all outside Elsie's front
door right now and I don't want to see hide nor hair of

you ever again.' She stood up. 'I've always told you I never wanted you in the first place, so now you're old enough, you can look after yerself.'

With that parting shot, she flounced from Elsie's kitchen and out of the front door, leaving them staring after her.

'She's not normal, that woman. Sorry to say it, Jen, but she ain't got a maternal bone in her body. Ah well . . .' Elsie heaved herself up and went to the front door. 'Best get your things back upstairs into Ronnie's room. Looks like you'll be staying with us again.'

'Oh, Aunty Elsie,' Jenny jumped up. 'I never thought. Oh dear, what have I done?'

Elsie paused and turned to look at her. 'What are you on about?'

'Bobby. I never thought. What about Bobby's job? Will Mr Jenkins sack him?'

For a moment Elsie stared at her and then she burst out laughing. 'Don't you worry about our Bobby, darlin'. He'll likely not want to work there any more when he hears what's been going on.'

'I'll bloody well thump him.' Bobby punched his fist into the palm of his other hand, wishing it was Donald Jenkins's nose he was bloodying. 'Just wait till I get me hands on him. I'll teach him to lay a finger on you.'

'Now, now, calm down, Bobby. Jenny's going to stay with us and she's not going back there.'

'I should think not, indeed. And neither am I.'

'Don't say that, Bobby. I don't want you to lose your job because of me.'

But Bobby was shaking his head. 'I've got another job. On the railway. I heard this morning. I'd've been leaving Jenkins anyway. It's better pay and it might mean it'll be a reserved occupation and I won't get called up.'

'Oh Bobby,' Elsie threw her arms around the embarrassed young man and hugged him, 'that's wonderful.'

Grinning with embarrassment, Bobby extricated himself. 'I didn't tell you before, Mam, because I didn't know if I'd get it and I didn't want to get your hopes up. I knew you'd be pleased.'

'Pleased! You can't even begin to guess how much, darlin'.'

Jenny, too, was smiling. 'Any jobs going for girls on the railway?' She was half joking, but Bobby took her question seriously. 'I don't know, but I can ask, if you like.'

'Well, I need a job. I want to pay my way here—'

Mother and son both spoke at once: 'There's no need.'

'You can help me about the house and—' Elsie began.

Jenny put her hands up, protesting laughingly. 'It's very good of you, but I must look for work. I'll go back to the authorities and see what they want me to do. I would like to stay here – really I would, but I shall get work.'

Forty-Nine

Jenny had been staying at the Huttons' house for almost a month. Rumours about her mother were flying around the neighbourhood.

'You do want me to tell you what I've heard, Jen, don't you?' Elsie asked worriedly. She didn't want to upset the girl any more and yet Jenny had settled in well with them and didn't seem unduly worried about her mother. Not that Dot Mercer deserved her daughter's concern, Elsie thought wryly.

Jenny sighed in answer to Elsie's question. 'What's she up to now? Not in trouble with the law, is she?'

'No – no. At least, not that I've heard. No, it's Mr Jenkins.'

Jenny's tone hardened. 'What about him?'

'It's true what she told us. He has left his wife and moved in with her.'

Jenny stared at Elsie open-mouthed. 'Never.'

'S'true. Gladys heard it from the folks next door to where yer mam's living, so it must be true.'

'Did – did she say anything about me?'

'No, darlin'. Sorry.'

Jenny was silent, wiping the same plate with the tea towel over and over until Elsie forced a laugh and said, 'If you dry that much more, Jen, you'll wear the pattern off.'

341

'Oh – sorry.' She put the dry plate down on the pile and picked up another wet one from the draining board.

'What's his wife had to say about it?'

'Plenty, by the sound of it. Went round there one night – to yer mam's – and caused a right old to-do. Wonder we didn't hear it. Tried to drag him home by his ear, so Gladys heard, but she was no match for yer mam.'

Jenny smiled thinly. 'Mum must think he's worth hanging on to, then? I wonder how long this one'll last.'

'Aye, well, we'll see. But don't you worry your head about it, Jen. You're all right with us. Though it won't be easy for you living in the same street with folks' tongues wagging. You know, darlin', I don't understand why you've never gone back to those nice people you were evacuated to. Don't get me wrong, Jen,' Elsie added swiftly, 'you're more than welcome here. Me an' Bobby love having yer.'

'What about Sammy when he comes home on leave? Will he mind?'

'Oh, you know our Sammy. Nothing bothers him. Besides – ' her face fell as she added, 'he won't be here very long, will he?' She paused a moment, sparing yet another thought for her loved ones away fighting the war. Then she took a deep breath and returned to the previous topic. 'No, I just wondered, that's all. They seemed such lovely people. You couldn't stop talking about them when you came home. And when you all disappeared sudden-like, I thought that's where you'd gone, but when they came looking for you, I knew you hadn't.'

Elsie's last few words made Jenny catch her breath. 'What – what did you say?'

'I was surprised when they came looking for you, 'cos I thought that'd be where Dot'd've taken you.'

'What d'you mean – they came looking for me?'

'Those people you were with in – where was it?'

'Lincolnshire,' Jenny whispered, hope beginning to burst in her breast.

'That's it. Came all the way down on the train, they did.'

'When?' Jenny's tone was sharper than she meant it to be, but Elsie didn't seem to notice or to mind. Perhaps she caught some of the girl's eagerness. She wrinkled her forehead. 'It wasn't long after you'd gone and both our houses had got bombed. I remember that 'cos I was scrambling around on top of the heap of rubble trying to find me bits and pieces. Anything, really, but there was nothing left that was any good. They're nice people, Jen. Lovely. They even offered for me an' the boys to go to them if we wanted, but I told 'em I wanted to stay 'ere for when my hubby comes home on leave. Now let me think – when was it?'

Jenny waited with growing impatience. She put down the plate she was holding, but didn't pick up another. Her hands were trembling so much she was afraid she would drop it. She was gripping the tea towel to stop her hands from taking hold of Elsie's shoulders and shaking the words out of her. 'What did they want? What did they say?'

'They were trying to find you and they seemed real upset when I couldn't even tell them where you'd gone. You could have written to them, Jen,' she added, with a note of reproach in her tone. 'Come to think of it, you could have written to us too. We've all been wondering where you were and if you were all right.'

Neatly ignoring what Elsie had said about herself and her family, Jenny said quietly, 'Mum said they'd sent me back because they didn't want me any more.'

Elsie snorted wryly. 'Didn't look like that to me.'

'Do – do you really think they'd like to – to see me again?'

Elsie stared at her and then said quietly, 'I've never been so sure of anything in me life.'

'Oh Aunty Elsie.' Jenny dropped the tea towel she was still holding and flung her arms round the woman's neck. 'I must go and see them. I have to.'

Elsie returned her hug. 'Just so long as you aren't going because you think you're a trouble to us, 'cos you're not.'

'No – no, I'm not. You've been so kind.'

Elsie held her at arm's length and said seriously, 'You go, darlin', but if it doesn't turn out the way you want it to, then you come straight back here. D'you hear me?'

Jenny nodded, her eyes shining.

'And this time, you just keep in touch. All right?'

'I will, Aunty Elsie. I promise.' She couldn't tell this trusting woman that the only reason she'd never written to them had been because she dared not do so. Postmarks could be traced and Arthur had forbidden either of them to write letters to anyone, least of all to Elsie, who might be questioned by the police in their efforts to track down Arthur Osborne.

Jenny couldn't wait to get there and yet she was filled with trepidation too. What if Aunty Elsie was wrong? What if they'd just been down in London for some other reason and thought they'd look her up to see if she was all right? That didn't mean they wanted her back.

But she was older now. She'd left school and started work. She was quite capable of taking the train to Lincolnshire and seeing for herself. She'd soon know by their attitude whether they were pleased to see her or not.

'You're not going to come back, are you?' Bobby said quietly.

Jenny forced a laugh. 'I'll be home on the next train if they don't want me.'

'They'll want you, all right. *I* never thought they didn't.'

'But why would Mum say that? Let's face it, she never wanted me, so why didn't she take the chance of offloading me for good? Well, at least for the rest of the war.'

Bobby laughed wryly. 'There's no telling what goes on in yer mam's mind. Oh sorry, I shouldn't—'

Jenny held up her hand. 'Don't apologize. We always tell each other the truth, Bobby. I know exactly what my mum is.' She sighed and shook her head. 'And what she thinks of me, so that's why I can't understand why she didn't just leave me in the country and forget all about me.'

'All the other kids in the neighbourhood were coming back. We were back.' He pulled a face. 'We hated it where we were. I wish we could have come wiv you.' He grinned. 'I'd've stayed there.'

Jenny smiled weakly, the memories of her happy time with the Thornton family flooding back. And yet with it came the ache in her heart for Georgie. Where was he? Was he really safe, as she'd always believed? Or had she been deluding herself, clinging to a vain hope? Perhaps that was what Charlotte and Miles had come to tell her. They'd had some news of Georgie.

Now she couldn't get to Ravensfleet quickly enough.

Fifty

The train seemed interminably slow and it was crowded – as seemed usual these days – with troops being moved from one place to another. Several seemed to be going home on leave, their faces grey with exhaustion. Maybe they'd been at the front of the fighting and their weariness and the haunted look in their eyes was because of what they'd endured. And yet, despite their weariness, there seemed to be a feeling of optimism. Everyone hoped that 1945 would bring the end of the war.

The March day was cold and blustery and Jenny huddled into her corner of the carriage, willing the train to go faster. There was a group of four airmen in their smart blue uniforms who reminded Jenny so sharply of Georgie that tears sprang to her eyes.

'You all right, pet?' one of them asked, with a broad Geordie accent.

'I'm fine.' She smiled through her tears. 'It's just – just you all remind me of someone I used to know.'

The young airman's face sobered. 'Lost, is he?'

'The last I heard, they said so. They just said he was missing, presumed—' She couldn't bring herself to say the word, but the airman knew only too well.

'Aye, well, we've all lost some of our best mates, but it'll not be long now. War'll soon be over.'

'Will it?' Jenny couldn't help the doubt in her tone but he was confident. 'Just you wait an' see. Can't say more than that.' He tapped the side of his nose and winked at her. 'Careless talk an' all that.'

He continued to sit beside her until the train drew into Thirsby station, where she had to change for the train that would take her the short distance to Ravensfleet. She shared the sandwiches Elsie had packed for her with him and asked him about his home town of Newcastle. His eyes grew misty as he talked about his family.

'This isn't the train for Newcastle, though. Did you get on the wrong train?'

The airman grinned. 'No, I'm on me way to see me fiancée. She lives near Cleethorpes.' He paused and then asked, 'You got a boyfriend?'

Jenny hesitated and then shook her head. She turned her face away to look out of the window, but not before he'd noticed her bleak expression. 'Carrying a torch for your young airman, a' you, pet?'

Her throat was too full of tears so she just nodded. How uncomfortably perceptive he was, she thought. When the train pulled into the station where she had to get off, he helped her with her suitcase – the very same one that Charlotte had given her when she'd gone back to London; she refused to call it going home. This was coming home. Home to her was Ravensfleet and the Thornton family. And now she was back. But what sort of welcome awaited her?

As she stood on the platform, waving goodbye to the airmen, she suddenly felt very alone and apprehensive.

She dragged her case to where the train for Lynthorpe was almost ready to leave. The train rattled through the Lincolnshire countryside and as she watched the flat fields flashing by as they drew nearer and nearer to the

Ravensfleet station, she felt more and more as if she was coming home.

The little station was bustling when she stepped down, pulling her case after her. She stood a moment to catch her breath and look about her. The walk from the station to the manor was quite a distance, so she asked the porter if she could leave her suitcase in the left-luggage office and collect it later.

'Course you can, duck.'

When she heard the Lincolnshire voice, she knew she was home at last.

Leaving her suitcase in his care and carrying only her small handbag, she left the station and walked through the streets. On her way, she passed the cottage where the two old ladies – the Miss Listers – lived. Jenny shuddered as she remembered that dreadful time. Then on past the Tomkinses' house towards the manor. Her heart beat faster as she neared the gate where she paused a moment.

The wind blew in from the sea and she drew her coat more closely around her. Already, she could smell the salty air. She rested her hand on the stone gatepost. The wrought-iron gates were gone. For the war effort, she supposed. Somewhere they'd been melted down to make Hurricanes or Spitfires for those brave young airmen to fly. Maybe Georgie . . .

She shaded her eyes and she saw two figures on the smooth front lawn; the lawn where Miles – and Georgie – had played football with all the evacuee kids who'd been given lessons at the manor. Now someone else was playing football. A tall man and a little child. Tears blurred her eyes and she dashed them away impatiently. As her vision cleared, she saw that the child was a little girl – a toddler, no more than three, with curly hair – running towards the man who was squatting down and reaching towards her with open arms. The child reached him and he stood up, swinging her high into the air and, even from here, Jenny could hear the infant's merry laughter. He was tall but, as he turned to walk back to the house, she saw that he was limping. As the breeze ruffled his curly blond hair, her heart missed a beat and then began to thump madly. Suddenly she felt dizzy and had to lean against the gatepost.

He'd almost reached the steps leading up to the front door when something made him look round. Perhaps he'd felt the intensity of her gaze, and, catching sight of the figure standing uncertainly in the gateway, he turned and began to walk towards her. Nearer and nearer he came, still carrying the little girl in his arms.

Overwhelming joy flooded through Jenny. 'Georgie,' she whispered. 'Oh Georgie, it is you. You're safe, just as I always knew you would be.' But she could not find her voice to speak out loud, could not call to him or even walk towards him; her legs refused to move. He was smiling as he came towards her, but it was the smile with which he might greet a stranger. He didn't recognize her. She felt a pang of disappointment; he didn't know her. She'd carried his image in her heart over the years, but he'd forgotten her. But then a curious look crossed his face. He set the little girl down on the ground, but still kept hold of her hand. Now he was staring at Jenny, a small frown on his forehead.

Jenny glanced at the child; a pretty little girl with dark brown curls and huge brown eyes. But it was her cheeky smile, so like Georgie's, that made Jenny catch her breath. Her glance went back him and her lips parted in a question. But the words were stilled on her lips for a slow smile was spreading across his face now.

'Jenny. You've come back to us.' He moved towards her, stretching out his free arm. 'Oh Jen, little Jen. You don't know how glad I am to see you.'

Still she couldn't speak, not even when he put his arm around her shoulders and kissed her hair. 'This is wonderful. Father and Charlotte will be over the moon. They've never stopped thinking about you. *We've* never stopped wondering where you were and if you were all right.'

He drew back a little and looked down into her upturned face and she, in turn, gazed up into his eyes.

'You've still got those beautiful blue eyes.'

'You – you,' she found her voice at last, 'nearly didn't recognize me, did you?'

Georgie chuckled. 'It took me a moment, you've grown so. Quite the young lady now and a very beautiful one.'

She felt the blush creeping up her face and wondered if he was teasing her, but his tone, though light, was serious. His eyes, too, told her he was speaking the truth.

'We must go and find Father and Charlotte. Come on, little one, up you come.'

He took his arm from around Jenny's shoulder and picked up the child again.

'Is she – ?' Jenny's courage failed her. The child must be Georgie's. He must have fallen in love with some girl while he'd been in the RAF and . . .'

'This is Louisa. Say "hello" to Jenny, Lou-Lou.' The child gazed at Jenny but did not speak. Instead she stuck her thumb in her mouth. Georgie laughed. 'Don't tell me you're shy. Not my Lou-Lou.'

Jenny's heart plummeted. The little girl was his; he was married with a child. 'So – so she's—'

'She's a little miracle, that's what Louisa Alice is, Jen. You know my father always desperately wanted a daughter?' he began to explain as they walked up the drive towards the house.

'I remember,' Jenny said quietly.

Georgie grinned, quite happy in the knowledge that he and his brothers had always been very much wanted children. But Miles had always dreamed of having a little girl; a daughter he would one day walk up the aisle on her wedding day. 'But for a long time it seemed poor Charlotte couldn't have children. And then – it was such a surprise – she found she was expecting. Of course Father had such mixed feelings, having lost my mother when I was born.'

Jenny nodded, remembering the stories she had heard when she'd stayed with them before. Relief flooded through her. The child wasn't Georgie's. She was Charlotte's and Miles's.

Georgie glanced down at her. 'For a while, he thought you would become that daughter, but then your mother demanded we send you back. Father was heartbroken when you went. Both of them were.'

Jenny stopped, appalled at what she was hearing. 'But – but Mum said *they'd* sent me back. That – that they didn't want me any more.'

Georgie too stopped and turned to face her. His face darkened with anger. 'Well, I can assure you, Jen, nothing could be further from the truth. They wanted you to stay. For ever, if you could have done.'

He hoisted Louisa into his right arm and put his left around Jenny's shoulder again. 'But now you've come back to us and everything will be all right.'

Joy surged through Jenny as she climbed the steps into the house.

At last, she was home again.

Fifty-One

As soon as they entered the hall, Georgie was shouting at the top of his voice. 'Father! Charlotte! Come quickly. Just look who's here.'

Charlotte came to the top of the stairs. She paused a moment, staring down at them. 'Oh! Oh!' And then she was running down the stairs as the door to Miles's study flew open.

They both spoke at once, recognizing her instantly. 'Jenny, oh Jenny.' And then she was enveloped in a bear hug, first by Charlotte and then by Miles, who held her a long time, murmuring, 'Jenny, my little Jenny. You've come back to us.'

There was no mistaking the warmth of their welcome and now Jenny felt guilty for having ever doubted them.

'We've been so worried about you,' Charlotte said as she led everyone to the morning room and ordered tea.

Jenny glanced about her; nothing had changed much and yet everything was different. Charlotte and Miles had their own daughter now. Maybe . . . but she pushed such thoughts aside and basked in the happiness of the moment. They all talked at once, the words spilling out in their need to catch up on the lost years.

Their news came out bit by bit, but first Jenny wanted to know about Georgie, wanted to hear what had happened to him.

'I got shot down over the French coast,' he told her briefly. 'I was rescued and taken prisoner.'

'But he escaped several times from different prison camps and ended up in Colditz.'

Georgie chuckled. 'It was a prison camp in a castle – the place from which the Germans said no one could escape.'

'But Georgie did and managed to get to Switzerland,' Miles took up the story. 'They're a neutral country, so eventually he got all the way home.'

'Is that when you got hurt?'

This time it was Charlotte who said quietly, 'No, that was later. Once he was home, he had to go back into the RAF, although they were good and gave you quite a long leave, didn't they, Georgie?'

He nodded and added, with a nonchalance that belied his brave exploits, 'I crash-landed coming back to base but at least I was at home. Bust my leg pretty badly and so, no more war for me.'

'And the others?' she asked. 'Philip and Ben?'

Their faced sobered and she could see her question was causing them pain. They glanced at each other before Miles said quietly, 'Poor old Philip wasn't so lucky. He got very badly wounded. We got him home and nursed him. Charlotte' – Miles smiled lovingly at his wife – 'was wonderful to him. But sadly, he died.'

'I'm so sorry,' Jenny said. 'He was kind to me.'

'Was he?' There was surprise in Georgie's tone.

Jenny nodded. 'He was home on leave and he read *The Wind in the Willows* to me.'

'Did he now?' Georgie said softly. 'Good old Phil.'

Now she hardly dared ask the next question, but she had to know. 'And – and Ben?'

Now they all smiled fondly. 'Ben – the quiet one. He

354

got the George Cross for bravery and is some big shot in the army now.'

'He transferred to training new recruits but now he's in London at the War Office. He's not in the fighting either now,' Charlotte said and then bit her lip, adding softly, 'but there's always the bombing – these dreadful doodlebugs. Are they very bad?'

'The V-2s are the worst,' Jenny said. 'There's no warning with them.'

There was a brief silence before Jenny took a deep breath and asked, 'And Louisa?'

A young nursery maid had taken the child upstairs, but it was as if her presence was still in the room. 'Georgie's told me that she's your daughter. How old is she?'

Miles must have heard the wistful note in her tone, as if she feared there was no room for her here any more.

'She was born in December 1941. Philip didn't live long enough to see her, but he knew a baby was coming.' He glanced at Charlotte. 'It was he who suggested calling her Louisa after my first wife. And Charlotte, as generous as ever, didn't object.'

'Did – did Philip know Georgie was safe?'

'Oh yes, but at that time, of course, we thought he would be a POW for the rest of the war.'

Jenny laughed. 'If I'd known, I could have told you he'd try to escape.'

Charlotte shuddered. 'It was a good job I didn't know what he was up to until he arrived home. I thought he was safe and all the time – ' She shook her head and glanced at him. There had always been a special bond between Charlotte and Georgie and, feeling it, Jenny felt excluded.

'We came to London to tell you he was safe,' Miles said, 'but you'd gone and your neighbour didn't know where.'

'Aunty Elsie? Yes, she told me you'd been, but not until the day before yesterday. She never thought to mention it before. We've been back in London for a while.'

'And you didn't think to come earlier?' Charlotte asked gently.

'I wanted to – so many times – you've no idea, but Mum told me that it was you who'd sent me back – that you didn't want me any more. I – I did write after I left here.'

Charlotte gasped. 'We never received any letters from you. And I wrote to you several times.'

Jenny shook her head and said heavily, 'I never got them.'

Miles exploded with anger. 'How could she? How could she say such a thing? And she must have intercepted the letters too. That blasted woman—'

'Miles!'

'Steady on, Father. She is Jenny's mother!'

Miles was immediately contrite. 'I'm sorry, Jenny. I shouldn't speak about her like that. But you've no idea what agonies we've been through wondering where you were and if you were all right. For all we knew, you might have been killed in the bombing.'

Jenny shook her head, 'It's all right, but – but when I tell you where I've been and – and what I've been doing, you – you really might not want me any more.'

The three of them stared at her in disbelief. 'What could you possibly have done that would turn us against you?' Miles said gently.

Jenny bit her lip and hung her head.

'Come on, you can tell us. Where's my feisty little girl gone?' Miles tried to lighten the mood, but, to his horror, tears filled Jenny's eyes.

She was so afraid to tell them and yet she couldn't deceive these wonderful people.

Georgie moved his chair closer to her and put his arm around her. 'Whatever it is, Jen, you can tell us. We'll help. Are – are you in trouble?'

She shook her head. 'No – no, but I could have been.' And then she told them everything, even down to the smallest detail. About how they'd left London in the middle of the night. All about Arthur and his thieving that had involved her. A maid whom Jenny hadn't seen before brought in tea and Charlotte poured for all of them and handed round dainty cakes. But all the time they listened whilst Jenny spoke, haltingly at first, and then with more confidence, though she twisted her fingers together nervously.

She knew, only too well, that her happiness could be shattered almost as soon as she'd found it again.

Georgie's comforting arm was around her shoulders the whole time she was telling her sorry tale and, whilst Charlotte's face turned pale, Miles's grew red with suppressed anger. At last, Jenny fell silent and hung her head. Then she felt Georgie squeeze her shoulders and Charlotte touch her hand. By this time, Miles was pacing the room.

'They ought to be locked up – the whole lot of them.' He was thumping his right fist into the palm of his left hand. 'If I had my way . . .'

Charlotte, recovering her composure, managed to smile. 'You're safe now, Jenny. Don't listen to Miles ranting. He's just getting it off his chest. He's – ' she glanced at Georgie, seeking agreement – 'we're all just so upset to hear what you've been through. But you're safe now,' she repeated it again, impressing upon her that whilst Miles would like to do goodness knew what to Arthur Osborne and the others, he would not endanger Jenny.

Miles paused in his pacing. 'D'you think I should – ?'

'No!' Charlotte and Georgie chorused and then Georgie added, 'If you report any of this to the police, they'll want to question Jenny.'

The struggle with his conscience was evident on Miles's face. 'I know, but . . .'

Jenny looked up at him. He was such a good, kind man and so honest. It wouldn't sit well with him to keep the knowledge to himself. She stood up suddenly, Georgie's arm falling away from her shoulders. She crossed the small space between herself and Miles and put her hand on his arm. She looked up into his face and saw the anxiety there. She didn't want to cause Miles – or any of them – a moment's worry. 'I don't want to cause you any trouble. It'd be better if I went back.'

Miles's response was swift and definite. 'No.' He put his arm around her and pulled her close. 'Never. Not now you're back with us, we're not letting you go again.' He pulled back from her a little and looked down into her upturned face. 'You do want to stay with us, don't you?'

Her voice was husky as she whispered, 'More than anything in the world.'

Miles held her tightly as if he would, indeed, never let her go. Despite the fact that he now had his very own daughter, Jenny knew in that moment that he meant every word he'd said.

At last, she was loved and wanted.

Secure now in the knowledge that she was truly home, Jenny pulled Miles back to sit down again with Charlotte and Georgie. Charlotte was smiling. 'Your room's waiting for you. We haven't altered a thing since you left and the nursery is waiting too, but – ' she laughed at her own foolishness, 'of course, you're too big for toys now, perhaps.'

Shyly, Jenny said, 'Perhaps, but I'd love to play with Louisa, if – if you'd let me.'

'*Let* you?' Georgie laughed. 'She'll be thrilled to have a big sister and that's how you must think of yourself from now on. As our much-loved sister.'

Jenny smiled weakly at him, touched by his words, and yet the very last thing she wanted to be was Georgie's *sister*.

Fifty-Two

After Miles had fetched Jenny's suitcase from the station, they talked until dinner was announced by a beaming Kitty. When the servants – though at the manor they were never called that – had heard that little Jenny had come back, Mrs Beddows had immediately baked the girl's favourite cake without sparing a thought for wartime rationing. 'Madam won't mind just this once,' she said, nodding in agreement with her own statement as she beat butter and sugar into a creamy mix. Kitty smiled. She'd been allowed to keep her job at the manor because she'd volunteered to join the local ARP and had been spared being requisitioned into war work in a factory somewhere. Mrs Beddows – with Charlotte's full approval – was relaxed about the hours Kitty worked in the house. Many times she was called in to do the night watch and came home exhausted. But, to help out, Charlotte had employed a fifteen-year-old girl from the village. Joan was willing but very shy and she scuttled back to the kitchen every time Miles or Georgie spoke to her. It had been she who'd served the tea in the morning room and had run back to the kitchen to report that someone called Jenny had arrived and that everyone seemed delighted to see her. And she was even more amazed when both Mrs Beddows and Kitty – and even Wilkins – threw up their hands in delight and went about their work with broad smiles on their faces. It

360

wasn't long before Jenny came to the kitchen and Joan watched with wide-eyed amazement when the new-comer flung herself into Mrs Beddows's floury arms.

Just before dinner, Georgie took Jenny up to the nursery, where he sat Louisa on his knee – just as he had so long ago with Jenny – and began to read her a bedtime story. Jenny sat on the rug at his feet, watching his face illuminated by the flickering firelight and falling in love with him all over again.

As he finished reading and Louisa was already falling asleep against his shoulder, he smiled down at Jenny and murmured, 'She's a little young for *The Wind in the Willows* at the moment.' Though she forced herself to smile back at him, Jenny felt a flash of jealousy. That book was their story – hers and Georgie's. She didn't want him reading it to anyone else but her. And then she realized how childish she was being. It was time to grow up. Louisa was no threat to her; she was Georgie's half-sister.

Over dinner, the family talked and talked and the conversation was still in full flow when they took coffee in the drawing room. Charlotte wanted to know if Jenny had been able to keep up with her painting and Jenny blushed with pleasure when Georgie assured her that he still had all the pictures she'd done for him.

'They were here waiting for me when I got home. Charlotte told me,' he said softly, 'that you were ada-mant I was still alive.' His blue eyes held her gaze as if silently thanking her for the faith she'd had.

When she'd heard all their news, at last Jenny brought the subject back to herself. She could still see the worried expression in Miles's eyes and knew the honest man would never know a moment's peace if she didn't encourage him to do the right thing.

She took a deep breath and said, 'Miles, I think you're right. We should go to the police and tell them everything.'

She saw Charlotte and Georgie glance at each other, but for once they said nothing. Miles sighed heavily. 'But I don't know what the outcome will be, my dear, if we do.'

'She was only a child,' Charlotte put in softly. 'Surely—'

'But old enough to know right from wrong,' Georgie said soberly. 'That's what they'll judge her on.'

'But she was helpless in the face of what her mother and Arthur Osborne ordered her to do.'

Miles ran his hand through his hair. 'I know, but will the police see it that way? And what about Dot?' He glanced at Jenny. 'We don't want to get her into trouble.'

Jenny shrugged, her expression hardening. 'She wasn't bothered about me getting caught, was she? Besides' – she grinned ruefully – 'Mum will wriggle her way out of it. If whoever questions her is a man, she'll charm him so that he ends up thinking she's been the victim in all this. And, to be honest, she didn't do a lot. She didn't go out at night all that often with Arthur . . .' Her voice trailed away and she hung her head.

'Do you know where Arthur is now?'

Jenny shook her head. 'He left when we were in Sheffield. When – when we moved in with Jim He was the butcher I told you about.'

'And he – the butcher, I mean – was arrested?'
She nodded.

'So, we needn't worry about him, then. Was there

anyone else? This man she's living with now, what's he do?'

'He's a grocer, but he won't have anything to do with the black market. I think he's honest – at least in his business. When I worked for him, there was no funny business with the coupons like there had been with Jim.' She laughed wryly. 'The only thing he's done is leave his wife, but I don't suppose they can arrest him for that, can they?'

'But you said he was – er – trying to get a little too friendly towards you? Wasn't that why you went to Elsie's?'

Jenny bit her lip and nodded. 'He didn't really do anything – I didn't give him the chance.' She shuddered. 'He was just – creepy.'

'Then perhaps we'll be able to keep Dot out of it,' Charlotte said hopefully.

'Not really,' Miles said. 'They'll probably want to interview her.'

'You needn't worry about that if they do,' Jenny said firmly. 'Like I said, my mum can talk her way out of anything. As long as I never have to go back . . .'

'No, never,' they all chorused and Jenny's eyes filled with tears of happiness and relief.

The following day, after further discussion over break-fast, they all agreed that Miles should send for the local bobby. He came in the middle of the afternoon and was shown into Miles's study where they were waiting: Miles, Charlotte, Georgie and Jenny. Joan was looking after Louisa in the nursery. PC Webster was every-one's idea of a village bobby; middle aged, rotund and balding but with a kindly, smiling face that could, when necessary, turn very stern. The local youngsters misbehaved at their peril, yet each and every one of them knew that they could run to him for help at any time.

'Hello, young Jenny,' he greeted her at once as he came into the room, sat in the chair which Miles had placed for him and set his helmet carefully on Miles's desk. 'It's nice to see you back. On holiday, are you?'

'No,' Miles said gently. 'She's back for good. Jenny's going to live with us from now on.'

The constable glanced around at the solemn faces before him and realized at once that he had not been called here to make a social visit.

'Ah,' he said, seeming to understand something of the reasoning behind Miles's statement. But, as an upholder of the law in all it's intricacies, he was obliged to ask, 'How old are you now, love?'

'Fifteen.'

'Mm. And has your mam agreed to you coming to live here?'

'She threw me out,' Jenny told him and Miles added, 'This is all part of what we have to tell you, Mr Webster. I think if Jenny tells you everything that has been happening to her since the time she left us, you will understand – and agree – that she should live with us.'

Harry Webster nodded but he warned them, 'I am here officially, you understand?'

Jenny bit her lip and nodded, but still she hesitated to begin. Georgie moved his chair closer and took hold of her hand. 'Tell Mr Webster everything, Jen, just like you told us yesterday. It'll be for the best.'

She looked up at him trustingly. 'I know. I know it is, only I – I don't want to go to prison.'

There was a startled silence in the room.

'Aw now, lass, I don't reckon it'll come to that, but I can't say if I don't know the story, can I? But whatever it is, the fact that you're coming forward of your own free will counts very much in your favour. So, on you go, love, and don't be frightened. Tell me everything, there's a good lass.'

So she told him everything, just as she had related it all the previous day. The policeman listened solemnly until the girl's voice faded away as she ended, '. . . And so, when Aunty Elsie told me that Miles and Charlotte had come looking for me in London, I – I thought that Mum must have got it wrong.' She gazed at Harry Webster. 'They wouldn't have come all the way to London to tell me about Georgie being alive if – if they hadn't been bothered about me. And Aunty Elsie said she was sure they – they wanted me. They even offered to take her and her boys, she said.' Here Jenny smiled at Charlotte and Miles. 'She thought that was really kind.' She turned back to PC Webster. 'And they'd brought lots of food for me, but they gave it to Aunty Elsie. She was ever so grateful.'

Harry Webster pretended to frown, but his eyes were twinkling as he looked at Miles. 'Nothing contraband, I trust, Mr Thornton?'

'Of course not, officer,' Miles said, indignantly, but he, too, was smiling.

Harry Webster turned back to Jenny, who was regarding him with her bright blue eyes and waiting, trembling a little, for his pronouncement.

'Well, young lady, I don't think I'll be getting my handcuffs out today. It seems to me that, although you knew what you were doing was wrong, you were forced into it by your mother's – er – friend. I can see that there wasn't much else you could have done other than run away, you being only twelve or thirteen at the time, like.'

'I did try to run away,' Jenny said. 'Once. I'd got my suitcase packed and a bit of money saved up and I knew where the station was. Only Uncle Arthur came home and said we were moving. And we did. We did another "moonlight". But I was going to run away and try to get back to London. I knew Aunty Elsie would take me in. If she was still alive, that is.'

'What do you mean, darling?' Charlotte asked softly. 'Why did you think Elsie might have – have died?'

'Because of the bombing.'

'Oh yes,' Charlotte blushed a little, 'how silly of me. We saw that your house and hers had been bombed. For a dreadful moment, we thought – ' She glanced at Miles, remembering how they'd been so fearful that Jenny had been hurt or even killed.

'I am afraid, however,' Harry was saying, 'that my colleagues may feel they need to question your mother. Just to see if she has any idea where this Arthur Osborne might be.'

'She won't know. He's long gone and she's got this other feller now.'

'Ah yes,' Harry consulted the notes he'd been making as Jenny talked. 'Mr Jenkins. Is that right?'

Jenny nodded.

'And you're sure there's nothing more you want to tell me about him?'

Jenny shook her head. 'He never really did anything – you know – but I just didn't like him.'

'I'm sure your "feelings" were right, love. You did well to get yourself out of there.'

'Will you be questioning him?' Miles asked.

Harry shook his head. 'Not at the moment, Mr Thornton, but I shall report everything to my superior and he'll take it from there. But Jenny can forget all about it now. There'll be no further action as far as she's concerned, I can assure you of that. Now she's back with you, I'm sure she won't be getting into any more scrapes, at least none that are on the wrong side of the law, that is.' He ended with a rumbling laugh as he heaved himself out of the chair and picked up his helmet.

When the policeman had left, his rotund form wobbling a little on his bicycle, Georgie tweaked Jenny's nose playfully. 'Father was right, as he usually is. Now you can forget all about it.'

'I just hope Mum doesn't get arrested.'

'I don't think for a minute she will, Jen. Like you say, she'll talk her way out of anything and besides, rather like you, she was under Arthur's thumb.'

'I'll find out from PC Webster how things go,' Miles promised. 'He'll keep us posted about your mother, I'm sure.'

'Thank goodness that's all over,' Charlotte said, getting up. 'And now we have the weekend to look forward to. Felix is coming. You remember Felix, the artist, don't you, Jen?'

'I remember you talking about him, but I never met him.'

'Didn't you?' Charlotte said in surprise. Then she wrinkled her forehead. 'Come to think about it, I don't think he did visit in the early years of the war.' She smiled. 'Too busy trying to protect his precious paintings from the bombing, I expect.'

'And don't forget Cassandra is coming this weekend,' Georgie put in. 'She's got seventy-two hours' leave.'

Margaret Dickinson

Jenny glanced at Charlotte and saw the delight fall from her face at the mention of someone called Cassandra. 'Ah yes,' she said quietly. 'I'd almost forgotten.'

'Who's Cassandra?' Jenny asked, innocent of the bombshell that was about to fall.

'Cassandra is my girlfriend, Jen. She's in the Women's Auxiliary Air Force. She was stationed where I was after I got back. She's lovely. You'll like her, I know you will.'

Jenny stared at him, wondering how he could be so stupid. How could she ever even begin to like any girlfriend of Georgie's when she was so desperately in love with him herself?

368

Fifty-Three

Cassandra was certainly lovely to look at, but there was no way Jenny would ever take to her in a million years. And to Jenny's surprise, Charlotte didn't seem to like the girl either. Though she was polite and charming to her as she was to everyone, there was not the warmth in her tone or in her actions with which she'd welcomed Jenny or greeted Felix, who arrived on the same train as the smartly dressed Waaf. But Miles fussed around Cassandra, making sure she had everything she needed. In the kitchen, Jenny heard Mrs Beddows give a wry snort. 'Men! They fall over themselves for a pretty face. "Handsome is as handsome does", that's what I say.'

'She's very beautiful,' Jenny said, setting the dirty plates she brought from the dining room on the kitchen table. Whilst there were extra guests and Kitty was on ARP duty, Jenny had offered to help Joan.

'I'm frit of serving posh guests, miss,' the young girl told her fearfully.

'You needn't worry about Mr Kerr. He's an old darling.' Already Jenny was charmed by the flamboyant artist. He seemed to know all about her and her ambition to be an artist. Charlotte had obviously told him. 'And as for Cassandra – ' Jenny sniffed dismissively – 'you certainly needn't bother about *her*.'

Some of the anxiety left Joan's face as she giggled. 'You sound as if you don't like her much, miss.'

Georgie's mine, Jenny wanted to shout, but she bit her tongue and smiled weakly. 'Maybe she'll improve on further acquaintance,' she said, rather grandly, and stuck her nose in the air. Then she dropped the charade and chuckled along with Joan. 'But I doubt it.'

'Last time she came,' Joan began, confiding in the girl who was about the same age as she was, 'I had to act as her lady's maid.'

Jenny's eyes widened. 'She's been here before? I thought this was her first visit.'

'Oh no. This is her third – at least, I think it is. Isn't it, Mrs Beddows?'

'Isn't it – what?' Mrs Beddows was putting the finishing touches to a trifle, her tongue caught between her teeth as she set the cherries on top of the whipped cream. Jenny watched her. 'D'you know, I haven't tasted cream since I left here.'

Mrs Beddows smiled as she glanced up and winked at her. 'That's the advantage of living in the country, lass. The master's been able to see that none of us go short and he keeps on the right side of the law, though quite how he does it, I don't know.'

'He makes sure we all get a fair share and not just in this house neither,' Joan said knowingly.

'And how d'you know a thing like that, missy?'

''Cos me dad ses, that's how. Me dad ses there's not a finer feller in this country than Mr Thornton, even though he's a stranger.'

'A stranger? Mr Thornton?' Jenny was appalled. 'How can you say that? He's lived here years.'

Mrs Beddows was bending double with laughter. 'You're never a local in the countryside, lovey, unless you've been born here.' She straightened up. 'Mind you, Mr Thornton's better thought of than most townies. I

370

came with him when he moved here and I reckon I'm only just beginning to be accepted by the locals, but I'm still "'er what come here with the squire".'

Memories came flooding back. Name calling in the playground at school when she'd been here before had included the derisory 'townie' amongst other names. Jenny shuddered and tried not to think about that time. And yet it had turned into a happy experience, but that had all been down to Miles and Charlotte and, of course, Georgie.

'There – all done.' Mrs Beddows stood back to admire her own handiwork. 'Now just you be careful carrying it upstairs. Which of you is going to take it up to the dining room?'

'She is.' The two girls pointed at each other and spoke at the same moment. There was a pause before Jenny sighed and said, 'Oh, all right, then. I suppose I'll have to.'

'You won't get the sack if you drop it,' Joan said. 'I might.'

'I don't think so, but you shake so much when you go in there, you most likely would drop it.' Jenny picked up the trifle and cast a wicked glance at Joan. 'If I do trip up with it, I'll just have to mind I'm chucking it in the direction of Lady Muck.'

'Now, now,' Mrs Beddows chastised gently, but Jenny could see the older woman was having difficulty in keeping a straight face.

'So – how many times has she been here before, then?'

'A couple of times.'

'And?'

'And – what?'

'How serious is it?'

'With Georgie, you mean?' Mrs Beddows shrugged. 'He seems very – ' she paused, not quite knowing what word to use in front of the young girls. In her own mind she'd have said he was 'besotted' but the word didn't sound quite seemly to use about Georgie. It made him sound weak and the brave young pilot was no such thing. She sighed inwardly. And yet didn't love make you weak? She supposed he must love the girl, but the cook couldn't see why. Miss Hoity-Toity was her name for Cassandra. She glanced at Jenny, still standing holding the trifle. 'Now, don't you drop that, Jen, else you'll have me to deal with – not the mistress.'

'You still haven't answered my question,' Jenny said doggedly. The glass bowl in her hands was beginning to feel cold and slippery so she set it down on the table again. 'Please, Mrs Beddows, tell me.'

The cook stared at her as she heard the urgency in Jenny's tone – the yearning. My goodness, Mrs Beddows realized with a pang. The poor child fancies herself in love with Master Georgie. Oh dear, oh dear. She's in for some heartache, there's nothing so sure. She pulled in a deep breath. There was no point in lying to her, no point at all, but she couldn't bring herself to say more than, 'I think he's very fond of her.'

Jenny stared at her for a moment then picked up the trifle and carried it carefully up the stairs and into the dining room to place it in front of Charlotte to serve. Fond. Mrs Beddows had said 'fond'. That was nothing much to worry about, but as she took her place at the table once more, next to Felix Kerr, she saw Georgie's eyes on Cassandra's lovely face and to Jenny's jealous eyes his feelings for the young woman were a whole lot more than 'fond'.

'Now tell me, young lady,' Felix said, putting his arm

around Jenny's shoulders as they all finished eating and rose to go into the drawing room. 'Have you kept up your painting?'

Jenny bit her lip. 'I've tried.' She hoped Miles and Charlotte wouldn't tell Mr Kerr what she *had* been doing while she'd been away. 'But it was sometimes difficult to get paper and paints. I did quite a lot, but I had to leave them all behind when we went back to London.'

Overhearing their conversation, Charlotte said, 'Your table's still waiting for you in the studio upstairs. We've never moved it. You can go up there any time you want to. Help yourself to whatever you want, darling.'

'Studio?' Cassandra's eyebrows, plucked into a neat curve, rose a little. 'You have a studio, Mrs Thornton? Are you an artist, then? I hadn't realized.'

Jenny felt a stab of pleasure. Despite her air of superiority, Cassandra had not been invited to call Charlotte by her Christian name and yet, from the moment she'd arrived here as a scruffy little urchin, Jenny had been made to feel part of the family at once. No such courtesy had been extended to Georgie's girlfriend, it seemed. She risked a glance at Georgie's face. Was he upset by the fact? It didn't seem so. He was ushering Cassandra across the hall and into drawing the room, his arm protectively around her waist. As Cassandra sat down and crossed her shapely legs, she asked, 'What do you paint?' She made it sound as if Charlotte was a mere amateur.

Before Charlotte could even open her mouth to reply, Jenny saw Felix's eyes sparkle with mischief. 'Obviously you don't know very much about the art world, Miss Willoughby, or you would have heard of Charlotte Thornton. Her work sells exceedingly well in the best gallery in London.'

Since Jenny knew that the outlet for Charlotte's paintings was Felix's own gallery, she understood the twinkling in his eyes.

'And Felix is a very well-known artist, Cassandra,' Charlotte said gently, no doubt feeling guilty at Felix teasing their guest. 'You must have heard of Felix Kerr.' But Cassandra's next words must have wiped away any feeling of embarrassment. The young woman wrinkled her forehead as she drawled, 'No, I can't say I have, but of course Daddy's in banking. He doesn't move in the arty circles.' She said the last two words with a scathing tone, as if such a thought was anathema to her and her family.

'He must be finding it difficult just now,' Felix said easily. 'As we all are. The art world has virtually shut down.'

'They've taken a lot of the valuable paintings out of the city, haven't they?' Miles said, handing out the cups for Charlotte whilst she poured.

Felix nodded. 'Away from the bombing.'

'We have a portrait gallery at Willoughby Hall,' Cassandra said, accepting a cup of coffee. 'But Daddy has had all the paintings wrapped up and put down in the cellars until the war's over.'

'Very wise,' Miles murmured. He smiled across the room at Jenny. 'You must take up your painting again in earnest, Jenny. You showed real promise.'

'I still have your picture of the beach in my bedroom,' Georgie said, grinning.

But it was Cassandra's face that was the 'picture' on hearing his words.

'You'll be going to school here, I take it,' Felix said, still addressing Jenny. A moment's fear crossed her face as she remembered her last so-called welcome to the village school. 'Well, I've left. I've been working. I would have liked to have stayed on because I – I missed so much when – when we were moving about. But I don't suppose I could go back now.'

'Then we'll engage a tutor to help you catch up,' Miles said. 'Maybe we could get you into the grammar school in Lynthorpe. Perhaps you'd have a better chance of getting into art college from there.'

Jenny almost dropped her cup and saucer as she stammered, 'Art college?' Suddenly, her face was alight with hope and joy. Art college! She'd only ever dared to dream such a thing and now here was Miles talking as if it could really be possible. Even when Jim had suggested it, she'd known, deep down, that it would never happen. Not while her mother was around. But if Miles and Charlotte were suggesting it, then that was entirely different. If she could go back to school, catch up with all the lessons she'd missed as Miles was promising, then maybe – just maybe – she could make something of the scruffy little urchin, the city street kid.

And maybe then Georgie would forget all about his toffee-nosed girlfriend. But first she had a lot of growing up to do. She knew he was watching her, she could feel his gaze upon her, but at this moment her brilliant blue eyes, wide and shining, were fastened on Miles's face. 'Do – do you really think I could?'

'Why not?' Miles said, spreading his hands as if it was the most natural thing in the world. Jenny turned her gaze to Charlotte. 'Am I good enough?'

'You showed a lot of promise for your age when you were with us, Jenny,' Charlotte said seriously. 'But we'd need to see how you've progressed.'

Jenny's face fell. 'I haven't had anyone to advise me. Mum—' She stopped, unwilling to say anything else derogatory about her mother. Enough had been said already.

'Don't worry,' Charlotte promised. 'I'll help you.'

'And so will I,' Felix promised generously, flinging his arms wide with one of his flamboyant gestures. 'And I shall be the first gallery in London to hang a Jenny Mercer painting.'

Everyone laughed, including Jenny. Only Cassandra stared stony-faced at them as if they had all gone completely mad.

Fifty-Four

The war news was encouraging. Georgie read the daily papers avidly. Allied forces were advancing across Germany and towards the end of March, he told the rest of the family, 'The Allies have crossed the Rhine and taken Cologne.'

Jenny was the happiest she'd ever been in her whole life, happier even than when she'd been at Ravensfleet before. The only shadow on her complete happiness was the presence of Georgie's girlfriend. But Cassandra had gone after her three days' leave and, for a while, Jenny could imagine that the girl didn't exist. Once again, Georgie became hers. At least, he would have done had it not been for Louisa, whom everyone called Lou-Lou. But Jenny felt no animosity, no jealousy towards her. In fact, she became as besotted with the merry child as everyone else in the family and played happily in the nursery with her for hours on end.

'My little sister,' she murmured in Lou-Lou's ear when the little girl held up her arms to be cuddled. 'My darling little sister.'

Georgie spent many hours with both girls. He read to them, entertained them and they went out walking together, though now with his wounded leg, he couldn't walk as far as the beach. 'And before anyone suggests it,' he said firmly. 'I am not taking to a wheelchair or even taking to using a stick.'

'I could drive you down the lane to the sandhills,' Miles said. 'You could make it from there, couldn't you?'

'Oh do try, Georgie. I want to go picking samphire again.'

'It won't be ready yet.'

'I know. But we don't have to wait for that,' Jenny insisted. 'I've not seen the sea since I came back and I want you to be there when I do. Please, Georgie.'

So one warm April morning they all set off on a trip to the beach with a picnic hamper packed by Mrs Beddows.

'I've not been on a picnic since I was here before,' Jenny said, completely forgetting in her excitement that she was supposed to be acting like a grown-up.

'Then this will be the best picnic ever,' Miles said, loading the hamper, rugs and folding chairs into the car boot. They arrived at the spot where the lane gave way to sand. Jenny scrambled out and ran ahead, up the slope of the dunes where she stood breathing in the sea air. The tide was coming in, but there was still a stretch of smooth, untouched sand though the barbed wire was still there. She turned to see Miles carrying the basket towards a sheltered hollow in the sand-hills. Jenny ran back to the car. 'Let me help. What shall I carry?'

'You take the rugs and I'll manage a couple of the chairs,' Georgie said. 'Charlotte's got her hands full with Lou-Lou.'

Soon everything had been transported to their picnic spot.

'Let's build a sandcastle just far enough up the beach so that the tide comes in and swirls round the moat,' Georgie said, dropping any pretence of being an adult himself now.

Charlotte shaded her eyes and looked out to where the sea lapped the sand. 'Can we get right to the water's edge through the barbed wire?'

'We can now. Someone's cut a hole over there. Look.'

'Now, I wonder who could have done that?' Miles murmured.

Charlotte laughed. 'Alfie. He hates the barbed wire. I hope he doesn't get into trouble.'

'I haven't seen Alfie yet. Is he still working at Buckthorn Farm?'

'Yes, but he's stayed on at school. He got a transfer to the Grammar School and he wants to go to agricultural college, like Ben did, but he still works on the farm at weekends if you want to see him.'

Jenny nodded. 'I'll take Lou-Lou in the pushchair and walk over to see him tomorrow if it's fine.'

'Father, did you bring the buckets and spades?'

'Of course. With *three* children,' he chuckled, counting Georgie as one of them, 'I'm hardly likely to forget.'

'Four,' Charlotte corrected him and promptly sat down on the rug to peel off her shoes and stockings. Picking up her small daughter, she began to pick her way across the mud and the shingle, beyond where the samphire grew to the beach. 'Come along, children,' she called gaily. 'Let's get building this castle.'

The next half-hour was happily spent whilst Georgie, Charlotte and Jenny constructed a sandcastle with a moat. Even Louisa dug with her little spade.

'Now a bridge with a tunnel underneath it,' Georgie said, lowering himself on to the sand, his wounded leg sticking out awkwardly as he made the bridge.

'Shells,' Charlotte said. 'We need shells for windows and doors.'

Louisa, watched over by Miles, picked up handfuls

of sand and threw them in the air, squealing with delight. Now she picked up a shell and held it out to her mother.

'Clever girl,' Charlotte laughed. 'Press it into the side of the castle, like this.'

It was such a truly happy day for them all, but especially for Jenny, who could begin to put the dark days of life with her mother and the string of 'uncles' well and truly behind her.

The castle completed, they watched the tide creep nearer and near. At last a wave reached it and swirled around the moat.

'Now it's a real castle,' Georgie said. But it wasn't long before the tide encroached even more and began to wash away the walls and the towers. Louisa's face crumpled and she began to cry as the waves demolished the last sign of their castle.

'Don't cry, Lou-Lou,' Jenny promised, gently wiping away the child's tears. 'We can soon build another one. Let's go and have our picnic now.'

They sat and ate their picnic in the sheltered hollow in the dunes but Louisa was still hiccuping sadly as they packed up and carried her back to the car.

'Perhaps it wasn't such a good idea,' Georgie said worriedly. 'I didn't think it would upset her.'

'Don't worry,' Charlotte said. 'Even at Lou-Lou's age, you have to learn that life has its ups and downs. If she never knows anything worse than seeing her sand-castle washed away by the sea, she'll be a very lucky little girl.'

'Yes, but she's so little to start having to learn about life's disappointments,' Georgie murmured, his eyes still anxious.

'Never too young, Georgie dear,' Charlotte said softly. 'She'll have forgotten all about it by the time we get home and the next time we build one for her we'll teach her how to have fun jumping on it herself before the tide can reach it.'

And indeed, by the time they reached the manor, Louisa was fast asleep against Georgie's shoulder.

But as it turned out, there were to be no more sandcastle-building expeditions for the moment. The very next day, Georgie received a letter telling him to report for a medical.

'You haven't got to go back, have you?' Jenny was trembling with fear and Charlotte looked anxious. 'They can't make you, can they? You're wounded. Besides, it'll soon be over, won't it?'

'I'm still in the RAF. I won't be flying any more.' Jenny was shocked by the look of sadness on his face. She couldn't understand why he would even want to when all she could think of was keeping him safely at home with all of them. And away from Cassandra. Her heart sank at the thought. Perhaps that was why he wanted to go back, so that he'd be nearer her. Maybe he'd even be on the same station as Cassandra. 'But they'll probably find me a desk job somewhere or train me to work in the control tower on an airfield. They sometimes do that with crocked-up pilots.'

Jenny's voice rose a pitch as she said, 'But – but they bomb airfields, don't they? You'll be in danger.'

Georgie put his arm around her and drew her to him. 'Look, Jen, I've only been at home because I'm recovering. I always knew I'd have to go back as soon as they said I was fit enough.'

'But you're not fit enough. You're still limping.'

Georgie grinned ruefully. 'I'll probably always have a limp, Jen. I don't think that's ever going to get quite better.'

Jenny stuck her chin out stubbornly. 'Then when you go for this medical, limp more.'

Georgie laughed. 'I can't do that, Jen. I'm no shirker. Besides, it's high time I went back and did something useful.'

Before she could stop herself, the words burst from her mouth. 'You're going to be with *her*, aren't you?'

For a moment Georgie frowned, then, as understanding dawned, he looked incredibly sad. 'Oh, Jen,' he whispered, touching her hair gently, 'don't you like Cassandra?'

She stared at him for a long moment before saying harshly, 'No, I don't. And she doesn't like me.'

'Oh, Jen, I'm sure—'

But she didn't stay to listen to any more. She turned away from him. 'I've got to go. Charlotte's taking me into Lynthorpe to buy me some new clothes. I've an interview with the headmaster of the grammar school tomorrow.'

'Jen, don't go like that – ' he called after her, but Jenny hurried away. She didn't want him to see the tears that were already streaming down her face.

Fifty-Five

Both Charlotte and Felix Kerr had been as good as their word. Jenny had hoped that Charlotte would encourage her to draw and paint again and would offer guidance, but she hadn't expected Felix to take such a keen interest. He was a frequent visitor to the manor and always arrived laden with presents for all of them and usually he brought painting materials or art books for Jenny. 'When this wretched war is finished, you shall come to London and I'll take you round all the galleries,' he offered. 'Would you like that?'

Jenny hesitated.

'We'll both come – if we may,' Charlotte said at once, sensitive to how Jenny must be feeling about the city just now. The bombing must have left her with bad memories and the trauma of her home life was obviously still fresh in the girl's mind.

'Of course, of course.' Felix spread his arms wide. 'Miles too. We'll make a special occasion of it. It'll be something to look forward to.'

Georgie, keen to get back into some sort of active service, was declared fit enough to undertake a sedentary occupation. 'I've been posted to Scampton.'

'Where's that?' Jenny asked with a belligerent note in her tone.

Miles and Charlotte were already smiling as Georgie explained, 'About forty-five miles away.'

Jenny's heart lifted. He'd be able to get home often – if he wanted to. But she couldn't stop herself asking, 'Is *she* there?'

'No, Cassandra is on an airfield in the south of England – the station where I flew from. That's how I met her.'

'So – why aren't you going back there?'

'Because I can't fly any more.' They could all hear the disappointment in his voice that had more to do with not being able to fly than with his girlfriend. Yet not one of them could sympathize with his feelings; they wanted him safe.

'But,' Georgie was saying, 'there's a vacancy for some sort of desk job at Scampton so that's where I'm going.'

'Do you know what you'll be doing?' Miles asked. 'Will you need training?'

'They haven't said. I'd hoped to be in the control tower, but I think those jobs are usually taken by Waafs.'

More girls! Jenny thought with anguish. She bit her lip, but in that moment she realized she was being rather childish about the whole business of Cassandra – and any other girl he might meet. She couldn't really expect him to wait until she grew up. He was nine years older than she was. Georgie was a handsome young man who was obviously going to have girlfriends. But there and then Jenny decided – quite deliberately – that she must act in a more adult manner. She must try to get him to begin to see her as a grown-up, not as some silly schoolgirl, who still pouted and stamped her foot when things didn't suit her.

So she smiled bravely and gave him a swift hug. 'So you'll be able to get home often.'

'Of course. I'm going to get a motorbike. It'll use a

lot less petrol than a car and it'll mean I can get down to see Cassandra.'

Jenny felt a physical pain in her chest and she turned and ran from the room. The vow to be more grown-up hadn't lasted many minutes.

Charlotte, sensitive to the girl's feelings for Georgie, watched her go with troubled eyes.

Later, she found Jenny in the studio. She sat down in front of her own easel near the window and regarded the painting she was working on with a critical eye. Without looking round, Charlotte said softly, 'If I tell you something, Jenny, you won't say anything to anyone else, will you?'

Jenny glanced up at her, but Charlotte was still looking at her own painting.

'No,' the girl said quietly and added a little bitterly, 'I'm good at keeping secrets.'

'It's just that – I don't like Cassandra very much either.'

The thought that she'd been right made Jenny smile a little smugly. 'I thought so.'

Now Charlotte turned round to look at her. 'Did you? Oh dear! Was it obvious?'

'Not to her,' Jenny said with wisdom beyond her years. Though she didn't realize it yet, she was already quite adult in a lot of ways. It was only where Georgie was concerned that jealousy made her childish. 'Only to people who know you well.'

'So – you think Georgie might have noticed?' Now Charlotte was worried and Jenny considered her question carefully.

'I don't think he's noticed it yet,' she said slowly, 'but—'

'If I let it show next time she comes, he might?'

'Well, I could see it and he's known you an awful lot longer than I have.'

'Mm.' Charlotte was thoughtful and then she sighed. 'Oh dear, what fools we women are, Jen. I just want the best for Georgie and I don't think she's right for him.'

'Neither do I,' Jenny said at once and feeling safe in this little room with only Charlotte to hear, she added, 'There's only one person who ought to marry Georgie and that's me.'

Once the words were said, she couldn't take them back and she waited, holding her breath, fully expecting Charlotte to laugh or even be angry at her audacity. But Charlotte got up and crossed the room to her, kneeling down and putting her arms around her. 'Oh Jen,' she whispered as the young girl buried her head against Charlotte's neck.

They threw a party on Georgie's last night, which happily coincided with Ben coming home on leave and also with another of Felix's frequent visits. Ben hadn't altered except that he seemed taller. Perhaps it was all the military training that made him carry himself more erect.

'So you're going to be one of the "chairborne" now,' he teased Georgie, slapping him on the back. It was a jovial term used in the RAF for those who didn't fly but who sat at a desk. 'Thank goodness for that. At least we'll know you're comparatively safe.'

'Why "comparatively"?' Jenny asked, sitting down at the dinner table next to Georgie and across the table from Ben and Felix. Miles and Charlotte sat at either end of the long dining table. Jenny was determined to be very grown-up tonight. Charlotte had helped her to wash her hair and it now hung in waves and curls to her shoulders. And she was wearing a pretty dress, which Charlotte had bought for her.

Ben glanced at Georgie before saying quietly, 'Because the enemy try to bomb airfields and it's a bomber station where Georgie is going. So it's what they call a prime target.'

Jenny nodded. 'Like London. They tried to demoralize us, but they reckoned without us cockneys. We don't give in that easy.'

'How was it when you went back?' Ben asked quietly, sensing that Jenny could handle talking about it now.

'We always went to the shelters or to the nearest underground sometimes. That was the best place.' She grinned. 'We'd share food and sing songs and the kids would play, then we'd all settle down on the platforms to sleep.' Then her face clouded. 'But I wasn't there long.' She glanced up at Miles. 'We did a moonlight – thanks to Uncle Arthur.' She didn't know how much Ben had been told, but she rather thought he would have heard about it. There didn't seem to be any secrets within the Thornton family. But they might not, of course, have told Felix.

Miles cleared his throat and seemed to speak directly to Felix. 'Jenny spent some time in Derbyshire and that's why we couldn't find her when we went to London to tell her that we'd heard Georgie was safe.'

'I remember.' Felix nodded.

'So it wasn't until she got back there recently that one of their neighbours told her we'd been looking for her.' Miles reached across the corner of the table and put his hand over Jenny's. 'And so here she is back safe and sound with us.'

How neatly Miles had turned the conversation away

from the traumas Jenny had suffered and yet had managed to give a plausible explanation to their friend. As long as Felix didn't ask awkward questions about her time in Derbyshire, but it seemed he was content and turned the conversation instead to Charlotte's painting and then, once more, to thoughts of Jenny's future. The art world was his life and he never tired of talking about it. And Jenny never tired of hearing about it. She was even beginning to hope that it was a world in which, one day, she might have a part.

'So,' he asked her, 'how did you get on in your interview with the headmaster?'

Jenny grimaced. 'I've got to sit some exams.'

Miles took up the story. 'But he did say that if Jenny can reach the required standard in the examinations he's going to set her, then she can be admitted and take the School Certificate at the end of the summer term. He also said that because teachers, and the education authorities too, are well aware of how the war has disrupted children's education, they are keen to be helpful whenever possible.'

'Really.' Felix beamed. 'How wonderful. And . . . ?'

Miles chuckled. 'The headmaster and the art master looked at the paintings Jenny has done since she's been back with us.'

'And . . . ?' Felix prompted again.

'They say she shows remarkable talent.'

'Ah, what sensible people. We know that, but I always fear that others aren't going to be blessed with our perception.' Everyone around the table laughed. 'So – what's next?'

'One of the teachers from the school has agreed to tutor Jenny in the evenings and at weekends. He'll set work for her to do each day and—'

'But she must leave time for her art.'

'Of course.' Miles inclined his head in agreement. 'Everyone realizes that is of paramount importance.'

'The teacher, Mr Lomax,' Charlotte explained, 'is a committed young man but he was very distressed when he failed his medical for the armed forces at the beginning of the war. He says this is a way he feels he can "do his bit".'

'I'd've thought he was already doing it by continuing as a teacher,' Felix spread his hands, 'but I'm hardly going to argue with him if he's going to help Jenny.'

'We'll make sure he has everything he needs and I shall fetch him from Lynthorpe each day.' Miles laughed. 'Though it might have to be in the pony and trap. The only thing that bothers me is that he's refusing to take any payment for tutoring Jenny.'

'Don't press him any more, Miles, if that's the way he feels,' Charlotte said softly. 'He might begin to feel insulted.'

'No, no, I won't.'

'And I'll work ever so hard to repay him,' Jenny promised. 'To repay all of you.'

'You being here is all we want.'

'But if I get to college then – then I'd be going away again, wouldn't I?'

'Yes, but that would be very different. You'd always come back here. Or at least we'd hope you would.'

Jenny nodded vigorously.

'Would you really like to go to art college, Jen?' Georgie asked.

'I think so. Can you become an art teacher in a school, then?'

Felix laughed. 'So you don't want to become a famous artist with your pictures hanging in every gallery

389

in the land or the rich and famous clamouring for you to paint their portrait?'

'It'd be nice, but I don't think I'll be good enough.'

'Don't underestimate yourself, my dear. You have a natural talent that we all' – he glanced round the table to include all the Thornton family – 'intend to see is nurtured and brought to its full potential. There's just one thing,' he added, wagging his finger at her and pretending to be serious though she could see his eyes were twinkling. 'I shall do everything I can to prevent you running off and getting married and having hordes of babies.'

'Now that's a little hard, Felix,' Georgie laughed. 'Jenny's a pretty girl and Father and Charlotte will have young men queuing halfway down the driveway when she's a little older.'

Round the table everyone laughed, but it was not cruel laughter, just the gentle sort of teasing that goes on within a real family. Even Jenny joined in, though she knew she was blushing and so avoided catching Charlotte's eye.

Fifty-Six

'Hitler's committed suicide.' Miles rushed into the dining room on the first day of May waving the newspaper. 'It'll all be over now.'

'Are you sure?' Charlotte hardly dared to believe it. 'Won't there be someone to take his place?'

'Oh they might try, but the Russians are already in Berlin and the Americans will be there any day if they're not already. I think the war in Europe will be over in a matter of days, though defeating Japan might take a little longer.'

Miles was right and on 7 May, General Montgomery, along with other high-ranking officials, accepted the Germans' surrender.

'It's over. It's really over.' Charlotte cried tears of joy. 'The boys will be coming home for good.'

With the morning post came more exciting news.

'Where's Jenny?' Miles emerged from his study waving a letter.

'She's just playing with Lou-Lou in the nursery before she settles down to her lessons. Why?'

'Right, let's go and find her.'

Charlotte's heart lurched, but she could tell from Miles's face that it was not bad news. 'What is it?'

'You'll see in a minute,' he promised as he led the way upstairs.

Miles flung open the nursery door with a flourish.

Jenny and Louisa, kneeling in front of the doll's house, looked up, startled.

'Jen, I've had a letter from your headmaster.'

Jenny got up slowly, looking anxious, but she saw that Miles was smiling.

'He's written to say that he's very pleased with your progress and that if you do well in your School Certificate examinations, there'll be a place in the sixth form for you if you want it.'

'If I want it?' Jenny laughed with relief. For one dreadful moment she'd thought she was going to be asked to leave the school where she'd settled in so well and was loving every minute. 'What a silly question!'

'You could probably go to art school sooner, but Charlotte and I feel that you'd do much better to go to school for another two years first and study for your Higher Certificate. How do you feel about that?'

Jenny's face fell. 'But I won't be earning anything, I won't be able to—'

Miles waved her worries aside. 'You're our daughter now – or as good as – and it's what we'd do for any of our children.' Miles had asked his solicitor about the legalities surrounding Jenny living with them permanently. Word came back that Dot had agreed to the arrangement – a little too readily, in Miles's opinion, yet he was grateful that she had done so. Now he continued happily, 'What we *have* done for the boys and what we'll one day do for Lou-Lou. So, what do you say? Shall I write and tell him you'd like to stay on another two years?'

'Oh yes, yes, yes,' she cried, flinging herself, first at Miles and then at Charlotte whilst Louisa clapped delightedly even though she didn't understand what the reason for all the excitement was. 'Thank you, thank you, thank you.'

'We have to go and see the headmaster next Monday afternoon after school to talk about what subjects you'd like to take in the sixth form.'

'Can I take art?'

'Of course. He understands that's what you want to do and he's promised that all the teachers will help you, especially, he said, the art teacher.'

'I couldn't have a better teacher than Charlotte and Felix,' Jenny said loyally.

'That's sweet of you, darling, but the school teacher will know just what's required to get you into a proper art school.'

Jenny felt suddenly nervous and yet excited too. 'Oh, I'll work so hard for you. I won't let you down.'

Charlotte put her arms around her and hugged her. 'We know you won't.'

'Now we've a double celebration,' Miles said happily.

'Is Georgie coming home? I can't wait to tell him.'

'He will be soon, I expect, but you'd better write to him. He'll be thrilled for you.'

'I will. I'll do it now and walk down to the post office.'

She turned and ran to the room next door to the nursery that was still her bedroom.

'She's growing up so fast,' Miles murmured as he picked Louisa up and set her gently on the rocking horse.

'Sixteen in August,' Charlotte answered.

'I expect we'll soon have young men knocking at the door just like Georgie predicted.'

Charlotte glanced at her husband. Men – even her beloved husband – could be so blind in matters of the heart, she thought. Softly she said, 'Not a word to a soul, Miles, but our Jenny's heart is already captured.'

Miles blinked and then stared at her. Then his face cleared, 'Oh Alfie, d'you mean?'

Charlotte chuckled and shook her head. 'Closer to home than Alfie. A lot closer to home.'

She could almost hear cogs whirring in his head. 'You don't mean – ?'

'Indeed I do, but promise me you won't way a word and you certainly mustn't tease her or even hint as much to him. She's very sensitive about it.'

Miles glanced at the closed door through which Jenny had disappeared a moment before. 'So that's why she doesn't like Cassandra,' he murmured.

Charlotte gave a most unladylike snort. 'Well, I'm not exactly enamoured of Georgie's choice either and that has nothing to do with good old-fashioned jealousy.'

Miles laughed and put his arm around her shoulders. 'Oh, I don't know. We all know he's always been your golden boy. No doubt you think if he marries Cassandra he'll move away and we won't see much of him.'

'She'd see to that.' Charlotte couldn't keep the bitterness from her tone.

'But isn't Jenny awfully young for him, even supposing he were to – well – think of her in that way?'

'She seems so now, yes, I grant you. But there're only nine years between them. Another couple of years and she'll be an adult.' She laughed. 'There are several more years than that between you and me, now aren't there?'

'But he could get married before, well, before Jenny grows up.'

'Yes,' Charlotte agreed flatly. 'Indeed he could.'

*

Now that the war was over, Charlotte and Jenny fully expected both Georgie and Ben to be demobbed and to return home. Only Miles knew differently. 'There's still a lot of work to be done. It'll take time before everyone is allowed to come home, except on leave, of course. The soldiers who are still abroad will be first home and rightly so. Some of them might not have seen their families for years.'

'Of course. I hadn't looked at it like that, but you're right.' Charlotte smiled. 'We'll just have to be patient a little longer.'

But when Georgie came home on leave, it was to tell them that he thought he would stay in the RAF for a little longer. 'There's a lot of paperwork and organization still to be done and my commanding officer thinks I can be useful, even with a limp,' he joked. Then he shrugged. 'And I really don't know what else I'd do anyway. I've not trained for anything other than flying.'

'I'm sure that other opportunities to do with commercial flying might arise after the war,' Miles murmured.

'I don't think I'd pass a medical now, would I?'

'It'd be worth a try. They can only say no.'

Georgie's face brightened. 'You're right.'

'But flying's dangerous,' Jenny blurted out before she could stop herself.

'Quite right,' Charlotte said firmly. 'We want you safe now, Georgie. We've had enough worry over the last six years.'

'Oh you two!' He put an arm around each of them. 'What shall we do with them, Father?'

Miles smiled at the three of them standing before him. How he loved them all. And part of him understood the women's anxiety, but being a man, he could understand his son's point of view too. Georgie had to find something to do with his life now the war was over. And he loved flying. It was as simple as that.

But then Georgie went and spoilt the moment. 'I must go,' he said, dropping his arms from around Charlotte and Jenny. 'I'm meeting the two o'clock train. Ben will be on it and Cassandra too. She's coming for the weekend.'

Fifty-Seven

At three and a half, Louisa was adorable. She could wrap each member of the family around her little finger and Jenny was no exception. When Jenny wasn't at her lessons or painting, the little girl followed her everywhere.

On the Saturday morning she begged Jenny to take her to the beach. 'We can pick samphire for Mrs Beddows,' she pleaded.

'All right,' Jenny agreed, pleased to have an excuse to get out of the house when Cassandra was around. 'Get your wellingtons on and we'll go.'

But as they were rummaging in the hall cupboard for their boots, Cassandra appeared.

'Going out?'

'Lou-Lou wants to go to the beach to pick samphire.'

'What on earth's that?'

'It's a plant that grows on the marshes near the beach.'

'Mrs Beddows will cook it for lunch,' Louisa informed her solemnly.

'You actually pick something off the beach that we eat? Ugh!'

Jenny hid her smile. 'It's quite nice really. Right, you ready, Lou-Lou? Bye, Cassandra.'

'I'll come with you. I've nothing to do this morning. Now Ben's home too, Georgie's gone off round the estate with his father and brother.' She pulled a face. 'I'm not into looking at smelly pigs and mournful-looking cows.'

Jenny hid her smile. 'Of course,' she said, making a valiant effort to be friendly. 'I'm sure Charlotte's boots will fit you.' She opened the hall cupboard door again and fished out a pair of dusty boots.

Cassandra slipped off her shoes and tried on the boots. 'They're a wee bit loose, but they'll do. Is there a headscarf in there I could borrow? I only had my hair done yesterday before I came.'

Again Jenny searched through the clothes hanging in the cupboard and on the shelves. Louisa was jumping up and down. 'Come on, Jen.'

'Here you are, Cassandra, and you'd better take this pair of gloves. It can get very cold on the beach, even in June.'

They set off, taking the back way through the gardens of the manor, crossed the main road and walked down the long lane leading to the sandhills, Louisa skipping beside them.

'My, it's a long way,' Cassandra said, pausing to catch her breath and shading her eyes to look how far they still had to walk.

Jenny hid her smile and walked on, leaving Cassandra, struggling in boots that were a size too large to catch up. When they reached the dunes, Jenny said, 'Hang on a mo, I've to pick up the sticks and rags. There's a box they leave somewhere beside the path. Now where is it? Ah, here is it.' She opened the lid of the wooden box and picked out an armful of sticks and white squares of rags. 'They're left here for anyone to use.'

'What are they for?' Cassandra asked.

'Marking the track through the marshes in case a mist comes down. It's very easy to get lost and lose your sense of direction if a sea fret comes in.'

Cassandra's mouth curved in a sneer, but she said nothing.

As they headed towards the place where the samphire grew in profusion, Jenny marked their path carefully, just as Georgie had shown her all those years ago. Now, she was showing his little sister. 'You stay close beside me, Lou-Lou. Don't go running off now, will you?'

Young though she was, Louisa had already been carefully instructed about how dangerous the marshes and the sea could be if care wasn't taken.

With the final marker in place, Jenny stood up and looked about her. 'We must watch for the tide coming in too. It forms creeks and you can easily get cut off.'

'Really,' Cassandra said off-handedly. She looked down at the plants growing at her feet. 'Is this the stuff we've to pick?'

'Yes. I've brought a bucket. Now, be careful, Lou-Lou, mind the stems don't cut your hands.'

'I know how to do it. Mummy and Daddy bringed me last year.'

Jenny stared at her. 'Do you remember?' The child would only have been two and a half then, but Louisa was nodding solemnly. 'Daddy marked the path just like you've done.'

Jenny marvelled at the young child's memory; Louisa was remarkably bright.

They began picking samphire, but Cassandra soon bored of the job. She couldn't grasp the stems properly wearing the gloves and she had no intention of soiling her hands. She wandered off towards the beach and the sea, heading for the hole in the barbed wire so that she could reach the water's edge.

'Don't go too far, Cassandra,' Jenny called, but the young woman merely raised her hand, waggled her fingers and carried on walking.

Jenny stood up and glanced towards the landmark they'd always used; the mill. It was still clearly visible. She bent again and plucked more samphire.

'Mrs Beddows will be pleased,' Louisa said and Jenny smiled.

'Has she shown you how to cook it yet?'

The little girl shook her head solemnly. 'She ses I'm too lickle to be near hot pans yet. But she's promised to teach me when I'm growed up.'

After a few minutes, Jenny stood up again, checking about her. She glanced towards the sea. The tide had turned and was coming in now, quite fast. And further out to sea, there was a mist forming.

'Come on, Lou-Lou, time to go. The tide's coming in and I reckon there's a mist coming too.'

Louisa didn't argue; she understood at once.

When they'd put all that they'd picked into the bucket, Jenny glanced around for sight of Cassandra. 'Now where's that wretched woman gone? Oh my, she's right down at the water's edge.'

Jenny bit her lip. She was tempted, very tempted, to leave Cassandra to her fate, but she pushed the wicked thought aside. 'Come on, Lou-Lou, I'll take you back to the sandhills and you must stay there – you promise me – while I go after Cassandra.'

Louisa was a good little girl and Jenny was sure she would do as she was told and yet she was afraid to leave such a young child on her own for what might take some time. But luck was on her side for once. When they crested the sandhills, she could see a figure in the fields to the right. And, better still, she knew who it was. She cupped her hands around her mouth and yelled at the top of her voice.

'Alfie, Alfie.' The wind whipped the sound away and it took several attempts before he turned and saw her waving frantically and beckoning. Sensing her urgency, Alfie began to run towards her as she took hold of Louisa's hand and set off down the hill to meet him.

'We were picking samphire,' she explained quickly, 'but Cassandra has wandered off towards the sea. The tide's coming and there's a sea mist blowing in. I'll have to go after her, but I can't risk taking Lou-Lou. Alfie, will you take her back to the manor?'

'I'll take her to Buckthorn Farm. Mrs Thornton's there visiting her father. I'll come back as soon as I've handed Louisa over to her ma. But she'll not get far – this Cassandra – because of the barbed wire.'

'She has – she's got through a hole and got right to the sea.'

'Oh heck – I made that hole.' He looked suddenly guilty.

'Don't blame yourself. It's her own silly fault. I did warn her.' As she handed Louisa over into Alfie's safe keeping, she turned and began to run back towards the sandhills.

'Be careful, Jen,' Alfie's anxious voice drifted back to her. 'I'll come as soon as I can.' She raised her hand in a wave of acknowledgement, but ran on as fast as she could.

Fifty-Eight

Jenny ran on until she felt as if her lungs would burst. Panting hard, she climbed the sandhill again and slid down the other side. The mist had rolled in even further, almost covering the place now where she and Louisa had been picking samphire. The white markers hung limply against the sticks. And worst of all, she could no longer see Cassandra.

'Cassandra!' Jenny yelled at the top of her voice. She listened but could hear no answer. Again and again she shouted, all the time moving towards the sea. As she threaded her way through the hole in the barbed wire, she too was lost in a swirling white mist and now she couldn't see the shore or the sea. But her hearing was acute and she could hear the waves. Jenny swallowed her fear and kept on calling and then listening in turn. She came to the first creek – the tide was coming in fast now. She waded through it. Gaining hard sand on the other side, she shouted again then was suddenly still. Was that an answering cry? She called again and yes – very faintly, she heard Cassandra screaming, 'Jenny – Jenny?'

'Cassandra! Cassandra, keep calling but stand still. Stay where you are.' Jenny moved forward, carefully now. She had to find the young woman, but it would help no one if she injured herself or lost her bearings. At the moment, she was sure she was still heading directly towards the sea. 'Keep shouting, Cassandra.' And this time the answer definitely sounded nearer, but to her left.

'Jenny – help me. The water's coming in. I'll drown.' Cassandra sounded hysterical but at least her frightened cries were leading Jenny to her. Nearer and nearer. 'There's barbed wire—'

'Stand *still*, Cassandra. I can't find you if you keep moving about.'

'But the sea's coming in.' She was screaming in terror, but now Jenny was getting closer to her with every step. And then suddenly she felt two hands grasp her arm, clinging desperately.

'You're all right, Cassandra. Calm down.'

'But we're lost. No one'll find us in this fog. We'll drown. The sea—'

'We'll be all right if you just calm down and do exactly as I tell you.'

'Oh Jen, thank you, thank you for coming for me. I'm so sorry I—' Whatever she'd been going to say ended in a scream as a wave hit her legs and caught her off balance, knocking her to her knees. She clung to Jenny, sobbing hysterically.

'Now listen, Cassandra –' Jenny grabbed Cassandra's shoulders, hauled her to her feet and shook her. 'We have to find our way back to the hole in the wire.'

'We can't. We don't know which way it is.'

'Just stop panicking and let me think.'

After she'd come through the hole, she'd turned to her left, following the sound of Cassandra's voice. So the sea would have been on her right. So, now, they had to turn round and walk back with the sea on their left.

'Where did that wave hit you?'

'On my leg.'

'Which leg?'

'Why does it matter which leg?' Her voice was rising to a high-pitched squeak again. 'Just get us back.'

Jenny tightened her grip on Cassandra's arm. 'Because,' she said, trying hard to hold on to her patience, 'I need to know where the sea is. It needs to be on our left. So, if the wave hit your right leg, we're facing the wrong direction.'

'Are you sure?'

Jenny bit her lip and pulled in a deep breath, praying that she was right. 'Yes,' she said firmly, with more confidence in her tone than she was actually feeling inside, but at that moment, as if coming to their aid, the sea sent another wave crashing into them both and now Jenny knew for sure. 'This way,' she said, turning Cassandra around and pulling her along.

The water was swirling around them now, getting deeper and deeper. 'Keep going,' Jenny urged. She was supporting the weeping girl now, almost half carrying her. 'We'll be all right,' she kept repeating, but it was obvious that Cassandra didn't believe her. She clung to Jenny, leaning heavily on the younger, slighter girl.

'Now – about here we need to turn again towards the sandhills so the sea needs to be behind us.' But now they were walking in the shallows of the incoming tide and it was difficult to know. The water was suddenly deeper and Cassandra gripped Jenny even tighter and screamed again. 'We'll drown, we'll drown.'

The mist cleared a little for a brief moment and Jenny cried, 'Look out, there's the barbed wire in front of us. Thank goodness. Now, all we've got to do is find the hole.'

Cassandra, a little calmer now, snivelled like a lost child. 'I cut myself on the wire back there.'

Suddenly the sand beneath their feet dipped and they almost tumbled forwards into the water, clinging on to each other to stay upright.

'You've brought us the wrong way,' Cassandra shrieked. 'We're going into the sea.'

'No, we're not. It's only a creek. It's the way the tide comes in. Come on. It won't be deep.'

'I can't, I can't.' And, stubbornly, Cassandra stopped and refused to budge.

'Oh Cassandra, for Heaven's sake, pull yourself together. I thought Waafs were supposed to be courageous.'

'I can't help it. I hate the sea.'

'Then what on earth made you go towards it?'

Just when Jenny was at her wits' end to know what to do next, she heard the sound of voices through the mist. She took a deep breath and yelled, 'Here, we're here!' She felt Cassandra jump at the suddenness of Jenny's shouting, but then she began to call too. 'Help! Oh help us!'

And then Jen recognized Georgie's voice. 'Stand still, Jen, then I can find you. Keep shouting.'

'Over here. We're here.'

In only a few minutes, they heard someone splashing through the creek in front of them.

'Georgie – here,' Jenny called again and then his tall figure was looming up out of the mist. He threw his arms around them both and hugged them before saying, 'Let's get you both home. You must be frozen. Hang on to me.' He placed himself between them, but Cassandra still refused to step into the water. 'I can't. I can't.'

Jenny felt Georgie let go of her. He turned and picked Cassandra up in his arms. 'Hold on to my coat, Jen. Don't let go.'

Carefully he stepped into the water, Jenny following closely behind. Cassandra was clinging to his neck and still giving little shrieks of terror.

'You're quite safe now, Cassandra,' Georgie said firmly. 'You all right, Jen?'

'I'm fine.' But she wasn't really. She was starting to shiver with the cold and the shock and her teeth were chattering. Georgie found the hole in the wire immediately and once they were through it he set Cassandra down on the sand, but she still clung to him.

'We're quite safe now. There's no more water to go through. Come, Charlotte is waiting near the dunes with blankets and a hot drink.'

They stumbled up the beach, Georgie's progress hampered by Cassandra's clinging hands, Jenny's because she was so cold.

'Thank goodness.' Jenny looked up to see Charlotte and Miles hurrying towards them. Soon they were sitting on the sand wrapped in blankets and sipping hot tea laced with whisky.

'The car's just over the dunes. Let's get you home.'

'And a hot bath and bed for both of you,' Charlotte ordered. 'You've both had a frightening experience.'

'C-Cassandra has hurt her-herself on the b-barbed wire,' Jenny stammered.

'I'll phone for Dr Bennet as soon as we get back,' Miles promised. 'Now up you get. You take my arm, Jenny.'

They walked along the foot of the dunes until they came to the gap leading to the lane. Miles had brought his car as close as he could and they were all soon squashed into it and heading homewards.

'I'll never, ever go near the sea again,' Cassandra

vowed as she leaned her head against Georgie's shoulder.

'There, there,' he comforted, as he might have spoken to Louisa. 'It's all over now and you're safe.'

Jenny swallowed the lump in her throat and blinked back the tears, not caring, for once, if Georgie saw them. He would only think they were tears of relief after their nightmare experience.

Reaching the manor, they both had a hot bath and went to bed. Charlotte ran up and down stairs with hot drinks. 'The doctor's on his way.'

'I'm fine,' Jenny insisted and then shivered violently.

'We'd be happier if you'd allow the doctor just to check you over, Jen.'

Jenny raised a watery smile. 'Have I any choice?'

'Not really.' Charlotte chuckled. 'Miles is insisting.'

Miles, not Georgie, as she might have hoped. Jenny sighed inwardly, set the empty cup down on the bedside table and snuggled beneath the covers. 'I'm just so tired,' she murmured and closed her eyes.

Charlotte crept out of the room. When the doctor arrived shortly afterwards, Jenny was still asleep.

'Best thing for her,' Dr Bennet said when he'd dressed Cassandra's scratches and pronounced her fit and well, though perhaps a little overwrought. Speaking of Jenny, he went on, 'We'll not disturb her now, but if you have any reason for concern, let me know and I'll come at once. Just let her rest over the next few days. No school-work until she feels ready.' He'd heard about the young girl working hard at her lessons. 'How's she getting on?'

'Fine. She's got a place at the grammar school in the sixth form in September if her exam results are acceptable.'

'Good for her.' He paused and then asked, 'I take it she's come to live here permanently then, has she?'

'We all hope so.'

Cassandra stayed in bed for two more days, hovered over by a worried Georgie, but Jenny was up and about the next morning claiming she was fine and wanting to get back to her school books. 'Mr Lomax will be cross if I haven't finished all the work he set me. The exams start next week.'

So, though Charlotte kept a close eye on her, they allowed Jenny to work quietly in the studio at her studies. They knew just how important it was.

'And,' Charlotte murmured softly to Miles, 'it'll keep her mind off fretting about Georgie running up and downstairs every five minutes waiting on Lady Muck's every command.'

Fifty-Nine

'I'm going home,' Cassandra declared the very first time she felt able to come downstairs for lunch.

'Oh darling, must you?' Georgie tried to argue. 'I thought you had a whole week's leave.'

'I have, but I'm not staying here a moment longer.' She shuddered dramatically. 'Every time I look out of the window, I remember . . .'

'Very well, then, I'll take you back tomorrow – '

'No, this afternoon. I want to go this afternoon.'

'But I don't know if there are trains to Nottingham—' Cassandra's parents lived in a grand house somewhere just outside the city.

'There must be,' Cassandra snapped. 'Even from this godforsaken place.'

There was an awkward silence round the table. No one spoke until Georgie rose and said quietly, 'I'll telephone the station to ask.'

'Charlotte, please may I leave the table?' Jenny said, afraid that if she stayed she would say something to Cassandra that Georgie wouldn't forgive her for. 'I must get on. 'Bye, then, Cassandra.'

Cassandra didn't even glance at her. 'Goodbye, Jenny.'

She passed Georgie on his way back from Miles's study. 'There is a train later this afternoon. I'd better take her home. Bye, Jenny. Take care of yourself, won't you?' He touched her shoulder and smiled down at her, though the worried look never left his eyes.

'Bye, Georgie.' To her chagrin, her voice was husky. She cleared her throat and forced a smile. 'See you soon.'

'Thank you for all you did to help Cassandra. But for you she might have – might have—'

'Don't mention it,' she said off-handedly and turned away. She didn't want his thanks for saving the life of the girl her darker side would sooner have left to drown.

Later that afternoon, Charlotte sought out Jenny in the studio. 'I hope I'm not interrupting, but there's something you ought to know.'

'There's nothing wrong, is there?'

'Yes – and no – it's about Georgie and Cassandra,' Charlotte answered.

Jenny waited, her heart thumping.

'I think – I mean – it rather sounds as if it's all over between them.'

Jenny's eyes widened. 'What happened?'

'After you came upstairs, Georgie came back into the dining room having found out there was a train.'

'I know – I met him in the hall. We – we said "goodbye". I thought he was going with her.'

'So did he, but when he said he would get his things together Cassandra said there was no need. She was going back on her own. "You can take me to the station," she said, "but there's no need for you to come with me." '

'What did Georgie say?'

'He asked her why, of course, but she just stood up and told him she thought that it'd be better if they didn't see each other any more. Oh, Jenny, you should have seen his face. I didn't like her, but I hated seeing him so hurt. I think he's very fond of her.'

Jenny snorted. 'I don't know why – she's a cow and a half.'

'Did she ever thank you for saving her life? Because we all know you did.'

Jenny shook her head. 'Not really.' In a small voice she added, 'Georgie did, though.' She paused and then asked Charlotte, 'How are we to handle this? I mean – do I say anything to him?'

'It's difficult. They were quarrelling all the time she was packing. We could hear their raised voices down in the drawing room. I'm surprised you didn't hear them too. But then this room *is* pretty well tucked away at the top of the house.'

'Raised voices? Georgie?'

'Yes, she even got our darling Georgie mad!'

'Oh!' Jenny was silent for a moment, unshed tears prickling her eyes before she said, 'He must really love her, then.'

Charlotte had no answer.

None of them knew how to deal with the situation. Jenny kept out of the way as much as she could. Mr Lomax arrived at five o'clock to tutor her for two hours until dinner. Feeling that the presence of a comparative stranger might ease the atmosphere about the table, Charlotte invited him to stay for the meal, but it turned out that it hadn't been necessary.

Georgie came down from his room just before seven and sought out Charlotte. 'Please excuse me from dinner. I'm really not hungry. I'm going for a long walk.'

Mr Lomax, however, was an entertaining dinner guest. He talked non-stop and didn't seem to notice that the others around the table were unusually silent.

'He's like that all the time,' Jenny told them after he'd left, 'but he is a good teacher,' she added hastily in case Miles should think the man did more talking than teaching. 'He seems to know an awful lot about all sorts of things. He's found out what books I'll be needing at the grammar school. And' – she smiled despite the ache in her heart over Georgie – 'he says Mr Boswell – that's the art teacher – can't wait for me to start.'

Charlotte was glancing at the clock for the umpteenth time. 'Georgie should be back by now. It's getting dark.'

Jenny jumped up. 'I'll go and find him.'

'Oh Jen – do be careful what you say.'

'I will.'

She headed for the hall cupboard to find boots and a coat and then set off down the drive to take the long path across the flat land to the beach. She was sure that was where he'd have gone. She climbed the dunes and stood on the top. The marsh below and the beach beyond it were already in shadow. She took a deep breath, pulling in the bracing, salty sea air. The waves breaking on the shore sounded so loud in the deepening dusk. She looked to right and left, but there was no sign of a lonely figure walking the shore. She bit her lip, suddenly even more anxious than before. Where was he?

She began to walk down the dune towards the marsh, the little white flags with which she'd marked the path to where the samphire grew were still fluttering and at the end of the line was the bucket they'd used. It had been forgotten in all the drama that had followed.

'What we picked will have died by now,' she murmured as she moved towards it.

She emptied the bucket and collected the sticks and white rags, carrying them back to the wooden box in the dunes. It was as she was closing the lid that she heard a voice close by.

'Jen.'

She jumped and stared through the gloom. '*There* you are,' she said and couldn't hide the relief in her voice. But then, quite deliberately, she adopted a firm tone. 'You ought to come home, Georgie. Charlotte's worried.'

'You go back and tell them I'm fine.'

She climbed to where he was sitting. 'No, that won't do.' She grasped his arm and tried to pull him up.

To her surprise, he chuckled. 'You're a determined little madam, aren't you? Do you always get your own way?'

'Yes,' she answered, even though it wasn't quite true.

She didn't think she'd ever have what she most wanted where Georgie was concerned.

As they walked home, Georgie said, 'I expect you know what's happened?'

There was no point in lying and perhaps she was the one who could speak most candidly about it. 'Yes, I do. And I'm sorry – at least, I'm sorry she's hurt you. But to be honest, Georgie, she wasn't right for you.' She held her breath, fearing she'd said too much, too soon. She was afraid she'd make him angry again and this time his anger would be directed at her.

But Georgie merely said mildly, 'What makes you say that?' He didn't sound angry – just curious.

'She was hard and selfish. There was no gentleness

one who'll be as loving towards you as you'll be to
them. She was all take and no give.'

Still, he said nothing so Jenny went on. She'd said
too much to hold back now; it might as well be said.
'She didn't fit in here, Georgie. She was a townie like
Alfie calls me.'

'But you fit in.'

'That's because I love you – all.' She couldn't help
the merest hesitation before the last word and prayed he
hadn't noticed. 'And I love it here. You taught me to
love the sea, but to respect it. You, and all your family,'
she said, more carefully now, 'were so kind to me when
I first came and even now, you've all welcomed me back
and just look what your dad and Charlotte are trying to
do for me.' Bravely she pushed aside her overwhelming
love for this man at her side as she added, 'I've got a life
to look forward to, thanks to them.'

He put his arm about her shoulders and hugged her
to his side as they walked. 'Don't you ever leave us, Jen,
will you? I couldn't bear it if you left.'

As they walked homewards through the darkness,
Jenny's heart was singing.

414

Sixty

In August, there was a double celebration at the manor. On the fourteenth, Japan finally surrendered to the Allies and Jenny's sixteenth birthday exactly a week later had Charlotte and Miles planning a huge party for the following Saturday.

'We'll invite everyone,' Miles said, never happier than when he was planning a party. 'We never really celebrated VE day, did we?'

'No,' Charlotte said soberly. 'It was difficult when so many are mourning those they've lost in the war and besides, whilst there was fighting still going on against the Japanese, it didn't feel as if it were really over.'

Miles put his arm around her shoulders. 'But now it does. And Philip and all those whom we've lost would be the first to say we should celebrate the peace. It's what they made their sacrifice for.'

Charlotte nodded. 'You're right, of course. So, who are we going to invite?'

Miles flung out his arm as if to embrace the whole of Ravensfleet and the surrounding district. 'Everyone we know and even some we don't – if they want to come.'

Jenny glowered. 'Not the Miss Listers.'

'Come now, Jen. You wouldn't be so mean to a couple of lonely old ladies, would you?'

Jenny hesitated, torn between the bitter memories of the two horrible old women and the kindly man

415

standing in front of her who was magnanimous enough to forgive and forget most things.

'All right,' she said grudgingly and then smiled suddenly and, as always, it was like the sun appearing from behind a thundercloud. 'They'll be good company for your dad, Charlotte. Oops! I'm sorry, I shouldn't . . .'

But Charlotte was laughing. 'You're right, darling. We'll make sure we sit them together.'

Georgie threw himself into the preparations whenever he was home on leave.

'I've been thinking,' he said one evening over dinner.

'Swings, roundabouts, a coconut shy?' Miles smiled. Already Georgie had been full of ideas for their party. It was becoming more like a church fête every day. Thinking that his idea was something to do with the preparations for the big day, the family was quite unprepared for what he was about to say.

'No, Father, about what I should do now. The RAF found me a "chairborne" job whilst the war was still on and I'm willing to stay on a few more months until we get all the lads home, but I don't really want to sign on as a regular. I want to fly.'

'Fly!' they all chorused and Charlotte groaned. 'We thought you might have forgotten about that idea.'

'Hoped, you mean,' Jenny muttered.

Only Ben, home for good now that his job at the War Office was finished, was silent, calmly helping himself to more vegetables. Glancing at him, Jenny wondered if Georgie had already confided in his brother.

'Yes, there are all sorts of opportunities opening up. Exciting advances have been made in the aircraft manufacturing industry because of the war. I can train to be a civilian pilot and—'

'But will they let you fly?' Charlotte asked worriedly.

'I mean . . .' She fell silent, the colour rising in her face. She didn't want to refer openly to his wounded leg, but they all knew what she meant.

Georgie, sitting next to her, touched her hand. 'If Douglas Bader, who lost both his legs in a flying accident, was allowed to rejoin the RAF and take part in the Battle of Britain, then I'm sure I can.'

'But even if you pass the tests – and they'll be stringent – will anyone employ you, Georgie?' Miles said bluntly.

Georgie chuckled. It was the first time he'd really laughed since Cassandra had left. 'I'll employ myself.'

'What!' Now even Ben looked up.

'I want to buy my own plane and set up my own business.'

'Doing what exactly?'

'I don't know yet,' Georgie said cheerfully. 'But I'll think of something.'

There was a moment's silence around the table as they stared at him. And then, as if on cue, they all dissolved into laughter. His optimistic plans were so typical of Georgie.

The party, which turned into a garden party because the weather treated them kindly, was a huge success. Miles hired a group of musicians to play and there was dancing on the patio outside the drawing-room windows.

'May I have the pleasure?' a voice she remembered spoke in her ear. Jenny turned to see Billy Harrington standing there. A taller Billy, who looked broad and strong and tanned. 'Mester Warren said you were back. I'm surprised we haven't seen each other before.'

'I didn't know you'd come back too,' she said, giving him a bear hug.

His face sobered for a moment. 'I never left, Jen, and I'm never going back to London. The Warrens say I can stay. I'm working for them full time. Dad doesn't want me back – he's said so – and I don't want to go.'

'What about Frankie?'

'He went home. Can't blame him. He missed his folks. I get a letter now and again. He's doing all right. Got a job in an office.' He grinned. 'Thanks to Mester Thornton and the lessons we had at the manor, Frankie took to the learning lark and he went on with his education. But I'm better suited to working with me hands. I love it here.'

'So do I, Billy. I'm back for good too.'

'Mrs Warren told me you're staying on at school.'

Jenny nodded, a little embarrassed in case her childhood friend should feel she was 'getting above herself'. But Billy's next words dispelled any misgivings. 'Good for you, I hope you get what you want an' all. You deserve it.'

'So do you, Billy. I'm glad you're happy. Now, how about that dance? Not that I'm much of a dancer, I'm afraid.'

'Neither am I,' Billy admitted, 'but let's give it a go.'

They shuffled around the area set aside for dancing, talking and laughing more than dancing until Alfie tapped Billy on the shoulder and demanded to be allowed to dance with Jenny. After that, she was never without a partner, but the one person she longed to ask her to dance sat in a chair with his wounded leg stretched out in front of him looking lost and lonely.

As dusk settled over the grounds, Jenny could bear it no longer. She went and stood in front of him and put her hands on her hips. 'Now, I'm sure even with a limp, you can dance better than Billy or Alfie. Come on,' she held out her hand. 'If you're planning on flying again, I'm sure you can manage a waltz.'

He looked up at her, but his smile did not reach his blue eyes like it usually did. But, good-naturedly, he got up and put his arms around her. 'I haven't done this in a while,' he murmured close to her ear.

'Then it's high time you did.'

'Cassandra liked dancing, but I couldn't manage all the jitterbugging.'

Jenny didn't know what to say so she concentrated on trying to follow his steps. As the music came to an end, Georgie didn't release her but looked down at her murmuring, 'Little Jen, sixteen already and looking very grown-up tonight. But don't ever change, will you? You'll always be my "Little Jen".' Gently, he pressed his lips to her forehead, before letting his arms fall and stepping back. 'People are starting to leave. We'd better go and wish them goodnight. Come on.' He held out his hand to her and together they walked round the house to the front door, where Miles and Charlotte were already seeing their guests off. As an appropriate farewell, the musicians played 'There'll always be an England'.

In the shadows of the trees on the edge of the lawn, Alfie and Billy stood together.

'I don't reckon either of us stands a chance, do you, mate?' Billy murmured.

'No, and I was going to ask her if she'd go out with me.'

'Me too.' Billy laughed wryly and then added quietly, 'I just hope he doesn't break her heart, that's all.'

'He'd better not,' Alfie muttered fiercely, 'else he'll have me to reckon with.'

It seemed Georgie was the only one who couldn't see Jenny's love for him shining out of her eyes every time she looked at him. And it was the same even when he wasn't there and someone just mentioned his name. Felix, too, had observed them together tonight and guessed the truth.

'Poor child,' he murmured to Charlotte. 'I hope she won't let it affect her studies. She has such a wonderful future.'

'She won't, Felix, I'm sure of it. Her work – her talent – will be the making of her. And who knows, in time Georgie might come to his senses.'

And then Felix echoed Billy's sentiments, 'I just hope she doesn't break her heart over him, that's all.'

But Jenny was made of sterner stuff than either Billy or Felix had given her credit for. She knew exactly where she stood with Georgie and whilst she might dream that one day he'd fall in love with her, reality was filled with hard work and the promise of fulfilling a different kind of dream.

Sixty-One

With the same tenacity she'd had when she'd always believed that Georgie was still alive when he'd been posted missing, Jenny now threw herself into life in the sixth form. Her examination results had been better than anyone had dared to hope and her place at the grammar school was justified.

'We're so proud of you, darling.' Charlotte hugged her the morning the results arrived and Miles rang Felix at once to invite him to join them at the weekend. 'We're celebrating,' he said.

Whilst the country tried to get itself back to some sort of normality after the war, Jenny buried herself in her schoolwork. Louisa turned five and started at the local village school. Things were still difficult, but there was an air of optimism and enterprise and hard work was being rewarded. Georgie had passed all the tests to be able to fly again and with Miles's help had bought an aeroplane to set up a commercial business locally.

'There's a small airfield opening up just north of Lynthorpe,' he explained to the family. 'I've been in touch with the owner and we're going to run pleasure flights for holidaymakers. Now the town is getting back on its feet after the war, I'm sure it'll work.'

'I don't want to put a dampener on your idea, which I think is a good one, by the way,' Miles put in a word of caution, 'but what about in the winter months? And will you be able to get aviation fuel?'

'Pleasure flights won't be the only thing we'll do. We hope to use it to ferry lightweight goods for people, maybe even abroad. And, of course, people too. Businessmen who want to get to Europe quickly. That sort of thing. Of course, there's a lot of paperwork to go through and licences to obtain and, yes, the fuel might be a problem, but we'll get there.'

At the end of two years, Jenny achieved such good results in her final school examinations that she earned a place at Lincoln Art College.

'You'll still be able to come home every weekend. I'll fetch you and take you back,' Miles promised.

'But petrol's still on ration. Are you sure?'

He put his arm around her shoulders and chuckled. 'Either that or Georgie can fetch you in his plane.'

Georgie, it seemed, was throwing himself into his new venture.

'Is it to try to forget Cassandra?' Jenny asked Charlotte when she was home for the weekend having been at college for just over a month.

'Partly perhaps.' Then she smiled. 'But it's so like Georgie anyway. Full of plans and ideas.'

'He seems happier.'

'I think he is, but I do catch him in a pensive mood sometimes when he thinks no one is watching.'

Jenny giggled. 'But of course you always are. And Ben? How's he now?'

'Oh, you know Ben. Never says much, but he's settled back into running the Ravensfleet Estate as if he'd never been away.'

There was silence between them as they thought about the third brother – the one they'd lost. 'There's something you perhaps ought to know, now that you're really part of our family for good.'

Charlotte's words gave Jenny a warm glow. 'What is it?'

'Miles asked me to tell you. We've both seen how friendly you are with Alfie – ' She held up her hand as Jenny opened her mouth to speak. 'Oh I know, I know, it's only a friendship, but we think you should know that Alfie is – ' Charlotte licked her dry lips before finishing – 'Philip's illegitimate son and therefore, Miles's grandson.' Jenny's eyes widened as Charlotte went on, 'When the Thornton family first came here, Lily Warren, as she was then, was a maid here at the manor and she and Philip, well – ' Again she paused, not wanting to speak ill of either Philip or Lily. 'They were very young.'

Jenny touched her arm. 'I understand. And Miles didn't want Philip to marry her.'

'Oh goodness me, no, I mean, yes, he did. There's no snobbery about Miles, but Philip adamantly refused. So, later, Eddie asked Lily to marry him and he took on Alfie as his own. He's a wonderful man. He's never shown even a hint of favouritism between Alfie and his own children.'

'Does Alfie know?'

Charlotte nodded. 'When he knew he was dying, Philip asked to see him and they got to know each other. Lily told him then and, one day, Alfie will inherit Buckthorn Farm.'

'How? It's yours, isn't it?'

Charlotte laughed wryly. 'My father always wanted a son and when the Thornton boys arrived, he took a shine to Philip and made a will leaving the farm to him.'

'And cutting you out?'

Charlotte nodded.

'Didn't you mind?'

'Dreadfully, at first, but then Miles asked me to marry him. I was already in love with him, so it no longer mattered to me about my so-called inheritance.'

'You fell in love with Miles before he fell in love with you? Just like me, then. Maybe one day . . .'

There was silence between them until Charlotte changed the delicate subject by asking, 'And how are things going at college?'

'It's wonderful,' Jenny assured her. 'I absolutely love it.' Charlotte watched Jenny's eyes sparkle as she began to talk about the second love of her life. How she'd changed since they'd first seen her as a belligerent, scruffy street urchin, so lost and lonely. Now, she'd blossomed into a lovely, confident young woman who would one day take the art world by storm, according to Felix. She had a number of would-be suitors at college and even two heartsick young men nearer to home, but whilst she was friends with all of them, she held them all at arm's length.

The months and years seemed to fly by and before she realized it, Jenny was coming to the end of her time at the college. One weekend when final examinations were looming, she arrived home in a thoughtful mood.

'Is anything wrong?' Charlotte asked.

Jenny hesitated for a moment before the words came tumbling out. 'The principal called me into his office on Friday morning and said that he thought I should try for a place at the Slade in London.'

'Really? How marvellous.'

'Charlotte, I can't go there. Even if I won a scholarship or something, it would cost so much to keep me, especially in London.'

'I'll have a word with Miles—'

'No, no, I won't let you. You've done so much for me already—'

But Charlotte placed a gentle finger on the girl's lips and murmured, 'Not another word.'

'I'm absolutely shattered,' Jenny said when she arrived home again having finished all the examinations at the end of her final term.

'Too much partying at the end of term, I expect,' Georgie teased her.

'I did go to one, but only after exams had finished.'

'You've been working too hard,' Charlotte said as Jenny leaned her head back against the cushions on the sofa and closed her eyes.

'No, it's not possible to work too hard. Not when it's something you love doing anyway.'

'When do the results come?' Miles asked, but Jenny didn't answer; she was already asleep.

'Do you remember,' Georgie said softly, 'when she first came to us, how we stood at the door of her bedroom watching her sleeping, clutching that moth-eaten old teddy bear?'

'You mean Bert?'

'I wonder where he is now?'

Charlotte chuckled. 'Oh he's still with her. He's just been to art school.'

'Bless her,' Georgie said fondly. 'So, there's still the little girl inside the lovely young woman, then?'

'Oh yes,' Charlotte murmured softly. 'Our little Jenny's still here.'

The three of them tiptoed from the room and left her to sleep.

Felix arrived unexpectedly the night before Jenny's results were due.

'I couldn't miss such a great day.'

'Oh dear.' Jenny was nervous. 'I do hope you're not going to be disappointed.'

But Felix only beamed.

The following morning Jenny was pacing up and down the hall with the front door wide open, waiting anxiously for the arrival of the postman.

'Do come and get your breakfast, darling,' Charlotte urged.

'I couldn't eat a thing. I feel sick. Oh, there he is.'

She rushed out of the front door and down the steps, running halfway down the drive to meet the postman on his bicycle. There were only two letters and both were addressed to Jenny. Ignoring one, she tore open the other, which held her results. The whole family and Felix – and even Wilkins – hovered in the background watching from the doorway. Louisa hopped up and down and clapped her hands.

'What's it say, Jen? Have you passed?' she called excitedly, but then they all saw Jenny burst into tears, standing there in the middle of the drive, shaking and sobbing.

Georgie, followed by all the others except for Wilkins, reached her first.

'Oh darling,' he put his arms around her and pulled her close. 'What is it? Is it bad news? I can't believe it.'

'No, no, look.' With trembling fingers she held out the piece of paper to him. As Georgie read it, a huge

grin spread across his face and then he passed the letter
to Miles and Charlotte, whilst Louisa begged, 'Tell me,
please tell me.'

Felix, it seemed, didn't need to read the letter; he was
beaming from ear to ear. But in their excitement no one
seemed to realize that he already knew what the letter
contained.

'She's only gone and got the highest grades in her
year,' Georgie said. 'That's all.' He picked her up and
swung her round. 'I knew you could do it.'

When they returned to the house, Miles called, 'Wilkins, champagne all round. We'll have a champagne
breakfast. This calls for a real celebration. And open a
bottle for below stairs too, won't you?'

'Thank you, sir.' Wilkins gave a little bow. 'And may
I on behalf of all the staff, offer Miss Jenny our hearty
congratulations.'

'Oh thank you, Wilkins.' And then she startled the
reserved manservant by kissing him on the cheek. 'Tell
Mrs Beddows I'll be down to see her and the others
later.'

As they all sat down to breakfast, still talking excitedly, Felix said calmly, 'Aren't you going to open your
other letter, my dear?'

'Oh yes. I'd almost forgotten it.'

As she slit it open and read it, the colour suffused her
face. She looked up and met Felix's benign expression.
'How – ?'

'What is it, Jen?' Georgie asked, but for once in her
life Jenny didn't seem to be paying him any attention.
She was still staring at Felix.

'You know, don't you?'

He nodded.

'But you know I can't go.'

427

'Not go?' Felix was scandalized. 'Of course you must go.'

The others were mystified and, strangely it was the quiet one of the family, Ben, who asked. 'Go where, Jenny?'

But Jenny was lost in a trance, still staring at the letter she held in her trembling hands.

'Jenny has been offered a place at the Slade in London,' Felix explained.

Charlotte clapped her hands. 'Oh darling, that's wonderful!'

'But I didn't apply. How can I have been offered a place there when I didn't even apply?'

Felix's smile broadened. 'Ah, now I might have had a bit of a hand in that. I have very close connections with the Slade, you see, and – well – I might just have mentioned that there was this remarkable pupil who was sure to get top marks in all her examinations and that she would be a most worthwhile candidate for a place there. But I promise,' he held up his hand almost defensively, 'that I didn't pull any strings. I only suggested that you should be considered. You have been offered a place solely on your merits.'

'But how do they know my work?'

Felix chuckled again. 'My professor friend has been in touch with Lincoln. He knows all about you and has seen examples of your work.'

'How?'

'We-ell, he visited my gallery and – as you know – I have one or two of your paintings on show.'

'You *know* a professor at the Slade?'

'Of course,' Felix waved his hand airily. 'I know everyone in the art world who is worth knowing.'

'But – but I can't go. It'll cost a fortune – especially living in London.'

'You might be entitled to some sort of grant,' Miles said, 'but if not, we'll support you, you know that.'

'Jenny – don't you *want* to go?' Charlotte asked gently, guessing what was holding Jenny near to Ravensfleet. London was a long way away from Georgie.

Jenny bit her lip and glanced down at the letter in her hand. She pulled in a deep breath, knowing that the decision she was about to make might alter the course of her life. She looked across the table into Charlotte's deep violet eyes. She could read the love there – and the concern. Intuitively, she knew Charlotte was encouraging her to make her own life and not to miss such a wonderful opportunity by waiting around for something that might never happen. Or rather, for someone who might never love her in the way she wanted him to.

Jenny swallowed and smiled tremulously. Her voice was husky as she said, 'Of course I want to go. But what about the expense?'

'You can come and live with me,' Felix offered generously. 'At least you can live at my flat. I'm away so often, I'll hardly notice you're there.'

That part was true. Since the end of the war, Felix's business had blossomed and now he travelled the world. 'I won't charge you a *huge* amount for your board and lodging.' His eyes were twinkling as he added impishly, 'Perhaps a painting now and then.'

'I thought you said her paintings were going to be worth a fortune once day?' Georgie said.

Felix gave an exaggerated sigh. 'Me and my big mouth.'

And so it was settled. Jenny would accept the place

at the famous art school and would stay at Felix's flat in the city during term time, coming home to Ravensfleet during the holidays.

There was only one other cloud on her bright horizon – other than leaving Georgie, of course.

'I suppose,' she said slowly. 'I shall have to visit my mother.'

To this no one made any answer; that decision was entirely Jenny's.

Sixty-Two

Leaving Ravensfleet was hard and she shed a few tears at the station when Miles and Charlotte waved her off. But once term started, Jenny found she was so busy that she hadn't time to brood, although not a day went by that she didn't think about Georgie and all of them at the manor and wonder what they were doing.

And there was no denying that she loved her life. She could never have dreamed that the scruffy little evacuee urchin could have ended up a student at the famous art college and living in a luxurious apartment nearby. When he was home, Felix insisted on expanding her education by taking her to the theatre, the ballet, the opera and, of course, every art gallery in the city. They got on well. Despite his creative talents, Felix was not a temperamental man; he was easy-going and generous. But there was one thing that he insisted she should do.

'You should see your mother, my dear, and visit your old friends. Have you told them you're in London?'

Jenny bit her lip and shook her head.

'I thought not.' He said no more, but his words had pricked her conscience. So, the following Saturday morning Jenny announced at breakfast that she would go to the East End to see if her mother was still there.

'Haven't you been in touch with her at all since you left?' Felix was appalled.

'Only through Bobby and Aunty Elsie. I've been

431

writing to them. But Mum made it very clear she didn't want anything more to do with me.' Felix was still looking shocked. She glanced at him. Perhaps he didn't know the full story.

'Did – did Charlotte ever tell you what happened?' When Felix frowned in puzzlement, she added, 'Why I left home and – and went back to Ravensfleet.'

He shook his head slowly, his gaze never leaving her face. 'I presumed – perhaps incorrectly – that your mother had sent you back to them towards the end of the war when the doodlebugs started.'

Jenny sighed.

'Look, if you'd rather not tell me, I'm not prying.' But she could see that Felix was itching to know, even though he said candidly, 'And if it's a secret, you'd certainly better not tell me. I never could keep a secret. I'd certainly have been no good as a spy in the war.'

Jenny giggled. 'I think you'd have made a very good one. No one would ever have suspected you.'

'That's true,' Felix agreed. False modesty was not one of his strong points either.

Her face sobered. 'I don't mind you knowing, Uncle Felix. I – I just hope you won't think too badly of me.'

So she told him everything and in the telling, all the nightmare of her life with Dot came flooding back. At the end of her story she was in tears and Felix felt guilty for having pressed her to tell him. 'I shouldn't have asked. I'm so sorry, my dear. And of course you have no duty to see your mother. Not ever again, if you don't want to.'

She smiled through her tears. 'No, I should go. I owe it to Aunty Elsie if not to Mum. And then there's Bobby. I'd like to see him again.'

'Oho, do I detect a little romance?'

Jenny shook her head and opened her mouth to explain, but then she closed it again quickly. The time for confidences was gone. If Felix couldn't keep secrets then there was no way she was going to tell him about her feelings for Georgie. Instead she said, brightly, 'I'm far too busy for such nonsense, Uncle Felix.'

Little did she guess that Felix knew all about her feelings for Georgie. The flamboyant artist was a better keeper of secrets than he gave himself credit for.

When she knocked on the door of the terraced house where she'd last seen Elsie and her family, she didn't recognize the tall young man who opened it. The Hutton family must have moved. 'I'm sorry, I thought . . .'

The young man's mouth widened into a grin; a grin she'd have known anywhere.

'Jen!'

'Bobby!'

They both spoke at once and then he was stepping into the street, picking her up and swinging her round.

'Mam,' he hollered. 'Just look who's turned up like a bad penny.'

Elsie appeared in the doorway drying her hands on a towel. She stared at Jenny for a moment before recognition dawned. 'Blimey, ain't you a sight for sore eyes, darlin'. Come on in. Have yer seen yer mum?'

Bobby set her down on the ground but grasped her hand and pulled her into the house. 'Get the kettle on, Mam. This calls for a celebration.'

When they were seated in the small kitchen, Jenny said, 'Where is she now? D'you know?'

Elsie nodded her head in the direction of the house at the end of the street. 'Still there with his nibs.'

'Oh!'

'S'all right, Jen. If you want to see her, I'll come with you,' Bobby said. His grin broadened. 'I always looked out for yer, didn't I?'

'You did, Bobby, and I'll never forget it.'

''Ere, don't you talk posh now? Don't she talk posh, Mam?'

Elsie smiled. 'She talks very nicely, Bobby, and don't you tease her.'

'I'm sorry, I didn't mean to—'

'Don't you apologize, Jen. We want to hear everything. Oh, I know you've written letters, but it ain't the same as hearing you tell us face to face.'

They sat around Elsie's kitchen table until the clock on the wall struck twelve. 'Oh look at me, yer dad'll be home for his dinner any minute and 'ere's me gossiping. He'll 'ave me guts fer garters.'

But as she got up from the table, Elsie was smiling. Sid Hutton would no more harm a hair of his wife's head than fly to the moon.

'Your mam told me in her letters that your dad had come back safely. Is he all right?' Jenny asked Bobby softly.

'Yeah, right as ninepence, he was. We was lucky. Dad, Ronnie and Sammy all came back. Sammy got wounded, but he's recovered well, though he'll always limp a bit.'

Like Georgie, Jenny thought.

Soon all the family arrived home and the little house was filled with merry chatter and laughter. It felt as if the years dropped away and Jenny was back in the bosom of the family that had always felt like her own; more so than life with Dot had ever done. At last Sid glanced at the clock on the mantelpiece and with one accord the menfolk of the household stood up.

'Time we was going, Elsie love.' He kissed her fondly and reached for a scarf from the peg behind the door. The boys, too, wound identical scarves around their necks. Jenny stared in amazement, until, noticing her puzzled look, Bobby laughed and said, 'It's the Hammers' colours, Jen – claret and blue. Mam knitted us one each. We're off to the match. We always go when it's at home.'

Jenny's face cleared. 'Of course. How could I have forgotten?' The memories came flooding back once more. Arthur had never missed a home match, though Jenny now wondered if his attendance hadn't had more to do with his nefarious business activities than actually enjoying the football.

'Hope you win.' Jenny smiled as she and Elsie stood at the door waving them off.

Now that the house was quiet, Elsie asked seriously, 'Are yer going down to see yer mam, Jenny?'

The girl sighed. 'That's what I came for, except for seeing you all, of course.'

'Of course.' They smiled at each other. 'Like me to come wiv yer?'

Jenny shook her head. 'No. Thanks all the same, but I'd best do this on me own.'

'He'll be at the shop this afternoon, if that's any help.'

Jenny nodded. 'Then I'll go now.' She stood up and hugged Elsie; she couldn't put off the moment any longer.

As she walked down the street, her legs were trembling and her palms felt sweaty. It was ridiculous, she thought, feeling like this when she was only going to visit her own mother.

'Oh, look what the cat's dragged in.' Dot opened the door to her knock. She hadn't changed a bit; she was still dressed in a short skirt, her dyed blond hair brassier than ever and her make-up plastered on her petulant face even more thickly.

'Hello, Mum. Just thought I'd – er – come and see you.'

Dot shrugged and turned away as if she really wasn't bothered one way or the other, but she left the door open for Jenny to follow her. Entering the kitchen, Jenny glanced around her and when she saw that Donald Jenkins wasn't there, she began to breathe more easily.

'Did you get my letters, Mum? You never replied.'

'Oh yeah,' Dot said vaguely, drawing on her cigarette. 'But I'm not much of a letter writer, Jen, you know that. And after you accused my Donald like you did, well, I didn't really want to know.'

'You'd believe him rather than your own daughter, would you?' The words were said without malice or reproach; Jenny was merely stating a fact, but Dot turned on her. 'Don't you dare come back here in your fancy clothes and talking all posh and start that again. He's a good man. He's the best thing that's ever happened to me and you're nothing but a dirty little trollop that's landed on her feet. So don't you come here causing bother. I've got a good one in Donald, I have. He's not a spiv like Arfer.' She smiled maliciously. 'The coppers come asking me about him, but o' course I couldn't tell them anything.'

Jenny held her breath, expecting an onslaught of accusations. The police must have paid her mother a visit after Jenny had confessed to PC Webster. But it seemed as if her name hadn't been mentioned as Dot went on, 'Did you see it in the papers? About Arfer?'

Jenny shook her head.

'Got caught, 'ee did. Up in Manchester. Got done for black market trading. Six months, 'ee got. Just think, we could've got done an' all if we'd still been with him.'

Jenny didn't quite know what to feel. Arthur Osborne had been a criminal, there was no denying that and she'd hated him for involving her in his activities. And yet in a lot of ways he'd been good to her. Her drifting thoughts came back to what her mother was saying, 'I 'ad a lucky escape there, and from that Jim, but now me an' Donald are doing all right together, see? So don't you spoil it.'

'I've no intention of spoiling it for you, Mum. And I'm glad you're happy. I just wanted to make sure you're all right, that's all.'

'I'm all right and I always will be.' She fluffed her hair with the gesture that Jenny remembered so well. 'I've still got me looks.'

Jenny gazed at her with pity. Maybe once, when she'd been a young girl, Dot had been pretty, but now the years, and the way she'd lived, had taken their toll. But she was lucky. She still had a man at her beck and call and she appeared to be as happy as she ever would be. Jenny felt any burden of guilt slip away. She could leave now with a clear conscience. She'd always keep in touch with her mother, but she could get on with her own life without forever looking back over her shoulder.

After a long silence when it was obvious that they had nothing to talk about, Dot said, 'You'd better go. He'll be home soon.'

Jenny nodded, kissed Dot's cheek and left the house.

Sixty-Three

At last life seemed to be settling down for Jenny; she was truly happy living in London in Felix's apartment, working hard at college and at home, too, for Felix gave her free run of his own cluttered studio and there her talent really blossomed. Once her homework was done, she painted for pure pleasure working in every different media and honing her skills. Her paintings of London scenes were pounced upon eagerly by Felix and carried off to his gallery.

'You're getting better and better, my dear.'

There was only one cloud on her otherwise clear blue horizon: Georgie. Whenever she visited Ravensfleet, he was as kind and affectionate as he always had been, but now Jenny wanted more. So much more.

'But at least he hasn't found another girlfriend,' she comforted herself.

Another Christmas came and Jenny and Felix travelled together to Ravensfleet to be met at the station by Miles in the motor car.

They saw him standing on the windswept platform, huddled in a thick overcoat. To Jenny's perceptive eyes, he looked suddenly much older than she remembered him. Maybe it was just the winter weather.

'Is everyone all right?' was Jenny's first question as she scrambled into the back seat, leaving Felix to take the front passenger seat.

'Fine,' Miles said as he started the engine. 'How are you both? Good journey?' He was asking all the usual questions and yet he seemed distant, as if there was something on his mind that was troubling him. Felix, however, didn't seem to notice. He chattered on the short journey to the manor, but Jenny was acutely aware of Miles's silence.

Charlotte opened the front door as the car drew to a halt in front of the steps. Smiling, she threw her arms wide to envelop them both, but Jenny could see that the smile did not reach her eyes. 'Come in, quickly. We've tea waiting, you must be frozen.'

Amidst the flurry of their arrival, Jenny had no opportunity to question Charlotte, but later, as she took her suitcase up to her old room, Charlotte followed her and closed the door behind them.

'Charlotte, what's the matter and don't tell me "nothing" because I know there is something.'

'I won't,' Charlotte said softly. 'Let's sit down, here on the side of the bed.'

As they sat together, Charlotte took her hand. 'Darling – '

Fear clutched at Jenny's heart. 'Georgie? It's Georgie, isn't it? Oh – he's had a crash in his aeroplane. He's—'

'No, no, nothing like that. I promise you – he's fine.' Charlotte bit her lip. 'But it *is* about Georgie.'

'Then tell me quickly.'

'Cassandra's back.'

Jenny stared open mouthed at Charlotte. Then she ran her tongue round her lips. 'How? What happened?'

'Georgie's business is flourishing and expanding. He's got another plane and taken on another pilot. A pal from his RAF days. They make a great team. Georgie was doing some work for a businessman in Nottingham and he went out to dinner with him one evening and there was Cassandra. She came over to their table and started chatting. The following day she rang Georgie and asked to meet him.' Charlotte sighed. 'I don't know what passed between them, but they've started seeing each other again. Oh Jen, I'm so sorry.'

Despite her heart feeling as if it was dropping like a stone and her hopes and dreams once more fading into the mist, Jenny asked, 'Is that what's troubling Miles?' Jenny asked.

Charlotte nodded. 'Darling, he's known for a long time how you feel about Georgie and he's worried – as I am – about you.'

'Has she altered at all?'

'No, she's just the same. She sticks her nose in the air at just about everything. The house is too cold for her. There's nothing to do. No dancing, no parties. And she's for ever referring to here as "this Godforsaken place".'

'And Georgie? Is he happier now she's back?'

Charlotte wrinkled her brow. 'Hard to tell. He's fond of her, I'm sure – though I'm sorry to have to say it. But maybe this time there is a wariness about him where she's concerned. You know, as if at the back of his mind he thinks she might up and leave him again.'

Jenny laughed wryly. 'Let's hope she does.'

'And there's one more thing to tell you. She's coming for Christmas.'

'Right,' Jenny said firmly, 'then I'm declaring war. I was too young to do much about it before, but now I'm going to fight for him.'

*

440

Georgie's greeting when he arrived home that night was as affectionate as ever. He picked her up and swung her round just as he had when she'd been a little girl. But, of course, Jenny made no objection. She hugged him back and, for two pins, would have snuggled on to his knee and begged him to read to her.

Cassandra, when she arrived, was just as beautiful, but still had the same haughty, disdainful expression on her face.

'Shame the samphire's not in season,' Jenny murmured to Charlotte, who chuckled deliciously and whispered back, 'Oh, you wicked girl!'

Miles and Charlotte were polite to their guest but Ben disappeared as often as he could, pleading being short-staffed on the farm over the Christmas holidays. 'The animals still need feeding.'

'Can't you get someone else to do it?' Cassandra said, fixing yet another cigarette into a long holder and lighting it. Jenny saw Charlotte and Miles exchange a glance. Miles smoked a pipe but in deference to the rest of the family he only ever smoked in his study. Cassandra hadn't even asked if anyone minded; she just lit up whenever she felt like it.

'Would you like a walk this morning?' Georgie asked her.

'A walk?' Cassandra was appalled. 'In this weather?'

'A drive out to the airfield, then? I'd like to show you my new plane.'

Before she could answer, Jenny chipped in, 'Charlotte said you'd got another one. I'd love to see it.'

Failing to inspire interest in Cassandra, Georgie turned to Jenny. 'I'm hoping to license it to carry passengers. In the summer I want to take the holidaymakers up in it to show them the sights from the air, like I planned.'

'I'll be your first passenger.'

Georgie grinned at her. 'You're on. But it won't be yet. It's got to pass it's airworthiness test first.'

'Easter?'

'I hope so. I want to start taking the visitors up by then.'

'Let me know and I'll come home.'

'I'm not sure I ought to let you,' Felix said, his eyes twinkling. 'People with a talent like yours shouldn't endanger themselves.'

'Georgie will look after me,' Jenny said and was delighted by the glare Cassandra gave her.

Despite Cassandra's moodiness, they managed to have a merry Christmas. The only time she smiled was when she opened her numerous presents. Georgie had showered her with several expensive gifts.

'She hasn't got much family. Only her mother and father,' he explained.

'You don't have to excuse yourself,' Charlotte said softly. 'Look how your father has always spoiled all of us and he still is doing.' She laughed as she pointed to her own pile of parcels under the tree. 'And Louisa has a veritable mountain to open.'

'It's a shame she's too old to believe in Father Christmas any more,' Georgie murmured. 'I used to love creeping into her room when she'd finally gone to sleep with a pillowcase stuffed with presents.'

'Happy days. But one day you'll have children of your own and you'll—'

'Cassandra doesn't want children,' he blurted out. 'She's made that very clear already.'

Charlotte stared at him with something very close to

horror on her face. 'Doesn't want children! Oh my dear, you'd be such a wonderful father.'

His eyes clouded. 'I'd certainly like the chance to try,' he murmured.

'Then—' Charlotte put her hand on his arm. Out of all the family, only she would have dared to say such a thing to him. 'Do you really think she's the right one for you?'

'I – think so, Charlotte. She's pretty and vivacious. She's the life and soul, as they say, of any party.' Georgie was spending more and more time at Cassandra's home near Nottingham.

'But?'

He shifted uncomfortably. 'But nothing, really. I mean, her parents approve. They always make me very welcome. They throw a big party nearly every time I visit. They're big on parties.'

'And we're not, you mean?'

'No, no, Charlotte, I didn't mean to imply—'

Charlotte touched his hand quickly. 'No, I know. City people are very different to us country bumpkins.'

'Oh now Charlotte—'

She laughed. 'It's all right, I'm teasing you. We can't alter just to please her, but we've tried to make her welcome in our own way.'

'You have, you have.'

Serious now, she added, 'We all just want you to be happy, Georgie. Just be sure she's the one, that's all I ask.'

He nodded and said huskily, 'I will. I promise.'

Jenny went back to start the spring term with a heavy heart. She hadn't won the war against Cassandra; she couldn't even claim a small victory. Cassandra had spent most of her time in the morning room reading glossy magazines that she'd brought with her. The only time the girl had brightened up had been when Georgie suggested going to a New Year's Eve dance in Lynthorpe but even then she came back grumbling about 'clod-hopping farmers'. The day after New Year's Day, she insisted that Georgie should drive her back to Nottingham.

'She's not right for him,' Miles burst out as soon as the car had driven off down the drive and Georgie and Cassandra were safely out of earshot. He ran his hand through his thinning hair. 'I thought it before and I haven't changed my opinion.'

'Well, she certainly wouldn't do for me,' Ben said, showing an unusual spurt of anger. 'Why on earth is he so blind? Can't he see for himself the one person who'd be perfect for him? The girl who's loved him devotedly for years.'

Miles frowned and shook his head, trying to stop the usually taciturn Ben from saying any more, whilst Charlotte cast an anxious glance at Jenny, who was trying to stop the colour rising in her face. Now Ben seemed to realize that, for once in his life, he'd opened his mouth and put his size-ten boot right in it! He cast an apologetic glance at Jenny. 'Sorry! I've said too much.'

Jenny sighed and glanced around the room at them, including Felix, but they all avoided meeting her gaze. Only Louisa looked puzzled. Then, suddenly, she sidled up to Jenny and took her hand. With a child's candour she said what none of the others dared to put into words. 'It's you, isn't it, Jen. You love Georgie, don't you?'

There was no point in trying to deny it. 'I always have,' Jenny admitted. 'Ever since the moment he came into the bathroom when I was a scruffy little evacuee screaming the place down because your mummy was trying to give me a bath.'

Louisa leaned her head against Jenny's shoulder and squeezed her hand. But now even she could think of nothing to say.

Sixty-Four

Jenny threw herself back into her work and life at college. Felix was full of plans.

'As soon as your end-of-year exams are out of the way, we must have an exhibition of your work in my gallery. In fact, I've been in touch with my friend at the Slade and have offered to have a special students' exhibition. What do you think about that?'

'It's a splendid idea,' Jenny said.

'Just your class, I thought, to start with. Do you think they'd like that?'

'They'd love it and be so grateful, Felix.'

'I don't want gratitude,' Felix chuckled. 'I want to be the one who discovers the next generation of famous artists and you, my dear, are certainly going to be one of them.'

When their tutor announced the proposal to Jenny's fellow students, her friends were ecstatic and, as she had predicted, grateful for the great man's interest.

'He's a fabulous artist in his own right, you know,' they told her. 'And to think you've been friends with him for years.'

'He's been very good to me,' Jenny was swift to acknowledge. 'I don't think I'd be here at the Slade if it hadn't been for him.'

'Don't knock it, kid,' one of her classmates said and

the rest agreed. 'And don't feel you have to apologize. Because of you, we're all getting the chance to show our work in a prestigious gallery. And we promise not to be jealous if your work has pride of place.'

As the time for the proposed exhibition drew close, Jenny confided in Matthew Baxter, one of the students in the same class to whom she'd become close. 'I don't know whether I'm excited or just plain terrified.'

'Well, I know. I'm petrified. It's almost more important than the exams. It could launch our careers.'

The exhibition was set to run for a month and a grand opening night was fixed for the week after the students had finished their exams.

'It'll give everyone time to finish any work they want to exhibit,' declared the ever-thoughtful Felix. 'And put the thought of exams behind them for a while.'

It was a frantic week but everyone loved the excitement and the tension. Those who had no work to finish turned up at the gallery every day to help or just to be a part of it. Every student in Jenny's year was represented, each allowed to show a maximum number of three works of art in whatever medium they chose.

As the evening of the grand opening drew closer, Jenny's nerves got worse. 'Oh Matt, I feel sick.'

'What on earth have you got to be nervous about?' he laughed. 'The whole thing's being put on by your mentor and your family's coming to London to support you. What more could anybody want?'

She grinned ruefully at him, realizing just how very lucky she was to have such wonderful support. Even Georgie was coming, though she did wish that he wasn't bringing Cassandra too.

They arrived and booked into a hotel the day before the grand opening.

'And this afternoon,' Charlotte said firmly when Jenny joined them for lunch, 'you and I are going shopping. You must have a lovely new dress for tomorrow night.'

'Oh, I couldn't let you—'

Miles chuckled and touched her hand. 'Don't spoil Charlotte's fun. She doesn't get the chance very often to go shopping in Knightsbridge.'

'And you must have your hair done too.' Across the table Charlotte and Jenny exchanged a fond glance; they were both remembering another time when Jenny's blond curls had caused such a problem.

'Me too,' Louisa piped up. 'Can I have my hair done in a salon, Mummy?' It was the first time she'd come to London and the young girl was wide eyed with wonder.

'I can show you all the very best shops,' Cassandra offered. 'And I know a very chic hairdresser. He's quite famous.'

'That's very kind of you.' Charlotte smiled. 'We'll be glad of your help.'

So the four 'girls' set out for an afternoon of shopping and pampering. If only, Jenny couldn't help wishing, Cassandra wasn't there. But, in fact, the girl was a great help. She knew the best stores, the best salons and even the best restaurants.

'We couldn't have done without you,' Charlotte said generously, when they arrived back at the hotel laden with parcels.

'I enjoyed it,' Cassandra said and sounded for once as if she meant it, but then she spoilt it by adding, 'Nice for you to see how the other half live for once.' And then she flounced away to her own room to try on the new gown she'd bought for the occasion.

'Who does she think she is?' Jenny stormed.

'Don't let her worry you, darling, tomorrow tonight is *your* moment.' Charlotte put her arms around Jenny and held her close. 'We're all so proud of you.'

Jenny hugged her in return. 'I don't know how to thank you all. Just think what my life would have been like if I hadn't met you.'

'And I dread to think what mine would have been like if Miles hadn't brought his family to live in Ravensfleet all those years ago. I'd have been an old spinster still living with my irascible old father, I've no doubt. So, we've both been lucky.' She held Jenny away from her and traced the line of the girl's cheek with a gentle finger as she said huskily, 'I just hope that one day you'll find the happiness you deserve with – with someone who'll love you.'

Tears sprang to Jenny's eyes, but she smiled through them. 'You know there's only one person for me, but he doesn't seem to notice me. Not in that way, does he?'

'Well, maybe that'll alter. Tomorrow night, you, my dear girl, are going to be the belle of the ball, or rather the exhibition.'

'Not while the beautiful Cassandra's there.'

'Oh, you just wait and see.'

When they arrived at the gallery the following evening, Jenny stepped inside to be greeted by Felix, his arms spread wide. 'My dear girl, you look stunning.'

Jenny and Charlotte exchanged a smile. They had spent most of the afternoon getting ready. Charlotte had recreated the sophisticated style the hairdresser had suggested, piling her hair on top of her head with soft tendrils framing her face. Then she had shown Jenny how to apply make-up and now, in the midnight-blue gown they had bought, Jenny did indeed look amazing. And she'd been thrilled to see Cassandra's mouth twist with jealousy as Georgie had kissed Jenny's hand with a gallant gesture when they'd gathered in the foyer of the hotel to await the taxi.

And now she was being whisked away by her friends into the mêlée of students and their families milling around the gallery trying to search out which paintings belonged to which artist.

When everyone had arrived, Felix stood on a dais at one end of the long room and clapped his hands. 'Ladies and gentlemen, may I have your attention for just a moment, please. Welcome to the Felix Kerr Gallery. I hope you have a wonderful evening, but before I let you loose, there are just one or two things I'd like to say. Not only members of the students' families are with us tonight, but also tutors from the art school and members of the press, together with some of my friends and colleagues from the art world. This is a chance for all of us to see the artists of tomorrow. All the paintings are, of course, for sale but they are being shown anonymously. You'll see that the names on the drawings and paintings have been covered up and this is deliberate because I want you to buy a picture you like and not because it is the work of your offspring.'

A murmur rang amongst his listeners, but Felix raised his voice. 'I realize you must think that a little unfair, but not all the students have family here and yet they deserve to have an equal chance of selling their work. The students' – he cast a glance of mock severity at his protégés clustered together in one corner of the room – 'have all been issued with dire threats if they give so much as a hint to any of you as to which is their work. So, now, please wander around and most of all – enjoy your-selves.' His words were greeted with polite applause. 'Oh, and just one more thing. I have been in conversation with the school and, if tonight is successful, we hope to make this an annual event and because of this I am inaugur-ating a Student of the Year Award. The recipient has been chosen by their tutors. Not by me, I hasten to add. Even I don't know at this moment who has won. The prize will be a trophy and five hundred pounds to help further their studies.'

Now the applause was more enthusiastic and as Felix stepped down, chatter broke out throughout the room. Jenny threaded her way through the crowd dragging Matthew in her wake.

'This is Matthew Baxter. Matt, this is Mr and Mrs Thornton, Louisa, Georgie and Cassandra.' She hesitated a fraction before adding, grudgingly, 'Georgie's girlfriend.'

'Pleased to meet you all.' Matthew smiled. 'Can I get you anything to drink?' Waiters were now moving amongst the throng, carrying trays of canapés and glasses of champagne. As Jenny and Matthew went off to acquire drinks for the party, the rest of them wan-dered around the room, studying each picture carefully.

'Felix is a crafty old so-and-so,' Miles murmured. 'But I can see his point about not divulging who the artist is. It does give them all a fairer chance, but I think this one rather gives the game away, don't you, Char-lotte?' They'd come to the far end of the room where a small portrait hung. 'I rather think we know who painted this one, don't we?'

'Oh my,' Georgie said, staring at the oil painting. 'That's me.'

Charlotte and Miles exchanged a glance. They could see the love that had gone into every stroke of the brush.

'That's amazing.' Georgie was still gazing at the picture.

'Isn't it just,' Cassandra murmured, her eyes narrowing. 'However long did you have to sit for her to do that?'

'I didn't,' Georgie said. Jenny had painted the portrait from memory and yet it was perfect, every bit as good as if he'd sat in front of her for hours.

Jenny, arriving back with a plate of canapés and drinks, felt the colour flooding her face. 'He – Felix wasn't supposed to put that one in the exhibition. I told him it would give the game away, but he insisted. I'm sorry.'

'Sorry?' Georgie turned to grin at her. 'Don't be sorry. It's great. You've made me look even more handsome than I already am.' As ever, Georgie had diffused an awkward moment and turned it into laughter. His grin faded as he held Jenny's gaze. 'It's magnificent,' he said quietly, 'but I'm going to break Felix's rule and buy it.'

'You – don't have to – '

'I know, but I want to,' he said softly, his gaze never leaving her face. 'I'll treasure it always.'

'Come along, darling,' Cassandra said, hooking her arm through his. 'We mustn't let Jenny hog the limelight all evening.'

As she pulled him away, Georgie cast a rueful smile over his shoulder before he disappeared into the crowd.

'Am I mistaken,' Miles whispered softly to Charlotte, 'or do I detect the green-eyed monster rearing its ugly head.'

'Mm,' Charlotte murmured. 'Let's hope so.'

*

452

The evening was a huge success and when Felix announced the winner of the first Student of the Year Award – Jennifer Mercer – the rafters rang with the generous applause from her fellow students. Matthew lifted her off her feet and swung her round. 'No one deserves it more than you, Jenny.'

'It's nepotism,' Cassandra said loudly to anyone around her who cared to listen. 'We all know she's Felix's protégé and I bet the college have given it to her because they want to keep on his good side.'

'Well, that's where you're wrong, young lady,' Felix countered, coming up behind them at that moment. 'It was done completely anonymously. Each student submitted one work of art to be judged and it wasn't until the decision had been made that the name was revealed. Rather like tonight.'

Cassandra raised an eyebrow. 'You can hardly call her painting of Georgie "anonymous". It's obvious.'

But Felix only beamed. 'Only to the family. No one else here knows who Georgie is. Besides,' he added, putting his head on one side like a naughty schoolboy who's been caught out. 'I do *own* the gallery. And on that occasion, I even pulled rank on the artist herself. She said exactly the same as you and didn't want it in the exhibition, but it's the finest example of portraiture you'll see in a long time, so – in it went. And now, if you'll excuse me, some of my guests are leaving.'

As he moved away, all a red-faced Cassandra could say was, 'Well, really!' And her temper was not improved when she sought out Georgie to find him standing once more in front of the portrait of himself, gazing at it with a thoughtful expression on his face.

Sixty-Five

It was just before the end of term. Exams were over and the exhibition had been a huge success and the students had sold at least one painting each, though Jenny had the sneaky feeling that Felix had kindly bought any that had been left so that no student felt left out. There was a suspicious new stack of paintings against the wall in the storeroom behind the gallery.

Jenny was packing ready for the journey home at the end of the week when the telephone in Felix's apartment rang. Felix was out so it was Jenny who answered the call, to hear Charlotte's worried voice at the other end of the line.

'Oh Jen,' she said at once. 'It's Georgie. He's – he's had a crash in his new plane.'

Jenny's heart felt as if it stopped and then began to thump painfully. She felt cold and her legs gave way. She sank to the floor, still clutching the receiver in her hand, her fingers white.

'He's – he's not – '

'No, no, but he's badly hurt. His wounded leg is – is smashed so badly, they're – ' Charlotte dissolved into tears – 'they're talking about amputating it.'

Jenny swallowed hard but her voice trembled as she said bravely, 'But if it's to save his life – '

'Yes, yes, of course. How sensible you are, Jen.'

'I'm coming home. I won't wait till the end of the

week. I'll ring the college now. They'll understand.' Jenny found herself taking charge, making quick decisions. 'I'll be with you by tonight.'

They talked a little while longer. Miles, it seemed, was in a state of shock, convinced he was going to lose another son.

'He'll be fine. He's strong and he's everything to live for.' Jenny bit her lip before adding with a generosity she hadn't known she possessed, 'Have you sent for Cassandra?'

'Not yet. I rang you first. I'm sorry, I must go. Miles wants to go back to the hospital.'

'Where is he?'

'Lynthorpe at the moment, but if they do decide to operate, he'll have to go to a bigger one.'

'Where?'

'Miles is going to talk to the doctors. He wants to make sure Georgie has the very best treatment available wherever it is.' Charlotte's voice broke. 'But come home as soon as you can, darling. We need you.'

When Jenny told Felix, he offered, 'Do you want me to come with you?'

'I'll be fine once I get there, unless, of course, you want to come.' She knew how fond Felix was of all the family and how worried he'd be.

'I would, only I've so much on here, but if I can help in any way, you promise you'll let me know and I'll drop everything and come at once.'

'I'll ring you every day, Felix.'

He took her to the station and saw her on to the train, hugging her tightly and reminding her, 'Don't forget to ring. Every day.'

The journey seemed interminable; far longer even than when she'd travelled the same route as an evacuee child. But, at last, the train drew into Ravensfleet and Jenny dragged her trunk and her suitcase on to the platform.

'At last.' She heard Miles's voice behind her, and she turned to see him coming towards her with his arms spread wide.

'How is he?'

'Holding on.'

'Are they going to operate?'

'Yes. The leg's so badly damaged that without an amputation he'll – he'll – oh Jen.' Miles hugged her to him. 'Thank goodness you've come home. We need your strength and your faith.' He drew back, fished in his pocket, pulled out a white handkerchief and blew his nose hard. 'Come on, let's get you home. Charlotte and Ben are waiting for us.'

'Isn't anyone at the hospital with him?' Jenny wanted to know.

Miles's voice hardened. 'Cassandra arrived about an hour ago, so we came away.'

'She'll be staying with us, I suppose.'

Miles sighed. 'Can't really refuse in all fairness, now can we?'

'Of course you can't. She has a right to be with him. But – I would like to see him.'

'Of course you must. Let's go home first and then we'll go back to the hospital. We'll go as soon as you're ready. She's had an hour or so with him now and visiting time will soon be over.'

As soon as they'd dumped her trunk and suitcase at the manor, Miles, Charlotte and Jenny set off at once to

Lynthorpe. As they drew into the car park behind the small cottage hospital they saw Cassandra pacing up and down outside the entrance, smoking.

'I'm not allowed to smoke in there,' she informed them as they approached. 'Oh hello,' she added, noticing Jenny. 'I thought it wouldn't take you long to come running to his bedside. Well, you can be the one to stroke his fevered brow and hold his hand. I'm no good around sick people.' She glared at Miles, as if it was his fault. 'Is it true they're going to take his leg off? He's going to be in a wheelchair?'

Before Miles could even answer, Jenny spoke up. 'They might have to, yes, to save his life. But if I know Georgie, he won't be in a wheelchair for any longer than necessary. Douglas Bader was his inspiration when he wanted to start flying again and the thought of what that man achieved after he lost both his legs will help Georgie again. He'll be back on his feet in no time. You'll see.'

Cassandra's mouth twisted in a sneer. 'But he won't ever take me dancing again, will he?'

'Is that all you can think about?' Jenny began angrily, but Charlotte put a warning hand on her arm and whispered, 'Not now, darling. She's upset.' She turned towards Cassandra. 'We're just going in to see him, then we'll take you home.'

'I'm not staying. I'm going back to Nottingham. I'll come again at the weekend.'

'I don't know if there's another train today – '

Again her lip curled. 'I have my own car now. Daddy bought it for me.' She threw down the stub of her cigarette and ground it with the toe of her pointed shoe. 'I'll be off before it gets dark. The roads round here are—' She stopped and then muttered, 'Oh what's the use!' and stalked off towards a vehicle parked a little way off.

Miles put his arms around Jenny and Charlotte. 'I could say I hope that's the last we see of her, but I rather doubt it will be. Come on, let's go and see him.'

He didn't look as bad as Jenny might have expected. He had a cut on his forehead and a black eye, but he was awake and watching the door.

'Jen,' he said as soon as he saw her. He stretched out his hand. 'I knew you'd come.' There a slight inflection in his words as if he was insinuating he'd doubted that Cassandra would.

Jenny took his hand and sat down by the bed. 'Course I have.'

'But term's not over yet, is it?'

'Almost.'

'But you've finished your exams? You haven't come before you should have, have you? Not on account of me.'

'They're finished. They were finished before the exhibition. I'd have been coming at the weekend any way.' She leaned towards him, a bantering note in her tone. 'You just got me out of all the boring end-of-term rubbish.'

He closed his eyes. 'That's all right, then.' His voice began to slur, as if he'd been drinking. 'Sorry, the pills they've given me are just beginning to . . .' His eyes closed.

After a moment, Charlotte said, 'He's asleep. Perhaps we should go.'

'Just another minute or two,' Jenny pleaded.

Miles touched her shoulder. 'We'll wait outside. You'll have to come out when the bell goes for the end of visiting anyway. In the meantime, we'll go and see if we can find Sister. See how he's doing.'

Jenny nodded, her gaze fastened on Georgie's face, his hand safely in hers. How she wished she could sit here all night watching over him.

'They're taking him to London tomorrow by ambulance,' Miles said as they climbed into the car a little later. 'To one of the big hospitals there. Sister says it's the best in the country for – for what he's got to have done.'

'Is it definite, then? He – he's going to lose his leg?'

'The final word will rest with his surgeon, but yes, it seems likely.'

They were all silent, busy with their own thoughts, on the way home.

'I must ring Felix,' Jenny murmured, 'to let him know what's happening. I promised.'

Ben and Louisa were waiting for them in the hall, anxious to hear the news. Louisa burst into noisy tears and climbed on to Miles's knee. 'I love Georgie, Daddy. I don't want him to die.'

Jenny felt tears prickle the back of her eyelids, but bravely she blinked them away. She had to be strong for everyone's sake. 'He's not going to die, Lou-Lou. We won't let him.'

'I'm going to book rooms for us in a hotel in London,' Miles said. 'Whoever wants to come, can do. I don't care what it costs. We need to be near him – at least until he's over the operation.'

They all stared at him, but no one dared voice the secret fear locked within their hearts. *If* he survived.

It all happened quickly then. Georgie was taken to

London and the surgeon decided that the operation should be done without delay. When Miles, Charlotte, Louisa and Jenny arrived at the hotel and rang the hospital for news, it was already underway.

'You won't be allowed to visit him today,' the nurse told Miles gently, 'but Sister says she'll allow you a brief time with him in the morning, if he's up to it.'

'Thank you, Nurse. May I ring again later to see—'

'Of course. Please feel free to phone any time.'

Miles thanked her and gave details of the hotel where they were staying.

As he replaced the receiver, three pairs of anxious eyes watched him. Miles forced a smile. 'He's in the operating theatre now.'

'When can we see him?'

'Tomorrow morning – if he's well enough.'

The hotel was a good one, the rooms comfortable, the food excellent, but none of the family could eat much. They were all too worried. And only Louisa slept well. Miles and Charlotte whispered together into the early hours, trying to comfort each other, trying to cling to hope.

Jenny, in a twin bed in the same room as Louisa, tossed and turned for most of the night, rising heavy-eyed and with a headache.

After they'd had breakfast in the dining room, they gathered in Miles and Charlotte's room. 'What time can we go to the hospital?'

'I'll ring them to ask—'

But he got no further for the telephone at the side of the bed rang suddenly, making them all jump. Louisa clung to Jenny, wide-eyed and fearful.

When Miles answered it, they were relieved to hear

him say, 'Hello, Ben. No, no news yet. We'll keep you posted, I promise.'

They spoke a little longer and when the call ended, Miles telephoned the hospital. Once more, the other three clustered around him. When at last he finished the call and turned to them, he was smiling. 'He's come through it very well. He's awake and asking where we are. So, come on, look lively.'

As they climbed into the car in the hotel car park only minutes later, Charlotte said, 'We haven't told Cassandra.'

'Don't know her phone number,' Miles said cheerily.

'But she might go all the way to Lynthorpe and he won't be there.'

Miles snorted. 'I doubt it.' As he started the car and manoeuvred it out of the car park, he sighed and relented. 'I suppose you're right. We ought to let her know what's happening. Have you got her number with you?'

'No, but it's in the address book at the side of the telephone in the hall at home. Ben could give it to us if we ring him.'

'Right. I'll do it later.'

When they arrived at the hospital, the sister in charge of the ward greeted them. 'Only two at a time and I can only give you five minutes each. He is in a single room, but it's outside visiting hours. I'm sorry.'

'It's good of you to let us come at all, Sister.'

'You can come again during visiting hours this afternoon, but it'll still only be two at a time.'

'We understand. We only want to do what's best.'

The sister smiled. 'I wish all our patients' families were as thoughtful. Come, I'll take you to his room.' As

461

they followed her along the corridor, she said, 'He's doing well. He's a strong young man and Mr Parkinson – he's the surgeon – is very hopeful. Here we are. Who's going in first?'

'You and Charlotte go,' Jenny said to Miles, holding herself firmly in check. She longed to rush into the room and gather him into her arms. 'Louisa and I will go in after you.'

Charlotte squeezed her hand and followed Miles into the room, whilst Jenny and Louisa sat on two chairs in the corridor.

'It's scary, isn't it?' Louisa whispered when the sister had left them. They watched the nurses scurrying backwards and forwards and saw patients being wheeled up and down, some in wheelchairs, some lying flat on trolleys.

'Where are they taking them?' Louisa said.

'Goodness knows. Some for X-rays, I expect. Maybe – maybe some for operations.'

Louisa watched the goings-on with round eyes, imagining all sorts of dramas that went on in this place.

The door to Georgie's room opened and Miles and Charlotte were smiling. 'You two go in now. He seems fine.'

Jenny took Louisa's hand and they tiptoed in, holding their breath and only letting it go when they saw him propped up in bed and smiling at them.

They went to either side of the bed and each took hold of one of his hands. 'How – how do you feel?'

'Great! Surprisingly, though I've been warned it's probably still the anaesthetic. I'll probably feel worse tomorrow. But don't you worry, I'll soon be home and – ' his voice shook a little – 'hopping around.'

Jenny leaned closer. 'Think of Douglas Bader.'

She felt him squeeze her hand. 'I will, Jen.'

'Promise?'

'I promise.'

The five minutes were up all too quickly and the sister was shooing them out of the door.

Back at the hotel, Miles telephoned Ben and obtained Cassandra's number. The girl answered herself. 'Thank you for letting me know,' she said stiffly. 'I'll drive down first thing tomorrow.'

Miles replaced the receiver slowly. 'She's coming tomorrow.'

Jenny clicked her tongue. 'That means she'll hog one of the places all the time, I bet.'

'Mm, maybe.'

'What is it, Miles?' Charlotte asked, perceptive as ever.

He sighed. 'I'm not sure, but – there's something. I can't put my finger on it.'

'I can,' Jenny said. 'She's sulky because he won't be able to take her dancing any more and because she thinks he's going to be a cripple in a wheelchair. But she's wrong. Georgie won't let this stop him. He'll be flying again in no time – just like his hero did. You'll see.'

'Oh I do hope he won't,' Charlotte murmured, but even she knew there'd be no stopping him.

'And he's not a wounded war hero any more,' Jenny went on. 'Now his injury was caused by an accident and there's no honour in it. Not for her. She can't bask in reflected glory.'

Miles and Charlotte stared at her. 'You know, Jen,' Charlotte said, 'you do have a knack of hitting the proverbial nail right on the head.'

The telephone rang. It was Felix, who, having

obtained the hotel number from Ben, was ringing to find out how Georgie was and if there was anything he could do. 'I'm so sorry I couldn't put you all up here, but as soon as there's better news, you must let me take you all out to dinner. Are you sure there's nothing I can do now?'

'Not at the moment, Felix,' Miles said. 'But thank you.'

'I'll keep in touch, then. Love to the girls, especially my protégé. Tell her I've sold another two of her paintings and one of Matt's too. Got a very good price for them.'

'Oh darling, congratulations!' Charlotte said, hugging her delightedly.

But, to their surprise, Jenny's lip trembled and she dropped her head.

'What is it, Jen? Aren't you pleased? You're really on your way. You have such a wonderful career ahead of you, just as we've always believed. Whatever's wrong?'

Slowly Jenny raised her head, the tears running down her face, her chin trembling. But her voice was resolute as she said, 'I don't want to sound ungrateful – you know I'm not – but I'd give all of it up – everything – in a moment, if I could make sure that Georgie's going to be all right.'

Sixty-Six

'She really does love him, doesn't she?' Miles said later to Charlotte in the privacy of their room.

'Yes.'

'I only wish that other bloody girl wasn't in the way,' Miles said, thumping his fist against the palm of his hand. 'And if only Georgie wasn't so blind. Cassandra's no good for him, never was, and especially not now. But Jen . . .'

'I think he still sees her as a little girl.'

'Well, he shouldn't, because she's not. She's bright and talented and beautiful. Why on earth can't he see it?' Miles paced the floor.

'I thought he was beginning to see her in a different light. You know, at the exhibition. I saw him watching her with a mixture of pride and love – yes, love – on his face.'

Miles turned and spread his hands. 'Then why?'

'Because I think he loves her like a sister. The same way he loves Louisa.'

'Then I'm sorry – very sorry – for both of them. Georgie, because Cassandra's not right for him and Jenny, because – ' He didn't need to say any more.

Charlotte put her arms around him. 'But there's nothing we can do, darling.'

'I know, I know,' Miles said sadly, 'but at least

Georgie's going to be all right. He's going to get better.'

The following afternoon when they arrived at the hospital, they met an angry Cassandra storming out of the entrance and marching towards her car.

'What is it? What's happened?' Charlotte asked, hurrying towards her, even though Miles muttered, 'Let her go.'

Cassandra turned and glared at them all, but her furious gaze came to rest on Jenny. 'Her! She's what's the matter.'

'Me? What have I done?'

Cassandra stepped towards her. 'He's worse today.'

Charlotte gasped and her hand fluttered to her mouth. Jenny bit her lip and Miles moved agitatedly as if he didn't want to hang about chatting in the car park. He wanted to go in to see his son. But Cassandra's anger held them all there.

'They say it's normal after the anaesthetic wears off. But he has a fever they're worried about.' But Cassandra didn't seem worried at all and her next words shocked them. 'But I'm done here.' Still, she was facing Jenny. 'He's all yours and you're welcome to him. I won't be coming back.'

'Why? What's *happened*, Cassandra?' Charlotte persisted. She was sure there was something that the girl wasn't telling them. 'Please tell us.'

Cassandra was still glaring at Jenny. 'I was sitting by his bedside, holding his hand.' Her mouth curled. 'Trying my best to play the "good little nurse" bit, all tea and sympathy.'

'And?'

'Well, like I told you, he's got a fever and he's out of it a lot of the time, doesn't know what he's saying, but I suppose – like when someone's drunk – you get the truth then.'

'Cassandra, I really don't understand what you're talking about,' Charlotte said, trying hard to hold on to her patience when she felt like shaking the girl.

'He was delirious, I know that, but he was shouting out a name, calling for – for someone.'

'Who? Whose name was he calling?'

Now Cassandra's face twisted into ugly malice. '*Hers!* "Jenny," he kept muttering. And not just once. Over and over again, until I couldn't stand it any longer. It's her he wants.'

No one spoke, no one even attempted to contradict her because no one there wanted to. They all wanted what she was saying to be the truth.

'So, I'm off. Goodbye and I can't say it's been nice knowing you.'

With that, Cassandra turned away and walked towards her car without a backward glance.

'She must have got it wrong.' Still Jenny didn't dare to believe it.

Charlotte put her arm around the girl's shoulders. 'Come, let's go and see how he is.'

To those who loved him so, today Georgie looked terrible. His face was red and sweating and he was thrashing about the bed so much that the young nurse who'd been put in charge of him on one-to-one nursing was almost in tears from trying to keep him calm.

'He's so strong,' she said helplessly to Miles. 'Please, can you talk to him, it might calm him.'

Miles tried, Charlotte tried and even Louisa, but it was only when Jenny took his hand, squeezed it and

467

said firmly, 'Now, Georgie, no more of this. You must lie still', that he ceased his restlessness and lay still. She took a damp flannel and wiped his forehead. 'That's better. Now try to sleep, get some rest and – ' Jenny smiled and leaned closer to whisper – 'and "Hang spring-cleaning!" '

'Oh miss, are you a nurse, 'cos if you aren't, you ought to be!'

'Now, will you just look at that,' Miles said in wonderment. Then he turned to Charlotte. 'But what's she talking about spring-cleaning for?'

Charlotte chuckled, relieved to see that in the space of only minutes, Georgie already looked more peaceful.

'It's the beginning of *The Wind in the Willows*.'

'Ah, yes, of course, I see now.'

'I don't,' Louisa said.

'When she first came to us as a little evacuee, Georgie used to read it to her.'

At that moment, the sister came in. 'Whatever are you all doing in here? Nurse Benson, you should know better. This patient is only allowed one visitor at a time today seeing as he's—' She stopped suddenly and stared at Georgie, who was now lying quietly, his eyes closed, his breathing more regular, even though still a little fast.

'Sorry, Sister, but I couldn't manage him. I was so frightened he was going to harm himself and then his family came in and tried to calm him, but it wasn't until his sister here took hold of his hand and spoke to him that he responded.'

'I'm not his sister. I'm Jenny.'

Both the sister and the nurse stared at her. '*You're* Jenny!' they both exclaimed together then glanced at each other, perplexed.

'Then who was the other one? We thought she was his girlfriend.'

'She was,' Charlotte said quietly.

'Oh heck, Sister,' the little nurse said, 'I called her Jenny because that's who he's been asking for.'

Sister nodded. 'I know. I called her that too.'

Charlotte couldn't hide her laughter any longer. 'No wonder she was angry. Oh dear. Oh Miles . . .' She clung to his arm, overcome by a fit of the giggles.

'Please excuse my wife,' Miles said, but he, too, was grinning. 'You see that was Cassandra and, yes, she was his girlfriend, but no longer, I think, and we're all – er – shall I say, rather relieved.'

'Ah,' Sister said, understanding at once. Then she turned back to Jenny. 'Well, my dear, it is a little unusual for us to allow someone who isn't a close relative to stay with a patient who is – I have to tell you – at the moment very ill – ' At her words both Charlotte and Miles sobered immediately. 'But since it seems that you are the only one who can keep him calm, we will allow you to stay. That is, if his family don't mind.'

'Of course not. We want whatever is best for Georgie.' Miles smiled at Jenny. 'And though she's not related to us, she is very much part of our family.'

Sister smiled. 'It sounds to me as if she very soon will be. Now, shoo, the rest of you. You can come back this evening and if he's a little better, I'll let you have ten minutes with him. Nurse, will you fetch Jenny a cup of tea and when you've done that you can take a break yourself.' Her smile widened. 'I can see he's in safe hands.'

*

Georgie slept through the evening and all through the night, only waking early in the morning when the sister began to change his dressing.

Jenny had sat by his bedside all that time, refusing to leave him except to answer the call of nature and to have a bite to eat at the sister's insistence.

At last Georgie opened his eyes and blinked at her. 'What are you doing here, Jen?'

'This young lady has been here all night, holding your hand and willing you to get better.' The sister looked up and smiled. 'And I think it's worked. We'll take your temperature in a moment, but I can see just by looking at you that it's down.' She turned to Jenny. 'Now, my dear, if you'd leave us for a little while, you can come back for a few moments and then I really think you should go back to the hotel and get some rest yourself. Mr Thornton has already been ringing up to see how things are and I asked him to come and fetch you in about half an hour.'

When Jenny opened her mouth to argue, Georgie laughed. 'Don't argue with Sister, Jen. She can be a dragon when she's roused.'

Twenty minutes later, Jenny was allowed back in to say "goodbye" for the moment.

'Where's Cassandra?' Georgie asked her.

'Georgie, I'm sorry. She's gone.'

There was a long silence before he murmured, 'And she's not coming back, is she? I thought as much. Can't handle sickness and – and cripples.'

'You, a cripple?' Jenny forced a bantering note into her tone, though all she felt like doing was bowing her head and sobbing. 'Don't make me laugh. You'll be up and about on your tin leg in no time. Your dad's already thinking of making enquiries about hospitals that treat – ' she faltered over the word, but it had to be said – 'amputees.'

'But you're still here, aren't you, little Jenny? You've been here all night.'

'Hey, not so much of the "little". I'm a big girl now.'

He turned his head on the pillow and looked into her face, staring at her as if he was really seeing her for the person she was now. 'You won't leave me, will you?'

'No, Georgie, I'll never leave you.'

'But you're going to be a famous artist and travel all over the world. You won't want to be stuck in Ravensfleet with a—'

She put her finger against his lips. 'Don't you dare say it.'

He caught hold of her hand and pressed it to his lips. 'How blind I've been. Searching for love in all the wrong places when it was here all the time.'

Firmly, he replaced her hand. 'Go and get some rest, but you will come back, won't you, Jen? Promise?'

'Oh yes,' she breathed. It was the easiest promise she'd ever made in her life.

As she walked out of the hospital and towards Miles waiting in the car, she lifted up her face to the early morning sunshine, closed her eyes for a moment and whispered a prayer of thankfulness.

The war that had so changed all their lives had been over for some time, and now Jenny's own private battle was won too.

At last, at long last, Georgie loved her.

FOR MORE ON

MARGARET DICKINSON

sign up to receive our

SAGA NEWSLETTER

Packed with **features, competitions, authors'
and readers' letters** and **news of exclusive events,**
it's a 'must-read' for every Margaret Dickinson fan!

Simply fill in your details below and tick to confirm that you would
like to receive saga-related news and promotions and return to us at
Pan Macmillan, Saga Newsletter, 20 New Wharf Road, London, NI 9RR.

NAME _____

ADDRESS _____

_____ POSTCODE_____

EMAIL _____

☐ *I would like to receive saga-related news and promotions (please tick)*

*You can unsubscribe at any time in writing or through our website where you can also see
our privacy policy which explains how we will store and use your data.*